W9-AYM-400

Praise for #1 *New York Times* bestselling author Lisa Jackson

"Lisa Jackson takes my breath away."
—*New York Times* bestselling author Linda Lael Miller

"When it comes to providing gritty and sexy stories, Ms. Jackson certainly knows how to deliver."
—*RT Book Reviews* on *Unspoken*

"Bestselling Jackson cranks up the suspense to almost unbearable heights in her latest tautly written thriller."
—*Booklist* on *Malice*

"Provocative prose, an irresistible plot and finely crafted characters make up Jackson's latest contemporary sizzler."
—*Publishers Weekly* on *Wishes*

Praise for *New York Times* bestselling author B.J. Daniels

"After reading *Mercy*, B.J. Daniels will absolutely move to the top of your list of must-read authors."
—*Fresh Fiction*

"Daniels is truly an expert at Western romantic suspense."
—*RT Book Reviews* on *Atonement*

"Action-packed and chock-full of suspense."
—*Under the Covers* on *Redemption*

"Fans of Western romantic suspense will relish Daniels' tale of clandestine love played out in a small town on the Great Plains."
—*Booklist* on *Unforgiven*

#1 *NEW YORK TIMES*
BESTSELLING AUTHOR

LISA
JACKSON

NEW YORK TIMES BESTSELLING AUTHOR

B.J. DANIELS

SHADOW
OF DOUBT

Previously published as *A Husband to Remember* and
Undeniable Proof

ISBN-13: 978-1-335-00885-5

Shadow of Doubt

Copyright © 2019 by Harlequin Books S.A.

First published as A Husband to Remember
by Harlequin Books in 1993
and Undeniable Proof by Harlequin Books in 2006.

Recycling programs
for this product may
not exist in your area.

The publisher acknowledges the copyright holders
of the individual works as follows:

A Husband to Remember
Copyright © 1993 by Susan Crose

Undeniable Proof
Copyright © 2006 by Barbara Heinlein

This edition published by arrangement with Harlequin Books S.A.

For questions and comments about the quality of this book,
please contact us at CustomerService@Harlequin.com.

® and TM are trademarks of Harlequin Enterprises Limited or its corporate affiliates. Trademarks indicated with ® are registered in the United States Patent and Trademark Office, the Canadian Intellectual Property Office and in other countries.

Printed in U.S.A.

CONTENTS

Lisa Jackson is a #1 *New York Times* bestselling author of more than eighty-five books, including romantic suspense, thrillers and contemporary and historical romances. She is a recipient of the *RT Book Reviews* Reviewers' Choice Award and has also been honored with their Career Achievement Award for Romantic Suspense. Born in Oregon, she continues to make her home among family, friends and dogs in the Pacific Northwest. Visit her at lisajackson.com.

Books by Lisa Jackson

Illicit
Proof of Innocence
Memories
Suspicions
Disclosure: The McCaffertys
Confessions
Rumors: The McCaffertys
Secrets and Lies
Abandoned
Strangers
Sweet Revenge
Stormy Nights
Montana Fire
Risky Business
Missing
High Stakes

Visit the Author Profile page
at Harlequin.com for more titles.

A HUSBAND TO REMEMBER

Lisa Jackson

Prologue

Steam rose from the jungle floor. The earth smelled damp though the tropical sun beat mercilessly through a canopy of thick leaves. Her lungs burned, her calf muscles ached, and she swallowed back the fear that drove her higher and higher through the hills of the island. Over her own labored breathing, she heard the surf pounding the shore far below the cliffs, but still she ran, ears straining for sounds of the man in pursuit.

Help me, God, please. Her legs were scratched from the vines and brambles and her sandaled feet tripped over exposed roots and rocks. She scrambled up the overgrown trail, hoping that at the ridge, high above the sea, there would be a place to hide, a fork in the path that would at least give her a way to escape.

"¡Pare!" a deep voice commanded. "Stop!"

He was close, much too close!

"¡Dama! ¡Por favor! ¡Pare!"

Panic ripped through her as the path broke free of the dense foliage and she found herself on the rocky cliffs. The sun was bright, nearly blinding as it reflected off the water. Staying near the shadows of the forest, she headed upward still, to the north, away from the town.

Terror, stark and deep, propelled her forward. Sweat streamed down her face and her breathing was loud— too loud. Heart thundering, she saw the grimy bricks of the old mission, its cross long disappeared, the walls beginning to crumble. Though deserted for years, the mission held her only hope. There was still a chance that someone was there, a tourist or local who could help her.

She started up the final hill. Biting her lip against the urge to cry out, she ran along the trail that rimmed the cliffs. Pebbles fell, dislodged by her feet to mingle with the angry white foam that swirled far below, pounding the rocky shore.

Just a few more yards.

Unless no one is there.

Unless the man chasing her already had someone there.

Behind her the man was scrambling up the trail, closing the distance. *Hurry! Hurry! Hurry!*

Tears stung her eyes, but still she ran, hearing his loud breathing, hoping that he didn't have a gun.

"Stop!" he yelled again. So close. So damned close.

A huge hand touched her shoulder and her footing gave way. Her ankle twisted and she cried out. Falling, she tried to clutch the tufts of dried grass and sharp rocks, but her fingers found only air. Her body pitched over the edge of the cliffs, soaring high above the rocky beach.

She tried to scream just as the blackness engulfed her.

Chapter 1

Voices, distant and jumbled, echoing from somewhere in the darkness, somewhere just out of reach, beckoned to her.

"You wake up now," a woman said in thickly accented English. "*Dios,* it's time for you to stop this sleeping. *Señora,* can you hear me?"

She tried to respond but couldn't, though the voice had become familiar and kind, one of the voices that ebbed and flowed on the tide of her consciousness. She'd heard many voices often in the darkness and knew that they were friendly. They were voices she could count on, voices that would help—unlike the voices in her dreams, the voices that caused her to scream in silent horror as she replayed the chase through the jungle over and over.

If only she could open her eyes.

"*Señora*—can you hear me? *¿Señora?*" The nurse was trying to talk to her again. "Your husband…he is here. Waiting for you to wake up."

Husband. But I don't have a husband…

She swallowed. Lord, was that sand in her throat? And the taste in her mouth—horrid and bitter. Metallic. Her stomach burned and her eyelids peeled back for an instant. Light streamed through the swollen slits, causing an explosion of pain in her brain. In an instant, she saw a huge woman leaning over her—a woman in white, with large breasts, worried expression, dark skin and black hair pulled into a tight bun covered with a stiff white nurse's cap.

Intelligent brown eyes stared into hers, and the nurse began speaking in rapid-fire Spanish that she couldn't begin to understand. Where was she? A hospital, she guessed, but where?

She couldn't focus, couldn't read the name on the pin clipped to the nurse's huge bosom. "The doctor, he is on his way, and your husband, we have told him you are waking up."

I'm not married, she tried to say, but the words wouldn't form, and another wave of blackness engulfed her.

"Oh, no…she is sinking again…" More Spanish as the nurse barked orders.

The darkness was peaceful and calm and cool.

"We are losing her again!" the big nurse's voice called from the darkness. "*¡Señora! ¡Señora!* You wake up. You just wake up again!" She felt strong fingers around her wrist, moving quickly, trying to edge her back to consciousness, but the sinking had begun and she floated steadily downward to the black void, grateful for the relief it brought.

"Nikki!" A man's voice called to her, but it was too late.

Nikki?

"Your wife, she will wake up soon," the nurse said.

I'm no one's wife. I'm... Panic seized her as she searched for a name, a memory, anything she could recall. But there was nothing.

"Nikki, please. Wake up." The husband again. *Husband?* Her eyes fluttered for a second and she focused on a hard face, a very male face. Severe, bladed features, thick brows and stormy blue eyes pierced through the fog in her mind. His lips were thin and sensual, his nose a little crooked, and she was certain that she'd never seen him before in her life.

"Nikki, come on. Wake up..."

But the darkness washed over her again, pulling her into its safe, silent vortex, to a place where she didn't have to wonder about her past and she didn't have to think why this man, this stranger, was claiming to be her husband.

The fragrance of carnations and roses drifted through the ever-present odor of antiseptic, and she heard music, a soft Spanish ballad interrupted by occasional bouts of static as the melody drifted through her sleep, dragging her awake. She tried to stretch, but her muscles rebelled and she felt as if she'd been lying in one spot forever. She ached all over and her head—Lord, her head—pounded with an intensity that brought tears to her eyes.

Slowly lifting a painful eyelid, she stared at a ceiling

of white plaster. The lights were dim, but waning daylight streamed through a single window and kept the room from total darkness. She blinked and swept her gaze around the room—a hospital room, from the looks of it, with white stucco walls, tile floor and two single beds, one bare of bedding and unoccupied.

She felt, rather than saw, the man. Turning her head slightly and sucking in air against the pain, she faced a stranger who was slouched in the single chair. Unshaven, shirt wrinkled and rolled at the sleeves, jean-clad legs stretched in front of him, he was tall and swarthy, his features set and grim, his lips clamped shut in a harsh, thin line. His gaze was trained past her to the hallway door, and the sound of the music accompanied muted voices and the rattle of a cart being pushed through the corridor.

A tingle of foreboding touched all her nerve endings when she looked at him. There had to be a reason he was here—but what? And who was he? Mean-looking, with a square jaw that meant business and shoulders wide enough to hide the back of the chair, he appeared not to have slept for the past week. Aside from his rumpled clothes, his black hair was mussed and hung past his collar, and there was an air about him that seemed almost dangerous.

As if he suddenly sensed that she was staring at him, his gaze swung quickly back to the bed, and eyes as blue as the Caribbean focused on her with such unerring intensity that a shiver of dread chased up her spine. *Don't be silly,* she told herself. *He's obviously a friend.* And yet there was something disturbing about him, something she should remember, something important.

Something desperate. She tried to remember, but pain screamed through her head.

She expected him to smile, but instead the corners of a blade-thin mouth tightened a bit when he saw that she was awake.

"Nikki."

Was that her name? It seemed to fit, and yet... She tried to say something, ask him who he was, but her voice failed her and her mouth felt gritty and dry. She licked her lips and tried to sit up, but pain exploded in her head.

"Hey, wait a minute." He was on his feet in an instant, big, callused palms pressing gently on her shoulders as he held her down. "Take it slow, Nikki. You'll get your chance to talk, believe me."

He knew her, but she was certain she'd never seen him before in her life.... No, there had been an instant of wakefulness when these same cold blue eyes had searched hers. She willed herself to remember, but the pain in her head caused her to wince and she felt like she might throw up. There was something she should know about him. Something important.

He offered her a sip of water from a glass on the table, bending a straw so that she could drink. The water was warm and tasted slightly metallic, and after a few swallows she shook her head and he set the glass back on the tray.

"Who...who are you?" she asked, her voice rough and squeaky, like a neglected instrument that needed tuning.

For just a second she thought his eyes slitted suspiciously. "You don't know?"

"No... I..." Panic gripped her as she searched her

memory, or what had been her memory. Nothing surfaced. *Nothing.* Not just about this man or this hospital or herself. "I... I don't remember...." But how could that be? She tried to concentrate, but no single event of her past—no person, no place, no favorite pet or book—would swim to the surface of her memory. "Oh, Lord," she whispered, her heart hammering, her palms beginning to sweat. "I don't remember...."

He shoved his hair from his eyes and seemed about to say something, but stopped himself short, and the sharp glance he shot her way said, without words, that he didn't believe her.

"Who *are* you?" she demanded. She knew instinctively that she shouldn't show any kind of weakness to this man.

"You're serious about this amnesia?" he scoffed in a whisper.

"I don't—"

Suddenly he leaned over the bed, took her face between his hands and pressed his lips upon hers with the intimacy of a kiss that bespoke of a thousand kisses before. His lips molded against hers with a warm possession, and her heart, already beating in fear, began a wild tempo that pulsed through her veins. He groaned softly into her mouth and whispered, "I've missed you, Nikki. Oh, God, I was scared." His lips claimed hers again with a depth of passion that caused her to tremble and melt inside before she could collect her senses.

Stop this madness. Stop it now!

Even though his mouth and hands were persuasive, she couldn't respond, because deep in her heart she knew the kiss wasn't right—the passion and caring of this man were all wrong. There wasn't any logic involved in her thinking, just a gut feeling that the man wasn't being honest with her. She tried to struggle, but the IV tube in her arm restrained her and his mouth moved slowly, sensually against hers.

"Thank God you're safe." Again he kissed her.

A quiet cough from the doorway caused him to stand straight and flush up the back of his neck. Embarrassed, he managed a smile for the nurse who filled the doorway. "She's awake," he said, shrugging with the innocent guile of a child caught stealing a cookie from the jar. All trace of the coldness she'd sensed in him had been quickly hidden.

"*Dios.* We thank the Virgin." The nurse, a big, buxom woman with copper-colored skin and eyes as black as obsidian, moved to Nikki's bedside. Smothering a smile over the tender scene she just witnessed, she shooed the man back away from the bed where he suddenly hung like a lovesick puppy.

Nikki tried to explain. "I don't know what's going on, but—"

"Shh, *señora.* Please." With trained fingers, Nurse Consuela Vásquez, according to the nametag pinned to her ample bosom, took Nikki's pulse, blood pressure and temperature. Nikki tried to protest, to ask questions, but she was told by the big woman to wait. "First we see how you are doing. Then you tell us everything. Okay?"

Impatiently Nikki waited, wanting to wiggle from beneath the stranger's stare, for his eyes, as she was examined, never left her. Finally, when Nurse Vásquez had checked the IV bag and scratched Nikki's vital information on her chart, she offered Nikki a sincere and relieved smile. "Well, Señora Makinzee, you wake up. *¿Qué tal se siente hoy?*"

Nikki's brows drew together and she shook her head. "I… I don't understand. I don't speak Spanish."

"She wants to know how you feel," the man interjected.

"Like I've been run over by an eighteen-wheeler."

"¿Cómo?"

The corners of the stranger's mouth curved upward just a little as he explained to the nurse, and Consuela Vásquez chuckled.

"Sí. You are lucky to be alive. Your husband…he save your life."

Nikki's gaze moved to the man leaning over the bed. He wasn't smiling any longer and his gaze had suddenly become unreadable. Like a chameleon, always changing. "He did?" she whispered, her heart hammering and sweat collecting along her spine. She wanted to confide in the nurse, to explain about the frightening blackness that seemed to be in the spot that should have held her memory, but hesitated, wondering if it would be wise to admit as much while this man—this man who had kissed her so passionately while she was lying helplessly in the bed—was standing nearby. "My husband? But I'm not married."

The nurse's smile collapsed. "He is your husband, *señora.*"

Nikki shook her head, but a jagged streak of pain ripped through her brain and she was forced to draw in a sharp breath. "I'm not married," she said again, her gaze locking with that of the stranger, the man claiming to have married her. Was it her imagination or did the skin around the corners of his mouth tighten a little?

"But, Señor Makinzee—"

"McKenzie. Trent McKenzie." His eyes didn't warm

as he said, "You remember, we were married just before we came to Salvaje for our honeymoon."

Dear God, was he telling the truth? Why would he lie? But certainly she would remember her own wedding.

"My name is—" She squinted against the blinding pain, trying to see through the door that was locked in her mind.

"Nikki Carrothers," Trent supplied.

That sounded right. It fit, like a favorite pair of old slippers.

"Nikki Carrothers McKenzie."

The slippers were suddenly too tight. "I don't think so," she said uncertainly. Could she possibly have been married to this man? Eyeing him, she mentally removed several days' growth of beard, the tired lines of strain around his eyes, the unkempt hair. He could be considered handsome, she supposed. He was just shy of six feet with a thick chest that tapered to slim hips and muscles that were visible whenever he moved. *Lean and mean.* For there wasn't a trace of kindness in his eyes and she knew that undying love wasn't one of the reasons he'd had for staying at her bedside.

"No memory?" the nurse asked.

Try, Nikki, try. She squeezed her eyes shut for a second, willing her memories—her *life*—to come back to her. "None. I... I... I just can't," she reluctantly admitted, her head throbbing.

Consuela's worried expression deepened. "Dr. Padilla will be in soon. He will talk to you." She turned questioning eyes to Trent and then, after promising a sponge bath and breakfast and a pill for pain, she hurried out the door with a rustle of her crisp uniform.

Trent followed the nurse into the corridor, and though Nikki strained to listen, she heard only snatches of their conversation which was spoken in whispered Spanish. What was she doing here in this foreign country—in a hospital, for God's sake—with no memory?

Her heart thudded and she tried to raise her arms. Her left was strapped to the bed, the IV taped to her wrist. Her right was free, but ached when she tried to move it. In fact, now that the pain in her head had eased to a dull throb, she realized that she hurt all over. Her legs and torso—everywhere—felt bruised and battered.

Your husband. He save your life.

Her throat tightened. What was she doing with Trent McKenzie?

She glanced around the room, to the thick stucco walls and single window. Fading sunlight was streaming through the fronds of a palm tree that moved in the wind just outside the glass, causing shadows to play on the wall at the foot of her bed. The window was partially opened and the scent of the sea wafted through the room, mingling with the fragrance of the roses, two dozen red buds interspersed with white carnations in a vase on the metal stand near the table.

The card had been opened. Pinned to a huge white bow, it read: "All my love, Trent." These flowers were from that hard-edged man who claimed he was married to her? Nikki tried to imagine Trent McKenzie, in a florist's shop, browsing over vases of cut lilies, bachelor's buttons and orchids. She couldn't. The man who'd camped out in her hospital room was tough and suspicious and had a cruel streak in his eyes. No way would he have sent flowers. And no way would she have married him.

But why would he lie?

If only she could remember. Her head began to throb again.

Somewhere down the hallway a patient moaned and a woman was softly weeping. Bells clanged and footsteps hurried through the hushed corridors. Several people passed by the doorway, all with black hair and dark skin, natives of this island off the coast of Venezuela. When Trent had mentioned Salvaje to her, Nikki had flashed upon a mental picture of the tropical island. The picture had been from a brochure that touted Salvaje as a garden paradise, a quaint tropical island. There had been pictures, small captioned photographs of white, sandy beaches, lush, dense foliage, happy natives and breathtakingly beautiful jagged cliffs that seemed to rise from the sea. Nikki's pulse skyrocketed as she remembered a final photo in the brochure, a picture of an abandoned mission, built hundreds of years ago at the highest point of the island. The mission with the crumbling bell tower and weathered statue of the Madonna. The mission in her nightmare.

She convulsed, her heart hammering. What was she doing here on Salvaje, and why did this man, the only other American she'd seen, claim to be her husband? If only she could remember! She slammed her eyes shut, fighting against the bleak emptiness in her brain, and heard the steady click of boot heels against the tile.

He was back. Her body tensed in fear, but she forced her eyes open and told herself that he'd inadvertently given her a glimpse of her memory when he had mentioned Salvaje, the Wild Island, and if she could, she should try to get him to give her more information, hoping that any little piece might trigger other recollections.

He strode to her bed, towering over her with his

cynical demeanor and lying eyes. Nikki, tied to the rails, forced to lie under a thin sheet and blanket, felt incredibly vulnerable, and she knew instinctively that she hadn't felt this way before the fall. "Dr. Padillo has been called," Trent said with a little less rancor. "He'll be here within the hour. Then maybe we can get you out of here."

"Where will we go?"

"Back to the hotel and pack our bags. Then we'll grab the first flight to Seattle as soon as you're well enough to travel."

Seattle. Home was the Pacific Northwest. She almost believed him. "We have a house there?" she asked, and she noticed the hardening of his jaw, the slight hesitation in his gaze.

"I have a house. You have an apartment, but we planned that you'd move your things over to my place once we returned."

"We...we got married in Seattle?"

His gaze, blue and hard, searched hers, as if he suspected that she was somehow trying to trip him up.

"By a justice of the peace. A quick ceremony before we came here for our honeymoon."

No big wedding? An elopement? What about her family—her parents? Surely they were still alive. Her stomach knotted as she tried to concentrate on Seattle—the city on Puget Sound. In her mind's eye she saw gray water, white ferries and sea gulls wheeling in a cloud-filled sky. Memories? Or a postcard she'd received from some acquaintance?

Trent rubbed his shoulder muscles, as if he ached from his vigil. She watched the movement of his hands along his neck and wondered if those very hands—

tanned and callused—had touched her in intimate places. Had they scaled her ribs, slid possessively along her thigh, cupped her nape and drawn her to him in a passion as hot as a volcano? And had she, in return, touched him, kissed him, made love to him? Had she fingered the thick black strands of his hair where it brushed his nape? Had she boldly slid her hand beneath the waistband of his worn jeans? She bit her lip in frustration. True, Trent was sexy and male and dangerous, and yet…if she'd made love to him, if her naked body had twined with his, wouldn't she remember?

He turned to face her, catching her staring at his back, and for a second his hard shell faded and a spark of regret flashed in his eyes. Nikki's lungs tightened and she could barely breathe, for beneath the regret, she also saw the hint of physical desire. He glanced quickly away, as if the emotions registering in his eyes betrayed him.

"Who are you, really?" she asked.

His jaw slid to the side. "You honestly don't remember me?"

"Why would I lie?"

"Why would I?"

She lifted the fingers of her left hand just a little, wiggling her ringless fingers.

His lips thinned. "Hospital rules. Your jewelry, including your wedding ring, is in the safe."

"No tan line."

"No time for a tan. We just got here when you fell."

"I fell?"

"On the cliffs by the old mission. You're lucky to be alive, Nikki. I thought…you could have been killed."

Fear took a stranglehold of her throat. "I don't remember," she lied, not wanting to hear any confirmation that her nightmare had been real, that the terror-riddled dream that had chased her in her sleep wasn't a figment of her overactive imagination.

The back of her throat tasted acrid. "Were you chasing me up on the ridge?" she asked, her voice little more than a whisper.

He hesitated, but only for a heartbeat. "You were alone, Nikki," he said, and she knew he was lying through his beautiful white teeth. "There was no one else."

"Where were you?"

"Waiting. At the mission. I saw you fall." His face went chalk-white, as if he relived a horrid memory. "I think it would be best…for you…to go home. You'd feel safer and forget the accident."

Accident? The breath of fear blew through her insides, and she wished she could run again, that her body would support her and she could get away…to…where?

"I don't think I'd feel safer—"

"But you would be. With me."

"I don't even know you," she said, stark terror beginning to seize her throat.

Sighing, he shoved a hand through his unruly mane. "Maybe we shouldn't talk about this. The doctor doesn't want you getting upset."

Her patience snapped and she threw caution to the wind. "I can't remember anything! I don't remember my life, my job, my parents, my family, and I certainly don't remember you! I'm already way past upset!"

His mouth twisted heartlessly as his cruel mask slipped easily back into place. "I think we'd better wait for Padillo. See what he has to say."

There was an edge to his voice that caused sweat to gather at her nape. She couldn't remember the men she'd dated, but she would swear on her very life that none of those men would look like a rough-and-tumble backwoodsman with hawk-sharp eyes, angular features and scuffed boots. She noticed the beat-up leather jacket tossed carelessly over the back of his chair and the worn heels of his boots. He moved restlessly as if he were a man used to looking over his shoulder. Her throat went dry with fear. He was a con man? Someone sent to kidnap her? Or was he really her husband?

Her mind raced with a thousand reasons why she might be kidnapped, but she didn't think she was rich or famous or the daughter of some tycoon. She didn't feel like a political radical or a criminal or anything…. But for some reason this man wanted her, or the people in the hospital, to think that they were married.

She couldn't remember much, but she was convinced this impostor was *not* her husband.

But who would believe her on this island? Certainly not Nurse Vásquez, who obviously thought that Trent was besotted with her. But maybe the doctor. If she could talk to Dr. Padillo alone, perhaps she could convince him that something was very wrong.

Trent peered out the window, as if he were searching for someone in the parking lot below.

"I think if I really was married to you, I'd know it," she said.

"You'll remember," he predicted, though no warmth came over his face. He rested his hips on the sill, his gaze shifting from her to the crucifix mounted on the wall, the only decoration in the otherwise stark room. "As soon as I get you out of here."

"But you can't," she said, desperation creeping into her soul. Alone with this man—with no recollections of the past?

He smiled with cold patience. "I'm your husband, Nikki, and now that you're awake, I'm going to ask the doctor to release you as soon as you're well enough to go home."

Chapter 2

"So she wakes up!" the doctor said, poking his head into Nikki's hospital room. Short and round, with a wide smile, dark eyes and a horseshoe of gray hair, he strode into the room with the air of a man in charge. "*Buenos días,* you are the sleeping beauty, *si?*"

Nikki felt anything but beautiful. Her entire body ached and she knew her face was scratched and bruised. "*Buenos días,*" she murmured, glad to finally see someone who might be able to help her.

The doctor picked up her chart from its cradle at the foot of the bed and scanned the page. His lab coat, a size too small, strained around his belly, and when he looked up and grinned a glimmer of gold surrounded a few of his teeth. Small, wire-rimmed glasses were perched on his flat nose. "I'm Dr. Padillo," he said as he dropped the chart and moved in close with his penlight, carefully peeling back Nikki's eyelid and shining the tiny beam in her eye. *"¿Qué tal se siente hoy?"*

"Pardon?"

"She doesn't speak Spanish." Trent's voice caused her to stiffen slightly.

With the small beam blinding her, Nikki couldn't see Trent, but she sensed that he hadn't moved from his post near the window. He'd spent hours sitting on the ledge or restlessly pacing near the foot of the bed.

"Dr. Padillo asked how you were feeling today." As the penlight snapped off she caught a glimpse of him, leaning against the sill, one hip thrown out at a sexy angle.

"The truth?" Nikki asked, blinking.

"Nothing but," Trent said.

"Like I was ground up into hamburger."

Padillo's eyebrows shot up and he removed his glasses. *"¿Cómo?"*

Trent said something in quick Spanish and the doctor smiled as he polished the lenses of his wire-rims with the corner of his lab coat. He slid his spectacles back onto the bridge of his nose. "So you have not lost your sense of humor, eh?"

"Just my memory."

"Is this right?" he asked Trent and Nikki was more than a little rankled. It wasn't Trent's memory that was missing, it was hers, and she resented the two men discussing her.

"Yes, it's right," she said a little angrily.

Scowling, Padillo checked her other eye, clicked off his light and glanced at Trent, who had shoved himself upright and was standing in her line of vision. His features were stern and the air of impatience about him hadn't disappeared. Dr. Padillo rubbed his chin. "You are a very lucky woman, Señora McKenzie. We were all worried about you. Especially your husband."

"Worried sick," Trent added, and Nikki thought she heard a trace of mockery in his voice. His cool gaze flicked to her before returning to the doctor.

Shifting on the bed, she grimaced against a sudden pain in her leg. "I feel like I broke every bone in my body."

Padillo smiled a bit, not certain that she was joking. "The bones—they are fine. And except for your—" he glanced at Trent *"—tobillo."*

"Your ankle. It's sprained but not broken," Trent told her, though she would rather have heard the news from the doctor himself. The thought of Trent and Padillo discussing her injuries or anything else about her made her stomach begin to knot in dread.

"Sí. The ankle, it is swollen, but lucky not to be broken."

She supposed she should believe him, but lying in the hospital bed, her body aching, Trent acting as her husband or jailer, she felt anything but lucky.

"Your muscles are sore and you have the cuts and scrapes—contusions. Lacerations. You will be—" he hesitated.

"Black and blue?" Trent supplied.

Doctor Padillo grinned. *"Sí.* Bruised. But you will live, I think." His dark eyes twinkled as he touched her lightly on the arms and neck, lifting her hospital gown to expose more of her skin as he eyed the abrasions she could feel on her abdomen and back. "This must be kept clean and covered with antibiotic cream so that she heals and does not get the infection," he told Trent.

To underscore his meaning, he pointed at a scrape that ran beneath her right arm and the side of her ribs, and the air touched the side of her breast.

A tide of embarrassment washed up her face and neck, which was ridiculous if Trent really was her husband. Surely he'd seen her dressed in much less than the hospital gown. Her breasts weren't something new to him. Yet she was grateful when the thin cotton dropped over her side and afforded her a little bit of modesty.

The headache that had been with her most of the time she was awake started thundering again and hurt all over. Her entire right side was sore and she was conscious of the throbbing in her ankle. Padillo listened to her heartbeat through a stethoscope and asked her to show him that she could make a fist and sit up. She did as she was bid, then hazarded a glance in Trent's direction, hoping that he had the decency to stare out the window, but his eyes were trained on her as if he had every right to watch as the doctor examined her.

"Ooh!" she cried when Padillo touched her right foot.

The doctor frowned slightly. *"Tiene dolor aquí."*

"What?"

"He says you have a pain there—in your foot."

"Mucho pain," she said, gritting her teeth.

"Sí." Padillo placed the sheet and woven blanket over her body again. "It will be…tender for a few days, but should be able to carry your weight by the end of the week." Stuffing his hands in the pockets of his coat, he added, "We were wondering if you were ever going to wake up."

"How long was I—?"

"You were in a coma for six days," Trent said, and from the looks of his jaw he hadn't shaved the entire time she'd been under. She supposed that it was testament to his undying love that he'd spent the better part of a week keeping his vigil, and yet there was something about him that seemed almost predatory.

Again she looked at his harsh features, trying to find some hint in her memory of the rugged planes of his face. Surely if she'd married him, loved him, slept in the same bed with him, she would recall something about him. She bit down on her lip as he returned her stare, his eyes an opaque blue that gave no hint of his emotions. Desperation put a stranglehold on her heart.

"The nurse will give you medication for the pain," Dr. Padillo said, making notes on her chart before resting his hip on her bed. "Tell me about the—*Dios*," he muttered, snapping his fingers.

"Amnesia," Trent supplied.

"*Sí.* Have you any memory?"

Nikki glanced from the doctor to Trent and back again. She needed time alone with the doctor and yet Trent wasn't about to leave. "Can we speak privately?" she asked, and Padillo's brows drew together.

"We are alone…." He glanced up at Trent, his furrowed expression showing concern.

"Please."

"But your husband—"

"*Please,* Doctor. It's important!" She wrapped her fingers into the starched fabric of his white jacket.

"It's probably a good idea," Trent said with a nonchalant shrug. As if he had nothing to hide. "She's a little confused right now. Maybe you can straighten things out for her and help her remember."

I'm not confused about you, she thought, but bit hard

on her tongue, because the truth was, she didn't know a thing about herself.

Trent let his fingers slide along the bottom rail of the hospital bed. "I'll be in the hall if you need me." As he left the room, his bootheels ringing softly, he closed the door behind him, and Nikki let out a long sigh.

"That man is *not* my husband," she asserted as firmly as she could.

"He's not?" The doctor's eyebrows raised skeptically, and he eyed Nikki as if she'd truly lost her mind.

"I—I'm sure of it."

"Your memory. It has come back?"

"No, but…" Oh, this was hopeless! She clenched a fist in frustration, and pain shot up her arm. "I would remember him. I know it!" Unbidden, hot, wet tears touched the back of her eyelids, but she refused to cry.

Dr. Padillo patted her shoulder. "These things, they take time."

"But I would remember the man I married."

"As you remember the rest of your family?"

She didn't answer. The haze that was her past refused to crystallize and she was left with dark shadows and vague feelings, nothing solid.

"Your home? A pet? Your job? You remember any of these things?"

She closed her eyes and fought the tears building behind her swollen lids. She remembered so little and yet she felt like she was trapped, like an insect caught in the sticky web of a spider, vulnerable and weak. She stared at the IV tube draining into her arm, the iron sides of the bed, the gauze on her arm and the tiny room—her prison until she could walk again.

If only she could remember! Why was Trent posted

like a wary guard in her room day and night? Surely he trusted the hospital staff to take care of her. Or was his concern of a different nature? Was he afraid she might escape?

She closed her eyes as the questions pounded at her brain. Why the devil was she on this little island off the coast of Venezuela? And why in God's name wouldn't this doctor believe her? There had to be a way to convince him!

"I've never set eyes on Trent McKenzie until I woke up a little while ago."

"See! That is wrong. He is the one who brought you to the hospital." Padillo smiled reassuringly. "Give it some time, Señora McKenzie. You Americans. Always so in a hurry."

"Please, call me Nikki."

"Nikki, then. Do not rush this," Doctor Padillo said gently. "You have been...lucky. The accident could have been much worse."

The tone of his voice caught her attention, and for the first time she wondered how she'd become so battered. "What happened to me?" she asked, looking up at him and trying to ignore the horrible feeling that the man to whom this doctor was going to release her was inherently dangerous.

"I've talked to your husband as well as the *policía*. They concur. You and Señor McKenzie were walking along the hills by the mission. These hills, they can be very...*escarpado*...uh, sharp...no—"

"Steep," she supplied, her nightmare becoming vivid again. The jagged cliffs. The roaring sea. The dizzying heights and the mission with its crumbling bell tower.

"*Sí.* Steep. The path you were on was narrow, near

the cliffs, and you stumbled, lost your footing and fell over the edge. Fortunately, you landed on a…*saliente— Dios*…you call it a…"

"A ledge," Trent supplied as he opened the door and heard the tail end of the discussion. His gaze was pinned to Nikki's and his mouth was a thin grim line. "You slid over the side and landed on a ledge that jutted beneath the edge of the cliff. If you'd rolled another two feet, you would have fallen over a hundred feet into the sea."

Her body jarred as she remembered pitching in the air. *So the nightmare was real. Oh, God, help me!* Her throat closed in fear, but she managed to whisper hoarsely, "And you saved me?"

His lips tightened a little. "I couldn't save you from falling over the edge—I was already at the mission. But I heard you scream." His jaw clenched. "I followed the sound and ran back to the spot where you'd fallen. Fortunately I could climb down and carry you back."

Was he lying? "How did you get down to me?"

"It was tricky," he admitted as he rolled up the sleeve of a cotton work shirt. "But I've climbed mountains."

"So you didn't see me fall?"

His eyes locked with hers, and he hesitated for a fraction of an instant. "I'm sorry. I shouldn't have gone on ahead."

Nikki wasn't convinced he was telling the truth, but the pain in her body was intense and she knew arguing with these two men was useless. Could Trent possibly be her savior as he claimed, or had he been the man chasing her, the man who pushed her over the edge? But if so, why would he have brought her back for medical care? Oh, Lord, her brain hurt.

Shuddering, she thought about her nightmare, her

feet losing their purchase on the rocky trail, her body pitching toward the rocky shore hundreds of feet below the ridge. Deep in her heart she'd expected that the horrid dream was real, but she shivered with a fear as cold as the bottom of the sea. She hadn't fallen over the edge, she'd been pushed, chased by someone… someone darkly evil. Her gaze moved to Trent's face, so severe and determined. It was hard to imagine that he had saved her from death…. She almost cried out, but forced the tremors in her body to subside. She couldn't show any sign of weakness to this stranger who claimed to be her husband, and she had to come up with a plan, a way to escape the hospital and find out who she was. Oh, God, if her head didn't ache so badly, if she could bear weight on her ankle, she'd find a way to uncover the truth.

A shadow crossed her face as Trent bent over the bed. "I'll be back in a minute," he promised, his breath fanning her face. He kissed her lightly on the lips and there was a warmth in the feel of his mouth against hers that caused her heart to trip. Was it possible that she'd fallen in love with this brash, uncompromising man? Nikki couldn't remember anything about her past, but she didn't believe for a second that she would marry a man so damned intimidating, a man who just by his mere presence seemed destined to dominate everyone he met. Certainly she would have chosen a kinder, wiser individual—a thinking man.

His lips moved against hers, and it was all Nikki could do to lay stiffly and unresponsively on the bed. Trent lifted his head and, straightening, smoothed the wrinkles from his shirt as he winked at her. The smile curving his lips was positively wicked—as if he and she shared some dark, indecent secret. He patted the edge of the bed, then walked with the doctor out of the room.

Silently fuming, Nikki thought of a million ways to strangle him. His little show for the doctor was just an act. Or was it? There was no passion in this kiss, not like the one before, and yet she'd felt a spark of emotion, a tenderness she couldn't equate with Trent McKenzie or whoever the hell he was. She ground her teeth in frustration and willed her memory to surface, but only vague images drifted into her mind. She remembered a grassy field and riding a horse—no, a pony, a spotted pony. She'd been bareback. A dog had trailed after the chubby little horse, nearly hidden in the tall grass. There had been apple trees—an old orchard, perhaps—in the corner of the field and a copse of oak and fir trees on the other side of the fence line.

Had the pony been hers? She imagined cattle grazing on the stubble in the next field, but the image turned cloudy and she was left with an emptiness that she couldn't fill. "Damn it all," she muttered as she tried and failed to summon any other thoughts about her past.

What about Trent? Your husband? Any memory of him at all eluded her completely.

She shifted on the wrinkled sheets and sucked in her breath at the sharp pain at her ankle. From the hallway, she heard Trent and Dr. Padillo, talking softly in the flowing cadences of Spanish. Of course they were discussing her, but she couldn't hear or understand them. Frustrated, she tried to sit up, but fell back against the pillows. If only she could climb out of this bed, march down to the police station, or the airport, or the American embassy, if there was one on this godforsaken island, and demand to know who she was and how she got here.

Tears threatened, and she stared at the crucifix on the wall. "Give me strength," she whispered as Nurse Vásquez returned with her medication. She thought of refusing the drugs, knowing she needed a clear mind, but the pain was too great and she was thankful for the tide of sleep the tiny pills would bring her. She swallowed the sedative eagerly, waiting for the pain to slowly erode and drowsiness to overcome her. Closing her eyes, an old commercial message wafted through her brain. *Calgon, take me away...*

When she woke up...then she'd try to remember.

"I want her released as soon as possible." Trent eyed the little man who was the most highly recommended doctor on the island. However, there couldn't have been more than three physicians on Salvaje, so Trent wasn't going to linger here, hoping this man knew what he was doing. Too much was at stake.

"But you have time...you are on your honeymoon." With a knowing grin, Padillo patted Trent's arm. "Be patient."

"We have to get back to the States."

"Why must you leave so soon?"

"We'd only planned to stay a week," Trent explained, trying to keep his temper in check. He was used to doing things his own way. Having Nikki in the local hospital was inconvenient. Damned inconvenient. Probably even dangerous. *Don't get paranoid,* he told himself, but he hadn't slept much in five nights and he was strung tighter than a bowstring. Right now, he wanted to shake some sense into the little doctor, to convince Padillo to release Nikki at that very moment, but he couldn't tip his hand. Not yet.

"Salvaje is a beautiful place. You should stay here. Enjoy the climate," Doctor Padillo was saying as a nurse at the lobby waved at him in an attempt to get his attention. "Your wife…she has not seen much of the island."

"We can come back."

"You Americans," the doctor said, clucking his tongue. "Always in a rush."

If you only knew.

"I can release her within three days," Padillo said, though by the gathering of lines between his flat black brows it was obvious to Trent that the doctor wasn't happy about his decision. "But there are only a few flights to America."

"We'll find one."

"Doctor—" the nurse called, and Padillo waved her away, as if she were a bothersome insect.

"Then I'll have the necessary papers ready to sign."

"Good. Oh, and while you're at it, I'll need my wife's purse and personal belongings."

"Today?"

"*Sí*. I think she'd like to look through it before she goes home."

"If it is lost, the hospital cannot be responsible—"

"Don't worry," Trent said, thinking of the pretty woman with the battered face as she lay in a hospital bed a few doors down the dark corridor. "Just give me her belongings. I'll sign a release for everything."

Nikki wasn't sure of the time. She'd slept so much, she couldn't keep track, but it seemed as if two or three days had passed, with Trent forever in the room with her, the doctors and nurses flitting in and out, feeding her, forcing fluids down her, fiddling with the

IV, concerned that she eliminate, and assuring her she would be fine.

They seemed worried about infection, anxious about her temperature and her blood pressure, but no one showed the least bit of uneasiness about the fact that her memory had all but disappeared.

When Nikki had asked Padillo about her amnesia, he assured her that her memory would return and she would remember everything about her past, most likely in bits and pieces at first, but then, slowly, all the years of her life would blend together and she would know who she was, her family, what she did for a living. She'd even remember becoming Trent McKenzie's bride.

She wasn't so sure.

When she questioned him, Trent was reticent to talk to her about her amnesia. "Don't worry," he'd told her. "It'll come. Take it easy." She wondered if he'd been coached by the hospital staff or if there was a reason he didn't want her to remember her past.

He never gave up his vigil. Sitting with her day and night, refusing the next bed, looking the worse for wear each time she awoke, he was in the room with her. He didn't bother to shave, but did manage to change into a clean shirt one day. Was he devoted? She didn't buy it for a minute, yet she was certain that there was something tying them together, something worth much more to him than a wedding ring.

Had he kidnapped her and brought her to this tiny island off the coast of South America?

No—for he wouldn't have alerted the police to her accident, and Padillo himself had talked to the authorities. Unless the *Policía de Salvaje* were not sophisticated enough to know about crimes committed in the

States. Why would they doubt him? He made all the outward signs of caring for her. She, on the other hand, couldn't remember where she'd lived all her life. Of course they would believe him.

Her head began to throb, and Trent, sensing she was awake, shifted from his spot near the window to take a chair at the foot of the bed. He propped the worn heels of his boots against the mattress and folded his arms over his chest.

"Good morning," he drawled with a sexy smile.

She glanced at the windows. "It's afternoon." Her dry mouth tasted horrible.

"Well, at least you can still tell time."

"Very funny," she said, wishing her tongue didn't feel so thick. She moved her arm and was surprised that there wasn't much pain. Either she was healing, or the medication hadn't worn off.

"Feeling better?"

"I feel like hell."

He chuckled. "Glad to see you haven't lost your sunny personality."

"Never." Forcing her gaze to his, she said, "Who are you? And don't—" she lifted her sore right arm, holding out her palm so that he wouldn't immediately start giving her pat, hospital-approved answers "—don't give me any bull about being my husband."

His lips twitched and showed a hint of white teeth against his dark jaw, but he didn't argue with her.

"What do you do for a living?"

"I work for an insurance company."

"Oh, come on," she said, rolling her eyes to the ceiling. "You—a suit? No way." She would have bought a lumberjack, or a cowboy, or a race-car driver, but an insurance agent?

"Why not?"

"Give me some credit, will you? I may not be able to remember much, but I'm not a total moron."

"Believe what you want." His grin was smug and mocking and she would have given anything to be able to wipe it off his face.

"Oh, now I get it," she said, unable to stop baiting him. "You've spent the better part of the last week camped out here on the off chance I'd wake up and buy term life insurance or accident insurance—"

"I'm an investigator."

"That's more like it."

"For an insurance company. Fraudulent claims. Arson, suicide, that sort of thing." Cocking his head to one side, he said, "But the company would probably appreciate it if I could sell you some term—"

"Enough already. I believe you." She tried to sit up, couldn't and motioned toward the crank at the end of the bed. "Would you—"

Trent, dropping his feet, reached over. Within a minute she was nearly sitting upright. "Better?"

She rubbed the back of her hand where the needle marks from her recent IV were turning black and blue—to match the rest of her body. "Yes. Thanks."

He seemed less hostile today, and the restlessness which usually accompanied him had nearly disappeared. As he propped his boots on the mattress again, settling low on his back, he actually seemed harmless, just a concerned husband waiting for his bride to recover. She decided to take advantage of his good mood because she couldn't believe it would last very long.

"How did we meet?"

"I was working for the insurance company on a claim from someone who worked with you. Connie Benson."

"Connie?" she repeated, shaking her head when no memory surfaced. But the name seemed right. "Connie Benson?"

"You were both reporters at the *Observer*."

"I don't—"

"The *Seattle Observer*. You told me you've worked there for about six years."

A sharp pain touched her brain. The *Observer*. She'd heard of it. Now she remembered. Yes, yes! She'd read that particular Seattle daily newspaper all her life.... She remembered sitting at a table...sun streaming through the bay windows of the nook...with...oh, God, with whom? Her head snapped up.

"You remember."

"Just reading the paper. With someone."

He held up his hands. "Not me, I'm afraid."

She felt a niggle of disappointment. For some reason she'd hoped that his story could be proved or disproved by this one little facet of information.

"We met just about five weeks ago."

"Five weeks?" she repeated, astounded.

"Kind of a whirlwind thing."

"More like a hurricane. Five weeks? Thirty-five days and we got married?"

"That's about right."

"Oh, no." She shook her head, and his eyes grew dark. "I don't think I'd—"

"You did, damn it, Nikki! We hung out together as much as possible, decided to get married, found a local justice of the peace, tied the knot and came down here for our honeymoon."

She was still shaking her head. "No, I'm sure—"

His feet clattered to the floor and suddenly he was looming over her, his hands flat on the sheets on either side of her head, his face pressed close to hers. "Look, lady, I'm sorry if I destroyed all your romantic fantasies. But the truth of the matter is that we didn't have a long engagement or a big, fancy wedding."

"Why not?"

His sensual grin was positively wicked, and she wondered how she could have felt so comfortable with him only a few minutes before. With one finger, he traced the circle of bones at her throat in a slow sexy motion that caused her blood to flow wildly through her veins. "Because we couldn't wait, darlin'," he drawled. "We were just too damned hot."

"Liar." She shoved his hand away, but her pulse was jumping crazily, betraying her.

"That's the way it was. You can try to romanticize it if you want to, put me up on some white charger, give me a suit of shining armor, but it really doesn't wash, Nikki. I'm no hero."

Her heart was hammering, her breathing coming in short, quick gulps of air. *Oh, dear God!* Had she really married this...this sexy, arrogant bastard?

His glance slid insolently down her body. "I could lie to you. Hey, what the hell, you don't remember anyway, do you? So, if you want to believe it was all hearts and flowers, moonlight and champagne, holding hands as we walked along a beach, well, go right ahead."

"Why are you doing this?" she said through clenched teeth.

"I just don't want you to have any illusions about me. That's all."

"What about the roses?"

"The what?"

She moved her hand, motioning toward the stand near the bed. In the process, her fingertips scraped against his shirt, grazing the muscles hidden behind the soft blue denim. He sucked in a swift breath, his gaze locking with hers for a heartbeat. Her throat turned to sand and she imagined him on another bed, positioned above her, his body straining and sweating. Slamming her eyes closed, she blocked out the erotic image. He couldn't be telling the truth! He couldn't!

"Oh, the flowers. Nice touch, don't you think?" he said without masking any sarcasm.

"What do you mean? Are you saying they're just some kind of joke?"

"I thought you'd like them. That's all."

Her heart sank as he settled back in his chair again. Recrossing his ankles on the end of the bed, he asked, "Anything else you want to know?"

"Just one thing," she said, bracing herself. "Why did you marry me if you hate me so much?"

His lips flattened. "I don't hate you, Nikki."

"You've made a point to ridicule me."

"Because you can't or won't remember me."

Her heart ached, and she forced the words over her tongue. "Do you love me?"

He hesitated, his eyes shadowing for just a second, his emotions unreadable. Plowing a hand through his hair, he grimaced. "I guess you could call it that."

"Would you—would you call it love?"

Ignoring her question and the pain that had to be

obvious in her gaze, he stood and stretched lazily, his muscles lengthening, his body seeming more starkly male and dangerous than ever.

"Do you love me?" she said again, more forcefully this time.

A sad smile touched his face. "As much as I can, Nik. You can't remember this, but I may as well lay it out to you. I never much believed in love."

"Then why did you marry me?"

His jaw tightened and he hesitated for a heartbeat. "It seemed like the thing to do."

"Why?"

He shoved his hands into the back pockets of his jeans and walked to the door. Pausing, he sent her a look that cut right to her soul. "I married you 'cause you wanted it so damned much."

"Noble of you."

"You really don't remember me, do you? 'Cause if you did, you'd know I was anything but noble." He sauntered away, leaving her feeling raw and wounded as his footsteps faded down the hallway.

She let out a long, heartrending sigh. Everything was such a jumble. Nothing made any sense. *Think, Nikki, think! Trent McKenzie is not your husband. He can't be. Then who the hell is he and what does he want?* Squeezing her eyes shut, she forced her mind to roll backward. He'd told her she lived in Seattle, and that felt right. He'd mentioned she'd worked for a newspaper—the *Seattle Observer*—and that, too, seemed to fit. But nothing else—not the whirlwind romance, not the quick civil ceremony for a wedding, not the hostile man himself—seemed like it would be a part of her life.

So who was he and why was he insisting that they

were married? She tried to force her memory, her fists curling in frustration, her mind as blank and stark as the sheets that covered her.

In frustration, she gave up and stared out the window to the blue sky and leaves that moved in the breeze. Maybe she was trying too hard. Maybe she should take the doctor's advice and let her memory return slowly, bit by bit.

And what about Trent?

Oh, Lord!

"Señorita Carrothers!"

The woman's voice startled her. She turned her head toward the doorway and found a pretty girl with round cheeks and short black hair. Her smile faded slightly as she noticed the wounds on Nikki's face.

"*¡Dios!* Are you all right? We, at the hotel, were so worried—"

"Do I know you?"

"*Sí,* when you register—"

"Wait a minute." Nikki held up a hand but was restrained by her IV. She tried to think, to remember. "You're saying I registered as Carrothers. *Señorita* Carrothers?" Nikki asked, her heartbeat quickening. This was the first proof that Trent had lied.

"*Sí.*"

"Was I alone or was my husband with me?"

"Your husband?" A perplexed look crossed the girl's face.

From somewhere down the hallway, rapid-fire Spanish was directed at the girl in the doorway, and Nurse Vásquez, her guardian feathers obviously ruffled, appeared. Nikki couldn't understand the conversation but could tell that the nurse was dressing the girl down.

"Wait," Nikki said when she realized that Vásquez was sending away her one link to the past. "What's your name? Where do you work?" But already the girl was out of sight, her footsteps echoing down the hallway. "Please, call her back!" she begged, desperate for more information about herself.

"I'm sorry, Señora McKenzie. Strict orders from the doctor. You are to see no one but family members."

Nikki started to climb out of the bed. "But—"

"Oh, *señora,* please. You must rest…. Do not move."

"Don't let her leave!" Nikki ordered, but it was too late. The girl was gone and Nikki was left with a more defined mistrust of the man posing as her husband. As the nurse took her blood pressure, Nikki said, "Can't you at least give me her name?"

"I do not know it."

"Why was she here?"

"A visitor to Señorita Martínez, I believe."

"Please, ask Señorita her name and where she works." The nurse seemed about to decline, but Nikki grabbed her sleeve, her fingers desperate. "Please, Nurse Vásquez. It's important."

"*Dios,*" Nurse Vásquez muttered under her breath. "I will see what I can do."

"*Gracias,*" Nikki said, crossing her fingers that Trent wouldn't get wind of her request. For the moment, she would keep her conversation with the woman to herself.

Within the hour, she heard his footsteps and braced herself for another confrontation. He appeared in the doorway with two cups of coffee. "Peace offering," he said, setting a cup on the stand near the bed. Then he resumed his position near the window. "I didn't mean to upset you."

"I'd like to lie and tell you I'm fine, but I'm not."

He lifted a shoulder and took a long swallow. "I know. I wish I could change that."

"You don't have to spend day and night here."

"Sure I do."

"I'll be all right—"

"Wouldn't want my bride to get lonely." He offered her a sly grin, then sipped from his paper cup, letting the steam warm his face.

"I wouldn't be."

"I was hoping that being around me would jog your memory."

Slowly, she shook her head. "Don't be offended, but... I don't see how I would ever have wanted to marry you. True, I can't remember, but you don't really seem my type."

"I wasn't." He curled one knee up on the ledge and stared through the glass. "You were used to dating button-down types."

"So why would I take up with you?" she asked.

"The challenge," he said, his eyes twinkling seductively.

"I don't think so."

"That's where you're wrong." His lips turned down at the corners. "You've always been a risk-taker, Nikki. A woman who wasn't afraid to do whatever it was she felt she had to. Your job at the *Observer* is a case in point."

"My job?" she asked.

"Mmm. You're a reporter, and a damned good one."

For some strange reason, she glowed under his compliment, but she told herself to be wary. Instinctively she knew McKenzie wasn't the kind of man who praised someone without an ulterior motive. Her shoulder muscles bunched.

"You've been bucking for more difficult assignments since you signed on at the paper."

"And was I given them?"

"Hell, no. A few people at the *Observer,* those in positions of power, like to keep things status quo. You know, women doing the entertainment news, helpful household hints, local information about schools and mayoral candidates and whose kid won the last spelling bee. That kind of thing."

"That's what I wrote?" she asked, her brows drawing together. It sounded right, but she wasn't sure.

"Most of the time, but you were more interested in politics, the problems of gangs in the inner city, corruption in the police department, political stuff." He watched her carefully as he sipped the thick coffee.

"Who was my boss at the paper?"

"A woman named Peggy Henderson...no—Hendricks, I think her name was."

"You don't know?" she asked, incredulous.

He lifted a muscular shoulder. "Never met her." When she gazed at him skeptically, he snorted. "As I said, you and I, we haven't known each other all that long." Again, that soul-searing look.

"What about my family?" she asked, her fingers twisting in the sheets. He was giving her more information than she could handle.

"Your father's based in Seattle, owns his own import/export business. But he's out of town a lot. In the Orient. You have a sister back east and one in Montana somewhere, I think, and your mother lives in L.A."

"My folks are divorced?" Lord, why wasn't any of this registering? she wondered. Why couldn't she conjure up her mother's smile, her father's face, the color of her sisters' hair?

"Dr. Padillo didn't want you to rush things," Trent said evenly. "He thinks it's best if your memory returns on your own."

"And you disagree?"

"I don't know what to think, but I'm sure the best thing for you would be to get you home, back to the States, where an American doctor, maybe even a psychiatrist or neurosurgeon, could look at you."

Her throat closed. "Could my amnesia be permanent?" she asked, her heart nearly stopping. The thought of living the rest of her life with no recollection of her childhood, the homes she'd grown up in, the family she'd loved, was devastating. A black tide of desperation threatened to draw her into its inky depths.

A shadow crossed his eyes. "I don't know. But the sooner we get home, the better." This side of Trent was new, as if he were suddenly concerned for her emotional well-being. "Tomorrow Padillo's springing you. I'll pick up everything at the hotel, meet you here, and we'll take the first flight back to Seattle."

"I'd like to call someone."

He froze. "Who?"

"My editor, for starters. Then my mother, I guess." Was it her imagination or did his spine stiffen slightly?

"If the doctor agrees."

"Why wouldn't he?"

"As I said, I'm no medicine man. But I'll see if I can get a portable phone down here. If not, you can use the pay booth at the end of the hall."

"Now?"

"I don't think that would be a good idea."

"Well, I do." She forced herself upright, ignored the dull ache in her hip and leg, and slid over the edge of the bed. As she set weight on her right ankle, she winced, but the pain wasn't as intense as she'd expected. She didn't know the layout of the hospital, but she hoped to find Mrs. Martínez's room. If she couldn't get the information about the girl from the hotel from Nurse Vásquez, she'd check with Mrs. Martínez. There were more ways than one to skin a cat.

"Get back in the bed," Trent ordered.

"Not yet."

"Nikki, please—"

"Help me to the bathroom," she said, tossing her hair off her face and grabbing the light cotton robe that was thrown across the foot of the bed. It was hospital issue and not the least bit flattering, but at least it covered the gaps left by the hospital gown. Balancing most of her weight on her left foot, she shoved her hands down the sleeves and tied a knot in the loose belt. "Come on, *husband.*"

For a second he seemed about to refuse. "This is crazy."

"The nurse told me that whenever I felt like getting out of bed, I should. And I feel like it now."

Grumbling about hardheaded women without a lick of sense, Trent bent a little so that she could place her arm around his neck. He wrapped a strong arm around her waist and nearly supported all her weight himself. "Okay, let's go."

She was a little unsteady at first, but managed the few steps out of the room to the bathroom down the hall. She tried to ignore the warm impressions of Trent's fingers at her waist and concentrated on taking each tenuous step. The walking got easier and she became more confident.

If only she could ignore the smell of him, male and musk and leather as they paused at the bathroom door.

"¡Señora McKenzie!" A petite nurse hurried down the hallway. Concern creased her forehead and caused her steps to hurry along the smooth tile floor. *"¡Espere!"* As she approached, she slid a furious glance at Trent. *"¿Qué es esto?"* Her black eyes snapped fire and her thin lips drew tight like a purse string.

"She wants to know what's going on here," Trent explained. There was an exchange of angry Spanish, and finally Nurse Lidia Sánchez shoved open the restroom door with her hip and helped Nikki inside. "I guess she didn't like my bedside manner," Trent offered as the door swung shut.

Nurse Sánchez was still muttering furiously in Spanish, but Nikki didn't even try to understand her. Instead she stared at her reflection in the mirror mounted over the sink. Her heart dropped and all the tears she'd fought valiantly swam to the surface of her eyes. The swelling had gone down, but bruises and scrapes surrounded her eye sockets. Thick scabs covered the abrasions on her cheeks and chin. Her hair was dirty and limp and she barely recognized herself. She hadn't expected to be beautiful, but she hadn't thought it would be this bad. Beneath the bruises she could see traces of a woman who would be considered pretty and vivacious, with green eyes, an easy smile and high cheekbones. Her chin-length hair, a light brown streaked with strands of honey-blond, held the promise of thick waves, but today the dirty strands hung limp and lusterless.

Trent certainly wasn't posing as her husband because he was taken with her beauty. She winced as she touched the corner of her eye where the scab had curdled.

"Pase," Nurse Sánchez insisted as she held open the door to the lavatory. *"Ahora."*

Nikki followed her orders, but on her way out paused at the mirror again and caught Nurse Sánchez in the mirror's reflection as she attempted to wash her hands. "Do you know which room Mrs. Martínez is in?"

"Sí, room seven. You know her?" she asked skeptically.

"Just *of* her," Nikki said, wiping her hands and following the nurse back to her empty room. Trent wasn't anywhere to be seen, and she felt a mixture of emotions ranging from disappointment to relief. She had started to trust him, but the girl from the hotel had caused all her doubts to creep back into her mind. Somehow she had to find a way to talk to Mrs. Martínez in room seven.

Her bed had been changed, and she lay on the crisp sheets and closed her eyes. Her surface wounds were healing. Even her ankle was much better, but her memory was still a cloudy fog, ever-changing like the tide, allowing short little glimpses into the past life, but never completely rolling away.

She was certain she remembered a golden retriever named Shorty, and that she'd never gotten along with her sisters, who were several years older, but she couldn't recall their names or their faces.

Instinctively she knew that she'd always been ambitious and that she'd never spent much time lying around idle—already the hospital walls were beginning to cave in on her—yet she couldn't recall the simple fact that she was married to a man as unforgettable as Trent McKenzie.

She was in limbo. No past. No future. A person who didn't really exist.

At the sound of the scrape of his boot, she opened her eyes and found Trent at the foot of her bed. His expression was as grim as she'd ever seen. "There's good news and bad news," he said, his fingers gripping the metal rail of the bed until his knuckles showed white. "The good news is that you get to leave this place. Padillo says that you can leave tomorrow."

"And the bad news?"

"The airline we're booked on, one of the few carriers that flies to this island, declared Chapter Eleven yesterday."

"I don't understand."

His eyebrows pulled together, forming a solid black line. "They're in bankruptcy reorganization. Everyone who bought a seat on the plane is scrambling to get passage on the other carriers. The airport's a madhouse, and my guess is that we won't get out of here for at least two days."

"Two days?" she repeated.

"Maybe longer." His jaw was tight with frustration. "I booked us another room, and I was lucky to get one. I paid for a week. Just in case." He kicked at an imaginary stone on the floor. "Looks like we're stuck here for a while, Mrs. McKenzie. Just you and me."

Chapter 3

"Here it is—home, sweet home." Trent swung open the door of their hotel room and Nikki felt the cold hand of dread clamp over her heart. So she was here. Alone with her husband.

Swallowing hard, and still holding on to Trent's arm for balance, Nikki carefully stepped over the threshold of the second-story room. It was furnished with a single queen-size bed, a small round table with two chairs situated near the terrace and a single bureau. Matching night tables in an indiscriminate Mediterranean design were placed on either side of the bed.

"Come on. You'd better rest."

"I've done nothing but rest for the past week," she objected, though leaving the hospital, the bumpy cab ride and walking through the large hotel had been more difficult than she'd anticipated. Doctor Padillo had assured her that she would feel stronger with each passing day, and she certainly hoped so.

Trent hadn't lied about the problems getting off the island. Never easy, now leaving Salvaje was nearly impossible with the major carrier to the island in a state of flux. "You haven't found us another flight yet?" she asked, though she guessed from his silence in the cab that his attempts to fly home must have failed.

"I'll work on it."

A firm hand on her elbow, he guided her to one side of the bed, pulled down the covers and let her slide onto the clean sheets. She felt awkward and silly. If he were her husband, this was no big deal. If he weren't…she couldn't even imagine where being cooped up alone with him might lead.

"There's a phone here. Good luck getting an overseas line. Everyone who's stranded here is trying to call out."

"Great," she muttered, though she hadn't expected better. He'd tried to help her make a call to her mother from the pay phone at the hospital. She propped the second pillow behind her head while she scanned the room. It was airy and clean, with a paddle fan mounted from the ceiling and bright floral bedspreads that matched the curtains. The closet door was half-open, and she spied her clothes—at least, she assumed they were hers—hanging neatly. A yellow sundress, khaki-colored jacket and white skirt were visible. She'd hoped seeing some of her things would jog her memory, but she was disappointed again. It seemed as if she'd never put together the simple pieces of her life.

As if reading her thoughts, Trent opened a bureau drawer and withdrew a cowhide purse.

In a flash, she remembered the leather bag. "I bought

this in New Mexico," she said as he handed her the handbag and she rubbed the smooth, tooled leather. "From Native Americans. I was on a trip…with…" As quickly as the door to her memory opened, it closed again and she was left with an empty feeling of incredible loss. "Oh, God, I can't remember."

"A man or a woman?" he asked, his voice suddenly sharp.

"I don't know." She turned her face up to his, hoping he could fill in the holes, but he lifted a shoulder.

"I wasn't there. Before my time." He walked to the door, shut it and snapped on a switch that started the paddle fan over the bed moving in slow, lazy circles.

Nikki wasn't going to be thwarted. The keys to her life were in her hands and she was determined to find out everything she could about her past. Leaning back against the headboard, she tossed back the purse's flap and dumped the contents on her lap. Brush. Comb. Wallet. Tissues. Sunglasses. A paperback edition of a Spanish-English dictionary. A pair of silver earrings. Several pens. Address book. Passport. Small camera.

"All the clues to who I am," she said sarcastically.

"Not quite. I think I've got a few more." Reaching into the pocket of his jeans he withdrew a sealed plastic bag. Inside were a pair of gold hoop earrings, a matching bracelet and a slim gold band.

Her throat seemed to close upon itself, and she had to hold back a strangled cry at the sight of her wedding ring. Proof of her marriage. With trembling fingers she withdrew the tiny circle of metal and slipped it over her finger. "You bought me this?" she asked, her eyes seeking his.

"At a jewelry shop near Pioneer Square."

She licked her lips and stared at her hands. The ring was obviously a size too large.

"You wanted to keep it for the honeymoon, and we planned to have it sized back in the States."

"Is that right?" she said under her breath. Why couldn't she remember standing before a justice of the peace, her heart beating crazily, her smile wide and happy as the love of her life slipped this smooth ring over her finger. *Because it didn't happen!*

"I don't remem—"

"You will," he told her, his gaze steady as he stared down at her.

She shook her head, mesmerized as she scrutinized the ring. Her head began to throb again. "I should remember this, Trent," she said, her frustration mounting. "A wedding. No matter how simple. It's not something anyone forgets."

"Give it time."

Give it time. Don't rush things. It will all come back to you. But when? She felt as if she were going crazy and her patience snapped. "I'm sick of giving it time! Damn it, Trent, I want to remember. And not bits and pieces. I want the rest of my life back, and I want it back now!"

"I'd give it to you if I could." Plowing his hands through his hair in frustration, he spied her wallet. "Here." He tossed it into her hands. "Maybe this will help."

"Maybe," she said, though she didn't believe it for a minute. Sending up a silent prayer, she opened the fat leather case and sifted through her credit cards and pieces of ID. Nothing seemed to pierce through the armor of her past, and she was about to give up in futility when she saw the first picture.

"Dad," she whispered, her heart turning over as she recognized a photograph of a distinguished-looking man with a steel-gray mustache and jowly chin. For a second she remembered him in a velvet red suit and long white beard, tiny glasses perched on the end of his nose, as he dressed up as Santa Claus each year for his company party.... The memory faded and she tried vainly to call it up again.

"Hey...take it easy." Suddenly Trent sat on the edge of the bed, his warm hand on her forehead. "It'll come."

If only she could believe it. "So everyone says. Everyone who can remember who they are."

"It's been less than a week since you woke from the coma."

His harsh features seemed incredibly kind, and she felt hot tears fill her throat. She fought the urge to break down and cry because she couldn't trust him—even his kindness might be an act. There were other pictures in her wallet, some old and faded, none that she recognized, until she saw the family portrait, taken years ago, before her parents had split up. Her father still had black hair back then; her mother, a thin woman with a thrusting jaw, was a blonde. Her older sisters—why couldn't she remember their names?—looked about fourteen and twelve, and Nikki was no more than eight, her teeth much too large for her mouth.

"Janet," Trent said, pointing to the oldest girl with the dark hair. "Carole." The middle sister with braces. "Your mom's name is Eloise. She and your dad—"

"Were divorced. I know," she said, saddened that she couldn't recall her mother's voice or smile, couldn't even remember a fight with her sisters. Had they shared a room? Had they ever been close? Why, even staring at pictures of her family, did she feel so incredibly alone? If only she could sew together the patchwork of her life, bring back those odd-shaped pieces of her memory.

"Look, why don't you try calling your dad?" Trent suggested, though his eyes still held a wary spark. "He's still in Seattle and you always have been pretty close to him. Maybe hearing his voice will help." He snapped up the address book, opened it to the *C*'s and scanned the page. "It's still early in Seattle, so you might catch him at home."

He picked up the receiver and started dialing before she could protest.

"Have you talked with him?" she asked.

"No."

"You didn't call and tell him about the accident?"

"I figured he'd take the news better from you. I've never met him. As far as I know, he doesn't even know we're married, and since your life wasn't in danger, I didn't see a reason to worry him."

"And my mother—"

He held up a hand. *"¿La telefonista? Quiero llamar Seattle en los Estados Unidos. Comuníqueme, por favor, con el número de Ted Carrothers..."* He rattled off her father's number in Spanish, answered a few more questions, then, frowning slightly, handed her the receiver.

Nikki's heart was thudding, her fingers sweaty around the phone. "Come on, Dad," she whispered as the phone began to ring on the continent far away. She was about to give up when a groggy male voice answered.

"Carrothers here."

"Dad?" Nikki said, her voice husky. Tears pressed hot behind her eyelids, and relief flooded through her. She felt like she might break down and sob.

"Hey, Nik, I wondered if I'd hear from you."

"Oh, Dad." She couldn't keep her voice from cracking.

"Is something wrong, honey?"

"No, no, I'm fine," she assured him, shooting Trent a grateful glance. "But I did have an accident…." She told him everything she could remember or had been told of her trip, leaving out her amnesia so that her father wouldn't worry. As she talked, bringing up the fact that Trent McKenzie had been the man who had rescued her, she let her gaze follow Trent, who, whether to give her some privacy or to get some air, left her and walked onto the veranda. The wind had kicked up, lifting his dark hair from his face and billowing his jacket away from his lean body.

"Nikki! You could have been killed!" her father exclaimed, all sounds of sleep gone from his voice.

"But I wasn't."

"Thank God. I knew going to Salvaje was a bad idea. I tried to warn you not to go."

"You did?"

"Don't you remember? I thought that was why you hadn't called, because you were still angry with me for trying to talk you out of the trip."

Now wasn't the time to mention her loss of memory. "Well, things worked out. And I got married to Trent."

"You *what?*" He swore under his breath. "But I've never heard you mention him. Nikki, is this some kind of joke? You could give me a heart attack—"

"It's no joke, Dad. I'm really married." *At least, that's*

what everyone tells me. She heard his swift intake of breath. "It…it was a quick decision," she said, giving him the same spotty information she'd gleaned from Trent.

"To a guy named Trent McKenzie. A man I've never even heard of?" *Here it comes—the lecture,* she thought. "Holy Mary! I can't believe it. What about Dave?"

"Dave?" A lock clicked open her mind.

"Dave Neumann. You know, the man you've been dating for about three years. I know you two had a spat and that you said it was over, but hell, Nikki, that was barely six months ago. Now you've gone and eloped with this…this stranger?" Anger, disapproval and astonishment radiated over the phone. "I know you've always been impulsive, but I gotta tell you, this takes the cake!"

"You'll meet him as soon as we get home," Nikki assured her father, though her stomach was tying itself into painful little knots.

"I'd damned well better. You know, Nikki, for the first eighteen years of your life I got you out of scrape after scrape—either with the law or school or your friends or whatever—but ever since you turned into an adult, you've been on this independence kick and nothing I tell you seems to sink in. I warned you not to go to Salvaje, didn't I? I knew that it would be trouble. Maybe if you'd told me you were going on your honeymoon, or at the very least confided that you'd found a man you were going to marry, things would have turned out differently and you wouldn't have ended up in some run-down, two-bit hospital!"

She felt her back stiffen involuntarily. "How would your knowing change anything?"

"Hell, I don't know. But you've gotten so damned

bullheaded and secretive! Lord, why would you try to hide the fact that you were getting married, unless you were ashamed of the guy?"

"It...it just seemed more romantic," she said, trying to come up with a plausible excuse.

"Romantic, my eye. Since when have you, the investigative reporter, the champion of the underdog, the girl who fought every damned liberal crusade, been romantic? Don't tell me he's one of those long-haired left-wing idiots who chains himself to nuclear reactors or sets spikes in old-growth timber to keep loggers from cutting the stuff."

"I don't think so, Dad," Nikki said, smiling to herself as she watched Trent lean against the railing, his broad shoulders straining the seams of his jacket. She couldn't imagine him in a protest march.

"Good." He sounded a little less wounded, as if the news had finally sunk in. "I just don't understand why you didn't bring up his name or have the guts to introduce me to him."

"It's...it's complicated. I'll explain everything when I get back."

There was a slight hesitation on the other end of the line, then a quiet swearword muttered under her father's breath. "There isn't something more I should know, is there?"

She felt sweat collect between her shoulder blades.

"I mean, if there was a...problem...you'd come to me, wouldn't you?"

She bit down on her lip. What was he saying?

"If you're in any kind of trouble..."

Oh, Dad, if you only knew.

"These days you don't *have* to get married. There

are all sorts of options...." His voice trailed off, and she realized what he was implying.

"I'm not pregnant, Dad."

A sigh of relief escaped him. "Well, I guess we can thank God for small favors."

"I'll call when I get home."

"You'd better. Now, wait a minute. Let me get my calendar. Where is the damned thing?" he asked himself, his voice suddenly muffled. "Okay, here we go. So when will you be back home? I'm supposed to take off for Tokyo next week."

"We'll be back as soon as we can catch a flight. There's a problem with the airline we flew on."

"I read about it. But there are other flights. Try and make it home before I leave."

"I will," she promised. They talked a few minutes more and she finally hung up feeling more desperate than ever. She had wanted to confide in her father, tell him that she wasn't sure of her past, couldn't remember the man who'd become her self-appointed guardian—her *husband* for God's sake—and yet she'd held her tongue. She was an adult now and responsible for herself, and she realized that the animosity she'd felt over the phone only scratched the surface of the rifts in her family.

Slowly, she pushed herself up from the bed and made her way to the veranda. The breeze, warm and smelling of the sea, lifted her hair and brushed against her bruised face. Thick vines crawled up the whitewashed walls of the hotel and fragrant blossoms moved with the wind. Poised on a hillside, the hotel offered a commanding view of the island. From the veranda, Nikki looked over red roofs and lush foliage toward the bay. Fishing vessels and pleasure craft dotted the horizon, and as she cast a glance northward, she saw the sharp cliffs rising from the ocean, the rugged terrain that wound upward to the highest point on Salvaje and the crumbling white walls of the mission tower.

Her heart seemed to stop for a minute and her teeth dug into her lower lip. Fear, like a black, faceless monster, curled her soul in its clawlike grasp, and suddenly she could barely breathe. She held on to the rail in a death grip and her knees threatened to buckle.

Trent had slid a pair of aviator glasses over his eyes and his expression was guarded. "Memory flash?" he asked, his jaw tense.

She shook her head. "Not really."

"Your father shake you up?"

She snorted and blinked against a sudden wash of tears. "A little. He's not too keen on the fact that he didn't meet you."

"He'll get over it."

"I wonder," she said. Leaning forward on her elbows, she ignored the cliffs and forced her gaze to the sea, where sunlight glittered against the smooth waves.

"Look. I know you don't remember me or trust me. That's all right. I can be incredibly patient when I have to be." That much she believed. Like a tiger stalking prey, Trent McKenzie knew when to wait and when to strike. That particular thought wasn't the least bit comforting. His lips grew into a deep line. "But I want you to know that I'll keep you safe."

She wanted to believe him. Oh, God, if only she could trust him, but she remembered the girl in the hospital, Mrs. Martínez's friend, and once again she doubted him. Her gaze flew to his and she trembled slightly. "I think I was the kind of person who took care of herself."

A cynical smile slashed his jaw. "Then I'll help."

Her heart cracked a little, and she noticed the handsome lines of his face disguised by the scruffy beard and dark glasses. It would be too easy to fall for him, to trust him because she didn't have much of a choice. But she was still her own woman, and though she'd grown to depend on him, she had to trust her own instincts, make up her own mind. "My father mentioned that I was going to Salvaje. I'd told him. But I hadn't mentioned you."

"Your choice."

"Why wouldn't I tell him?"

"Because you were afraid he might try and talk you out of it," Trent said simply, turning his face to the horizon again. "You and your dad don't always get along, Nikki, and he didn't like you taking off to some small island so far from what he considers civilization."

"So I snuck behind his back?" she asked, disbelieving.

"You just didn't mention me."

"Why not?"

He snorted and his eyes turned frigid as he assessed her. "Because you were afraid he wouldn't approve of me." He leaned an insolent hip against the rail and crossed his arms over his chest. "From what little I know of your old man, you were probably right. Ted Carrothers would probably hate me on sight."

"Why is that?"

"Because he had someone else picked out for you."

"Dave," she said, without thinking.

"That's right." The corners of his mouth pinched in

irritation and he shoved his sleeves over his elbows. "Remember him?" She shook her head, and he grinned that wicked smile. "Well, he was a real Joe College type. Big, blond, shoes always polished. Went to Washington State on a football scholarship and graduated at the top of his class. Ended up going to law school and joined a firm that specializes in corporate taxes. Drives a BMW and works out at the most prestigious athletic club in the city."

"This was a guy I dated?"

"The guy you planned to marry," he corrected.

"You know him?"

"I know *of* him."

Was it her imagination or did he flinch a little?

"How?"

"I checked him out," he said with more than a trace of irritation.

"When?"

"Before we left Seattle."

She wanted to argue with him, but there was something in his cocksure manner that convinced her he had his facts straight, that she had, indeed, been the fiancée of the man he described. "I assume you know why we broke up?"

He lifted a shoulder. "He was too conventional for you. Your dad loved him. Even your mother thought he was a great catch, but he wanted you to give up your career and concentrate on his. You weren't ready for that."

"Thank God," she whispered, then, realizing how that sounded, quickly shut her mouth. But it was too late. Trent's eyes gleamed devilishly, and Nikki was left with the distinct impression that he'd been conning her.

She plucked a purple bloom from the bougainvillea

and twirled the blossom in her fingers. Could she trust Trent? Probably not. Was he lying to her? No doubt. But what choice did she have?

He slapped the peeling wrought iron as if he'd finally made an important decision. "I've got to go out for a while. Check things at the airport. You want to come?"

She shook her head. "I'd like to clean up, I think."

"Just keep the door locked behind me."

"Afraid I might run off?" she asked, unable to hide the sarcasm in her words.

He glanced at her still-swollen ankle. "Run off? No. But hobble off—well, maybe. Though even at that I don't think you'd get far. Besides, there's really nowhere to run on this island."

Her temperature dropped several degrees at the realization that she was trapped. Her mouth suddenly turned to dust.

Trent cocked his head toward the French doors. "Come on, I'll help you into the bathroom."

"I can manage," she said stiffly, and to prove her point, she stepped unevenly off the veranda, walked into the bathroom and locked the door firmly behind her. Wasting no time, she turned on the taps of the tub and began stripping. As steam began to rise from the warm water, she glanced in the mirror, scowled at her reflection and noticed the greenish tinge to the bruises on her rump and back. The scabs were working themselves off, but beneath her skin, blood had pooled at the bottom of her foot and ankle. "Miss America you're not, Carrothers," she told herself, then stopped when she realized her name was now McKenzie.

"Nikki McKenzie. Nicole McKenzie. Nicole Louise Carrothers McKenzie." The name just didn't roll easily off her tongue. She settled into the tub and let the warm water soothe her aching muscles. As best she could, she washed her hair and body, then let the water turn tepid before she climbed out of the tub and rubbed a towel carefully over her skin and hair.

Wrapping the thick terry cloth around her torso, she walked into the bedroom, but stopped short when she found Trent lying on his side of the bed, boots kicked off, ankles crossed, eyes trained on the door.

His eyelids were at half-mast and his gaze was more than interested as it climbed from her feet, past her knees, up her front and finally rested on her face.

"I—I thought you'd left," she sputtered, clasping the towel as tightly as if she were a virgin with a stranger.

"I decided to wait."

"Why?"

"It didn't make sense to leave you alone in the bathroom where you could slip and hit your head, or worse."

"I'm not an invalid!"

"I didn't say you were."

"And I don't need a keeper."

He let that one slide. "I just wanted to be handy in case you got into any trouble."

"The only trouble I've gotten into is you," she said, willing her feet to propel her toward the bureau where she snatched clean panties, bra, shorts and T-shirt from one of the drawers. It crossed her mind that he'd un-packed her clothes, touched her most intimate pieces of apparel, but she ignored the stain of embarrassment that crawled steadily up her neck. After all, if she could believe him, they'd been intimate—made love eagerly. So who cared about the damned underwear?

She started for the bathroom. "Don't leave on my

account," he remarked, and when she turned to face him, her wet hair whipping across her face, she saw a glimmer of amusement in his cobalt eyes, as if he enjoyed her discomfiture.

"You mean I should just let the towel fall and dress at my leisure?"

"Great idea." He stacked his hands behind his head and watched her. Waiting. Like a lion waits patiently for the gazelle to ignore the warning in the air and begin grazing peacefully again.

Just to wipe the smirk off his face she wanted to let go of the damned towel, stand in front of him stark naked and call his bluff. Would he continue to tease her, playing word games, or would he avert his eyes, or, worse yet, would he, as he'd implied earlier, be unable to control himself and sweep her into his arms and carry her to the bed? How would she respond? With heart-melting passion? Oh, for crying out loud!

She turned on her heel and with as much pride as her injuries would allow, marched rigidly into the bathroom.

"Don't forget the antiseptic cream," he ordered as she slammed the door shut. Wrinkling her nose, she mimicked him in the mirror, trying to look beyond her skinned face and scabs. Some of the smaller scrapes were beginning to heal and her eye wasn't as discolored as it had been. "And stay inside," he ordered from the other side of the door. "The doctor warned you about getting too much sun."

"Yes, master," she muttered under her breath. Her teeth ground together as she thought of him barking orders at her. It seemed as if all her life someone was continually ordering her around. Her parents, her older sisters, her teachers, her editor at the paper, and now Trent…. She froze, her heart hammering wildly. She remembered! Nothing solid, but teasing bits of memory that were jagged and rough had pierced the clouds in her mind. Little pieces of her personality seemed to be shaping. Suddenly she was certain that she'd always been stubborn, resented being the smallest sister, the youngest woman on the staff of the *Observer!*

She'd also resented the fact that her work had been looked upon with a wary eye, just because she was young and sometimes because she was a woman. She'd had pride in her work, a great passion for journalism and an incredible frustration at not being taken seriously.

She wanted to share the news with Trent, to tell him that it was truly happening, her memory was coming back, but she held her tongue. She still didn't remember anything about him, about her trip to Salvaje, about the reasons she married him.

And what if she suddenly remembered that it had been he who had been chasing her, he who had pushed her over the cliff? She couldn't really believe that he'd want to hurt her, as he'd had plenty of opportunity to do so since the accident, but there was something deep in her unconscious mind, something dark and demonlike and frightening, that warned her to tread softly with this man. If he were dangerous and her memory was the key to uncovering his deception, he might turn violent.

A shudder of fear ripped through her. *Take it slow, Nikki,* she told herself. You can't trust him. Not yet. Until she had something more concrete, she'd keep her small discovery—that her memory was beginning to surface—to herself.

By the time she'd dressed, dried her hair and applied some salve to her face, he was gone, and she was grateful to be alone.

With the aid of her dictionary, she dialed room service and managed to order a pitcher of iced tea. She found some bills in her wallet and gave the waiter a healthy tip before locking the door behind him.

On the terrace, she poured herself some tea and looked through the pictures in her wallet again. There was one she'd missed earlier—a snapshot taken in the wilderness. A rushing river and steep mountains were the backdrop and two people were embracing before the camera. She recognized the woman as herself, but the man—blond and strapping with even features—wasn't Trent. *Dave,* she mouthed, though she felt no trace of emotion as she touched his photograph with the tip of her finger. No love. No hate. No anger. As if he'd been erased from her mind and heart forever.

"What a mess," she said, but decided not to dwell on her misfortune. She'd been feeling sorry for herself for nearly a week, but it was time to take charge of her life. She wasn't laid up any longer. She could walk, though admittedly she wouldn't win any races just yet, but she didn't have to depend upon Trent or a bevy of doctors to take care of her. She was a grown woman, and, if everyone were to be believed, a strong-willed and independent person who could handle her own life. An investigative journalist, for crying out loud.

She should be able to figure out if Trent was who he claimed to be. She watched the lemon dance between the ice cubes in her glass and decided that it was time to find out if Trent was her husband or an impostor.

Before it was too late. Before she made a horrible, irrevocable mistake.

Before she slept with him.

Chapter 4

The man was known as *el Perro,* the Dog, and Trent thought the name fit. Small and wiry, with long black hair tied in a stringy ponytail, *el Perro* slouched behind the wheel of the beat-up old Pontiac, squinting moodily through the smoke curling from the cigarette dangling at the corner of his mouth. His beady black eyes were ever vigilant as he surveyed the empty, dusty road. Harsh sunlight baked the hood of the car, filtering through the grime on the windshield and causing the temperature in the Pontiac to rise to over a hundred degrees, despite the fact that the windows were down.

The car was parked on a desolate patch of ground. Dry weeds grew heavy between the two dusty tracks on the hillside. Far in the distance, the sea was visible. Below, the town of Santa María stretched along the beach, whitewashed buildings almost blinding as they reflected the sun, and high above on the hill, the ruins of the mission were visible through the trees.

El Perro drew on his filterless cigarette, pulling smoke deep into his lungs. "You want me to watch this one." He jabbed a grubby fingernail at the photo of Nikki with her sisters, a copy Trent had made.

"Yes."

"Qué bonita."

Trent couldn't argue. Nikki Carrothers was one of the most beautiful women he'd ever met. Her smile was nearly infectious, her green eyes intelligent and warm, her hair thick and lustrous. But it wasn't her beauty that intrigued him. No. His fascination for her went much deeper. Too deep. He felt as if he were drowning. Nikki messed with his mind. She had from the first time he set eyes on her. He slid his gaze away from the photograph and gritted his teeth.

"She is in danger, eh?"

"She's in danger and she's dangerous. Both."

El Perro chuckled. "A *tigre, ¿sí?* Wild like the island."

"She's my wife," Trent said with a meaning that bridged the language and social barrier between the two men. Silently he cursed the fact that he had to deal with this lowlife. But *el Perro* came highly recommended. The best on Salvaje.

"You need another man to watch your wife?" With a disgusted snort, the sullen man said, "I trust no one but myself with my woman. No other man—"

Trent grabbed the front of *el Perro*'s shirt, the sweaty cotton wadding between his fingers. He shoved his face so close to the native's that he could see the pores in the smaller man's skin and acrid smoke from the Dog's cigarette burned Trent's eyes. "Get this straight, *amigo,* you're not to lay a hand on her, you're not to speak to her and you're not to be seen by her. You got that?" He gave the shirt a jerk.

El Perro's eyes slitted and he drew hard on his cigarette. Smoke drifted in angry waves from his nostrils. "You do not frighten me," he snarled, though his eyes grew black as the depths of hell. "For your money, I will watch your woman. She will never know that I am near."

"Good."

Releasing the other man's clothing, Trent settled back against the broken springs of the car, reached into his jacket pocket and withdrew a small envelope. He tossed the payment onto the stained seat and climbed out of the Pontiac, leaving the door ajar. "The rest when the job is done."

"How will I know when it is finished?"

"I'll find you," Trent vowed, surprised at the force of his emotions.

El Perro grinned lazily, showing off a slight gap between stained front teeth. "It is not always easy to find the tracks of the Dog, eh?" He tossed the butt of his cigarette out the open window.

"I'll find you," Trent promised, his lips drawing into a cruel smile. "You can bet on it."

No suits!

Not even a sports jacket. Nikki rifled through the clothes in the closet, searching for a clue to Trent's identity. She'd worked quickly, her fingers dipping into each of his pockets, rummaging through a denim jacket, two pairs of jeans, a pair of shorts and several shirts. For all her efforts, she discovered an opened pack of gum, loose change in American money, and a pair of nail clippers.

"Okay, Nancy Drew, what next?" she asked herself as she hobbled into the bathroom. His shaving kit was there and it held nothing more than shaving cream, a razor which obviously didn't get much use, a bar of soap, toothpaste and a brush. "Great. Just great," she muttered under her breath and wondered when he'd return. How much time did she have? If he were to be believed, the airport was overflowing with concerned tourists trying to make connections back home, and he would be standing in line for hours.

Feeling like a traitor, she picked up the telephone and with the aid of the operator, managed to get through to the hospital, though Nurse Sánchez was not on duty. Nor could Mrs. Martínez come to the phone. In heavily accented English, the hospital operator assured Nikki that Nurse Sánchez would call her when her schedule permitted.

"Great," Nikki mumbled in frustration as she eased back on the bed. There had to be a way to check him out. Another way. She picked up her address book and flipped through the pages, stopping at the section marked *M,* but nowhere in the pages had she scribbled Trent's name, address or telephone number.

Though the little book was half-full of entries, there wasn't even a notation for the man she'd married.

Names that were vaguely familiar caused little sparks to flare in her memory, though the faces that swam in her mind were blurred and fleeting.

In the section for people whose surnames started with *J,* she found Janet Jones, then saw that the address had been crossed out with a note to look under

C, where her sister Janet had landed after resuming use of her maiden name.

Her sister's face came to mind, and she remembered a teary confrontation where Janet had confided that her husband, the love of her life, had left her for another woman, a younger woman with no children and a lot of money. Janet had been nearly suicidal and she'd sworn off men for the rest of her life. It had been raining heavily outside, the water sheeting the windows of her apartment....

Nikki sucked in her breath. Suddenly she remembered where she lived—a small walk-up in the Queen Anne section of Seattle. The rambling old house had originally been built in the 1920s, and later divided into four apartments. Her studio was located on the uppermost floor in quarters originally designed for servants. The ceilings were sloped, the windows paned dormers, but there was a brick fireplace, tons of closet space under the eaves of the old manor, and a gleaming hardwood floor. Long and narrow, the roomy apartment was filled with plants and antiques.

Heart racing, Nikki remembered the braided rug she'd picked up at a garage sale, an antique sewing machine she used as an end table and a rolltop desk positioned near the windows. Her computer table was in the corner near a built-in bookcase and her lumpy couch, a hand-me-down from...from...oh, Lord, who gave her the camel-backed couch? Her great-aunt Ora!

Warm tears gathered in her eyes at the thought of her relatives, now with faces and names. She thought about her home, a place she remembered. Her sister Carole had been at the teary meeting as well, telling Janet to divorce the bum and get on with her life. As Carole rationalized, Janet could "take Tim to the cleaners."

Had there been happy moments with her sisters? Nikki concentrated, but no other memory of either woman drifted through the foggy corridors of her past.

Sniffing, Nikki tried to think of Trent, of the times he'd been there. Had he helped her cook in the tiny kitchen alcove? Had he been around to patch the leak in the roof near one of the windows? Had he swept her into his arms and made love to her there on the rug before the fire or on the daybed tucked under the eaves?

Her throat filled, but she remembered nothing but the incessant pounding of the rain when her sister had poured out her heart, alternately crying and swearing about Timothy Jones, DDS and SOB.

Heartened by the breakthrough, Nikki became impatient, trying to force more memories. She sifted through the address book again, stopping at the section marked *N*. Sure enough, David Neumann's name, address and phone number were neatly recorded. Yet she hadn't even scribbled Trent's number in the book. Strange.

She tossed the little address book aside and looked through her wallet, stopping again at the family portrait. Had Janet remarried since her divorce from Tim? And Carole? Did she have a husband?

Do you? a voice in her head demanded. She glanced at her wedding ring, shining and mocking, a symbol of possession that felt awkward around her finger. Why couldn't she remember Trent slipping the little band of gold on her hand? Had there been music at the ceremony? Probably not. A bridal bouquet? A wedding dress of any kind?

"Stop it!" she growled at herself. All she was doing

was creating a headache of mammoth proportions, and she didn't want to have to take any more medications for pain. Right now, while she had time alone, she needed a clear head.

In frustration, she walked back to the closet and pawed through her own clothes, half expecting to find a cream-colored linen suit suitable for a wedding, or a plethora of negligees, or …what? Discovering nothing, she turned back to the bed and her heart nearly stopped beating. The camera! Biting her lip, she picked up the 35 mm and checked the back. Nine pictures had already been taken. Her throat went dry. Surely, if she'd been on her honeymoon, some of the snapshots would be of Trent. Her fingers were sweaty as she clicked open the back of the camera, removed the film cartridge and slipped the undeveloped film into her purse. What would she do if Trent wasn't in the pictures? And, oh, Lord, what would she do if he was?

The shadows in the room were getting darker as the sun dipped behind the ridge of mountains to the west. It was still daylight, four in the afternoon by her watch. Trent would be back soon and she hadn't accomplished much. Her stomach growled, reminding her that she hadn't eaten since breakfast at the hospital, but she didn't have time for food. Not yet.

Propped on the bed, with her Spanish-English dictionary lying facedown on the night table, she gathered her strength and tried to dial her mother in Los Angeles, but was told by the operator that all outside lines to the United States were busy.

Wonderful, she thought sarcastically and made a mental note of the people she needed to call. Her family, of course, and her editor at the *Observer,* Peggy

Hendricks. Also, she'd call Connie Benson, a co-worker and close friend. If Nikki really had been seeing Trent in the few weeks before she'd flown to Salvaje, certainly someone she'd known had met him—a friend or a co-worker, if not the members of her family.

She had to work fast. Searching the room for an extra room key, she found nothing. Well, that wasn't going to stop her. She slung the strap of her handbag over her shoulder, locked the door behind her and made her way through the hall to the elevator.

With a groan of ancient gears, the lift arrived and she climbed in with an elderly couple and a teenage girl draped in a beach towel. With a deep tan and perpetually bored expression, the girl glanced at Nikki, flinched, then slid her eyes away. Blushing, Nikki noticed that the little old lady with apricot-tinted hair was staring at her face.

"My goodness, what happened to you?" she said, her eyes concerned behind owl-like glasses.

"I… It was an accident. I, um, fell off my bike," Nikki replied, hating to lie, but not wanting to tell her life story to the anxious woman.

The woman clucked her tongue. "Well it looks like it's healing. In a few days, you'll look much better. But you've got to keep the scabs soft. With vitamin E—"

"Phyllis, please." The gentleman shook his head. "I'm sorry, miss. My wife used to be a nurse and she can't ever give up her profession."

"It's fine," Nikki assured them both, glad to hear good old American English.

"Don't you go out in the sun too much," Phyllis advised as the elevator shuddered to a stop. "Wear a hat.

The sun's no good for you, anyway. Causes wrinkles. Just look at me."

"Come on, Phyllis."

The teenager slid out of the car as soon as the door opened, and the gentleman shepherded his wife toward the front doors. Nikki started toward the registration desk on the far side of the lobby.

The hotel was old, with thick plaster walls, paddle fans and rich-hued carpets spread over cool tile floors. In the center of the lobby, a screened aviary lent guests a view of brilliantly colored birds and lush tropical plants that flourished around a central pond and small waterfall. Goldfish and koi swam beneath the lily pads while a toucan screeched from an upper limb of a small palm.

If she were feeling better, if she believed that the man who claimed to be her husband was whom he said he was, if she could remember more of her past, Nikki knew she would enjoy this beautiful old hotel with its dark furniture, whitewashed walls, slow-moving fans and graceful ironwork.

She made her way to the desk and tried to speak with the thin man at the register, but her halting Spanish wasn't any better than his attempts at English. Trying to avoid staring at the scabs on her face, he forced a smile and located an older man with thick silver hair, glasses and a ruddy complexion.

"How can I help you, *señora?*"

Hiding her nerves, she told the man that her husband had mistakenly taken the room key and she'd locked herself out of her room. The lies came easier as she went on, and with very little explanation, she was given her own key. She asked to see their registration form, and the man, though his white eyebrows lifted slightly,

showed her the receipt Trent had signed. An imprint
of an American Express card identified him as Trent
McKenzie. Skimming the rest of the information, she
noted that he lived in Seattle, though the address meant
nothing to her. She forced her tired mind to memorize
the street and telephone number, then asked the man
behind the desk about a camera shop or a place she
could develop pictures.

"For the film?" he said, his lower lip protruding
thoughtfully. "On the waterfront. José's. He can get
you pictures in two, maybe three days."

Three days! "Doesn't anyone here do it in an hour?"

The ruddy man laughed. "Santa María is not New
York," he said. "Talk to José. Maybe he can…rush the
job for you."

She turned away and nearly tripped on a boy of about
five who was staring at her. His eyes were round and
he pointed at her face before running to catch up with
his mother, a tall, graceful woman in a voile dress. The
woman glanced at Nikki, offered a smile filled with pity
and promptly scolded her son for staring.

Nikki cringed inside. She wouldn't be able to get out
without drawing attention to herself. Though her scabs
were healing and her black eye had nearly disappeared,
she would still attract attention wherever she went.

She needed a disguise. Something simple. Dark
glasses and a hat with a scarf attached that she could
wrap over her face. With the traveler's checks still
tucked in her wallet, she could buy something inex-
pensive. All she needed was a shop, and certainly a
hotel this large catering mainly to tourists, would have
a little store.

Thanking the clerk, she walked as quickly as she

could down a corridor leading to an exit when she felt someone watching her. Her heart slammed against her ribs as she saw him, lounging lazily in a chair near the terrace doors, his eyes trained on her, one boot propped on a table. Slowly, Trent pushed himself upright. His face was impassive, devoid of emotion, as he approached his "wife."

"Been busy, haven't you?"

Oh, God, did he hear her ask about developing the film? Her throat was as dry as cotton. "I couldn't stand being in the room a second longer."

"So you decided to check up on me."

She wanted to deny it, but wasn't going to lie. Well, not much, especially when she'd been caught red-handed. She inched her chin up a notch. "Look, Trent, I can't recall diddly-squat about my past, I don't re-member you, or why—or even *if*—we were married. You haven't acted much like a bridegroom on his hon-eymoon, and I feel like you're hiding things from me, so why wouldn't I come down here and try to put a few of the pieces of my life together?"

"You *want* me to act like a bridegroom?" he asked, taking a step closer. "Is that what you want? To barri-cade ourselves into the bedroom for three or four days?"

"No, I—"

"It can be arranged, you know. Just say the word and I'll carry you upstairs and we'll get down to it."

"*You* don't understand—"

"You don't understand, damn it! I've tried hard not to rush you, Nikki. I figured that it would be better to wait until you wanted me as much as I want you." His lips flattened over his teeth and he grabbed the crook of her arm roughly. "You want to go upstairs? Now? Just you and me?"

"No!" her voice was strangled, and she felt fear mixed with awe at the pure animal lust in his eyes.

"I didn't think so." In disgust he dropped her arm and shoved his hair from his eyes. "This is driving me crazy!"

"You? At least you have a past."

"You will, too," he said, his voice harsh.

"Easy for you to say."

"Why can't you trust me?" he asked, his eyes an arresting shade of blue. For a second she saw a flicker of despair in his gaze, but it was quickly hidden.

"I don't know you."

He looked as if she'd slapped him. "Oh, hell, I'm not arguing about this again! Come on." He grabbed hold of her wrist and started for the elevator.

"No!" She refused to budge and nearly stumbled as he tugged on her arm. Several old men who had been smoking near a window cranked their heads in Nikki's direction.

"Let's go," he ordered through clenched teeth.

"I already told you I don't want to go back to the room."

His jaw worked and a vein throbbed at his temple. "Either you go willingly into the elevator or I bodily carry you up there."

"You can't—"

He leaned closer, so that his lips were nearly brushing her ear. "I've got news for you, baby. I can do anything I damned well please. You're my wife, I'm your husband and, if you haven't noticed, this ain't the good old U.S. of A."

"That doesn't mean—"

"This society isn't quite as sophisticated as ours. Women's rights haven't been an issue down here. In fact, I think it's legal for a man to do just about anything he wants to the woman he marries."

She could barely breathe. "That's archaic!"

"Welcome to Salvaje."

"Great place for a honeymoon," she muttered. "Who planned this vacation? The Marquis de Sade?"

"You."

She went cold inside. Who was this man, this monster, whom she'd married? He tried to propel her toward the elevator, but short of being dragged, she wouldn't move. Inching her chin up mutinously, she decided to call his bluff. "If you're going to carry me, then get on with it. If not, then let me go!"

Grinding his teeth, he dropped her arm again. "What is it you want from me?"

"Answers. Straight answers."

"I've given you answers."

"Not enough."

He closed his eyes for a second and pinched the bridge of his nose between his thumb and finger. "Okay," he said slowly, as if forcing himself to be calm, "why don't we go to dinner and you can ask me anything your little heart desires?"

He was mocking her, but she didn't argue. All she wanted was the truth. Again he took hold of her elbow, but this time his grip was less punishing, and he guided her through double glass doors to a restaurant with a garden. She insisted they sit outside, and Trent, though he looked angry enough to spit nails, didn't object.

The maître d' led them through the potted plants to

a private table positioned near the rock railing. Beyond the short wall was a view of the ocean, darkening with the coming night. The scents of jasmine and lemon wafted on the sea breeze and soft Spanish music floated on the air from speakers hidden in the lush vines and flowers surrounding the tables.

"It really is beautiful here," she said, nervously. She wondered how she would feel if she'd never fallen over the cliff, never lost her memory, and was deeply in love with this mysterious stranger who insisted they were wed.

"If you say so."

A waiter in red shirt and black slacks appeared, and Trent ordered wine for her and a beer for himself. The waiter glanced at Nikki, his soulful eyes lingering on her face a fraction longer than necessary before he disappeared.

"You sure you want to be here?"

"Of course I do."

"People stare."

"Let them. I'm not contagious," she said, and Trent settled back in his chair. Though he outwardly appeared relaxed, Nikki knew better. There was a restless tension lying just under the surface of his calm demeanor. Hands tented under his chin, he stared at her accusingly. "You should have waited until I got back before you came out of the room."

"I told you, the four walls and I had run out of conversation."

"I was only concerned that you might fall on that ankle."

"The ankle's a lot better."

He didn't respond, but glanced casually around the

garden, as if he were an interested tourist, but Nikki couldn't fight the impression that he was looking for something or someone lurking in the shadows.

The drinks arrived, and after quickly scanning the menus, Trent ordered for both of them. He exchanged words and a chuckle with the waiter and slid a sexy glance in her direction. Nikki refused to be intimidated, though her stomach was churning nervously. She thought of the camera in her purse and bit her lip. She couldn't very well develop the film with Trent around, and yet she saw no way of getting away from him today.

Placing her napkin over her skirt, she heard snatches of conversation from tables tucked between the pots overflowing with flowers. Quiet conversation and the clink of glasses were punctuated with soft bursts of laughter. People enjoying themselves, relaxed and happy, on a tropical island for a vacation.

"So you think you're ready to take on the town," he said, eyeing her.

"The whole island, if I have to."

He took a swallow from his beer, then picked at the label of his long-necked bottle. He scanned the garden slowly, as if gathering his thoughts, but his gaze was wary, his lips a little too tight over his teeth.

"How'd things go at the airport?"

"Not great. We got reservations out of here, but not for a few days."

Her heart sank a little. It was crazy, of course, and she wanted to return to her home and her life, but she felt cheated, as if she'd come to this Caribbean island with a purpose not yet served. Even if her plan had simply been to sightsee, she'd been robbed. And if this trip were truly her honeymoon, then it had become a disaster, because she and the man seated across from her were at odds, more enemies than lovers.

The waiter returned with steaming bowls of a thick fish chowder, which burned all the way down Nikki's throat. Her conversation with Trent lagged and she sipped her wine throughout the meal of swordfish, a spicy rice dish and sautéed vegetables.

She was nearly finished with her second glass of wine when the waiter returned with a dessert cart. She shook her head. "I can't," she insisted, and Trent grinned widely.

"I was beginning to think you were a bottomless pit."

"After watery gelatin, gooey oatmeal and wilted, tasteless vegetables at that hospital for the past week, everything looks good."

"Except dessert."

She grinned and finished her wine. "Maybe later."

"In bed?" he asked, his gaze locking with hers. She couldn't move for a second and unconsciously she licked a final drop of wine from her lips. She thought of the film hidden in a pocket of her purse. Would it develop into snapshots of Trent, smiling and carefree on his honeymoon? Bare-chested and incredibly sexy, with the wind in his hair and desire burning bright in his eyes? Suddenly the ring around her finger seemed heavy and tight.

Trent paid the bill, then helped her from her chair.

"I—I don't want to go upstairs yet," she admitted.

"You're not tired?"

"It's barely eight," she pointed out. "Besides, it seems like I've been in bed forever."

"Not with me," he said, and her pulse leapt wildly. He took her arm, and she wondered if he was being helpful, or making sure that she wouldn't bolt, that he wouldn't lose her.

Through the opening in the rail, they walked along a sandy path that wound through the grounds of the hotel. They crossed a wide flagstone patio and passed clusters of umbrella tables. Hurricane lanterns were lit, their flames warm and steady with the coming dusk.

"I tried to call my mother and my sisters today," Nikki admitted as they strolled past the pool. Children were still splashing in the water, but the sunbathers had left for the day, the chaise lounges empty.

"And?"

"No luck. The phone lines were jammed."

He nodded. "My guess is telephone service here isn't all that great to begin with, and now, with the airline fiasco, it's nearly impossible to call out. We were lucky to get through to your dad."

The night closed in around them. Insects droned and flitted around the lanterns and a million stars glimmered in the purple sky. Stuffing her hands in the pockets of her skirt, she said, "Tell me exactly how we met."

He slid her a glance. "It's not all that exciting."

"I don't care."

"I was working on a claim for Connie Benson. Her car had been stolen and I had some questions for her. You were with her when I showed up and we were introduced. Later in the week we ran into each other at a restaurant on the waterfront. We started talking and didn't stop until the place closed down. From that point on, we saw a lot of each other." He slid her a sly glance. "You practically moved into my place that first week."

"No!" She blushed as they walked, the heat climbing up her neck to redden her cheeks. "I couldn't be that impulsive."

"For God's sake, Nikki, why would I make this up?"

"I… I don't know," she admitted, wishing the holes in her memory would heal. "I realize I'm stubborn. 'Strong-willed,' I think my mother used to say, but I'm also somewhat methodical and careful, and I wouldn't marry someone I didn't know well."

"It felt right, Nikki, so don't beat it to death."

"Okay," she agreed, as they followed stone steps covered with sand. "Then what about you? You don't exactly seem like the marrying type."

"I'm not." He lifted a shoulder. "But with you—" Hesitating, he stopped near a crooked palm tree and his hands slid up her bare arms "—I lost my head." He said it with a sound of disgust. "Believe me, I tried to fight you, but—" his rough hands surrounded her arms and he pulled her against him "—I lost." His lips clamped over hers and his arms slid around her. Warning bells went off in her head, but she ignored them and felt the barriers she'd so carefully erected against him begin to erode. His lips were magical and demanding, warm with the promise of passions yet untouched. She trembled slightly, and his arms tightened around her, dragging her close. "You're a mystery to me, Nikki. I've never felt this way before. You make me do things that seem entirely irrational, and yet I do them willingly, *eagerly,* for you." His face was a mask of perplexity, as if he couldn't understand his own motives. "I thought when I met you that I would get you out of my system. We'd have a hot affair and that would be the end of it."

"Is that your usual relationship with a woman? A 'hot affair.'"

One side of his mouth lifted. "I don't have 'usual' relationships. In fact, I don't have any relationships at all."

"Am I supposed to be flattered?" she asked, not trusting him for a minute. She tried to step backward, to put some space between his body and hers, but the arms around her tightened like iron bands, holding her close, refusing to let her go.

"I'm just answering the questions."

"So you're into one-night stands?" she asked, her voice breathless, her gaze searching his face.

"I'm not 'into' anything."

"They're not safe, you know. Not in today's day and age."

"Don't lecture me, Nikki, 'cause it doesn't matter. Until I met you, when I saw a woman I was attracted to, I ran like hell. The last thing I wanted in my life was any emotional entanglements."

That much she accepted. But her heart was thundering and she couldn't ignore the feel of his body pressed anxiously against hers. Through the soft barrier of their clothing, her flesh was warmed by his. "But you want me to believe we're married."

"We are."

"I don't believe—"

"Believe," he commanded before kissing her again, his tongue rimming her lips, prying her mouth open so that he could taste all of her. Deep in a dark corner of her mind, she knew she should stop him, but she couldn't, not when her skin was on fire, her blood flowing wantonly.

He crushed her to him and her breasts began to ache. His hands moved slowly and sensually up and down her spine, touching the sensitive area at the small of her back.

"This…this can't happen."

"It is happening."

"No, please—"

"Listen, damn it!" he said, jerking his head back long enough to stare deep into her eyes. "I can't tell you anything else. I can't explain *how* it happened. It just did. It's not as if this was planned, you know. I took one look at you and told myself to make tracks and quick, but for some reason, and I can't explain why, I ran to you instead of away from you. Maybe it was because you weren't interested at first."

"I thought you said I was…. How did you so romantically put it? *So damned hot,* wasn't that it?"

"That was later." He grinned, running a hand down her back.

"But not much later."

"I kept pursuing you. You gave me the cold shoulder at first because of Neumann. You were still licking your wounds over him."

Dave. Her throat caught. She'd thought she loved him, planned to marry him, but he'd never intended to walk down the aisle with her. She couldn't remember their breakup, but suddenly felt the emotional abandonment, the pain and humiliation. Her memory teased her, rose to the surface of her consciousness only to submerge and leave her feeling raw and bereft.

"Are you saying I married you on the rebound?" she asked, her emotions electric and jumbled.

"I'm saying you didn't want to get seriously involved, but I wouldn't give up, and when things started getting hot and heavy, you insisted on marriage."

Would she have jumped so suddenly? Her father had said there had been six months since she and Dave had broken up. Would she have been so paranoid, so downright archaic to demand that this man marry her and prove that his intentions were honorable? "And you just happily went along with my idea," she scoffed, knowing instinctively that Trent McKenzie wasn't a man to be manipulated.

"I wanted you. Period." His voice was husky and raw, ringing with a conviction that tore at her soul. "I would have done anything to have you. Anything."

"Even marry me."

"Even that."

Her breath got lost in her lungs, and when his eyes touched hers, they burned with an inner fire that caused the denials to melt on her tongue. There was no doubt of his sexuality or the passion that simmered in his blood.

He lowered his lips to hers and kissed her softly at first, but with more hunger as each heartbeat passed. As her arms wrapped around his waist, she told herself to remember that this was the man who could not profess to love her, who often seemed cold and distant. So why now would he open his heart to her?

His lips moved over hers and his tongue rimmed her mouth, touching, enticing, prodding her lips apart to slip into the dark, wet recess. She closed her eyes and moaned as the tip of his tongue flicked against the roof of her mouth, dancing and parrying, teasing her own reluctant tongue to life.

Nikki's knees buckled, and his arms surrounded her, holding her close, pressing her against him, forcing her breasts against his chest. He prodded her legs apart with a knee that deftly cleaved her skirt and shoved her against the palm tree. Her blood was on fire, her breaths short and rapid, and the denials singing through her brain earlier all but silenced.

She knew that becoming intimate with him was taboo, that danger lurked in his dusky kisses, and yet she couldn't stop herself. Her body screamed for him, her breasts ached for his touch, and deep inside she felt a molten fire, like the boiling lava of a volcano about to erupt.

When he lifted his head, she sagged against him.

"This is how it's always been with us," he said, his breathing ragged, his gaze tortured. He smoothed a stray strand of hair from her face. "And that, lady, is why I married you."

Chapter 5

Now what? Come on, Nikki. You're a smart woman. Or at least you were once upon a time. So now what're you going to do?

Trust him. For God's sake, Nikki, follow your heart and trust him!

She stood on the veranda, her fingers curled around the iron rail, the breeze teasing her hair and brushing softly against her cheeks. From the open door of the hotel room, she heard water running, the sound of Trent in the shower. Trying to come up with a plan, she stared at the winking lights of Santa María. Strung jewel-like along the inlet, the city lights reflected on the water and kept the dark night at bay.

She didn't have much time. Soon she'd have to sleep with a man who, by casting her a single glance, could set her blood on fire. A mystery man who claimed to be her husband. A man she instinctively felt was dangerous. If only she could trust him. But trust, she knew from some vague experience in her past, was earned, not given casually. She rubbed her arms as if suddenly chilled and thought about the night ahead, sleeping in the same bed with him, feeling him close. Her stomach tightened and she knew she couldn't make love to him. Husband or no, she didn't trust him. She decided the best way to avoid making love to him was feigning sleep. Surely he'd understand that, after days of lying in the hospital, the move was hard on her and she was worn-out.

Truth to tell, she knew she'd barely sleep a wink with his body only inches from hers. What a mess, she thought, blowing her bangs from her eyes and glancing down at the garden patio where several people were still gathered, laughing and talking and sipping from island drinks. Older couples laughed over glasses of wine, and a couple in their mid-twenties held hands as they walked by the pool. Lovers, she thought, with just a twinge of envy.

Shaking off her worrisome thoughts, she hurried inside, and as she listened to the water still running in the bathroom, she quickly shed her skirt and blouse and yanked on a pair of satin pajamas. The fabric molded to her breasts and hips, and the deep *V* of the neckline offered a view of more of her skin than she would have preferred, but the pink pajamas were the most sedate bedroom apparel she'd brought to the island. It made sense, she supposed. A flannel nightgown and robe that would keep her warm through the wet and cold Seattle winters would have no business on a tropical island. *Especially on your honeymoon.*

The shower spray stopped, and her heart began an erratic tattoo. *Oh, God,* she thought, her throat so tight she could barely swallow.

Quietly, she slipped between the covers, rolled on her side and offered her back to the other side of the bed. Squeezing her eyes shut, she heard him running the water again, probably at the sink, taking his damned sweet time, while she prayed for sleep. She realized she was acting like a child, a neurotic virgin, but as she was still laid-up and vulnerable, she felt the best course of action was deception. Just until she had her full faculties back. Once her memory returned, she would be able to deal with him more openly.

However, the pretense bothered her more than she expected, and she realized that Nikki Carrothers, in her other lifetime, had never sunk low enough to deal in lies. *These are extenuating circumstances,* she told herself as she plumped her pillow and tried to relax.

The water at the sink stopped suddenly. Nikki tensed. Through her slitted eyelids she noticed the lightening of the bedroom as he opened the door. *Act groggy,* she told herself, though she felt a fool.

He didn't say a word. She heard his keys jangle on the nightstand near his side of the bed, felt the movement of the blankets as he threw back the covers, smelled the scents of soap and shaving cream and musk as he slid between the sheets and the mattress creaked. Her heart was thundering as he turned out the light on his night table and scooted closer.

She stiffened as his arms surrounded her waist with easy familiarity. He pressed his body against hers intimately, his breath warm against her neck, the stiff hairs of his chest brushing against the slick satin covering her back. "You're not fooling anyone," he said, his hand splayed possessively across her abdomen. "I know you're awake."

She didn't reply. *Fake it, fake it, fake it! Just breathe in and out as naturally as if you don't feel his warm body cuddling yours!*

"But don't worry. I won't force you."

Her muscles relaxed a little, and he took advantage of the moment, drawing her closer still. His legs, bare from what she could feel through her pajamas, tucked against hers and he seemed to fit perfectly, his knees and hips bending at the same angles as hers. She tried to remember this feeling of closeness and intimacy, of sharing a bed with him, but no pleasant, warm memory surfaced. He kissed the back of her neck, and her pulse jumped crazily. "There's no need to rush, darlin'," he said in a sexy drawl that caused her stomach to turn over in anticipation. "We've got the rest of our lives."

Oh, God, why couldn't she remember?

Trent knew he should keep his hands off her. Touching her like this was dangerous, and yet he couldn't resist. He hadn't lied when he'd told her that she was the most fascinating woman he'd ever met. From the moment he'd first seen her in Seattle, he'd wanted to make love to her.

And yet he had to hold back. She was still in pain, still confused, still distrustful. There was so much he wanted to tell her and so much he still couldn't divulge. But as soon as they were back in the United States and he was assured of her safety, things would be better. He smelled the lilac scent of her shampoo on the hairs that spilled across her pillow and the desire already flowing through his blood created an ache in his loins. It would be so easy to start kissing her, to brush his fingers across her breasts, to rub up against her and nudge her legs apart....

"Hell," he ground out, forcing himself to roll over and cling to the side of the bed. He'd never been a hero, and there had been a time in his life when he hadn't really cared what a woman thought of him before or after he'd taken her to bed. But now, with Nikki, things were different. Complicated. Dangerous.

He grimaced and stared at the ceiling, knowing she wasn't sleeping. Any way he thought about it, the night was going to last forever!

Nikki climbed out of bed as soon as the morning sunlight streamed through the window. Hazarding a glimpse of Trent, she felt her throat catch as she saw his face, cleanly shaven, in complete repose. His jaw was strong and square. Dark lashes brushed his cheek and his mouth was without its usual cynical twist. His black hair fell over his forehead and his bare shoulders, even relaxed, were sculpted with sinewy muscles. Bristly hair swirled over his chest and disappeared beneath the sheet. A handsome man, she thought, but who the devil was he? Husband? Lover? Enemy?

"Are you gonna stand there all day and drool over me, or are you gonna come back to bed and do something about it?" He patted the spot where she'd been lying without cracking open an eye.

"You—"

With a slow, deliberately sensual smile, he levered up on one elbow and the sheet fell away, revealing a washboard of lean abdominal muscles. "I what?"

"You were awake," she said, deciding it wouldn't be wise to insult him just yet.

"Mmm." He stretched his arms far over his head and settled back against the pillows. Yawning, his slumberous eyes dark with an unnamed passion, he said, "You're lucky I didn't try to take advantage of you."

She couldn't help rising to the bait. "Maybe you're the lucky one," she teased, hurrying into the bathroom and locking the door firmly behind her before she decided she was being childish. He was her husband—right? He could see her naked. Or could he? Taking in a deep breath she unlocked the door. He could make the next move if he wanted to.

Telling herself that things were as normal as they could be given the circumstances, she carefully applied a little makeup and was grateful that her face was beginning to heal. A few of the scabs had become loose and some had actually peeled away to reveal pink skin that contrasted vividly with her tan. All in all her body was healing, she decided as she applied antibiotic cream and vitamin E skin oil to her abrasions. If only her mind would mend as well.

After brushing her hair and changing into shorts and a T-shirt, she returned to the bedroom where Trent, dressed only in faded Levi's, was pouring coffee into two cups. "Cream, no sugar, right?" he asked.

"Yes." For years she'd tried to wean herself off cream, she remembered, but hadn't been able to drink coffee black. Somehow Trent had been around her long enough to know her habits. It was frustrating, this being in the dark.

Handing her a cup, he huddled over a newspaper at the table and she tentatively took a seat across from him.

She tried not to stare at the sharp angles of his face as she blew across her coffee, but she watched him, hoping that a glance, a gesture, a word would trigger memories of their whirlwind courtship and marriage.

"Tell me about your family," she suggested as he scanned the front page.

"Not much to tell."

"Your parents?"

"Still married and living in Toledo. Dad's retired from working in the steel mills. Mom's a nurse. She'll retire in a couple of years."

"Brothers?"

"Just one snip of a sister. Kate. Stubborn, single and a pain in the backside." He glanced up and smiled. "Anything else?"

"How did you end up in Seattle?"

Frowning, he folded his paper neatly on the table. "What is this—twenty questions?"

"Yes. Or thirty. Or fifty. Or a hundred. Whatever it takes."

"I didn't want to end up like my old man, with a bad back and a bum hip, so I managed to get a scholarship. That, along with working nights, put me through school. I graduated in law enforcement, decided I couldn't stand working for a boss and gravitated toward being a private detective. I moved around a lot. Things were slow and I heard about a job with the insurance company where I could make my own hours, and so I took it. I was living in Denver at the time and ready to move on."

"And that's it?"

"My life history."

She sipped from her cup and burned her tongue as

she considered his story—encapsulated as it was. He didn't say anything she could dispute, but it seemed so cold and sterile—no hint of warmth when he talked about his folks, no smile when he mentioned his home town, no mention of a family pet, or a friend, or anything that might show a hint of his emotions. As if his past has been manufactured and printed off a computer screen.

You're letting your imagination get the better of you, she told herself. *Why would he lie?*

He snapped his paper open again and scowled at the articles written in Spanish. "Makes you wish for a copy of the *Observer,* doesn't it?"

Crash!

Glass shattered on the veranda.

Nikki jumped, sloshing hot coffee onto her hands and the table.

Trent kicked back his chair. "Stay back," he ordered, his expression grim. On the balls of his feet, his muscles tense, his jaw tight, he said, "Stay back!" He threw open the French doors. A stiff morning breeze skated into the room, billowing the drapes and rustling the newspaper.

Despite his warning, Nikki inched forward and saw thousands of glass shards, the remains of a hurricane lantern, scattered over the decking.

Trent, seemingly oblivious to the glass and his bare feet, had run to the edge of the veranda, where he stood, surveying the grounds and nearby breadfruit trees, as if he expected a prowler to leap out at him.

He started to move, and she yelled, "Watch out or you'll cut yourself."

"I thought I told you to stay inside!"

"I don't like being ordered around."

"It's for your own good."

"I can take care of myself."

"Can you?" With a sharp glance over his shoulder, he raked his gaze up her body to land on the scrapes on her face.

Squaring her shoulders, she lifted her chin. "I may not know a lot about my past, but I'm sure that I was more than self-sufficient!"

The look he shot her spoke volumes.

"I don't know why you're so rattled, anyway," she said, motioning toward the sparkling shards of glass. "It was just the wind."

"Maybe." Apparently satisfied that no one was lurking nearby, he bent over and began picking up the larger pieces of broken glass.

"You were expecting someone?" Nikki, too, gathered the chunks of sharp glass and dropped the jagged pieces into a trash can.

"No." He shook his head, as if convincing himself.

"Then what is it you're afraid of?" she asked.

"Afraid of?"

"You act like you expect someone to jump out at us."

The lines around his mouth tightened a little. "I was startled, that's all." Angrily, he threw the last of the broken lantern into the metal trash can, and it clattered loud enough to wake the dead.

"You don't strike me as someone who would startle easily. Come on, Trent, something's going on. You want to get me off the island as soon as you can. You practically have me locked away in this hotel room. Every time I'm out alone, you act as if something awful is going to happen."

He followed her into the hotel room and leaned a

shoulder against the carved wood doorframe. Crossing his arms over his chest, he stared at her, his lips compressed, his eyes narrowed slightly, as if he were weighing a heavy decision. "You've already been hurt once and spent too much time in the hospital. I just don't want to take any chances."

"On another accident occurring?"

His lips thinned, and instinctively she backed up, steadying herself on the edge of the bureau. He still scared her a little, and yet she decided it was time for a showdown. She'd been walking a high wire with him, afraid that any misstep would send her plummeting into a black oblivion that she couldn't escape. She couldn't stand it a minute longer. "I get the feeling that you're hiding something from me."

"I'm not."

"Liar."

He advanced on her, his bare toes touching hers as they peeked from her sandals. For a second he didn't say a word, just studied the contours of her face, and her breath got lost somewhere between her lungs and throat. She stared into eyes a deep, mysterious blue, eyes that seemed to see into the most secret parts of her. Her palms began to sweat a little, and for a breathless instant she wondered if he was going to kiss her. *Get a grip, Nikki!*

"I just want to get you out of here before you really get hurt."

"So you're superstitious."

"I don't follow."

"Because the *accident* happened here, you want to leave. That doesn't make a whole lot of sense. Unless you think I'm only accident-prone when I'm on Salvaje.

Or unless you know something more than you're telling me."

"Like what?" Frowning, he locked the door firmly behind him.

"I have nightmares, Trent, and I relive falling over the cliff, only I don't just take a misstep and pitch toward the ocean on my own," she said, catching his full attention. His head snapped up and the muscles in the back of his neck grew strident. "I know someone was chasing me and that same person gave me a shove over the edge." The room was suddenly so close, she had trouble getting enough air into her lungs. His gaze narrowed on her, and he didn't move.

"Who?"

"I… I don't know. I don't remember. But it's so real, it's got to be true."

"You think I pushed you," he said, his voice flat, his nostrils flaring slightly.

Her pulse throbbed in her brain. "I don't know what to think. But I know that you haven't been completely honest with me."

"Oh, Lord," he said on a heavy sigh. Rubbing a hand around the back of his neck, he shook his head. When he looked at her again, his gaze had sharpened. "Part of your dream is real, part illusion. It's true I didn't see you fall over the edge. I was already at the mission, waiting for you. But no one was following us."

"You're certain?"

He didn't answer. "Why would anyone push you, Nikki?"

"I don't know." She shook her head, trying to remember.

"Oh, Nikki." Muttering a curse under his breath, he

placed his hands on either side of her body, trapping her against the bureau. He leaned forward, his nose nearly touching hers. "I know you don't like the idea, but you're going to have to trust me. I'll get you home. I'll make sure you're safe."

"You'll be honest with me?"

He hesitated, but only briefly, then one side of his mouth lifted into a sardonic smile. "Of course I will, darlin'," he drawled, and she knew in an instant that this man was an inveterate liar, a man who would say or do anything in order to accomplish his goals.

Despite all that, regardless of her gut feeling not to trust him, a part of her wanted to lean on him, rely on him, trust him with her life. If only she could let herself feel safe with him. He smelled clean and male and… She bit her lip as he tilted her chin with one finger and whispered, "Just trust me, Nikki. We'll be home soon and you can see your own doctor. You'll get your memory back. Things will be better."

Trust me. Her heart twisted. She wanted to trust him. More than anything in her life, she wanted to believe that he was telling her the truth, that they were married, that there wasn't anyone on Salvaje or anywhere else who would want to hurt her.

He kissed her then. Slowly and deliberately, his hands placed on either side of her head, his body pressed close to hers. His lips were warm and persuasive, his tongue a gentle prod against her teeth. She knew she should stop him, that kissing him was courting disaster, yet she closed her eyes and parted her lips willingly, and his hands moved slowly down her face to her shoulders and lower still to her buttocks. His bare chest rubbed against her T-shirt, and she was lost in the smell and feel of him.

With a groan, he drew her closer, pulling her hips against his so that she could feel the hardness of his desire against her abdomen. Her blood was pounding through her veins as his kiss deepened.

As suddenly as he'd grabbed her, he let go, swearing and planting his hands on his jean-clad hips. He closed his eyes and his jaw became hard as granite. "Son of a bitch. Son of a goddamned bitch!" Raking his hands through his hair, he growled, "I've got to get out of here…. *We've* got to get out of here."

She couldn't agree with him more. Being cooped up in the small room, with only each other, was playing with fire.

"Come on," he said, stuffing his arms through the sleeves of a bleached denim shirt. "Let's have some breakfast and then we'll check out Santa María. Do some sight-seeing. Something. Wait a minute." He closed the gap between them once more, and with his shirt still open, he surveyed her wounds. His thumb brushed across the scab still clinging to her cheek. "But we can't be out long. The doctor doesn't want too much sun on—"

"I know. I'll wear a hat," she said, angry with him or herself, she didn't know which.

"I just wouldn't want that beautiful face to scar."

"I'll be careful." She felt a sudden elation at the prospect of escaping the prison walls of the hotel room and realized this would be her chance, if she ever was alone, to have the film she'd found in her camera developed.

A sharp needle of guilt stabbed at her, but she quickly shoved it aside. She had the right to learn everything there was to know about her "husband," even if she had to sneak behind his back to uncover the truth.

He changed into walking shorts and a T-shirt, slipped a pair of aviator glasses over the bridge of his nose and headed outside. The sunbaked driveway to the front of the hotel was filled with idling cabs and cars. Trent took her hand and led her past the taxi stand to a shaded bench where the driver of a horse-drawn carriage was dozing.

At the sound of approaching footsteps, the horse—a big bay gelding—snorted, and the driver's black eyes opened. "Ah, *señor*," he said, tipping a wide-brimmed hat. "A ride for the lady?"

"Sí." Trent fished in his wallet for a bill and asked to be taken downtown.

"To see the beautiful *Santa María*—just like the name of Columbus, his boat, no?"

"Right," Nikki said, grinning. It felt good to be out in the sunshine, to see the shadows of swaying palm fronds play across the ground, to talk to someone other than Trent, to feel young and carefree despite the worrisome fact that she remembered so little of her past.

Trent helped her into the leather seats, and the driver climbed onto his perch and flicked his whip over the gelding's ears. The carriage began to creak as it rolled forward, bouncing a little on the uneven street of timeworn cobblestones.

With a hat to shade her face and huge sunglasses to cover her eyes, Nikki nearly felt normal. Sitting next to Trent, feeling the length of his leg rest against hers, smelling the soap and leather scent of him, she could almost imagine herself a bride on her honeymoon. Almost.

Trent threw one arm behind her shoulders, though he didn't draw her close, and his fingers tapped restlessly on the tucked upholstery supporting her head. His eyes, hidden by his aviator glasses, were restless, always on the move. His jaw was stern, his lips compressed, and never once did he seem to relax.

It was as if he was looking for something. Or someone. Expecting danger. Lines of strain carved his skin at the corners of his mouth and his fingers kept up their nervous beat. Like a restless, wary animal, he watched and listened.

Nikki refused to let his anxiety infect her. It had been ages since she'd been out among people, and she hadn't realized what a social creature she was. Delighted, she watched street vendors try to hawk their wares from umbrella-covered pushcarts parked on the street corners. Bicyclists and motorbikers vied for room with a few cars and ancient pickups that clogged the streets. Yet the old horse plodded on, undisturbed by the noise and motion of this lazy city.

Overhead, suspended from lampposts, baskets of flowers blazed in a profusion of color. Deep purple blooms and bright pink buds trailed from long vines and fluttered in the breeze, perfuming the air already filled with the scents of saltwater, fish and seaweed.

It was a glorious day. The sun was blazing with tropical heat, but the breadfruit trees and palms offered some shade. As the carriage moved slowly downhill, Nikki stared past the driver and haunches of the draft horse to catch glimpses of the ocean, azure and sparkling with sunlight. Schooners and fishing rigs skimmed the bay, and to the north, jagged rocks, small islands unto themselves, rose like the spiny backs of ancient sea monsters hidden deep in the water.

Involuntarily Nikki shuddered, and her good mood dissipated on the wind. She looked upward to the cliffs above the city to see the crumbling bell tower of the old mission, barely visible through the dense foliage of the hills. Why had she been running up the steep path and who had pushed her? For, despite Trent's claims otherwise, someone had deliberately shoved her over the embankment, hoping that she would plunge to her death on the rocky shoals.

The driver pulled the horse to a stop, and as Trent tipped the driver, Nikki hopped to the ground, careful to land on her uninjured foot. For a second she felt as if someone was watching her, and she turned quickly, looking at the throng of tourists crowding the street, half expecting to meet a stranger's malevolent gaze, but none of the tourists or locals wandering through a central square of shops and cafés near the park were paying her the least bit of attention. Most were walking slowly, a few had found a seat in the ornate wrought-iron benches to eat, read or smoke, still others threw scraps of food to the flock of birds that had gathered in the shade of several grapefruit trees.

She told herself that she was being silly—that some of Trent's tension had infected her, but she couldn't re-capture her lighthearted spirit of only moments before.

The sound of music from a steel-drum band floated on the breeze as Trent led the way along the sandy boardwalk that rimmed the water. People strolled along the docks, stopping to barter at outdoor booths and carts, chattering in a variety of languages.

At a small café, Trent ordered breakfast of fresh fruit,

fried bread and scallops. They sipped fresh orange juice and thick black coffee and watched the ocean, which glittered in the sunlight.

"You didn't tell me about any of the women in your life," she said as she finished her coffee.

"You didn't ask."

Leaning both elbows on the table and balancing her chin in her hands, she said, "I'm asking now."

He grinned. That slow, sexy smile that caused a nest of butterflies to erupt in her stomach. "All the gory details?"

"Every one," she replied, though a pang of jealousy surprised her. The thought of Trent with another woman was unsettling.

He took a long swallow from his cup, then frowned into the dregs. "There isn't really much to tell. I had a high school sweetheart in Toledo, but she ended up marrying another guy—someone more stable, which translates into dollars. The kid's dad owned one of the biggest steel mills in the Midwest. I moved from one college to another, didn't put down any roots or leave many broken hearts."

"You haven't been married before."

He shook his head.

"Never came close?"

"Not as close as you," he said, tilting his head to one side and surveying her. "You still don't remember Dave?"

She thought back, trying to conjure up some memory, some link to a man she'd nearly married. He was handsome and athletic—she'd seen that much in the snapshot she'd found in her wallet—but there was something else about him, a personality trait, that seemed to surface in her mind. "Not really, but I have this feeling he was very dominating."

Trent lifted a shoulder, but Nikki was on a roll. "That's right. Not overtly demanding, but always subtly suggesting that I should dress a little differently, act more sophisticated, get a job more suitable for a woman...." She felt an old emotion break through the void in her mind. "He...he took me somewhere once, to the symphony, or the opera, or something, and he bought me a dress because he didn't like the clothes I'd been wearing." She remembered opening the box, excited until she'd seen the black sheath with the gauze sleeves and skirt so short she wouldn't be able to sit comfortably.

"It'll look great on you," Dave had insisted, and to keep him happy, she'd worn the dress, even letting him tell her to pin her hair up in a French braid. All evening she'd felt uncomfortable. He'd introduced her to friends, showing her off as if she were another acquisition, just as he'd proudly displayed his new top-of-the-line sports car and his gold watch. Though he'd cared about her, Nikki had always gotten the feeling that his love hadn't gone past the surface, that if she'd been born ugly or scarred, he wouldn't have cast her a second glance. Lips curling wryly, she wondered what he'd think of her now with her battered face.

"I do remember Dave," she said. "In some ways he was like you."

Trent snorted, but his gaze never left her face.

"You know—demanding, arrogant, pushy," she teased, unable to resist baiting him.

He reached over and clasped his fingers over her wrist. "Watch it, lady," he warned, "or you'll find out just how pushy I can be." She might have been frightened, but the fingers around her wrist were warm, the curve of his lips seductive.

They wandered through the small town, and Nikki never stopped looking for a camera shop. As they window-shopped, pausing to finger trinkets of silver and gold, agate and shell, she never forgot the roll of film hidden deep in her pocket.

They passed carts laden with flowers, fresh fruit, hand-crafted jewelry, sweaters and kites. On the docks, fishermen sat and smoked while repairing their nets or selling their catches. Past the boardwalk, the white sand stretched in a lazy crescent surrounding the bay. Sunbathers lay on towels, soaking up rays, drinking from tall glasses. Children waded near the shore and snorkelers waded deeper into the glimmering surf.

An island paradise, Nikki thought. *A perfect spot for a honeymoon.* She almost believed it was true. However, one glance at Trent and her romantic fantasy crumbled. She remembered nothing of him. While staring at his rugged, handsome features, no image of being with him surfaced in her mind. Slowly she was glimpsing small, murky fragments of her memory, but never had Trent appeared in any of the tiny vignettes of her past. Why not?

Because he's a complete stranger, that's why!

That thought hit her like a blow, and she realized that she'd let herself get caught up in this ridiculous fantasy, that she was beginning to believe, if only a little, that he was her husband.

Even the undeveloped pictures might not prove that he wasn't her husband.

In the early afternoon, Nikki began to tire. They

stopped to rest at an outdoor café situated on the north
end of the boardwalk. Trent ordered drinks when Nikki
spied the sign, a painted board attached to a short stucco
building that housed José's camera shop, which was located less than a block from the café.

She hesitated, but told herself there was no time like
the present. The waiter deposited a frosty beer on the
table in front of Trent and an iced lemonade for Nikki.
They didn't talk much, just sipped their drinks slowly,
watching as the tourists, young and old, moved along
the street. The canister of film felt hot against her thigh,
and she watched the minutes roll by, hoping for some
excuse to leave him.

A loud woman in a straw hat, chasing a slim youth,
caught her attention before blending into the crowd that
drifted slowly along the street. The seconds ticked by.
Trent was nearly finished with his beer.

Nikki was taking her time, slowly drinking her
lemonade, hoping for a reason to leave the table. She
watched a black man without any teeth, who was playing a guitar in a doorway on the other side of the street.
A thin old dog was lying at his feet, sunning himself and
moving only to lift his head and sniff the air before letting out a low growl and lying back down again.

She felt Trent's eyes on her and took another swallow.
But her throat was nearly clogged and she had trouble
drinking. At a nearby table, a single man was nursing
a beer, and though his back was turned, Nikki felt as
if she'd seen him before...in the hotel lobby or... As if
he knew she'd spied him, he paid for his drink and left,
never once glancing over his shoulder.

You're imagining things, she told herself, turning back
to the guitar player who was playing the soft calypso

strains of an unfamiliar song. Nikki watched the crowd and noticed a tall, thin native dressed in white. A red sash was his belt and a green parrot was perched on his shoulder.

The dog lifted his head, sniffed, and spying the bird, jumped to his feet, barking loudly. The parrot flapped its great wings and squawked, trying to escape.

Nikki flinched, knocking over her glass and Trent's beer. Liquid and ice cubes sloshed across the table, beer foaming into lemonade as it drizzled over the edge, spilling onto her lap.

"What the devil?" Trent demanded, looking from the dog, now being dragged into the building by the toothless man, and the parrot, unable to fly away because of its leash, to Nikki.

"Oh, God, I'm sorry," she apologized, grabbing at her glass as it rolled toward the edge. "What a mess!"

Trent hardly blinked, just shouted to a passing waiter as Nikki dabbed at the table with a napkin. Her shorts were soaked, her blouse sprinkled with the beer and lemonade that still oozed through the cracks in the table and dripped to the brick patio.

"Señora, por favor..." A waiter with cloth in hand came to the rescue, and in the confusion, Nikki touched Trent's sleeve. "I'd better try to rinse this in the women's room," she said, motioning toward her clothes. "So that they won't stain."

"Let's just go back to the hotel."

"No!" Her fingers tightened over his arm. "We've had such a good time, let's not spoil it. Order another couple of drinks and I'll try not to be so much of a klutz." Without waiting for any further protests, she dashed into the building, ostensibly in search of a restroom.

She took the time to look back through the window and spied Trent talking with the waiter. Good. As quickly as possible, without causing a scene, she ducked through a side door and dashed along the shady side of the street to José's. Her ankle began to throb, but she kept running. A tiny bell tinkled as she entered the shop. A young, dark-skinned girl was at the register, helping another customer, a man with silver hair and a cane. Nikki waited impatiently, wishing she could push the older man aside. As he paid for his purchase, he turned, and his gaze collided with Nikki's. For a second, Nikki felt as if she should know the man, as if she'd stepped into the bottom of a dank well. A seeping coldness crept along her skin as she stared into eyes devoid of emotion. Her heart nearly stopped. The old man forced a smile that was well-practiced but friendly. The wintry feeling she'd experienced dissipated. "Pardon me, miss," he said in perfect English. With a tip of his straw fedora, he walked slowly out the door.

She gazed after him, but she didn't have time to wonder who he was—probably just some old guy who was surprised by her bruised face. She yanked her roll of film from her pocket and set it near the register. With the aid of her dictionary, and in halting Spanish, she asked the girl to process the film *pronto*. Nervous as a cat, she kept checking her watch while the pretty salesgirl took her sweet time about filling out the paperwork. Sweat began to collect on Nikki's palms, but eventually the salesgirl told her the film would be ready in two days. Nikki said a quick thanks and hurried out of the shop.

Breathless, she slipped back through the side door of the café and into the restroom, where, still dressed, she splashed her blouse and shorts with water before attempting to wring out all the liquid from the clumps of material she could squeeze in her fingers. She looked a mess, but couldn't worry about the half-baked job. Forcing her breathing to slow, she returned to the table where Trent, cradling his new bottle of beer on his stomach, was waiting.

He cast a glance at her wet clothes. "Okay?"

"Mmm." A fresh glass of lemonade was waiting on the clean table. She took a long swallow and hoped that she appeared calm, that she didn't show any sign of pain from her ankle or look as if she'd been running.

"Took long enough."

"It was a busy place." Smiling sweetly, she picked up a peanut from the dish on the table and popped it into her mouth. "I guess a lot of women had spilled on themselves."

He lifted a brow over the rim of his sunglasses but didn't comment. She wanted to squirm under the intensity of his gaze, but managed a smile as she lifted her glass to her lips. Feeling a tiny drop of sweat slide down her temple, she silently prayed he didn't notice that she was nervous as a mouse trapped in a rattler's cage.

"Cheers," she said, touching the rim of her glass to the top of his dark bottle. "To the honeymoon."

The muscles in his face flinched a little. "Cheers," he muttered, but his eyes didn't meet hers. Instead, he scanned the sea of people strolling past the umbrella tables situated in the courtyard.

Inwardly, Nikki breathed a sigh of relief. The lemonade was tart and cool, and now that she'd accomplished her mission, she could relax. They finished their drinks, and though Nikki protested, Trent insisted they return to the hotel.

She wanted to argue with him, but he was insistent and guided her back to the carriage stop. She decided it was better not to do battle just then. Besides, the sun was blistering, heat waving up from the cobblestone streets. Only the breeze off the ocean offered any relief. Nikki's face began to hurt again and her ankle throbbed.

Trent helped her into the carriage.

Two days, she thought, as the horse trudged slowly up the hill. Only two days. Then she would pick up the pictures. Finally she might have an answer or two about Trent McKenzie, the heretofore mystery man.

So what would she do if she discovered no sign of her "husband" in the shots? Worse yet, what would she do if he *was* in the photographs, holding her hand, kissing her, flashing his sexy smile toward the camera?

Her stomach did a nosedive. What if she found out that she really was married to this stranger?

Chapter 6

"I want to go back to the mission," Nikki said calmly as she shuffled the cards she'd been playing with for nearly an hour. Slowly but surely she was going out of her mind, cooped up with this man she wanted to trust, but couldn't let herself. She'd spent most of the time since they'd gotten back from the carriage ride pretending to play solitaire, surreptitiously studying him from beneath lowered lashes, willing herself to remember, knowing in her heart that a man like Trent McKenzie was unforgettable.

"You're not serious." He was stretched out on the bed, half listening to some Spanish program on the television while flipping through the pages of a sports magazine devoted solely, it seemed, to soccer. He'd been restless, as restless as she, since returning from the carriage ride. Like the clouds gathering in the tropical sky, the tension between them had grown heavy and oppressive.

"I'm dead serious, Trent. I think I should go back to the mission."

"Are you out of your mind?" He tossed his magazine aside.

"What mind?" she quipped, though the joke fell flat and he raked his fingers through his hair in the frustration that consumed them both.

She knew the mission was a dangerous topic, but going back up that trail was something she'd decided she had to do. Before they left the island. While she still had the chance.

Sitting at the table near the French doors, she looked back to his long body lying so insolently over the mussed bed covers and tried not to notice the dark hair on his legs or the open V of his shirt and the chest hairs springing from darkly tanned skin. She even tried to dismiss the concern and worry darkening his gaze.

She continued shuffling cards, listening to them ruffle rather than think about how that atmosphere in the room had become sultry. She'd caught him looking at her, staring at her with eyes that seemed to burn straight to her soul. She flipped a card faceup. The jack of diamonds. "I think if I went back up there, to the 'scene of the crime,' so to speak, I might remember something. Something important."

"There's no road that goes all the way to the mission. You'd have to walk, and that ankle of yours—"

"We could ride." She flipped another card. Queen of hearts.

"Ride? Ride *what?*"

"Motorbikes."

"Too bumpy."

She slapped down several more cards. "Horses, then. There's got to be some way up there."

"I don't think you're ready to go horseback riding."

"It doesn't matter what you think."

"Like hell!" He leaped from the bed and strode across the room. In one swift motion, he shoved her cards out of the way and placed his palms flat on the table so that his head was level with hers. "You're my wife, damn it. My responsibility. I'm not going to have you hurt yourself again and—"

"I'm a person!" she shot back, glaring at him, nose to nose. The air seemed to crackle between them, and she could see the streaks of gray in his blue eyes. "Whether you're my husband or not, I'm an adult. Able to make my own decisions." Oh, Lord, she'd had this conversation before. A long time ago. With…with someone else…. Her father! They'd been arguing— about trust and responsibility—and her father's face had been flushed, his lips tight with anger at his way-ward daughter.

"You can't decide anything until you're well!"

His words snapped her back to the present, and all the old anger mingled with her new fury. "And who decides that?" she demanded, thrusting her chin out mutinously. "You or God?"

His eyes sparked. "You are the most aggravating female I've ever met!"

"Great reason to get married, isn't it?"

Like a panther springing, he grabbed her. He dragged her into his arms, clamped his lips over hers and kissed her with a hot desire so wild she couldn't break free. Her blood was already pounding through her veins, and now his rough kiss caused her heart to thud and her mind to spin.

She yanked her head away from him. "Let go of me," she ground out.

"Not until you start making sense!"

He kissed her again. Harder this time. She tried to fight him, for she knew that kissing him, relying on him, giving herself up to him, was an irretrievable mistake. But his tongue was playing magic upon her lips, prying them open, pressing inward, and he'd all but climbed over the table to force his body close to hers.

Heat swirled inside her. Liquid and white-hot, desire coiled in wanton knots that slowly unwound and slid through her bloodstream.

"God, you make me crazy," he said when he finally lifted his head and stared into her eyes. His chest was rising and falling, his breathing torn from his lungs.

"You *are* crazy."

"Only with you, darlin'." He dropped his hands and gritted his teeth, desire still flaming in his hot blue eyes. By sheer force of will, he walked away from her. "Only with you."

Nikki rubbed her swollen lips and bit back another sharp retort. This was no time for her temper to take command of her tongue. If he chose to be autocratic, so be it. She'd wait him out. It shouldn't be all that hard. There was no way he'd spend an entire day tomorrow cooped up in the hotel, and when he left, she'd do exactly what she damned well pleased.

Flopping back on the bed, he picked up the phone and ordered room service for dinner. With one hand over the receiver, he asked, "What do you want?"

"Anything you order for me, O lord and master."

"Knock it off."

"I have no right to make decisions," she said sweetly, though her eyes were shooting daggers. "Remember?"

Jaw tightening, he ordered for her in Spanish, hung up and said, "Hope you like liver and chick-peas in a hot pepper sauce."

"My favorite," she replied with a smile.

Growling about unappreciative women, he strode to the veranda, slammed the door behind him and stared at the dusky sky.

Liver and chick-peas! Still fuming, Nikki went into the bathroom, locked the door and soaked in a tub of warm water. She didn't know if she could stand another moment of being alone with Trent.

Forty-five minutes later, refreshed and ready to do battle, she returned to the room and found him seated at the table, waiting. The dishes from room service had arrived and were still covered. A glass of white wine shimmered, waiting, next to her plate while a long-necked bottle of beer was sweating on the table in front of his chair. There were smaller dishes of bread, butter and dessert as well.

"Didn't want to start without you," he said, kicking out her chair as she rounded the table wearing a bathrobe over her pajamas.

"Noble of you."

He snorted as she took a seat opposite him. She felt his eyes linger on her a little too long before he slid his gaze away. "May as well eat. Wouldn't want that hot pepper sauce to cool down." With a flourish he lifted the lid from his dish and steam rose from the platter of whitefish, sautéed vegetables and pasta covered with a cream-and-garlic sauce. "Specialty of the house."

Nikki braced herself and uncovered her meal to discover that Trent had ordered the same for her.

"All out of the other stuff," he explained as he twisted off the cap of his beer.

"Sure."

"Maybe tomorrow." He was teasing her, and his eyes glinted seductively.

"After the ride to the mission."

"Don't start with me," he warned, his lips pulling into a harsh frown.

"Okay, okay!" She lifted her palms outward. "Truce."

"Is that possible?"

"God only knows," she said with a smile before lifting the glass of wine to her lips.

She tried her best not to antagonize him during the rest of the meal. They ate in companionable silence, and the food was delicious. Tender and flaky, the fish was the best she'd eaten in a long, long while.

She tried not to stare at him, attempted to make small talk, but there was only so much that could be said about the hotel, the weather and the town of Santa María.

She was nearly stuffed when he lifted the lids on two small dishes. "Oh, I couldn't," she said, shaking her head at the small custard cup filled with a crème pudding, covered by brandied bananas and drizzled in sauce.

"Come on. It's an island specialty." He poured them each a cup of coffee and added a slim stream of cream into her cup. She watched the lazy white clouds roll to the dark surface and wondered how many times in the past Trent had poured her a cup of coffee. How many times had they eaten, just the two of them at a table like this? How many times had they fallen into bed and made love until dawn?

Her throat felt suddenly dry, and she took a long drink from the coffee. She had to quit thinking about him like that—to stop her mind from running away with these fantasies. She glanced at him over the rim of her cup and her stomach turned over. He stared at her with such intensity, such hot-blooded desire, that she forced her gaze away.

Nerves tight, she tackled the dessert, eating most of the sweet concoction, until, belly stretched, she shoved the cup aside. "That's it. No more."

"You sure? There's more coffee—"

"No way. Go ahead." Yawning, she stretched in her chair and noticed that his eyes slid to the V of her neckline.

"Nah. I, uh, think I'll go clean up."

He shoved himself away from the table and walked straight to the bathroom. He locked the door behind himself and wondered how in the hell he'd get through the next few days. Didn't she know what she was doing to him? Didn't she care? Or had she changed so much since the accident? He didn't want to force himself upon her, not until she was ready, but damn, being this close to her, sleeping with her, for God's sake, and trying to keep his hands off her was driving him up the wall.

You're losing it, man.

Muttering under his breath, he turned on the shower spray. He kicked off his boots, yanked off his clothes and stepped under the ice-cold spray. Closing his eyes, he hoped the frigid water would temper his blood and take care of the erection that seemed to sprout every time he was alone with her.

The water stung. Sharp, cold needles against his skin. He leaned against the tiles and waited, forcing all thoughts of Nikki from his mind. He had other things to worry about. Tomorrow, first thing, he'd have to check with *el Perro,* just to make sure she wasn't up to any funny stuff. At the thought of the disgusting little man, Trent scowled, wishing he never had to deal with the likes of the Dog.

Unfortunately it was all part of the game.

Nikki took advantage of her time alone in the room. She was still angry that he thought he could tell her what she could and couldn't do. Well, he had another think coming. Trent wasn't going to get the best of her. She might not remember her past, but she wasn't some mindless wimp who didn't know what was best for her! With one ear tuned to the running water, she dug through his jacket and pants pockets and came up with his wallet.

"Bingo," she whispered, opening the leather with shaking fingers and a cat-who-ate-the-prized-canary smile. What would she do if she discovered he wasn't Trent McKenzie, that he had several aliases, that he'd lied to her? Her heart was pounding so loudly she was certain he could hear it through the closed door and above the shower's spray. With clammy fingers, she opened the wallet and held her breath.

The Washington state driver's license confirmed that his name was, indeed, Trent McKenzie, and that his address was the same as he'd listed on the hotel registration. His picture stared up at her, his harsh glare challenging her, and she felt like a thief. For a second she thought about returning the wallet, but she knew she might not get a second chance to discover more about him.

She told herself that going through his things was all part of investigative journalism, her job. Besides, if he truly was her husband, then he shouldn't mind. Quickly, she flipped through the cards stuffed neatly in special slots: social security, American Express, MasterCard, Visa, Puget Sound Insurance and an oil company card issued to Trent McKenzie. There were no pictures in his wallet, no clues to the inner man, but he was carrying a few hundred dollars in cash and traveler's checks worth nearly two thousand. She was about to flip the wallet closed when she checked one final recess. Her heart stopped beating as she read the permit to carry a concealed weapon.

Because he was a private investigator. She supposed she should feel comforted, but a knot of worry tightened in her guts and she bit her lip against the fear that shot like ice-cold bullets through her bloodstream.

The shower stopped and, with clumsy fingers, she hastily returned the wallet to his pocket. She slid between the covers, snapped off the light, settled her head on the pillow and again feigned sleep. The ruse of dozing wouldn't work indefinitely, she knew, but until she was ready to suffer the consequences of making love to her "husband," she was more than willing to sink to deception.

He left her alone the next morning. Exhausted, she'd fallen asleep sometime after midnight, despite his strong arm thrown around her waist and his warm, steady breath against her nape. Once in the middle of the night, she'd awakened and noticed that his hand had cupped her breast, as if he had every right to touch her anywhere he pleased.

She had shifted and the hand fell away, but it left her feeling empty and frustrated and wishing—oh, God, *wishing*—that she knew who she was.

He'd left a note on the nightstand, telling her that he'd be back before eleven and that she should order room service again.

"Not on your life," she said, flinging off the covers. She had to work fast. After dressing and combing her hair in record time, she dialed the overseas operator and was able to connect with the United States and the offices of the *Seattle Observer*. With any luck, Connie would be working the early shift. Nikki crossed her fingers. Within minutes, a pert female voice, thousands of miles away, answered on the fifth ring. "Connie Benson."

"Holding down the fort?" Nikki asked, her voice lowered though Trent wasn't due back for a few hours.

"Who is this?"

"Nikki. Nikki Carrothers."

"Are you kidding?" Connie said, her voice suddenly friendly. "I thought you were somewhere in the South Pacific."

"The Caribbean," Nikki corrected, trying to keep her voice steady. She took a deep breath. "On my honeymoon."

"On your *what?*" Connie screeched. "Hey, who is this? Is this some kind of joke or what?"

"It's no joke," Nikki said, explaining the circumstances as best she could, though she didn't admit to her amnesia. For now, she decided, the fewer people who knew about her loss of memory, the better.

"I don't believe it! You. Married." Connie chuckled, and Nikki saw the image of a red-blond, big-boned woman with freckles and laughing gold eyes. "Well, you know what they say—never say never."

"What's that supposed to mean?"

"You know, after that Dave fiasco, you swore off men for good. So who's the lucky guy and why didn't I meet him?"

"You know him," Nikki said, crossing her fingers. This was her first chance to catch Trent in a lie. "His name is Trent McKenzie and he works for—"

"The insurance company? Puget Sound Insurance?" Connie said on a long breath. "God, he's gorgeous!"

"Then you remember him?"

"How could you forget a man like that?" she said. "And you *married* him?"

I wish I knew.

"Let me tell you, if I ever snag a man like that I'll hire one of those sky pilots to write it in the sky over downtown Seattle and I'll have the biggest wedding this town has ever seen just to show him off! Come on, Nikki, why didn't you tell me?"

Nikki was ready for that one. "We wanted to surprise everyone."

"Oh, God, how romantic!" Again a long, envious sigh. "Wait until I tell Peggy. She's gonna flip. She'll think you'll want to give up your job, stay home and raise about fifty kids."

"I don't think so," Nikki said, but grinned. It felt good to speak to someone she knew she could trust. "So you remember introducing him to me?"

"Of course I do. It was that claim I had a few months ago. He was checking it out. Came into the office to talk to me, and you were there."

So far, so good. Trent's story was holding up, but there was still something wrong, something out of sync. "How's the job going?"

"Same old grind," Connie said. "It looks like there's been some scam down at the docks. One of the union bosses has been skimming off of the dues and there's a drug ring working out of Tacoma, but, of course, John and Max were given those assignments. I got to cover the arrival of Jana, that big-time fashion model from Europe, but other than that it's the same old, same old. You know, school district stuff, city council news, nothing earth-shattering. As for your friend Crowley, he's still up to his old tricks, but no one seems to be able to prove a thing. If you ask me, Max has dropped the ball on that one."

A little spark of memory flared. "Crowley?" she said nonchalantly, though her heart was thundering. There was something about that name, something important.

"Yeah. You know, Peggy went to bat for you to cover the story, but it was the higher-ups. Frank Pianzani, he's grooming Max for his job, so he put the thumbs-down on a woman covering the senator. Sometimes I think the women's movement never made it through the doors of the *Observer*. Sure, we can talk it up all we want, and report it—God knows we'll get all the information into the paper—but practice it? That'll never happen. Not as long as Pianzani and some of his pals are in charge."

Nervously, Nikki twisted the phone cord. "So tell me about Crowley."

"The good senator has been keeping his nose clean and his face out of the paper for the past couple of weeks," Connie said. "I've been too busy to pay much attention to him. Gotta get all the hot news on the school lunch menu, you know. Someone's got to report if they're serving hot dogs or jo-jos." She laughed and Nikki smiled. "You know, my most interesting story since you've been gone is whether there's too much fat in the food that the schools are serving."

"It's a dirty job, but someone's got to do it."

Connie laughed.

"I think I'll come back home and dig into the Crowley story again," she said, hoping Connie would fill her in on the details.

"I'd expect it."

"Just where did everything end?" Nikki persisted, her hands twining in the telephone cord. "What with getting married and all, I barely had time to think about it."

"Like I said, he's keeping a low profile. If he's into anything shady, he's hiding it well. Anyway, it'll wait until you get back. Besides, you know we agreed we shouldn't talk about it on the work lines."

"Oh." So this was big enough that they didn't trust other people at the paper overhearing their conversations? What could it be? Try as she might, she couldn't remember.

"You know, all this talk about the senator started about the time you met Trent."

"I... I...know," Nikki said, though she felt as if she'd been hit by a sledgehammer. Was there a connection between Trent and Senator Crowley and if so, what? *What was going on?*

"Look, I'll talk to you when you get home. And if you want, I'll nose around."

"That would be great."

"Consider it done!"

Nikki was more mystified than ever. Who the devil was Senator Crowley?

They talked for a couple of minutes longer, and Nikki explained that she'd be home in a few days. She didn't have a lot of time before Trent showed up again, but she was still reticent to sever the connection to her friend and her past.

She hung up and sighed. *So Trent hadn't lied.* She didn't know whether to laugh or cry. One thing was for certain, she couldn't give up trying to remember everything she could about her life before the accident, and the two items at the top of her list were Trent McKenzie and Senator Crowley.

Glancing at her watch, she decided she had time enough to talk to her mother. If she could get through. Her luck held and in a few minutes, her mother's high-pitched voice echoed in her ear. Eloise seemed genuinely glad to hear from her. Though the background noise was loud, and more than once her mother had to cover the mouthpiece to shout at one of her teenaged sons, she seemed relieved to hear from her youngest daughter.

"Thank God you finally called," she reprimanded gently. "Your father phoned. Told me about your accident, but didn't know where you were staying. Then dropped the bomb that you'd gotten married to some stranger. Nikki, I just never thought you would do anything so rash. Now, Janet, that's a different story. When she married Tim, I knew it was a mistake. I wouldn't be surprised if she called me up from Reno or some other place like that and told me she'd gotten married again. But you…well, you were always the sensible one. You know I was awfully fond of Dave…."

"I know, Mom," Nikki said, hating the deception. "But it didn't work out."

"And this Trevor, he's—"

"Trent, Mom. Trent McKenzie."

"I could've sworn your father told me his name was Trevor. That man, I tell you..." she grumbled, then let the rest of her thought die. "Look, just come down to L.A. as soon as you can. I'd love to meet him and so would Fred. He thinks of you girls as his own, you know."

Fred's affections, Nikki remembered, were anything but directed at his stepdaughters. And her mother knew it. Why she continually tried to deceive them all was beyond Nikki. Fred Sampas had never given any of Eloise's daughters a second glance. "Extra baggage," he'd once complained to a friend, and Carole, Nikki's middle sister, had overheard the comment. "Tell Fred I said hello," she said, hiding the sarcasm in her voice.

"I will, honey, but first you tell me all about your accident. Your father was sketchy but he said you're all right. He wasn't lying, was he? He wasn't just trying to spare my feelings."

"No, Mom, I'm okay. I've still got a few scrapes and a couple of bruises, but I'll be fine in a day or two." She filled in most of the details of her fall and recovery, and her mother, over the crackly long-distance wire, seemed satisfied.

"Thank the Lord you weren't hurt any worse! You know, Nikki, I don't know why you can't slow down a little. Now that you're married, you should take things easier, quit trying to prove yourself to that darned paper."

"Is that what I do?"

"Well, you want them to treat you like a man, and you're not one. I guess you know that now."

"I just want to be treated equally."

"There is no equal. Not in this world. Just like there's nothing fair. You know that as well as I do." Nikki didn't bother arguing, but she realized that she wasn't close to her mother and probably never had been. They talked for a few more minutes before Nikki's half brothers commanded her mother's attention and they had to disconnect.

Nikki fell back on the bed and tears burned at the corners of her eyes. Her mother and father had never been happy together, that much she knew, and the divorce had been, for them, a relief, but there had always been a bit of pain, and a little prick of guilt that Nikki had never dislodged. She was old enough to know that she hadn't caused the deep, angry rift between her mother and father, and yet she'd felt real jealousy that Eloise seemed so content with Fred and her new sons. She let out a slow, shuddering breath. "Quit feeling sorry for yourself," she chided.

This wasn't the time to dwell on the sorrows of her past, so she pushed her painful memories—tiny as they were—of her mother aside and concentrated instead on the call with Connie. Their conversation had served to whet her appetite to know more, find out everything she could, and the most certain way of throwing off the dark shadows of her nightmare was to face her past and the accident. The first step was the mission.

"Let's go!" Nikki, skirt bunched around her thighs, nudged her heels into the mare's dappled flanks. The little gray darted forward, galloping up the rocky path leading to the mission. Short, dark legs lengthened stride and the mare's ears flattened against her head. In the blur that was her vision, Nikki saw tall grass and wildflowers bend as the breeze over the ocean blew inland, carrying ominous clouds and oppressive heat. They rimmed the dark forest where, in her nightmares, she'd been chased in a life-and-death race for...what?

Nikki glanced at the gray sky nervously. Dressed in a skirt and a T-shirt, she wasn't ready for a tropical storm. Besides, she had to work fast. Before Trent caught up with her.

Renting the horse hadn't been easy. A driver of one of the horse-drawn carriages had told her of a man who had horses that could be leased for the day, but Nikki's halting Spanish, her half-healed face and the desperation in her tone had made the owner cautious. Only after paying him extra did she wind up with the spunky little mare.

"Don't worry about it," she told herself. But she felt anxious, partly because of the storm brewing, partly because she was deceiving Trent again and partly because, ever since leaving the hotel, she'd had the uncanny feeling that she was being followed. "Oh, stop being a ninny!" It was just the smell of the storm and the fact that her nerves were strung tight as piano wire. Nothing else.

Ignoring the pain that was beginning to throb in her ankle, she ducked her head closer to the horse's neck, smelling the scent of animal sweat and hearing the gray's breathing as she struggled uphill.

"We're almost there," Nikki said, hoping to encourage the horse. The wind in her hair and the pounding of hoofs against the gravel-strewn path reminded her of another time, another ride deep in the closed recesses of her mind. She was sure she had ridden often; the leather reins felt right in her hands. Instinctively she moved with the mare, anticipating subtle changes in the horse's gait, but she couldn't remember a single instance when she'd ridden.

It'll come, she told herself, frustrated that she couldn't control the timing of her memories. As they rounded a curve, the mission came into view, the once-white walls crumbling and gray in ruin.

The path veered closer to the edge of the cliff.

Nikki's heart nearly stopped and she drew back on the reins, yanking hard, causing the horse to shake her head and slide. "Whoa, girl, it's all right," Nikki said, as much to convince herself as the game little mare. Prancing and sidestepping, the gray snorted as she dismounted. Nikki could barely breathe, and the sound of the surf, pounding against rocks and sand hundreds of feet below, seemed to echo through her brain.

Fear, winter-cold and numbing, clutched her heart, but she made her way closer to the edge. Her throat felt dry and raw, her fingers twined in the leather straps of the reins as she inched toward the precipice and looked beyond the earth. Oh, Lord! Her heart plummeted as if to the angry depths below. Jagged black rocks pierced the swirling aquamarine water. Foam and spray swirled around the shore.

The nightmare seemed to close in around her. She felt herself falling over the side, and the edge of her vision seemed to grow dark. The hairs on the back of her neck lifted and she glanced swiftly over her shoulder, certain that she would see someone hidden in the shadows of the forest's growth, eyes hot as he spied upon her. Goose bumps stood on her flesh. For most of the day she'd felt she'd been followed but had never seen anyone tracing her tracks. Now, standing alone on the very ridge from which she'd been pushed, she felt alone and filled with a dread she couldn't name.

She turned back to the ocean. A flock of birds gathered in rookeries on the uppermost points of the rocks suddenly rose in a startled, frantic cloud toward the ominous sky. Rubbing her arms, Nikki tried to remember the birds. In all of her nightmares, the noisy flock hadn't existed. "Come on, Nikki, think!" she muttered under her breath in utter frustration. Why couldn't she call up anything, any damned thing? She kicked a stone in frustration and watched the pebble tumble over the cliff.

The image in her mind switched suddenly. With blood-chilling certainty, she remembered the feel of a harsh hand upon her shoulder, the reeling blow that had pitched her forward, over the edge—

"Nikki!"

She shrieked, nearly jumping out of her skin. The horse snorted, starting to rear, but Nikki held on to the reins and whirled around to find Trent, astride a sorrel gelding, emerging from the thick copse of trees. So he'd been following her! No wonder she'd been on edge. Steeling herself for another one of his lectures on going out alone, she watched as the sorrel raced up the hillside.

Trent moved with the horse, as if he'd ridden for years. His black hair was wild in the wind, his face tanned and harsh, his shirttails flapping. His eyes were covered with aviator glasses but his expression was severe. It didn't take a genius to realize that he wasn't pleased.

He leaped off as the gelding slid to a stop, and Nikki's already thudding heart accelerated.

"What the hell do you think you're doing?" he demanded, advancing on her.

"What the hell are *you* doing here? You nearly killed me, sneaking up on me like that and shouting my name!"

"I thought you might jump."

"Are you crazy?" she demanded, her fury seeping a little as she saw, behind his colored glasses, the fear in his gaze. She inched back from the edge and breathed in a deep, calming breath. Tossing her hair from her eyes, she reminded him, "I told you I wanted to come back here."

"And I said—"

"I know what you commanded," she said, poking an angry finger at his chest. Her horse, pulled by the bridle, followed her. "But I don't take orders from you or anyone else."

"You tried to sneak off behind my back!" He glowered down at her but she refused to be intimidated.

"That's right! Because you wouldn't bring me up here yourself." All her anger reignited in a blast of fury. "I'm tired of you telling me what to do for my own good. And I'm sick to death of lying around trying to piece together my life. If we're married, and I'm not saying I believe that we are, then you'd better get one thing straight, McKenzie, I'm not the kind of woman who wants to be coddled, or treated like a fragile doll, or commanded around like a slave!"

He stared at her, the wind moving his hair, his eyes hidden by the shaded lenses of his glasses, his mouth set in a thin, unbending line. In faded jeans, a white shirt with the sleeves rolled up and the tails flapping freely, he looked sexy and unpredictable and mysterious. Tanned and proud, he glared down at her, and Nikki didn't know what to expect.

"What if you would have hurt yourself?"

"I didn't. No thanks to you."

"No one knew where you were."

"You found me," she sassed back.

"I got lucky."

"Then there's nothing to fight about!"

"Like hell. If you haven't noticed, lady, there's a storm rolling in off the ocean."

"I've been through storms before."

"This isn't Seattle."

"*That* much, I remember." Angrily she wound the reins in her hands, the leather cutting into her palms. "You can come with me or you can go back to the hotel. I really don't care," she said as she placed her left foot in the stirrup and mounted. "I'm going up to the mission. I missed it last time around. Don't want to make the same mistake twice. Hiya!" She kicked her mare and the horse sprang into a gallop, leaving Trent to eat her dust.

"Serves him right," she told the gray. "I've never seen such an overprotective, arrogant, self-important macho jerk! I *can't* believe I married him!"

But he wasn't a man to be put off by a few strong words, or so it seemed as she heard the sound of approaching hoofbeats. Hazarding a quick glance over her shoulder, she saw Trent, riding hell-bent for leather, the gelding's longer strides easily closing the distance between the two horses. "How about that," she muttered, nudging her mount faster. She felt a perverse satisfaction that he'd been compelled to follow her. For some reason he'd taken on the responsibility of her protector, or at least that was what he had hoped she would think.

The mare was breathing hard by the time Nikki drew in on the reins near the mission. Dropping to the ground, she surveyed the ruins. The walls of the centuries-old church were still standing, though cracked and beginning to collapse from years of fighting a grueling and losing battle with the weather. The roof had succumbed long ago. Pieces of red tile were still visible, but there was a gaping hole exposing cross beams and rotting rafters.

The bell tower was beginning to crumble, the stone fence surrounding the mission in ruin and the place was deserted, as if only ghosts resided therein. Nikki felt a chill of apprehension as she tied the mare to a low-hanging branch of a breadfruit tree and walked through a sagging arch to an area where tangled weeds were all that remained of once-tended gardens.

"The monks who lived here left nearly a century ago," Trent said, tethering his horse before he followed her through the ruins. She slid through the opening left by a door no longer in existence and ventured into the church vestibule. The stone floor was cracked and weeds grew between the worn-flat stones leading to the raised platform which had once supported an altar. Vines grew on the inside of the walls, testament to the uselessness of the remaining roof.

"Why'd they leave?"

He lifted a broad shoulder. "Lack of interest, I suppose. The mission was already beginning to need a lot of repairs, and the population of monks had dwindled.

Salvaje wasn't as populated as some of the other islands. Off the trade routes, it also didn't develop as quickly."

"I'd think monks would like that kind of solitude."

"A few stayed, but eventually died. The last, Brother Francis, lived here until 1930, I think, but he was murdered in his sleep by a woman who swore he was the father of her child. Rumor has it that he still walks the ruins at night."

The ghost's footsteps seemed to crawl along her flesh. "You're kidding," she said. "Tell me you're kidding."

"I've never seen him myself, but a lot of the natives are superstitious and they believe that his soul is still earthbound."

"That's kind of creepy." Nikki ran her fingers along one rough wall, and encountered the web of a large black spider. She quickly stuffed her hand into the pocket of her skirt. "Why were we coming to visit this place the other day?"

"Sight-seeing."

Her brow puckered, and she remembered the dream, running through the steamy jungle, her feet stumbling as she broke from the dense foliage to the grassy headland rising over the sea. She'd heard a voice—a harsh male voice issuing orders to her in Spanish.

¡Dama! ¡Por favor! ¡Pare! She'd only run faster, the voice of her assailant spurring her upward toward the mission though her lungs had burned like fire with each breath.

"Oh, Lord," she whispered, leaning suddenly against the wall. Yes, she'd seen the path, taken it a few short steps, and then a heavy hand had pushed her over the edge and she was falling, falling…

"Nikki." She jumped at the sound of Trent's voice and the feel of his hand on her arm. "Are you all right?"

The vision faded and she was staring up at him, shivering though the temperature was sweltering, the humidity high enough to draw beads of sweat on her forehead. "I keep thinking about the dream."

"It's over," he said.

"I don't think so." She rubbed her arms and walked to a window which no longer held glass but offered a view of the changing horizon. Schooners, their masts devoid of sails, were harbored near the town, and the beach was nearly empty. Overhead, the bellies of heavy clouds had turned a deep purple hue and caused the ocean to swirl in dark, angry waves.

"We'll be home soon."

"And that will make everything right?"

"I hope so."

He was placating her, she could feel it, and she was torn between trusting him with her very life and running from him because he was dangerous—if not physically, at least emotionally. He kept her off balance; one minute she found him incredibly attractive on a purely sensual level, the next she feared he was part of some murky master scheme to do her harm. But why? Who was behind the plan? Why would anyone want to hurt her? Why did she feel like a pawn in some game of political intrigue?

The thought struck her like a lightning bolt. *Political intrigue. Politics!* She felt as if she'd inadvertently tripped over a major clue to her being on the island. But what? Her head was beginning to pound all over again. What was it Connie had said, that the women reporters at the *Seattle Observer* weren't allowed on the big, newsworthy stories? That they were kept away from political scandal and corruption and anything that could potentially be award-winning material? The thought was there, just under the surface of her consciousness, niggling at her, something that would give her a clue to her past as well as her present. She concentrated, but try as she could, the thought slipped away, into the black oblivion that was her past. Damn! Damn! Damn! Why couldn't she remember something this important?

"I think we should get back." Trent tugged lightly on her arm, but she yanked her hand back. She stared at the empty, ruined church and shook her head.

"Why did I pick Salvaje as a place for the honeymoon?" she demanded as suddenly as the question popped into her mind.

"I don't know. It appealed to you, I guess."

"But why not Jamaica or Bermuda or Hawaii? Why an isolated island like this?" She walked through the crumbling archway and viewed this island from the highest point. Little more than the top of a great, submerged mountain, Salvaje was as wild as its name. To the east lay the sea, a deep angry blue that looked as threatening as the darkening sky. To the west, the jungle, hot and sweltering and untamed. Far below, the city of Santa María, a small speck of civilization. She walked to the far side of the ruins, where the horses were tethered. Trent's arms surrounded her and he laced his fingers over her abdomen.

"Salvaje appealed to you."

"Didn't you think it was odd?" she asked, turning in his arms, wishing she could yank off his aviator glasses and stare into his eyes—search for the truth.

"We wanted to be alone." A stiff breeze ruffled his

hair and he adjusted his sleeves, already pushed over his forearms.

Her stomach did a strange little flip. "But there are tourists, other people…." He stared at her lips and she had to fight the urge to rim them nervously with her tongue. She saw him swallow and wondered what it would be like to touch his broad chest, to trace the small scar at his hairline, to feel his lips warm and wet against hers.

As if reading her thoughts, he lifted one side of his mouth in a crooked smile that caused her pulse to leap. "We'd better get going. There's one helluva storm brewing and we don't want to be caught out here."

"Don't we?" she said, thrusting out her chin as the wind billowed her skirt. "I thought you said we couldn't keep our hands off each other, that we were so hot we had to get married, that we came here because it was so damned isolated. So why is it now, when we are alone, not a soul in sight, you want to run back to the hotel?"

His back teeth ground together. "I'm only thinking of you."

"Are you?"

"Your injuries—"

"I don't believe you, Trent. This whole thing doesn't wash. I think I came here because…because of some story I was working on at the paper, or because I was running away from something or because I had to get away, but I don't believe that I came here to be alone with you—Oh!"

His mouth claimed hers. As the wind began to howl and the little mare whinnied and reared, Trent pulled her still closer and his lips molded firmly over hers. Gasping, she tried to struggle free, but he wouldn't let go.

His tongue gently prodded her lips apart to slip into the moist secrets beyond her teeth. Nikki knew she should stop him, that she was playing with fire by goading him, but she couldn't help it, and as his tongue flicked against the roof of her mouth, her knees threatened to buckle. The palms that pushed hard against his shoulders moved as her fingers curled to grab his shirt and feel the warm flesh beneath the cotton fabric.

Stop him, Nikki! Stop this madness! her mind screamed, but her reeling senses, already spinning out of control, demanded more. She couldn't get enough of the male smell of him, the feel of his hands splaying against her back, the taste of his mouth on hers.

Her heart was thundering wildly as, with his weight, he pulled them both to the ground. When he lifted his head from hers, he ripped off his sunglasses and searched the contours of her face. "You make me do things I shouldn't."

"Like…like this?" she asked, her voice catching as his blue, blue eyes gazed into hers.

"Like everything I've done since the first time I saw you."

Clouds moved through the sky as he traced the line of her jaw with one long, callused finger. "I told myself to stay away from you, that you were more trouble than I needed, to run like hell until I forgot your name."

"But you didn't," she prodded.

"Couldn't."

But still he didn't love her. She swallowed hard as he wrapped his fingers in her hair and settled his mouth on hers again. She returned the passion of his kiss. Their tongues met and danced, stroking and mating, thrusting and parrying.

Nikki's blood ran hot. Her body began to ache with a willful need that tugged at her heart and burned deep within her. He kissed her eyes, her cheeks, her neck. She was breathing so raggedly her breasts rose and fell, aching to be touched. She barely felt the first drops of rain.

Trent's lips moved easily down the column of her throat and his hands found the hem of her T-shirt, moving upward to scale her ribs, her skin feeling branded where he touched.

Don't do this, Nikki! Don't! one part of her mind screamed, while the other cast caution to the wind. So far she hadn't caught him in a lie. He was, after all, her husband, and even if he wasn't, he was the most damnably sexy man she'd ever met.

His tongue traced the circle of bones at her throat, and a liquid heat started to build deep within her. She moaned softly and he responded, slowly lifting her T-shirt over her head. As the cool air touched her bare skin, she felt her nipples stiffen, and the delicious warmth swirling within her, stretching and reaching outward from the deepest, most feminine part of her, caused all rational thought to cease.

He kissed the tops of her breasts, brushing his lips across the filmy lace of her bra. Had he kissed her this way before? She couldn't remember, but didn't stop his hands from lowering one strap to unleash her breast, its proud, dark nipple puckering in the wind.

"God, you're gorgeous," he whispered, his hot breath fanning the wet tracks of his kisses on her skin. "So damned gorgeous." She stared up at him. The darkening sky was a backdrop for his strong, chiseled features, a slightly crooked nose and a jaw that meant business. She reached upward, dragging his head downward so that his lips encircled her breast.

Like an electric current, a shock ripped through her. His teeth and lips tugged and played, his tongue tickled and teased, and she arched upward, thrusting her hips closer to his. "God, Nikki, we're playing with fire," he admitted as he stripped away her bra and kneaded the soft flesh of her breasts, pressing them together and burying his face in the deep cleft between.

"It's all right. We're married," she said, her equilibrium long gone, desire overtaking common sense.

Growling, he kissed her again, and one of his hands delved beneath the waistband of her skirt, sliding along her spine, touching deeper and deeper until she was writhing beneath him.

"Nikki—" he whispered roughly, as he withdrew his hand.

"Please." She bucked upward and he groaned, his eyes glazing.

"I don't think this is a good idea."

"You started it."

"We'll both regret it."

"Why?" she asked, sensing that he was trying to tell her something, to break the wall of passion that surrounded her mind.

"The doctor said—"

"He's not here."

"We're getting wet."

"Not the first time. We're from Seattle, remember?" She smiled up at him, teasing him, baiting him as rain began to pepper the ground.

His gaze moved from her just-kissed lips to her breasts, and his eyes turned smoky with passion again. "God help us," he said before his lips claimed hers again. Her fingers found the buttons of his shirt and ripped them free, so that she could touch the swirling black hair covering his chest, feel the muscles flex as her fingers grazed his nipples, watch his abdomen curve inward to allow her fingers access to the buttons of his fly.

"You make me crazy," he said.

"The feeling's mutual, I think."

With little effort, he stripped her of her skirt and kicked off his jeans. She saw him for the first time, naked and lean, strident muscles tense as he prodded her legs apart. "You're sure of this?" he asked.

"Trent, please."

Closing his eyes and muttering something under his breath, he thrust into her. Nikki gasped as she enveloped him, felt him start his magical rhythm. She moved her hips to his, and her fingers dug deep into the muscles of his shoulders as the tide of sweet pleasure washed over her in hot, anxious waves. He moved faster, and she kept up with his pace, her breathing wild, her heartbeat pounding in her ears, rain sliding down his smooth, sleek muscles.

"Nikki!" he screamed, throwing back his head. "Nikki, Nikki, Nikki!"

As if the universe exploded, she convulsed, her thoughts swirling, her mind soaring. She quivered in aftershocks and sighed in a voice she didn't recognize as hers as he fell against her, murmuring her name, his body glazed with a salty sheen of sweat.

"Oh, Nikki," he whispered hoarsely, his hands gently

brushing the wet strands of her hair from her face. Rain slid down his neck. His face was tortured and pained as he kissed her lips. "What have I done?"

Chapter 7

"...and stay in the room until I get back," Trent ordered through the open door of the cab. Rain ran down his neck and under his collar as Nikki sat in the back seat of a battered old Chevy that smelled of must, sweat and stale cigarette smoke. They'd returned the horses and now Trent was sending her back to the hotel. Alone.

"Where will you be?"

"Back at the airport, trying to find out how bad this storm is supposed to be and if our flight will take off tomorrow."

"I could come with you—"

His lips thinned in silent reproach. "Go back to the hotel and dry off before you catch pneumonia."

"I'm not going to—"

"I'll be there as soon as I can." He slammed the door closed and the cabbie stepped on the gas, leaving

Trent standing in a puddle of rainwater and a cloud of blue exhaust.

"Serves him right," she muttered, still steaming. After they'd made love, he'd become as sullen and brooding as before, insisting they return the horses and she go back to the hotel.

Wind whistled through the palms and banana trees that lined the street which was all but deserted as pedestrians waited for the storm to pass.

At the hotel, Nikki paid the cab driver and dashed through the rain to the hotel lobby. Her skirt was muddy, her hair lank and dripping as she took the elevator to the second floor and entered the room. As beautiful as Salvaje was during the mild weather, the island seemed dark and menacing in the storm.

Shivering, she stripped off her clothes and took a quick, hot shower, lathering her body and shampooing her hair with a vengeance. Her skirt was probably ruined, stained as the result of making love to Trent in the wilderness. The passion between them had been earth-shattering, and yet afterwards Trent had treated her no differently than he had before. He was still a cynical, overbearing bastard.

Dressed in a robe that covered her bra and panties, she sat before the bureau mirror and combed the tangles from her hair. The woman staring back at her looked better than she had a few days before. Most of the scabs on her face had fallen off, and though her skin was pink, with the right touch of base makeup, blush, lipstick and shadow, she would look almost the same as she had before she'd lost her memory.

The phone rang. She picked up the receiver on the

third ring and, telling herself that the caller had to be Trent, said, "Hello."

"For the love of St. Peter, why are you still on that godforsaken island?"

She couldn't help but grin when she conjured up a picture of the crusty man who'd spawned her. "Probably for the same reason you're forever on a jet between Seattle, Tokyo, Seoul and Sydney. Scheduling."

He chuckled a little. "Don't patronize me, girl. I'm worried about you, and won't feel right until your feet touch down on home soil. What with the storm warnings and all, it's enough to drive me nuts. I'm lucky I got through to you."

"It's good to hear from you, Dad," she said, flopping back on the bed and staring up at the ceiling, watching the blades of the paddle fan rotate slowly.

"Then you're not still mad at me?"

"No way," she said, wishing she could remember what they'd argued about before she'd left Seattle. He'd mentioned several times that he hadn't wanted her to fly to Salvaje, but she couldn't remember why.

"Good. 'Cause you were way off base."

"Off base?" she said, prodding him. "I don't think so."

She heard him exhale an exasperated breath. "'Course you were. Jim's above reproach. Always had been."

"Jim?" she repeated. *Jim who?*

"Why you thought that you had to investigate him after all these years… I don't know what got into you."

Investigate him? She didn't want to tip her hand, but she was dying to know who.

"He and I go way back, long before he was elected, and I won't have you trying to smear his name."

Elected? A politician? Oh, Lord. Her mind spun back to her conversation with Connie at the *Observer.* "You think I'm on a campaign against Senator Crowley," she said, gambling.

"Oh, for the love of Mike, of course the senator!" he growled in exasperation. "What's gotten into you?"

"Nothing," she lied, crossing her fingers.

"Well, you must be in love, 'cause you act as if you've lost your mind."

If you only knew, Dad. She wanted to confide in him, to tell him about her memory loss, but a feeling, a strange, uncomfortable warning buried deep in the depths of her mind, held her tongue. There was a reason, a reason she couldn't begin to fathom, that she couldn't talk things over with her father. She sensed it now—that unspoken barrier that existed between them had always been there. "So we fought about Senator Crowley," she said, trying in vain to remember.

There was a long pause on the other end of the line before her father said, "Honey, are you all right?"

"Fine. I'm fine," she lied. Why would she and her father argue about the senator? Connie had mentioned that Nikki was interested in some scam the senator might be pulling, but why would her father care? Was her father or his business involved? Did he think she was trying to smear the name of a good man, or did he think the senator was dangerous and he feared for Nikki's safety, or was there something else…something hidden much deeper in the recesses of her mind?

"When are you coming home?" Her father's voice was filled with concern.

"Tomorrow—unless the flight is canceled."

"We'll talk then."

"Dad! Wait!" Fortunately he hadn't hung up. "I... I bumped my head in the accident," she admitted, hoping the truth might elicit more information now that she so desperately needed it. "So I don't remember everything."

"You don't remember? For crying out loud, what's going on down there?"

"I've got a slight case of amnesia," she admitted, as rain sheeted against the French doors and wind began to rattle the panes. "Some things slip my mind. Like Crowley."

Her father swore long and hard under his breath. "I don't know whether to be worried out of my skull or relieved," he admitted, adding to her confusion, "but you get yourself on the first plane off that damned island and come home. I'll call Tom and—"

"Tom?"

"Tom Robertson. *Dr.* Robertson. The physician you've seen all your life. Hell, Nikki, now you've really got me worried."

"I remember *you,* Dad," she said, to alleviate his fears.

"Thank God for that!" His voice choked a little. "And when I meet that husband of yours, let me tell you, there's going to be hell to pay. I don't know what he's thinking, letting you—"

"Dad, I'll be all right," she said quickly. "Dr. Padillo thinks the amnesia is only temporary, and I'm already remembering a lot more than I did right after the fall. I'll be okay."

"Well, I don't know Dr. Whatever-the-hell-his-name-is from Adam, but I don't trust him. Could be a damned quack. You come home, Nicole. We'll take care of you."

She felt suddenly on the verge of tears. Here, at last, was her rock. "All right, Dad."

"Damned straight!"

He hung up still muttering oaths at doctors who had gotten their medical degrees by mail or worse! Nikki knew there wasn't any use in explaining that she had absolute faith in Dr. Padillo. The friendly physician seemed knowledgeable, competent and concerned, and if he'd only spoken more English, she would have been completely at ease with him. As it was, his prognosis had proved right on the money. Her wounds were healing according to his timetable and her memory was returning, in sharp little bits and pieces.

The only wild card so far was Trent. Her husband. The man who, with one cocky smile, could cause her heart to race out of control. The man to whom she'd given herself eagerly in the middle of a downpour.

Tomorrow she'd have answers. Once she went to the camera shop, she'd know if Trent had been with her before the accident. *And what if he wasn't?* a nagging part of her mind questioned. *What then? Will you be able to sleep with him? Will you confront him? What?* Without any answers to those questions, she considered her trip home to Seattle. Surely the familiar scenery would jog her memory.

But what would she do about Senator Crowley, and why did she feel that he was part of the reason she'd chosen Salvaje as a spot for her vacation...her honeymoon?

Her father's conversation echoed in her brain, names he'd spoken swimming in the murk that was her mind.

Dr. Robertson. Senator Crowley. She remembered a slight man with wire-rimmed glasses, an easy, gap-toothed smile and huge nose. Because she pictured him in a white jacket, she assumed he was the doctor. As for Crowley, she had no image of the man. Senator Jim—no, James—Crowley. How had she met him? Why did she care? What was the story that she thought surrounded him? Her skin crawled as she considered the fact that somehow Trent might be involved with the man. Maybe that was why he claimed they were married. Head beginning to pound, she stared down at her wedding ring, a gold band that was too big for her finger, and the circle of gold seemed to mock her.

Yet she'd made love to him. Abandoned herself to him as if he were indeed the man she loved. She couldn't help blushing when she remembered the intensity of his lovemaking and the wanton, wild way she'd responded, with no thought of the future. She'd lived for the moment, given herself wholly to the man, and now, lying on the bed she shared with him, she closed her eyes and knew, with gut-wrenching certainty, she'd make love with him again.

It was only a matter of time.

She must've dozed. Groggy, still lying on the bed, she heard the door of the veranda rattle. She rolled over, trying to ignore the sound, but the noise was persistent. As she stretched, she climbed off the bed and noticed the darkness outside. The storm was still blowing hard and Trent had been gone for hours. A pang of worry caused her to bite her lip, but she rationalized that Trent was a man who could take care of himself, probably better than any man she'd ever met. Of course, she thought wryly, she couldn't remember most of the men she had met. Her stomach growled and she wondered if she should order room service or wait for Trent.

The rattle sounded again. Rubbing the kinks from her neck, she walked to the glass doors and reached for the knob, when her hand paused in midair. She froze. The hairs on the back of her neck raised. Her throat gave out a strangled scream as she saw him. Someone. A figure on the veranda. The light from inside the room and the pelting rain distorted her view, but she knew very clearly that a man was on her veranda, a man with dark hair and wet jeans and a slick jacket. His features were blurred. He was about Trent's height and build, but... He vaulted the rail, his jacket billowing as he threw himself against the building, probably to climb down the vines.

"Oh God, oh God, oh God," she whispered half in prayer as she backed up, fumbling for the interior door, then suddenly stopping. What was to prevent him from going into the lobby and waiting for her? She ran across the room, checked the lock on the veranda doors and quickly threw the drapes closed. She checked the hall door, found it locked as well, and with trembling fingers dialed the main desk.

"I want to report a stranger lurking outside on my veranda, a Peeping Tom or something—"

"Señora, por favor—"

"Get me someone who can speak English. Oh, God! Uh, *¿Comprende Ud.?* Do you understand? There was a man, a damned Peeping Tom or worse, on my veranda! *¿Habla Ud. inglés?* I need help!"

The lock on the hallway door rattled. Nikki dropped the phone. Heart thudding, she reached for the bedside lamp—a weak weapon, but all she had—and watched in horror as the door swung open and Trent, his hair wet and plastered to his head, the shoulders of his leather jacket soaked, entered. She nearly collapsed against the wall and her fingers let go of the base of the lamp. "Thank God," she whispered.

Trent took one look at her face and his eyes slitted in concern. "What happened?" he demanded, crossing the room. "Nikki, are you okay?"

She nodded, though she couldn't find her tongue, and when he wrapped his arms around her, she sagged against him like a silly woman who couldn't take care of herself. Relieved, she clung to him, trying not to embarrass herself by breaking into tears. He smelled of the outdoors—rainwater, leather and salt air—and though she wanted to crumple into his arms like a lovesick fool, to trust him with all of her heart, to quit torturing herself with worries about him, she stiffened her spine and gently stepped out of his embrace.

"What's wrong?"

"I saw someone on the veranda."

"Who?"

She shook her head, trying to conjure up the man's image. "I don't know. Some man. It was too dark to recognize him, but he was built like you, had on a dark jacket…bare head…" She noticed Trent's dripping hair again and his flushed face. He seemed to be breathing hard, but there was no reason for him to spy on her. No reason on earth. Not when he had a key to the room. Her sick mind was playing games with her again.

Trent threw open the drapes and French doors. Rain and wind blew into the room as he dashed outside just as someone began banging on the hotel door. *"¡Señora McKenzie!"*

In three swift strides, leveling a staying finger at Nikki, Trent was across the room. "Who is it?"

"¡Policía!"

Trent yanked open the door, and two hotel security guards, weapons drawn, burst into the room.

"It's all right," Trent assured them, and one of the men, the beefier of the two, walked to the night table, picked up the phone, muttered Spanish into the receiver and hung up.

Nikki wrapped her arms around her middle and sat on a corner of the bed as Trent acted as interpreter. She told him of the man on the deck, and he, in Spanish, repeated it to the two guards. The questions about the man's identity and description were rapid, and Nikki had to admit that the figure she'd seen was dark and blurry through the rain-washed window.

"We have no idea who it was," Trent said as the security guards were finishing their interrogation. "At least, I don't. Nikki?"

She shook her head. Who would spy on her? "I can't imagine."

The guards talked between themselves and with Trent, even sharing a joke that Nikki couldn't begin to understand. They eventually left, apologizing to Nikki for her fright and promising to look for any suspicious characters.

"They assume it was just another burglary attempt," he said after he'd closed the door behind them. "There have been quite a few in the major hotels around here. A ring of thieves after rich tourists' money or jewelry."

"They wouldn't have found much here," she said,

unconvinced. Her eyebrows drew down over her eyes. "Besides, I'm not sure that it had anything to do with a robbery."

"Why not?" He threw both dead bolts before sitting on the foot of the bed and nudging off his boots.

"Because I've had this feeling that I've been followed."

He cast an interested glance over his shoulder, but didn't say anything.

"Earlier. When I was riding the horse, I felt it, and then you showed up, so I just assumed *you* were the reason I felt as if I'd been watched. But now... I'm not so sure." She tucked her feet up close to her bottom and hugged her knees.

"So you think the man on the veranda might have been following you?"

"Yes. But I don't know why!" Sighing in frustration, she decided to gamble a little. "I think it might have something to do with Senator Crowley."

Was it her imagination or did the cords in the back of his neck tighten a little?

"Crowley? What's he got to do with anything?"

"I don't know," she admitted, "but I talked to Connie at the paper and later my dad called. They both brought up our illustrious senator. Connie seems to think I was hoping to do a story on him, uncover some sort of political dirt, I suppose, and Dad... Dad was even stranger. He acted as if he and I had fought before I left for Salvaje, and that the argument had something to do with Crowley." Stretching, she fluffed her still-damp hair with fingers that shook a little. "The thing of it is, I don't even know what the man looks like. I could barely remember his name."

"James," Trent supplied as he kicked his boots into the closet. "Diamond Jim Crowley. Attorney-at-law, private businessman and senator. A Republican who hails from Tacoma." He pulled off his jacket and hung it over the back of the vanity chair before stretching out on the bed beside her. "Connie's right. You were interested in him. You thought he might be involved in something shady."

"What's that got to do with Salvaje?"

"Nothing."

"Then why did my father and I fight about him?"

"Because your dad is a die-hard Republican who owns his own business. You obviously don't remember, but you and your dad have always been about as far apart politically as any two people can get." He was moving closer to her, his head on the pillow next to her rump. Nikki tried to ignore the feel of his breath, warm even through her robe. She wanted to move away from him, told herself it only made sense, but there was an irresistible pull that kept her seated on the bed, her robe tucked around her legs, her breathing jumping irregularly.

"How shady?"

"Huh?"

"The senator. What was my theory?"

"I don't know. You wouldn't discuss it. Very hush-hush. I'm surprised your father and Connie knew about it."

Connie, too, had insisted that it was something they had to keep quiet. But what? Nikki racked her brain and felt Trent's wet hair rub against her thigh. Her stomach rolled over slowly as desire began to warm her blood.

"What did you find out at the airport?" she asked

to keep her head clear, but his hand encircled her bare ankle. Her heart dropped into her stomach and she could barely concentrate on anything but the warm grip around her leg.

"The storm's supposed to die down and we're booked on a flight that takes off at three. Barring any more catastrophes, we'll be home by midnight tomorrow."

She should have felt overwhelming relief. Instead the nagging feeling that she was leaving something in Salvaje, something undone, kept teasing at her.

He moved his hand. His fingers gently glided up the inside of her calf. Her throat grew tight and she could barely breathe. Biting her lip, she glanced down at him, his head angled on the pillow so that his gaze met hers.

"I don't know if this is such a good idea," she said in a voice she didn't recognize as her own.

His palm brushed her knee and moved upward. "I know it isn't."

"Maybe we should stop—Oh!" Her protests were cut off when he moved suddenly, shifting on the bed so that his body was stretched over hers, his lips finding her yielding mouth just as his fingers touched her panties.

"I can't," he admitted, his lips claiming hers with the same wild passion that had touched her soul only hours before. "Don't you know that by now? When I'm with you, I just can't stop."

Trent spied *el Perro* seated at the bar. The Dog was sipping from a tall glass and trying to make time with a long-legged redhead. The Luna Plata, or Silver Moon tavern, was busy for early afternoon, the air thick with cigarette smoke and laughter, glasses clinking, ice rattling, bawdy jokes thrown about in Spanish. The barkeep, a portly man with a handlebar mustache, was busy making drinks. Waitresses in short ruffled skirts and low-cut tight bodices wiggled quickly between the booths and round tables.

Trent slid into the empty stool next to the Dog. Their eyes met in the mirror behind the bar. As Trent ordered a beer, *el Perro* whispered something into the redhead's ear, grinned at her response and patted her on her rear as she slid from her stool. Only when Trent had paid for his beer did the two men move into one of the back booths near a loud poker game that protected their conversation.

"Your woman, she is sly like the fox, eh?" *el Perro* asked, his dark eyes burning with malicious mirth in the dark tavern.

Trent's blood boiled a little, but he managed a thin smile. "She's smart enough."

"Too smart for you, eh?"

"Maybe," Trent allowed, taking a long pull from his bottle.

El Perro snorted a laugh and lit a cigarette. "She leaves you to wipe the table and does her business alone."

"What business?" Trent asked, though he suspected he already knew. "You mean the camera shop?"

The smaller man exhaled a plume of smoke and seemed mildly disappointed. *"Sí."*

"I expected that."

"Did you know she met the silver-haired one?" *el Perro* asked, sliding a glance in Trent's direction. "The man with the cane."

Trent's composure slipped. His muscles tightened

and he held his bottle of beer in a death grip. "Crowley?" he whispered, his throat raw. "She met Crowley?"

"*Sí.*" El Perro was obviously enjoying himself, but Trent wanted to rip his throat out.

"And?"

"And nothing. She did not recognize him."

That didn't solve the problem. "What about him?"

"He looked long at her, but said nothing." The Dog leaned across the table. "The silver-haired one, I do not trust him, *amigo*. His eyes, they are dead."

Amen. Trent's fists clenched. "Anything else?"

"Nothing."

Trent pulled out a thin envelope and threw it across the table. "You were sloppy," he said. "She saw you on the veranda."

The swarthy man's brows drew together. He shifted his cigarette to one side of his mouth and counted the bills. "Sloppy. Not *el Perro*." Satisfied that the money was all there, he squinted through the trailing smoke of his cigarette. "I was never on your veranda, *amigo*."

Nikki checked her watch. Trent had been gone nearly forty-five minutes. He'd told her he was going down to the lobby to talk to the manager about tighter security, and she'd expected him by now.

The storm had blown itself out during the night, and the day was bright and clear, the afternoon sun once again streaming through the windows.

She glanced at the bed and felt her neck burn scarlet. How many times last night had they made love? Three times? Four? She couldn't remember. Not that it mattered, she supposed, but their lovemaking had been

so wild…so…desperate, as if they both knew it would
suddenly end. *Stupid woman with silly-girl dreams.*

Trent had promised her they could stop in the town
to do some last-minute shopping before they left, and
she was anxious to pick up the film. She would have to
find a way to ditch him again, for only a few minutes,
but that shouldn't be difficult.

She heard his key in the lock and smiled when he entered. "I thought I'd lost you," she said, but noticed the
air of urgency in his step, the grim line of his mouth.

"Not so lucky," he said, but never smiled. "Are you
packed?" He noticed the bags near the door and nodded.
"Good. There's a chance we can catch an earlier flight,
but we've got to get to the airport in twenty minutes."

Her heart dropped to the floor. "Wait a minute," she
argued as he picked up her suitcase and garment bag.
"I thought we were going into town—"

"No time."

"But you promised," she said, desperation gripping
her heart in a stranglehold. "I told you I wanted to go
shopping and—"

"Sorry."

"I'm not leaving until—"

"You're leaving and you're leaving now. With me,"
he said, his voice brooking no argument.

"In case you haven't heard, this isn't the Dark Ages,
McKenzie! You can't just order me around like you're
some lord and I'm your sorry little servant girl—Oh!"

He grabbed with hands tight as manacles circling
her forearms. "It's not safe here anymore."

"What do you mean?"

"The man on the deck. I think you were right. He
wasn't a burglar."

"Who was he?" she asked, trying to keep the fear from her voice.

"I don't know, but we're not sticking around to find out." He dropped her arms at a knock on the door and allowed the bellboy in to help with their bags.

Nikki was beginning to feel desperate. "It would only take a minute."

The phone rang loudly and Trent reached for the receiver. "Hello?"

The conversation was one-sided as he listened, and his eyes narrowed upon Nikki, his lips compressing.

"*Gracias,* I'll tell her," Trent said before slowly replacing the receiver.

Nikki's insides froze.

"That was Nurse Sánchez from the hospital. She says Mrs. Martínez's friend was a girl named Rosa Picano. She works at a hotel on the south end of the bay. Want to tell me about her?"

Leveling her gaze straight at him, she said, "I've wanted to tell you about her for a long time. She saw me in the hospital. She knew me. Called me Señorita Carrothers. Not Señora McKenzie."

One of Trent's eyebrows lifted. "And that surprises you?"

"Yes. Why would she call me—"

"Because there was a mix-up when we got here. At the first hotel. You signed us in while I took care of the baggage, and all of your credit cards, all of your identification, even your passport, is in your maiden name. It was easier to go by Carrothers."

"The girl didn't remember a husband."

"That's because I dealt with the manager directly because the plumbing in our first room didn't work."

She wanted to trust him, to believe in him and yet she couldn't. There were too many things left unexplained. "You're telling me the truth?"

"Yes, but I don't know what I can do to convince you," he said in irritation. "Come on. We've got a plane to catch." He propelled her to the elevator and through the lobby to the front of the hotel where a taxi was waiting in the circular drive. A copper-skinned cabbie shoved their bags into the trunk. "You can't do this," she hissed as Trent forced her into the back of the cab, climbed in beside her and ordered the driver in Spanish to get them to the airport.

"Watch me."

"I'll scream," she warned.

"Go right ahead. We're married, and as I told you before—on this island a husband's rights are rarely questioned. If I say something is good for you, whether you like it or not, that's the way it is."

"That's barbaric!"

His eyes glittered in anger. "Absolutely. That's why it works."

"But—" She wanted to argue, to scream, to pummel him with her fists as the cab driver turned onto the concrete slab of a road that drove them straight to the airport, avoiding the city of Santa María altogether. Her spirits sank as low as they had been since she'd woken up in the hospital all those days ago. At that moment she hated Trent!

"I want a divorce," she blurted out angrily.

His answer was a slow, sexy smile. "That's not what you were begging for last night."

Without thinking, she drew her hand back and

started to slap him, but he caught her wrist in mid-arc and clucked his tongue. "I wouldn't, if I were you."

"If you were me, you'd probably shoot me with that damned gun you've got a permit for!"

"Probably," he allowed, his smile returning as the palm trees gave way to the airport, which was hardly more than a few low-slung buildings and a couple of cracked runways. Nikki had no choice but to follow him into the terminal. She couldn't scream that she was being kidnapped, because he was only taking her home, and truth to tell, she did believe that there was some sort of danger on the island. Why else his case of nerves?

But there was something else here on Salvaje, something that had drawn her to this little speck in the Caribbean, some reason she had wanted to come here in the first place, and whatever that reason was, she knew in her gut that she hadn't found it.

She was still fuming as they boarded the small plane. She sat near the window, strapped her seat belt over her lap and listened to the flight attendant go over the safety procedures. She knew that Trent was watching her, but as they took off, she stared out the window, to the wild island where she'd lost her memory, the paradise she'd come to visit for her honeymoon, the place where she'd lost her heart to a man she alternately hated and loved. Oh, what a horrid mess!

The plane circled, and high above Salvaje, Nikki Carrothers McKenzie looked down to see the crumbling mission visible through the fronds of ancient palms. Her heart jerked painfully as she remembered her nightmare and the first day she'd woken up in the hospital and found herself married to a man she couldn't remember. Her throat grew tight as the island disappeared from sight.

They flew in silence until they reached Miami, where they went through customs, transferred planes and headed west. Nikki watched the movie, a romantic comedy she'd seen before, rather than have to make small talk with Trent. She dozed, ate, and after one final transfer, was on her way to Seattle.

Seattle. The largest city on Puget Sound. Sprawling around Lake Union and Lake Washington, with a series of freeways that could barely handle the traffic that had grown in recent years. She remembered the downtown area as incredibly hilly—she'd long ago given up a manual-shift car—and the waterfront as cool and windy.

She'd worked for the *Observer* for…five or six years. Leaning back against the headrest, she thought about her job and couldn't remember particular incidents, but knew that she had a deep dissatisfaction with her work and a burning need to prove that she was as good as most of the men on the staff. Slowly a memory surfaced.

"You know what they say. 'You can't fight city hall,'" Peggy had announced, slapping a file on Nikki's cluttered desk. Peggy, five foot two in three-inch heels was a petite redhead with big eyes, glasses that slid to the end of her nose and a temper that matched her coloring. "I tried, Nikki."

"I didn't get the story."

"'Racketeering,' and I'm quoting here, 'is better handled by men. They'll give the story the hard edge it needs.' End of quote." Peggy had reached in her purse, looking for a pack of cigarettes though she'd given up smoking eight months earlier. "Damn," she'd muttered under her breath. "It's enough to make me want to burn my bra all over again, and I gave that up in seventy-two."

Nikki, though furious, had managed a laugh. "We can't let them beat us."

"They think they're doing us a favor."

"Oh, so now taking the good stories is chivalrous." Nikki seethed inside. "Well, I guess we'll just have to prove them wrong."

"Nikki—" Peggy's voice held a warning note.

"I think it's Pulitzer Prize time."

"I don't like the sound of this," Peggy said, then wrinkled her nose. "Well, actually I do, but I'm supposed to go along with the decisions of the chief editor. That's my official stance."

Nikki had lifted a shoulder but knew what she had to do. The next big story that came along, wasn't going to pass her by. In fact, she'd been gathering information on a couple of stories, one of which was starting to look like it might be worthwhile—the one involving Senator James T. Crowley. "And your unofficial stance?"

Peggy pushed her glasses back to the bridge of her nose and her tiny chin was set in determination. "Go for it."

Now, circling above Seattle, Nikki's heart began to pound. So that's how she became interested in the senator, but she couldn't remember why. He was involved in something dirty, that much she'd determined, and somehow her trip to Salvaje—her *honeymoon*—was connected with the story. But how?

The plane began its approach, and Nikki glanced out the window. As they dropped through the clouds, a million lights, set in connecting grids, came into view. She tightened her seat belt. Soon she'd be home. Surely then her memory would return. She cast a glance at Trent. The mystery around him would be answered.

Her stomach twisted like a fraying rope. What if she found out they weren't married, that for whatever reason, now that she was back in Seattle, he had no further use for her? True, she believed that he cared for her, if just a little, but never once had he claimed to love her. Her heart tore a little and she told herself she was being a ninny. For the past ten days or so this man had been the very bane of her existence. So what if she melted when he kissed her, so what if she couldn't help staring at the way his hair fell over his forehead, so what if she tingled each time he took her hand in his?

Romantic fantasies! That's all. She'd been alone with him on a tropical island, sensing danger and adventure. Of course she'd become infatuated with him.

But it was over. She was home. He slid her a glance that echoed her own feelings and her heart turned to ice. Frowning slightly, Trent reached into the inner pocket of his jacket, withdrawing an envelope.

"I thought you'd want to see these," he said cryptically as he dropped the envelope into her lap. Her heart nearly stopped beating as she recognized the package containing photographs from the film she'd left at José's camera shop. "Go ahead, Nikki," he said with measured calm. "Open it."

Chapter 8

Nikki felt cold inside, as if a ghost had stepped across her soul. Only seven pictures had developed and those photographs were taken in a city near water, but a modern, busy city that she should recognize, a town that was far from the rustic Caribbean town of Santa María. She flipped through the few shots. Not one snapshot of Salvaje or Trent.

"Looks like Victoria," he said, when she just stared at the photographs and felt the hot stain of embarrassment climb up the back of her neck. "British Columbia."

She rolled her lips over her teeth. Victoria. She'd been there. Probably on her last vacation, the last time she'd used the camera.

"All that trouble for nothing," Trent remarked as she slid the snapshots into the envelope.

Clearing her throat, she slid him a suspicious glance. "Were you spying on me?"

"I was just trying to take care of you." His face was set in defiance, as if he dared her to argue with him. "But you never believe me."

"I don't know what to believe," she admitted. The plane touched down with a jolt and the chirp of tires on the runway. Nikki stuffed the pictures into her purse. Some investigative reporter she'd turned out to be. No wonder her stories had included covering the state fair, a Boy Scout jamboree and the governor's daughter's wedding. Hot stuff.

Now she was no closer to knowing if she was married to Trent than she had been before.

Once in the terminal, they picked up their bags and took a shuttle to the parking lot, where Trent's Jeep was parked. With more than its share of dents and a paint job that needed serious attention, the Jeep brought back no memories. She slid into the passenger seat that creaked beneath her weight, waited for Trent and was certain she'd never been in the Jeep before in her life.

Yet, here she was. With her "husband." Lord, when would she ever remember?

Tires humming on the pavement, the Jeep picked up speed, melding with the thick traffic that streamed northward into the heart of Seattle. A thick Washington mist drizzled from the sky and the wipers slapped rain off the windshield as Nikki peered desperately through the glass. Certainly here, in her hometown, she would remember. She waited, crossing her fingers and silently praying that with a rush of adrenaline and the familiar sights and sounds of Seattle, she would be instantly cured and her life would be complete—a past, a present and a future.

The rain-washed streets were familiar. The bustle, noise and bright lights of the city brought a familiar ache in her heart. Wispy fingers of fog rose from the asphalt. The chill wind of October blew eastward, crossing the dark waters of the Sound and rattling up the narrow, steep streets surrounding Elliott Bay.

Yes, this city was home. She'd lived here all her life and remembered driving downtown with her mother and sister, taking the monorail into the shopping district where they would wander through stores and meet their father for lunch. Those happy trips hadn't happened often and they were long ago, before the rift between Eloise and Ted Carrothers had become so deep it could never be repaired. Nikki, the youngest, had been oblivious to the undercurrents of tension between her parents in the early years, but as she grew older and approached adolescence, she'd begun to realize that her mother was deeply unhappy. Being married to a man who expected his dinner on the table at six-thirty without fail, his shirts washed, starched and ironed, and the house and children kept in spotless condition in case he brought a big client home for dinner had finally taken its toll.

The glass of wine her mother had consumed before dinner soon had stretched to two and eventually three. Sometimes Eloise had drunk an entire bottle before the meal, and as soon as the dishes had been stacked in the dishwasher, she had retired upstairs with a "headache."

Eventually she had barely been able to stay awake through the meal, and the fights that had erupted between Nikki's parents had rocked the timbers of their Cape Cod-style house in the Queen Anne district.

Nikki remembered lying on her bed, her quilt tucked over her head, trying to block out the sounds of anger that radiated throughout the old house. Even now, more than fifteen years later, the pain cut through her heart. She blinked back tears and told herself everything had turned out for the best—her mother was happy in Southern California, remarried to a real-estate man and living not far from the ocean, and her father, still single, seemed to enjoy his bachelorhood.

Trent wheeled the Jeep into the drive of an old English Tudor home that had been converted to apartments. The rig bounced over a couple of speed bumps before landing in a parking space beneath an oak tree with spreading branches and brittle, dead leaves.

Nikki stared at the building as she slammed the door of the Jeep shut. Home. Seeing the old house should bring back wave after wave of memories. Nervously, she scanned the house, trying to see past the windows which glowed brightly, though the drapes had been drawn against the night. Who were these people who lived so close to her? An old white pickup and a new Ford wagon were parked near the Jeep, but try as she might, she couldn't conjure up faces for the people who drove the vehicles and shared the same plumbing and roof with her.

Disappointed, she followed Trent as he carried her bags up the exterior stairs to the third-floor landing. Each step was covered with strips of rubber for traction and the rail was well used. Once on her small porch, Nikki fumbled with the keys and, hunching her shoulders against the steady drizzle, unlocked the door.

She dropped her suitcase and purse on the faded Oriental rug and breathed deeply of the musty, stale air. As if from habit, she kicked off her shoes and padded in stocking feet through the long, narrow attic that served as her living room and bedroom. Her hands trailed along the backs of chairs and across the dusty surface of the table, and a sense of belonging wove its way into her heart.

"It's good to be home," she admitted huskily, feeling, for the first time in two weeks, that she had some bearings. She glanced at the quilt tossed over the back of her camel-backed couch, smiled at the flowers, now dry and dropping petals, on a small table near one of the windows and noticed that her brass teapot was sitting empty on the stove.

"You remember?" Trent asked.

She shook her head and glanced back at him. Was there just a hint of relief in his gaze? "Not really. No images. Just feelings. But… I think it's coming." She crossed to a window and unlatched the panes, allowing the hint of an early autumn breeze to infiltrate the stuffy apartment as she walked to the fireplace. Cool, damp air swirled into the room and followed after her as she ran her fingers along the mantel, picking up a fine layer of dust, looking for any photographs or mementos of the man she'd married. There was nothing. Not a solitary snapshot to verify his claims.

Frowning, she eyed her desk. The calendar lay open to a date that was nearly two weeks past. Chuckling at the "Far Side" cartoon, she flipped forward two weeks. Every page was blank. Aware of Trent's gaze following her, she turned back a few pages, noted some of the appointments she'd made and kept, she supposed, but realized that there wasn't a single notation about Trent. Not even his initials. No dinner date or lunch appointment, no mention of a movie or drinks or anything. As if he'd never existed.

She glanced up at him, half expecting him to come up with some explanation, but his face was unreadable, allowing her to draw whatever conclusions she wanted. "Didn't we go out?" she asked. "You know, for dinner or something...a date?"

His mouth lifted in the corner and his eyes turned smoky blue. "We started out way beyond the dating stage."

"But there's no mention of you. Not one clue...."

Lifting a shoulder as if her concerns were unimportant, he balanced on the overstuffed arm of the couch. The muscles in the back of his neck tightened and he seemed to grapple for the right words. "It was all very spontaneous. I didn't analyze it. Neither did you."

She had no reason to believe him, no proof to substantiate what he was saying. Rubbing a kink from her neck, she sighed and glanced at the telephone recorder, its red light flashing impatiently. With a feeling of dread, she pushed the playback button and the tape rewound quickly.

The first four calls were hang-ups. Then Jan's voice, strained by older-sister concern, echoed through the room. *"Nikki? It's Jan. What the hell's going on? Mom called and said you were on some island in the Caribbean and you got married there, for God's sake. To some guy no one in the family's ever met."* Nikki's gaze collided with Trent's. *"Is this all on the up-and-up? Call me when you get back and be ready to spill everything! Geez, Nikki, what happened to you! This is just so... I don't know—impulsive, I guess. I thought you'd finally gotten over all that."* There was a weighty pause when

Jan sighed. *"Look, it sounds like we're trying to shut the barn door and the horse has already escaped. I guess I should congratulate you.... Well, just call me."*

"We don't have time for this," Trent grumbled as the phone buzzed and clicked over a series of hang-ups.

"Sure we do."

The next voice on the phone was a computer message about a fabulous deal on a time-share vacation in Colorado; the next, someone taking a survey about television programming.

The final call was more urgent. *"Nikki? It's Dave."* She stiffened. Trent's lips curled into a humorless smile. *"For heaven's sake, what's going on? I called your office and talked to Connie and she let it slip that you're married to a man you barely know! Is this some kind of a joke or something? Connie said you'd hardly dated him before taking off for that island. For crying out loud, Nikki, call me and tell me it's a lie or a joke or...or anything. I know we had some problems, but I thought we just needed a little time and space to work them out."* There was a lengthy pause and a long sigh. *"Look, if you're really married, I hope this guy is worth it, because you deserve the best...."* Nikki closed her eyes and she remembered Dave, big and blond, neat and tidy, spit and polish. At one time, he had seemed to care for her, but the images strobe-lighting through her mind weren't filled with love or tenderness or passion. She realized that she probably had never truly loved him. He'd just seemed like the right guy at the wrong time in her life. And he'd been the one who had wanted his "space" and a little more "time," if she remembered correctly.

His voice filled the emptiness again. *"But...well, if this is all a big lie, call me. Or if the guy doesn't turn*

*out to be Mr. Perfect, for God's sake, give me a buzz....
Believe it or not, Nikki, I miss you. I just didn't realize
how much until now.... What's the saying about being
a day late and a dollar short? Well, it seems to be the
story of my life. I love you, Nikki. I always will."* He
hung up abruptly and his words hung on the air, silent,
invisible sentinels that stood as strongly as a wall of
steel between Nikki and Trent.

"Eloquent," Trent muttered, his lips thinning into a
hard, flat line. "Maybe you married the wrong man."

"Maybe I'm not even married."

His mouth curved sardonically and he raked fingers
of frustration through his coal-black hair. "Right now I
don't give a good goddamn what you believe, but we're
getting out of here." He picked up the suitcase she'd
dropped and slung the strap over his shoulder. The fingers of his other hand wrapped around the handle of
her garment bag as he cocked his head in the general
direction of the door.

Nikki refused to be intimidated. "When did we get
married?" she demanded, not budging an inch.

"On the Friday we left. At noon."

Still standing at her desk, she glanced at that particular date on her calendar, but it was, aside from a reminder to pick up her dry cleaning and a note as to the
time her plane was scheduled to take off for Salvaje,
blank. As if Trent McKenzie, before he'd appeared at
her bedside at the hospital in Santa María, hadn't existed. "I didn't write it down."

"Of course not." Dropping both pieces of luggage, he
strode to the desk as if he'd walked through her home
a thousand times. "We didn't know when we were getting married until that day. So we just hightailed it down

to the justice of the peace and did the dirty deed." His eyes narrowed on her, as if he were challenging her to call his bluff.

"So it's on record."

"With the city of Seattle and King County," he said, reaching around her and drawing her into the circle of his arms. Sighing, he brushed a lock of hair from her face and struggled with his temper. "Come on, Nik. Throw some things together and we'll go to my place."

"Is that what we planned?"

"I think it's best."

"We could stay here."

"Nikki." He rested his forehead on hers. Tenderness softened his features. "We're both tired. Let's not argue—just get your things together and—"

"Wait a minute." She couldn't let him sweet-talk her. As warm and inviting as his embrace was, she yanked herself free and tried to think clearly. She was running on adrenaline now and she was back in her own home. No one, especially not a man she couldn't even remember, could order her around. "This isn't Salvaje, Trent. You can't use your caveman tactics on me."

"And I thought I was being nice," he said, rolling his eyes to the sloped ceiling.

"I want answers, answers you should have given me the first day I woke up."

His jaw slid to one side. "When we get to my place."

"How about right now?" She was on a roll and she wasn't going to stop. "Why did you follow me?"

"What?"

"On the island," she said, stepping farther from him, putting much needed distance between her body and his. When he held her, she found it impossible to think and remain level-headed. Right now, back in the United States, they had a helluva lot to straighten out. "You did follow me, didn't you?"

"I was worried about you."

"That's not an answer."

He muttered something and shoved his hands into his pockets. "I hired a man to keep his eye on you."

"You *what?*"

"A private investigator."

Her temper flamed white-hot. "You low-down, lying son of a—"

"Stop it!" he warned, his nostrils flaring slightly as his temper began to slip. "I wanted you to have a little freedom, but—"

"Not too much. You were just giving me a slightly longer leash, is that it? Why? So I could strangle myself?" She marched back to him and tipped her chin upward. Heat radiated from beneath her skin and she knew her eyes were throwing off sparks of fury. "You're keeping something from me. No, I take it back—not something, but everything. You've been pointedly vague when I asked about your family, you've sidestepped a million questions about our romance, and you act as if we're in some sort of dire jeopardy. Even now. When we're home. You told me I wasn't pushed over that ledge, and yet you're nervous as a cat, acting like someone's planning to do us—well, me, at least—in. What is it, Trent?"

"I told you I'd explain when we get home."

"We *are* home." She planted her hands on her hips and decided to force his hand. "Why don't you tell me what all this…secrecy and cloak-and-dagger stuff has to do with Senator Crowley?"

His jaw hardened a little. "So you're still onto that, are you?"

"Absolutely." She skirted him, walked to her computer and snapped the power switch. The machine hummed to life. "I figure I'll know everything I want to know and a lot of things I don't want to know about good ol' Diamond Jim when I find my notes in this thing." She tapped the top of the monitor with her fingernail. "Maybe your name will come up, too."

"We don't have time—"

"Don't we?" She whirled on him, her hair slapping her in her face. "What happened to 'all the time in the world.' Or 'the rest of our lives'? On Salvaje you wanted me to think we could take everything slow and easy, but now we're back in Seattle and it's rush, rush, rush. Are you going to enlighten me, Trent?" she asked as the monitor glowed.

Exasperated, she plopped into her desk chair, pressed a series of buttons and scanned her files. "Let's see, how about under 'Crowley' for starters?" Deftly, she typed the senator's name, but the machine beeped at her and told her no such file existed. "Okay." Her brow puckered and she tried to think. "How about 'government'?" Only a half-finished story on a mayoral candidate. "Politics" was no better. "This can't be," she said, typing quickly, one file heading after another. She reread her work-in-progress menu again. No Crowley. No Diamond Jim. No political intrigue. Something was wrong. Biting her lip, she brought up other menus, from articles she'd finished. Not a clue.

"Why are you so damned certain that you were working on this story?" Trent asked, eyeing the screen skeptically, then sauntering to the fireplace and picking up pictures of her family. He fingered a color photo of her sister, Carole.

"I wasn't assigned the story—not officially—but I have this gut feeling that…" Her voice trailed off as she noticed Trent move easily around the room, glancing through the windows, stuffing his hands in his back pockets, closing a closet door with a faulty latch, as if he knew the place inside out. As if he belonged.

Her throat went suddenly dry. Could he have erased her story on Crowley? Destroyed all records she had on the senator?

But why? Good Lord, her head was beginning to pound again. Maybe Crowley was the key to why Trent claimed to be her husband. Goose bumps raced up her arms. This whole theory gave her the creeps and it didn't make a lot of sense. She swallowed hard and kept her gaze on the screen, unable to look into Trent's eyes for fear he might read her thoughts. She didn't want to believe he would sabotage her. Why would he lie about something so easily checked? What would be the point? And if he planned to hurt her…well, he had ample opportunity in a faraway country where the United States government couldn't touch him. Her palms were slick with nervous sweat. "I think we need to talk," she said, switching off the computer and swiveling in her chair to face him. He met her eyes in the oval mirror mounted over the fireplace as the machine wound down. Nikki's throat squeezed, and his gaze, flat and unreadable, didn't falter.

"You're right. But we have to do it at my place."

"Why?"

"Because it's not safe here, Nikki."

"This is my home and—"

"For God's sake!" He whirled and stormed back to her, drawing her to her feet. "Get your things—now! We don't have a lot of time."

"You're serious about this danger thing?"

"Dead serious."

"And when we get to your place?"

"You can ask me anything you want. But move it, now, before it's too late!"

His harsh countenance convinced her. Swallowing a knot of fear in her throat, she stumbled to the closet and pulled out a couple of pairs of jeans and some sweaters which she stuffed into an empty bag. "Are you going to tell me what we're running from?" she asked, picking up her makeup case as he grabbed the suitcase she'd dropped on the floor. She struggled into her Reebok sneakers and denim jacket and glared at him. "Because I'm going to remember, damn it, and when I do, there will be hell to pay if I find out you're a fraud, Trent McKenzie!"

Trent had never been above telling a lie, not if the situation warranted stretching the truth a little, but this time he'd played out his hand and was about to ruin everything. He'd managed to get himself so emotionally tangled in his own web of deceit that he was trapped. Like a damned fly in a spider's web.

Mentally abusing himself, he took the corner a little too quickly and the old Jeep slid a bit before the tread-free tires caught hold of the slick street.

He slid a glance at her, small and huddled against the passenger door. Confused, half her memory gone, the other half distorted by people she couldn't even remember. He tightened his fingers around the steering wheel until they ached.

It wasn't supposed to happen this way. He wasn't supposed to care for her. When he'd met her he'd been attracted to her, of course—hell, what red-blooded American male wouldn't be? She was put together well, with curves in the right places and a face that could stop traffic. Whether she knew it or not, Nikki was a knockout. Even now, with the remainder of the abrasions from the accident casting parts of her face in pink, she was drop-dead gorgeous, in a way never exploited by fashion magazines.

Her eyes were clear and could cut to a man's soul, her hair was thick and wavy and shimmered under any light and her mouth was bowed into a thoughtful little pucker that caused the crotch of his pants to seem suddenly way too tight.

Her looks had attracted him, and her personality, part pit bull, part banty rooster and another part pure sexy feline, had kept him interested. He'd been around enough good-looking women not to fall into the usual traps, but with Nicole Louise Carrothers he'd swan-dived off a tall precipice and was still falling. Straight into the depths of emotional hell. The woman had a way of getting into a man's blood and there was no getting her out.

"Damn," he swore softly. She cast him a quick glance, then stared steadily ahead, through the rain-peppered windshield to the curving streets that wound along the shore of Lake Washington.

Tugging on the steering wheel, he pulled out of traffic and into a long drive that wound through tall fir trees and dripping rhododendron bushes no longer in bloom. The drive was lit by small lights. They rounded the bend, and the house, awash in the exterior lamplight, was visible through the trees.

"This is where you live?" she asked, her voice tinged with disbelief.

"Home sweet home."

He cut the engine in front of the garage and she stared up at the house, a long, rambling brick cottage that rose to two stories at one side.

"Somehow it doesn't fit with the Jeep."

"I just like to keep you guessing."

"That much, you do," she admitted, stepping out of his battered rig and hauling her makeup bag with her. Flipping up the hood of her jacket, she let out a low whistle.

Trent unlocked the door with a key on his ring.

Inside, the house smelled of cleaning solvent, wax and oil. As they walked along wood corridors, Trent snapped on the lights unerringly, his hands finding switches in the dark, but still Nikki felt cold as death. Though she couldn't remember her past, she was certain that she'd never set foot in this house in her life. The living room was situated near the back of the house. Furnished in high-backed chairs, ottomans and a couch in shades of cream and navy, the room offered a panoramic view of the lake, now dark and brooding, only a few lights reflecting on the inky surface.

Nikki stared out the window and wrapped her arms around herself. Brass lamps pooled soft light over mahogany tables and the smell of pipe tobacco and ash from the fireplace tinged the air in faint scents. "I've never been here before," she said flatly.

"You'll remember."

"I don't think so." A chill skittered up her spine. "I would remember this. I would remember being here with you!" She trailed a finger along the window ledge, then turned tortured eyes up to his, hoping to feel a sense of security, of belonging.

"You're just tired." His voice was rough as sandpaper. Jaw tight, he took her hand and walked along a short, carpeted hall to the bedroom, where he placed her suitcase on the foot of a massive king-size bed with square posts and a carved headboard. The carpet was thick burgundy, the quilt was patterned in tan, burgundy and deep forest green.

A fireplace filled one corner, and Trent struck a match to the bottom of his boot and lit the dry logs resting on ancient andirons.

She felt a sudden sense of trepidation as she looked around the room. Something wasn't right; she could feel it in the very marrow of her bones.

Flames began to crackle against desert-dry kindling and the moss popped as it was consumed by the hungry fire.

Trent straightened, rubbing the small of his back, then stretching. Nikki's heart turned over at the sight of a slice of his skin just above the waistband of his low-slung jeans, visible as his hands reached toward the ceiling. She noticed the smooth muscles of his back and the cleft of his spine. "It's been a long day," he said, shrugging out of his jacket and tossing it carelessly on the foot of the bed. "We should turn in."

The room felt suddenly close and she could barely breathe. She'd slept with him while they stayed in the hotel on Salvaje, but she'd salved her guilty conscience with the knowledge that she'd had no choice. She'd made love to him hungrily because she was a willing prisoner and the rest of her life had seemed so far away and remote.

But now they were back home. Or in a place he claimed belonged to him, and the prospect of falling into bed with him was suddenly terrifying. Now the choice was hers. Or, at least, it should have been. An American woman on American soil in her own hometown. He wasn't tying her to the bed, nor did he have to drag her here. True, he'd used his considerable powers of persuasion, but she had enough of her mind left to be able to say no if she'd really wanted to.

Truth to tell, she wanted to be with him. Here. Alone. As dangerous as he sometimes seemed, she couldn't stop wanting him. Maybe he hadn't lied. Maybe his story about the two of them held some water. The hot part was right. He yanked off his shirt, and Nikki watched as the firelight played upon tight, dense muscles sprayed with coarse chest hair.

He lifted a brow in her direction. "You want to take a bath or something?"

"You said you'd give me answers."

"That I did." He walked slowly to her, took the suitcase from her hand and dropped it onto the floor. With his gaze fastened to hers, he shoved her jacket over her shoulders and it dropped in a denim pool at her feet. "I just thought we should take care of a few more important things first."

"You're stalling," she said, but her voice was breathless, and she couldn't break the magnetic pull of his gaze as he searched her face.

He kissed her, his mouth molding over hers hungrily. Nikki closed her eyes and kissed him back, feeling the rough texture of his chest hair through her blouse, her fingers digging into the sinewy muscles of his shoulders.

"Nikki, oh, Nikki," he whispered roughly. Her mind spun backward to another time when she was kissing another man, a man whom she thought she loved. But his kisses held none of the passion of this man's, and she'd never felt the wild abandon that this man created deep in her soul. Yet they were confused in her mind, the then and now, the here and before. Trent or Dave? Her husband or fiancé? She couldn't think and she tried to regain her disappearing equilibrium. "Dave?" she whispered as his lips traveled down her neck and touched the sensitive skin below her jaw.

He froze. His hands dropped. Stumbling backward, Nikki almost fell on the bed. She was dazed, her body still anxious and wanting.

His face was a mask of fury. "What did you call me?"

"Oh, God," she said, her fingers trembling as she grabbed a clump of long hair and held it at the base of her skull. What had she been thinking? "I called you Dave," she admitted, seeing a streak of pain slash through his eyes. "I... I was confused."

He snorted and crossed his arms over the expanse of his chest. "You thought I was Neumann."

"No—not really," she said, shaking. Oh, Lord, why was she so rattled?

"But you called me—"

"I know. It's just that I remembered," she said, shaking her head as if to clear away the horrid cobwebs that kept wisping through her mind and distorting the past.

"Remembered what?"

"Kissing Dave."

"Great," he said, flinty anger sparking in his eyes. "Well, how do I compare?"

"Compare... No, I didn't mean to—".

"Just what the hell did you mean?" he demanded through lips that barely moved. Brow furrowed, deep lines cleaving his forehead, he raked a gaze down her front.

"You could be happy for me!" she countered, her temper flaring, her chin thrusting forward rebelliously.

"Happy!"

"This is a breakthrough."

"Wonderful." He snorted in derision. "And if we make love, are you going to pretend that I'm Neumann? And am I supposed to applaud?"

"You can do whatever you damned well want!"

"But it might just happen, right? You confusing the two of us?"

"Right. It's a chance we'll both have to take," she said, her breasts rising and falling with each uneven, furious breath she drew. Where did he get off, turning this around so that she felt like some cheap tramp? "Maybe you should take me home."

"This is home."

"Prove it," she threw out, angling her head up at him, letting her hair fall down one shoulder. "Show me the marriage certificate!"

The air between them grew still. Aside from the sizzle of the fire and the soft tattoo of rain against the window, there was no noise. Nikki knew she'd thrown her trump card on the table, but he didn't flinch, didn't move one solitary damn muscle.

"I don't have it," he said, his eyes moving to her lips. She tried not to notice, shifted her gaze downward, to the wide expanse of his chest, then lowered it still farther to rest on the huge silver buckle of his belt. Her throat tightened. This wasn't working.

"Where is it?" she asked, forcing her eyes upward to meet the smoky hue of his stare again.

"At my office."

"What?"

"Downtown. We left it there on our way to the airport." He stepped a little closer to her, close enough that she fought the urge to retreat. There was nowhere to run. Her calves were already pressed against the footboard of the bed.

"I don't believe you."

"Doesn't matter." He reached for her and she swatted his hand away. "You haven't believed me from the start."

"It matters. Big-time."

"We'll pick up the damned certificate." He reached forward again, one finger hooking on the V of her blouse. This time she didn't stop him. She couldn't.

"When?" she asked, hoping she wouldn't stammer, but hardly able to focus on the conversation. The tip of his finger brushed the flesh over her sternum and caused her blood to tingle and heat.

"Tomorrow. You'll want to go into the *Observer*. We'll stop by my office then."

Dear God, if only she could think clearly, but his touch was driving her wild. Standing close enough to feel his breath against her skin, she shivered as he slowly, and oh, so deliberately began working at the buttons of her blouse, his fingers prodding each tiny button free of its bond.

With all her willpower, she grabbed his wrist. "You're changing the subject."

"There is no subject." Leaning forward he kissed the shell of her ear and she melted inside.

"You—you could be lying to me."

"I could be." He nibbled at her neck. The blouse parted and he slid his hands around her. His fingers were warm and familiar against her skin as he pulled her closer.

"I need to know that you're telling the truth," she protested, though her mind was already spinning. "Please…"

"Later."

"Trent, please—" He cut off her pleas with his lips, hot and hard and wanting as they claimed hers. He groaned into her mouth and his tongue sought entrance past the barrier of her teeth.

"Come on, Nikki," he murmured, "let yourself go."

"I can't—"

"Of course you can. You're as hot and wild as that island we just left."

She sighed, and his tongue slid quickly into the wet interior of her mouth. Her knees threatened to buckle and a growing heat spread outward from her center and through her limbs. Her arms encircled his neck and his fingers scaled her ribs to cup her breasts.

Electricity shot through her bloodstream as he slid the blouse off her shoulders and kissed the swollen mounds above the lace of her bra. "God, you're gorgeous," he whispered, his lips wet and hot against her skin.

Lolling her head back, she gave him a full view of her neck. He nibbled and licked her flesh before returning to her breasts, which were now much too tight for her bra. With little encouragement, one rosy-tipped globe spilled free of the lavender lace and he eagerly swept the nipple into his mouth.

Nikki mewed deep in her throat as he tugged and suckled, laving the anxious point until she pressed her hips easily against him. "That's it, love, let go…." His fingers caught in the silky, honey-colored strands of her hair. His body weight pushed her gently and together they tumbled onto the cool quilt. Trent's mouth found hers again, his tongue probing, his hands moving to the small of her back to knead the soft flesh.

Nikki's thoughts were tangled, her emotions tied up in distant memories that teased the surface of her mind only to disappear again. But she wanted this man. Lust streamed through her bloodstream. She lowered her head and ran her tongue across his jaw and neck. Air whistled through his teeth as he sucked in his abdomen and she moved lower, enjoying the power of her body, watching in fascination as his flat nipples tightened at her touch. She took one tiny button into her mouth and he groaned, his fingers working anxiously in her hair.

"You're dangerous," he growled.

"So are you."

He tasted salty and male as he slipped her bra off her shoulders and pressed his lips to the hollow of her collarbone. "You make me do things I should never even think about," he said, his voice rough with emotion as he kissed her again. His fingers moved to her breasts and his thumbs grazed her nipples.

Thrusting her hips to meet his, Nikki was lost, her doubts all fleeing into the dark night. Her fingers dug into the rippling muscles of his back and she closed her mind to all the doubts and fears. She wanted this man, perhaps loved him, needed him as she was certain she'd needed no other. His touch set her ablaze and the drumming passion in her bloodstream refused to be denied.

Ignoring the future as her mind blacked out her past, she lived for the moment, for the hot-ice touch of his lips that burned against her skin and surrounded her heart.

She felt her jeans slide over her hips at his insistent tugging, blinked her eyes open long enough to see him kick off his faded Levi's as well.

"Tell me you want this," he whispered hoarsely.

"I want you."

Bracing himself on one hand, he palmed her breast, making the nipple stand erect again. "Tell me again."

"I... I want to make love to you," she whispered as he lowered his head and his lips surrounded her puckering nipple. "Ohhh."

"That's right." His breath was warm and teasing against the wet little bud, stoking the hungry fire within her. Again she arched up, her naked hips touching his. He held her for a moment, one hand cupping her buttocks. "God, Nikki, I don't want to ever stop," he admitted before prodding her knees apart and settling over her.

"Never," she murmured.

As rain slid against the windowpanes and the fire popped and burned, Trent claimed her as his own. He closed his eyes as she gazed up at him, her heart thudding, the tension in her tight as a piano wire. She reached upward and touched the dark strands of his hair, while capturing the sway of his lovemaking and moving her hips in time with his.

Lying with him felt so right against the soft, down-filled comforter. With firelight playing upon his sleek muscles and throwing red-gold highlights into his dark hair, he looked tough, and strong and male. His face was strained, little beads of sweat dotting his brow as he thrust into her, again and again.

Closing her eyes, she gave herself to him, body and soul, telling herself to trust him as her thoughts spun out of control, her blood ran hot, her body gathered the momentum of a steaming freight train. She felt their worlds collide, rocking her to her very soul, catapulting her into a realm of dizzying heights she was certain no woman before had ever scaled.

She heard a voice, realized it was hers and clung to him as he fell against her, breathless and covered in a sheen of sweat.

"Nikki, sweet Nikki," he murmured, crushing her to him. As afterglow claimed her, she snuggled against Trent, secure in the knowledge that for this night, this reckless, passionate night, nothing existed but Trent and the heart-stopping fact that she loved him.

Trent held her close, but the demons in his mind would allow no sleep. He'd made mistakes in his life, too many to count. And he knew he'd made more than his share with Nikki, but he couldn't help himself.

If he had to, he'd lie, he'd steal, probably even kill for her. But he knew that no matter how many times he told her, she'd never believe him.

He pulled her closer and kissed the hollow of her shoulder. She murmured his name and sighed softly, and the sound wrenched him to his very soul because he knew that, try though he might, he was destined to lose her.

He'd gone too far, let himself get caught up in his

own fantasy because he couldn't imagine ever living without her. Yes, he'd lied, and someday surely she would condemn him to the very bowels of hell, but he hadn't been able to stop himself. She was a woman the like of which he'd never met before and though he'd wanted to resist her, the task had proved too difficult.

"Oh, Nikki," he said on a sigh as he kissed her temple. "If you only knew."

Chapter 9

Hot, cloying air burned in her lungs and covered her skin like a moist, invisible blanket. She kept running, vines clinging to her legs, her feet stumbling as leaves slapped her face. Sweat poured from her skin and the sound of footsteps, heavy, evil and moving with the quickness of a jungle cat, crashed after her.

Help me!

The sound of the sea drew her like a magnet, though she knew the ocean was no savior. But the malevolence breathing hot upon the back of neck propelled her unwilling legs steadily up the hill, chasing her. Fear drummed in her ears and she sent up prayer after prayer.

Please, God, help me!

"¡Pare!" a deep voice yelled. Oh, God, he was so close! In her peripheral vision, she saw his shadow looming big and black and moving swiftly.

She ran harder, her lungs burning, her legs straining. "Nikki! Nikki!"

Trent's voice, somewhere in the distance.

The shadow stretched out its arm, targeting a gun toward her back. Nikki tried to scream but her voice froze in her lungs.

The gun cracked—

"Nikki! Nikki! Wake up!"

Shrieking, Nikki sat bolt upright in bed. Shaking, her voice raw from her own screams, she collapsed against Trent and lost a battle with hot, terrified tears.

"You're all right," he whispered against her crown. She buried her face into the curve of his shoulder, her fingers digging into his flesh. "Nikki, shh. You're safe now." His arms, strong and possessive, wrapped around her, and he cradled her against his chest, slowly rocking her, kissing her crown of mussed hair, willing his strength into her trembling body.

"It was so real," she whispered, her insides quaking. Swiping back a tear with her fingertips, she felt like a fool. Her fears had crystallized in the dream, the same damned nightmare she'd had off and on for two weeks.

"You were back on the island again," he said, holding her.

She nodded against him, her cheek rubbing his solid flesh. Over the sound of her breathing she could hear the steady beat of his heart. Squeezing back more tears, she leaned against him, her arms surrounding his naked torso, her sighs ruffling the dark swirling hairs of his chest.

Trent held her until her breathing was regular, until she no longer trembled in his arms, until the guilt eating at him was too great to bear. He stared at the clock. 5:00 a.m. The fire was reduced to a few glowing coals in a bed of cool ashes, and the rain had stopped. Through the window he saw the first few lights winking from the homes of early risers who lived across the lake.

Her arms tightened around him and he gritted his teeth against the deceit that tore at him like cat's teeth. For two weeks he'd lied to her, and sooner or later he would have to own up to the truth. He'd planned to set the record straight the minute their plane had touched down at SeaTac, but he hadn't, partly from fear, partly because he was so damned selfish. For the first time in five years he longed for a cigarette and a fifth of Jim Beam and wished the ache beginning to harden between his legs would go away.

Time was running out and the lie was growing bigger.

In a matter of hours, she would be able to check the records herself.

He hated weakness and he was weak where she was concerned. Had been from the beginning. That much hadn't been part of the lies. His lust for her had been overpowering and he'd given into carnal pleasure at the expense of her trust. Hell, what a mess.

The time was right. There was no going back. Slowly he disentangled himself from her. "Maybe you should try and get a little more sleep," he suggested, then mentally kicked himself for putting off the inevitable.

Yawning, she stretched, her hands reaching upward, the bedcovers slipping down to reveal her breasts, round, dark-tipped mounds that begged for his attention. The little peaks were tight from the cold and he had no trouble imagining what they would feel like in his hands or how they would taste....

"I can't sleep," she said, smiling a little.

His insides turned to jelly. Didn't she know how damned sexy she was with her gold-brown hair falling in sensual, tangled waves to her shoulders, and her eyes, still dark and slumberous, focused on him?

The hardness in his crotch was becoming unbearable. He slid to the side of the bed, threw his legs over the edge of the mattress and struggled into his suddenly too-tight Levi's. The room smelled of charred wood, perfume and fresh air, permeated with the heady aroma of sex.

"I can't sleep, either," he admitted, conscious of her gaze on his back. If he'd only known a few weeks ago how painful this would be, the consequences of his actions, he might have done something different. Now, of course, it was too late. Much too late. "There's something I've got to tell you." He was facing the opposite direction, but he sensed her stiffen, knew that her calm had given way to wariness again.

Hell, McKenzie, how could you have been such a fool? Turning, he rested his hips and hands against the edge of the bureau. "I don't know how to tell you this," he said, measuring his words and hating the brutal effect they would have on her. "But you were right. We aren't married."

For a moment there was no sound. Nothing changed except the temperature in the room, which seemed to suddenly drop to freezing. Her big eyes stared up at him, nearly uncomprehending yet she was wounded to her soul. "I... I don't think I heard you—"

"I lied."

She sucked in her breath, as if he'd physically slapped her, then closed her eyes for a minute, gathering strength, like clouds roiling before the storm. "We're not married," she clarified, her eyelids flipping open to reveal a face ravaged by fury, a face as white as death. "And never have been."

"That's right."

"Oh, God," she wailed, her gaze turning toward the ceiling in abject misery. "Why didn't you tell me? Why?"

"I couldn't."

Blinking hard, her lips flattening, her chin jutting in anger, she whispered, "I knew it. I just knew it and I let myself be fooled by you!"

"Nikki—" He took a step toward her, but she lowered her gaze and pinned him with all her righteous fury.

"You bastard. You miserable, low-life, lying bastard. You let me believe—"

"I had no choice."

"No choice?" she hurled back at him as she scrambled off the bed. For a second she hadn't moved, had seemed caught in a freeze-frame of time, but now she was all motion, her feet landing on the floor and her hands skimming the ground for the clothes. "No choice!" She snorted out his feeble excuse.

"They were going to kill you."

"They?" she repeated, her skepticism brassy.

"The men who were chasing you."

"Oh, now the story's changed. Lord, I've pulled some dumb ones in my life—well, at least, I *think* I have—but this must take the cake!"

"Yes."

"Convenient," she said, yanking on her jeans and her blouse before pulling a sweater over her head. She didn't bother with underwear as she grabbed the handle of her suitcase and started for the door.

His fingers locked around her wrist. "Where do you think you're going?"

"Home," she said succinctly. "The one I remember."

"You can't."

"I can damn well do what I please." She sneered down at the hand manacling her wrist. "Let go of me, McKenzie. Unless you want me to call the police and have you up on charges of kidnapping me and holding me hostage, as well as assault."

"I never hurt you." She blanched and he swore under his breath. "Not physically."

"Just take your damned hands off me before I scream," she warned, her eyes narrowing in pure hatred. A piece of his soul seemed to shred, but he held firm, his face tightening into a mask of impatience.

"You could at least let me explain."

"You had your chance. Over and over again. I *begged* you to tell me the truth, *pleaded* with you to be honest, and how did you respond? With lies and promises and God only knows what else!" She was nearly shouting by this time, her breathing uneven, her anger seeming to crackle in the air.

"So now you don't have time for the truth."

"From you? Never. I wouldn't know what to believe."

"For God's sake—"

She kicked him then. With the toe of her soft Reebok. She nailed him in the shin and jerked away, but he sprang on her like a cat and snarled, "Just a minute, darlin'."

"Go to hell."

"No, thanks. I've already been there," he shot back, his eyes snapping blue fury, his nostrils flared and his rugged face flushed.

"So have I." Glaring at him pointedly, she yanked

herself free, ripped the ring from her finger and tossed it at him. "I think this is yours."

He snapped the ring out of the air and the muscle in his face stretched taut. "I was only protecting you. It was the only way I could admit you into the hospital without a thousand questions being asked, the only way I could stay in the room and make sure that no one got to you—"

"Oh, is that what it was?" She cocked her head toward the bed. "You know, that's the first time a man's taken it upon himself to have sex with me to 'protect' me."

His teeth ground together. "You're impossible."

"At least I don't resort to lying to score."

"That's enough!" Both his hands opened and clenched, and Nikki had the distinct impression he wanted to put them around her throat and strangle her. Well, she wanted to strangle him, too! And yet a part of her—a silly, irrational, very feminine part of her still loved him. Lord, she was a fool! *Be strong, Nikki.*

"You're right about that, McKenzie," she said as she picked up her suitcase again and slid past him. "It's way more than enough!"

"For once, just listen."

"I've listened, Trent. Over and over again. And all I keep hearing are lies. Lies, lies and more lies! Thanks, anyway, I don't need any more!"

He didn't bother to try and restrain her and she didn't know whether to be grateful or sad. A part of her still longed for him to take her into his arms, but her realistic nature kicked that silly notion right out of her head. She didn't love him. She couldn't love him. She would never love him and never had. Anything

she had felt for him was a wasted, empty emotion—
a fantasy that made having sex with him convenient
and guilt-free.

Married to the man! Imagine! Even with the holes in
her memory she should have known he wasn't her type.

She threw open the back door and walked into the
gray light of dawn. Mist rose from the ground in ghostly
spirals, and the lake, down a steep incline covered with
fir trees still moist from the night's rain, was calm and
gray. The still water seemed to stretch for miles to the
opposite shore where, tucked in a dark ridge of hills,
house lights were beginning to glow.

In a flash of memory, she saw herself on a sailboat,
her father at the helm, her sisters, in fluorescent orange
life jackets, scrambling over the deck. The mainsail had
billowed, catching the wind, and the boat had dipped,
skimming across a choppy surface of whitecaps.

The wind had been winter-cold and raw, but Nikki
hadn't cared. Jan had complained about her hair losing
its curl. Carole was sure she had frostbite, but Nikki had
laughed in the wind, feeling the grip of frigid air tear-
ing at her ponytail and stinging her cheeks.

"Let's go all the way to Alaska," she'd cried, holding on to the boom for dear life.

"Aye, aye, matey," her father had replied and she'd
loved him with all her young heart.

"I'm not going to Alaska," Jan had yelled over the
cry of the wind. "I've got a date."

Nikki hadn't been impressed. "Big deal."

"It is a big deal! I have to get home in time to wash
and blow-dry my hair!"

"For Paul Jansen. Save me." Nikki had laughed.

"That's not a date. It's a death sentence," Carole

added with a wink to her youngest sister. "But Alaska's too cold." Carole's teeth had begun to chatter loudly. Her words came out in choppy little puffs. "C-can't we g-g-go to Hawaii or L.A. or…"

At the mention of the City of Angels, Ted Carrothers's grin had turned into a gritty scowl. Their mother had already moved to Southern California and had hinted to her daughters that there was another man in her life. "Just forget it," he'd muttered to his would-be sailor daughters. Then, spying Jan, he added, "Don't worry, you'll be home in time for your date."

"Good." She'd tossed her head and sniffed at her victory.

"No way! Come on, Dad," Nikki had pleaded, her dreams crumbling. She ached for adventure and she didn't want to go back to the empty house their mother had vacated two years earlier. "Let's sail into the Sound."

Her father had scanned the flinty sky, but even before he turned his eyes back on his youngest daughter, she'd known what he would say. The mood had been destroyed. "Ah, well, we'd better be heading back. I've got a lot of paperwork to catch up on if I'm going to be ready for the meeting in Seoul next week."

Now Nikki stood staring at the calm lake greeting the dawn. Steel gray and cold. She shivered and didn't realize Trent was beside her until a twig snapped beneath his boot.

"Second thoughts?" he asked. No longer was there any anger in his voice. Only regret.

She shook her head. "But thoughts, just the same." She was surprised how quickly they came now. All at once, in a jumble, sharp, vivid memories that last week had been lost to her.

He touched her shoulder and she flinched.

"I don't have my car," she said, as if in explanation. "Since I don't know the bus schedule, and cabs don't cruise by this section of town at daybreak—"

"I'll drive you."

"No way. I'll call a cab."

"Don't be silly."

"Silly?" She laughed mirthlessly. "I've already been played for a fool. I'm not really concerned with silly."

"You know what I mean. Get in the Jeep."

He actually sounded concerned. But then, he was a consummate actor. Hadn't he convinced her that they'd been married? That they'd *loved* each other? Her heart wrenched at his story. So simple. So deceptive. Despite the fact that no one she knew had known of their romance, they'd fallen in love, hightailed it to the nearest courthouse, tied the knot and flown off to a small, out-of-the-way island in the Lesser Antilles for a romantic honeymoon and while they were there she'd fallen off a cliff and nearly killed herself. Lucky for her he was around to snatch her from the jaws of death, carry her off to his bed and lie, lie, lie to her. Her fingers tightened around the strap of her purse.

"Come on, Nikki." His voice was a caress.

"Not if your damned Jeep was the last vehicle on earth." She hitched her bag on her shoulder and started for the main road. She'd stick out her thumb if she had to, though that might be a little risky.

His fingers clamped around her arm. "Get in the Jeep."

"You can't manhandle me."

"I'm doing you a favor."

She snorted. "Your kind of favors I can do without."

He propelled her toward the door of the rig, pulled on the handle, and with a groan of metal the interior was open to her. "Get in."

"I'm not going to—"

"If I have to shove that beautiful butt of yours into the seat, I will," he warned, and she believed him. Her pride still bleeding, she climbed into the damned Jeep and gritted her teeth as he slammed the door shut. This was crazy. Pure, dumb insanity.

He slid into the driver's seat and twisted the key in the ignition. He slammed the door shut and rammed the rig into Reverse. Within seconds they were driving along the rain-washed streets, joining the first few cars and trucks heading toward the skyscrapers swarming along the shores of Elliott Bay.

Inside the Jeep the air was thick. Steam rose on the windshield and Trent flipped on the fan. Cramming her back against the passenger door, Nikki told herself she was the worst kind of fool. She crossed her arms and glared at him. "Just who the hell are you?"

"I told you."

"McKenzie's your real name?"

"You saw my ID, didn't you? When you went through my wallet." The barb stung. Oh, well, Sherlock Holmes she wasn't.

"ID can be bought."

With a sigh, he flipped down the visor, ripped the registration from its holder and shoved it under her nose. "No aliases, okay?"

The beat-up vehicle was registered to Trent Mc-

Kenzie. He wheeled into the drive of her apartment building.

"Okay. So now I know your name." She shrugged as if she didn't care, but couldn't help asking, "What do you do for a living?"

"I'm a freelance investigator. Primarily I work on insurance fraud. I told you all this." He shifted down and the Jeep slowed.

"You told me a lot of things."

The rig slid to a stop, idling near the doorway of one of the first-floor apartments. "I didn't lie about the way we met, Nikki." He cut the engine, and when she tried to open the door, he caught her arm. "Just hear me out."

"I've heard enough. Two weeks of lies is more than anyone should have to swallow, don't you think?" She managed to pull on the door handle, breaking a nail in the process. Too damned bad. "You lied to me, McKenzie, and what's worse, when I knew you weren't telling the truth, you kept piling on more and more lies." Her words raced out of her mouth. "Not only that. You took me to bed, brought me back here under false pretenses, *used* me, and only when you knew the lies would begin to fall apart, did you finally come clean. But not until we made love! Excuse me, what I meant to say is not until we had sex!" So angry she was shaking, she threw off his arm. When he tried to reach for her again, she scrambled out of the Jeep, grabbed her suitcase and ran up the wet steps. He was on her heels, chasing after her, climbing the stairs behind her.

Her dream returned, surreal but no less terrifying as he followed her. It was as if they'd played this game before. At the landing, she whirled on him. "Leave me alone, Trent," she ordered, but he was too close. He planted his hands on the doorframe near her face, trapping her with his body.

"I can't, damn it. Look, Nikki, I didn't mean for it to turn out this way." His mouth curved into a self-deprecating frown. "I should have told you sooner, but I couldn't. Once you were released from the hospital, I... I wanted to stay with you. To keep you safe."

"To sleep with me."

"Yes!"

The air crackled with his admission, and Nikki's throat was suddenly clogged. "Well, lucky you," she said angrily, but the sharp honesty in his gaze cut through the armor of her defense. "You could have stopped things," she whispered.

"I would have."

"Sure," she mocked, and she finally worked up the nerve to ask a question that had been nagging at the back of her mind. "Just who do you think you were protecting me from?"

His lips thinned a fraction. "Crowley."

She sucked in her breath. "So I was right."

"Maybe."

She had a picture of the silver-haired man with his smooth black cane. She'd met him in the camera shop! Her heart nearly stopped. Yes, there was something deadly about him, the gleam in his eye was cold as an arctic well. But she didn't believe he had the strength or stamina to run her down through a jungle. "But he wasn't chasing me."

"I don't know that anyone was."

She felt as if she'd been kicked in the stomach. "But my dream. Everything else fits. And who was the man lurking on the veranda, huh? Was that you?"

"Of course not."

"Well?"

"I thought it might have been a man I had follow-ing you."

"Oh, great! Just great! Now you're trying to tell me that one of the so-called good guys is a Peeping Tom?"

"No. *El Perro* denied it."

"His name is *el Perro?* Doesn't that mean wolf or something?"

"Dog."

"Oh, come on." She threw her hands toward the sky—in desperation or supplication, she didn't know which. "This is too damned unbelievable."

"Is it?" He shoved his face so close she could see the small lines of impatience around his mouth. "You asked what I was trying to tell you and it's simple. You're in danger. From Crowley or one of his goons. Just because we're back in Seattle doesn't mean that you're safe. I overheard you talking to Connie. I knew you were onto Diamond Jim. That's when I started doing my research on you—because there was something about you I couldn't forget. The senator's dangerous, Nikki."

She felt her throat tighten in fear, then shoved the feeling aside. No man, especially not a pathological liar, was going to tell her what to do with her life. "I don't know why I should believe you." She reached behind her, found the doorknob and pushed. It didn't budge.

"Why would I lie?"

"You asked me that before and it took me two weeks to find the answer." She dug through her purse, came up with her ring of keys and wedged the house key into its lock. With a click, the latch gave way. She shoul-dered open the door and stood on the opposite side of the threshold. "I'd like to say something profound here, something you could remember me by, but I can't think of a blessed thing, so I'll just say goodbye."

"I'm not leaving." To prove his point, he stuck the toe of his beat-up leather boots into the apartment.

"I'll call the police."

"Fine." He didn't budge an inch, and she felt the steam rising from the back of her neck.

"You've spent the last two weeks bullying me, Trent McKenzie, but it's over," she lied knowing that, in her heart, it would never be finished between them. But she couldn't think of *that* now. "I'll have you up on charges of harassment, fraud and kidnapping. And if those don't stick, I'll find some that do. So you'd better haul yourself out of here."

He slid into the room, rested his hips against the wall, crossed his arms over his massive chest and nodded toward the phone. "Now *I* don't believe *you*."

She couldn't make good her threat, didn't dare call the police. Whatever story she was working on concerning Senator Crowley, it wasn't yet ready to break and she had to be careful that Diamond Jim didn't catch on to her. If she pressed charges against Trent, there was the matter of public record to consider, and there would be questions about their trip to Salvaje. Her story was half-baked and bizarre, her memory not yet a hundred percent. No, she had better keep the police out of this. For the time being. She looked up at Trent's impassive face and wished she could shake some sense into him. He had backed her into the proverbial corner and he knew it.

"Why don't you get ready for work and I'll drive you."

"You don't have to—" For the first time she realized she was missing her car. She half ran to a window, wiped the glass with her sleeve and stared down at the parking space assigned to her. Empty. Her red-and-white convertible wasn't in its usual spot. "I don't suppose you know what happened to my car?"

"My guess is it's at the airport."

"The airport!" she cried, her temper flaring again. If he'd only been honest with her earlier, she'd have her own set of wheels by now.

"But then again, maybe not. You didn't have a parking ticket on you."

"How do you know?" she demanded, but the answer was clear as the glass top of her coffee table. He'd been given her purse at the hospital when she'd been lying in that tiny room trying to piece together her memory—attempting to recall taking vows with the mysterious, bad-tempered man who had claimed to be her husband. He could have put anything in her purse or taken anything out. Hence, the wedding ring—that blasted symbol of deceit. "Oh, Lord, this is a mess," she said with a sigh as she sank onto the couch and closed her eyes. "What am I going to tell everyone? My entire family thinks I'm married. And Connie. What can I say to her?" She cast an accusing glare in his direction. "When you plot to turn someone's life upside down and inside out, you don't miss a trick, do you?"

Trying to stay calm, she rested the heel of one of her Reebok shoes on the tabletop and wondered how she was going to face the day. There would be questions about her accident, her face, her honeymoon, her husband. What would she say? What could she?

"You don't have to tell anyone what's going on."

"Oh, right! Next you'll be suggesting that I keep pretending that we're married." She lolled her head back on the couch and sighed.

She heard him skirting the coffee table as he walked to the fireplace. "What would it hurt?"

"It's a lie." She cracked open one eye.

"It doesn't have to be."

Her heart stopped for a second, before she found her voice. "Yes it does," she said, quietly. A part of her wanted to take the easy way out, keep the lie going until things settled down and to stay with this dangerous, erotic man. Then she could tell her friends and family the truth. Later she could leave him…or would she ever find the strength to let go? Slowly she shook her head and forced her gaze to meet his. "It'll only get worse."

As the words fell from her lips, she remembered her older sister, Jan, on bent knees, examining a cut on Nikki's chin as she had sat, white-faced and trembling, on the edge of the bathtub. "Geez, you look horrible," Jan had said.

"Thanks," Nikki muttered, fighting tears.

Her elbow ached and her face felt as bad as it probably looked. There was still gravel ground into the skin of her forearm and blood had dried all the way to her wrist. "So what happened?" Jan had asked, seeming uncertain as to how concerned she should be.

"I fell off my bike."

"And how." Jan reached into the medicine cabinet for a dangerous-looking brown bottle and gauze.

Tears welled in Nikki's eyes. Tasting blood in her mouth where her teeth had bitten into her lower lip, she told Jan the truth. Nikki had been riding her bike with her friend, Terry Watson, a devil-may-care girl whose sense of adventure appealed to Nikki. With her pale blond hair, round blue eyes and quick smile, Terry was popular and had a reputation for being a little bit daring. That day, while Nikki was supposed to have been studying for a history test at Terry's house, Terry had shoved her books aside and come up with an alternate plan. With only a little persuasion, Terry had convinced Nikki that they should ride their bikes down to the big Safeway store that was three miles away. The only trouble was that the store was located far beyond the boundaries their parents had agreed upon.

The girls had taken off, full of adventure, thrilled to be doing something just a little bit naughty. They had planned to be back by the time Terry's mom got off work. No one would have been the wiser.

The traffic had been wild, four lanes going fifty-five miles an hour, and the clouds that had been threatening all day suddenly let loose, pouring rain onto the streets, creating rivers flowing into the gutters and turning the day dark as night.

Headlights flashed on, tires sprayed water onto the sidewalks. Rather than ride to the crosswalk, Terry had decided to zigzag across all four lanes of traffic.

"Wait for me!" Nikki had yelled, and Terry, hearing her voice, had turned her head. A car, rounding the corner, had skidded as the driver slammed on his brakes. Horns had blared, tires had squealed. Nikki had squeezed on her brakes. The bike had shimmied in loose gravel, then slid. Nikki had fallen, scraping her knees and elbows and face, her bike flying into the traffic to be crumpled beneath the wheels of a pickup.

"Crazy kids!" The truck's driver had been livid. "I coulda killed you both!" Built like a lumberjack, with a full beard and snapping blue eyes, he'd walked over to Nikki, full of wrath until he saw the scratches on her face and arms. "Hey, kid, are you all right?"

"Fine," she'd stammered, though she felt wretched. But she'd known her injuries weren't nearly as bad as the fear that settled around her heart. Her parents would kill her when they found out.

A lady dressed in a long raincoat and huge round glasses speckled with rain, had climbed out of her small compact car with its emergency lights flashing. Shoulders hunched against the downpour, she'd said, "I think we should call an ambulance."

No! "I'm okay, really." Nikki had fought to hide her pain and she reached for the handlebars of her bike just as Terry, face pale as death, had wheeled up.

"We gotta get out of here," Terry had insisted.

"Now, honey, the police—"

That did it. Nikki had hauled her bike up on its bent frame and jumped onto the seat. The rear wheel had rubbed against the fender, and she was stuck in third gear, but she hadn't thought, just ridden, like the proverbial bat out of hell, as fast as her legs could pedal, all the way home.

"And that's what happened," she had admitted to her sister as she'd tried to balance on the edge of the tub.

Jan had rolled her eyes. "Big trouble, Nik. Big, big trouble." She'd swabbed Nikki's cuts with iodine and as Nikki sucked in her breath through teeth that felt looser than they had earlier in the day, Jan predicted, "Dad's gonna kill you."

He hadn't. In fact he'd been downright kind as he'd sat on the foot of her bed, hands clasped between his knees, his suit rumpled from the drive home. "I'm just thankful you're alive," he'd said, his voice filled with reproach.

Nikki had wanted to burrow down beneath the covers of her twin bed and never come out. She'd let him down and she felt miserable. Tears had drizzled from her eyes and she'd rolled her lips inward and clamped down hard to keep from sobbing.

"I hope you've learned your lesson. I trusted you to be where you'd told me you'd be. I thought I could believe you."

Nikki had blinked hard and swallowed that ever-growing lump in her throat. If only she could undo what had been done!

"But now…well, we'll have to start over, Nicole. Trust isn't just given out—it's earned, you know."

"I'm sorry, Dad. I'm so, so sorry."

"So am I, sweetheart, but this time sorry isn't good enough. You could've been killed. For the time being you're not to see Terry unless it's at school, and you're grounded for…well, until I can trust you again."

Her future had stretched out endlessly before her. She'd been certain she'd become an old maid before he believed her again. Oh, she'd wanted to die right then and there. *Take me, Lord, I'm ready. I can't stand the thought of being cooped up here until he trusts me again. He never will. Never, never, never!*

God, that had been a long time ago. Nikki rubbed her arms and realized that Trent was staring at her. Waiting for her to respond. "I'm not going to lie about it," she said, then realized how ridiculous her words sounded. "Well, I'm not going to lie anymore. I'll just say that it didn't work out, we rushed into things and that we're separated." Cringing inside, she heard "I told you so" being repeated to her over and over by her family and friends.

Pain darkened his gaze and he cleared his throat. "It would be best if we played along with the charade a little longer," he said, measuring the words.

"Why?"

"Until this mess with Crowley is straightened out."

A cold trickle of fear slid down her spine, but she hid it. "Why don't you tell me all about the good senator? And since we didn't go to Salvaje together, why were you down there? I can't imagine that you spend your vacations in the tropics hoping for some woman to lose her memory so you can pounce and take advantage of her."

His eyes flashed dangerously. He rubbed his chin and swore, as if he didn't want to divulge anything to her. "It's been rumored, but hushed up for the most part, that the senator's into taking bribes. Nothing's been proven, of course, and with public officials there's always a lot of conjecture, and our boy Diamond Jim is as slippery as he is popular. Nothing can be pinned on him—he just seems to slide away from scandal."

"What's this got to do with you?"

One of his fists closed for a second and a wave of tension tightened every muscle in the back of his neck. "I know the senator. I have a bone to pick with him."

"What bone?" she asked, surprised that he was opening up.

"It's personal."

"Don't you think I'm involved, *personally?*"

"Let's just say I wouldn't cry if he went down in flames."

"So you and I went down to the island independently."

"That's right. That's why Rosa, the clerk, recognized you and didn't know me."

"And then what?" she said, watching as emotions, strong and angry, played across his face.

"We weren't on the same flight. I'd followed Crowley earlier. You showed up a couple of days later and I recognized you and I thought you might be headed for trouble. I didn't want to blow my cover, so I just kept my eye on you. I figured, from overhearing your conversation with Connie at the *Observer* that you'd be tracking down Diamond Jim as well."

"So...you were following me."

"And Crowley."

She clucked her tongue. "Busy boy."

"By that time I'd done my research on you, your father, your boyfriends, your interests. Everything. I knew all about you."

"Charming," she muttered with more than a trace of sarcasm.

He ignored the dig. "Obviously Crowley knew you were onto him. He must've recognized you since he's in tight with your dad. But I don't think any feelings he has for your old man would affect his ambitions and you, lady, were and are a threat to him."

"How would he guess?"

"He's a powerful man with more than his share of connections. I wouldn't be surprised if one of your co-workers is in the senator's back pocket."

"Who?"

"That much I don't know," he admitted, scowling slightly. "So I kept dogging you and I knew you'd planned to see the mission because I'd overheard you talking to the concierge at the hotel, asking directions.

I made sure I got there ahead of you and then…" Guilt shadowed his eyes and he rubbed a hand over his mouth. "… I wasn't paying attention and suddenly I heard you scream. I ran as fast as I could and found you on the lower ledge. The rest you can figure out."

"What about the man who pushed me?"

Trent shook his head. "Didn't see him." When he realized she was about to protest, he held up a hand. "I'm not saying he didn't exist, I'm just telling you I didn't see him. He could've hidden, I suppose. All I was concerned about was getting you to safety."

"And deciding to pretend to be my husband."

"As I said, originally I did it so that I could stick close to you and keep you safe. That hospital didn't have the best security in the world and I thought Crowley might send one of his goons to make sure you didn't talk. That part worked."

"But only because I didn't regain my memory. What would have happened if I'd suddenly remembered everything?"

A muscle worked in his jaw. "That was one bridge I thought I'd cross when I came to it."

"And that's why you didn't…rush things in the bedroom."

He slid his jaw to the side. "I told myself that I'd keep my hands off you. Your injuries were enough reason."

"But—"

"Oh, hell, Nikki," he exploded, "I couldn't help myself! I knew it was wrong."

She blushed darkly. "You took advantage of me."

"So sue me! Call the damned police! Do whatever you have to, but, for God's sake, believe me! I couldn't keep away. I wanted to. Hell, I knew making love to you would be a mistake, but it was a risk I had to take."

"You didn't *have* to do anything."

He sighed loudly. "It happened, Nikki."

Her heart started to crack again, but she refused to play the part of the wounded victim. Unfortunately part of what he said made sense and the truth be told, she didn't want to leave him. Not yet. Not until she was stronger. Climbing to her feet, she said, "Okay, we'll go along with the charade, for just a few more days, until I can figure out how the hell to divorce you quietly. Then, a clean break."

"Fine." He seemed relieved. The lines of tension around his eyes became less prominent.

"But I am going to work."

He started to argue, thought better of it and nodded curtly. "I'll drive you and pick you up, then we'll go to the airport and try to locate your car."

There was no sense belaboring the point. At least the ground rules were set down, not that they might not shift at any minute. She found a set of towels in a cupboard and, after announcing she was going to take a shower, locked the bathroom door behind her and turned on the old spigots. Steam rose to the ceiling as she stripped off her clothes. So she wasn't married. Good. Soon Trent would be out of her life forever.

She pushed aside the shower curtain and stepped beneath the hot spray. As she reached for the shampoo bottle, she noticed her ringless left hand and bit down hard to keep from sobbing. What was wrong with her? He was a phony! A sham! A liar! No better than Judas Iscariot or Benedict Arnold!

So why did she still love him?

Chapter 10

"**C**ongratulations!" Connie, perched on the corner of Nikki's desk, dropped a white package with a big silver ribbon next to Nikki's computer monitor. Rawboned and strawberry blond, she'd grown up in West Texas and had never gotten rid of her drawl. Her long legs swung freely from beneath a short black skirt and when she smiled her eyes sparkled like liquid gold.

"What's this?" Nikki asked, but with a sinking sensation, she knew. The silver wedding bells on the wrapping paper gave the gift away.

"Open and find out."

"I can't."

"Sure you can." Connie pretended to look wounded. "Unless you want to wait until Trent's around—"

"No!" Nikki grabbed the package, read the card and pulled off the ribbon and wrapping paper. Inside was a cut-crystal vase with fluted sides. "Oh, Connie, it's beautiful," she said, feeling like a thief. "I... I don't know what to say."

Connie grinned. "You don't have to say anything. Now, check your schedule. Some of us want to throw you a belated wedding shower, probably early next month." She leaned over the desk and flipped through the blank pages of Nikki's calendar. "How about the tenth?"

"I... I don't think so," Nikki said, touched, but trying to come up with some reason to avoid the celebration. She felt like a phony and a fraud, a person who would lie to get whatever she wanted.

"It'll be fun. Jennifer knows a male stripper and—"

"Oh, Connie, really, don't," Nikki pleaded. Everything was snowballing too quickly and she felt as if her life was beginning to career off course. She touched Connie on the back of the hand and decided she had to confide in her friend. "Look, I've got to tell you something," she said, glancing over her shoulder.

Max Van Cleve was striding toward her desk. His wavy blond hair was combed perfectly, his white shirt starched.

"Later," Nikki said to Connie. "I'll tell you everything at lunch."

"What is it? Trouble?" Connie guessed from the lines of worry that seemed intent on permanently etching Nikki's brow.

"Just wait, okay?" She didn't want Max overhearing any of their conversation, and thankfully, Connie seemed to finally get the message.

"I hear congratulations are in order," Max said, showing off perfect white teeth. "How about a kiss for the blushing bride?" He was teasing, she knew. He'd been married to his wife, Dawn, for three years and the two of them still acted as if they were on their honeymoon. At that particular thought, Nikki's stomach did a little flip. Honeymoon. Salvaje. Trent.

"First of all, I don't blush, and secondly, I wouldn't want to make Dawn jealous," she quipped back. She felt like such a traitor. For years she'd prided herself on her honesty; she knew that much from the bad taste in her mouth every time she tried to lie.

"Me?" He pointed a finger at his chest. "Do anything to upset my wife? Never. Just the same, you owe me one." He rapped his knuckles on the edge of her desk and walked toward the reception area.

Nikki blew out a sigh of relief, ruffling her bangs in the process. It was good to finally be alone, though her peace lasted less then forty-five minutes, when Connie returned bearing a steaming cup of coffee and a toasted bagel.

"Fresh off the cart," she said, sliding the bagel, napkin, coffee and small container of cream onto a stack of Nikki's mail.

"You're a lifesaver." Nikki poured in the cream and sipped from the hot coffee.

"Well, I'm glad you're back. Things have been dull with a capital *D* around here since you've been gone." A set of slim gold bracelets jangled as she motioned toward Frank Pianzani's glassed-in office. "Worse than ever. Frank seems to think the only stories I can handle all have to do with triplets being born or teachers being fired. Heavy stuff." She winked lashes thick with mascara. "You'd think someone would tell that man we're closing in on the twenty-first century."

"I know just the woman to do it," Nikki said pointedly.

"Moi?" Connie pointed a red-tipped nail at her sternum and shook her head. "And chance losing my job? Uh-uh. I'll leave all that brave and noble business to someone else. I'm just a working girl."

"Sure," Nikki said as Connie strolled back to her desk.

She finished her bagel, dusted her fingers and sipped coffee while continuing to scan her notes, read her mail, skim the last few issues of the *Observer* and generally catch up with the rest of the staff. Time still seemed out of sync for her, and whether from jet lag, her amnesia or her stormy relationship with Trent, she couldn't concentrate fully on her work. Relationship. Ha! What she shared with Trent was no more than cold lies and hot sex.

That thought turned her stomach sour, and she tossed back the rest of her coffee, crumpling the cup and casting it into the wastebasket as she tore open an envelope. But work didn't come easily. She wasn't used to the noise and activity of the office. Secretaries clicked by in high heels, mail carriers pushed carts along the aisles between the cubicles housing individual desks, phones jangled, conversation wafted past soundproof barriers, and the fluorescent lights overhead hummed while offering a surreal light to the inner workings of the *Observer*.

She couldn't seem to dislodge Trent from her mind. His face swam behind her eyelids and his vague accusations against Senator Crowley kept playing back in Nikki's head like a record that was stuck. She twirled a pencil between her fingers and wondered about the connection between Crowley and Trent. Why was Trent so hell-bent to see Crowley destroyed?

Scratching the back of her head with the eraser end of the pencil, Nikki pulled up the files of stories she was working on before she left for Salvaje. Most of her work was finished and printed: old news. Only a few articles and interviews hadn't been completed, but not one of the articles had anything to do with politics or Diamond Jim Crowley. As she read over her work, trying to feel some connection to this job, she experienced an undercurrent of dissatisfaction, solidifying her earlier guess that she'd been unhappy here at the *Observer*.

Max had written an article on Senator Crowley a few weeks back, but the piece read more like a campaign advertisement than a piece of cutting-edge journalism. It was little more than a reminder that James Thaddeus Crowley was working hard in Washington, D.C., for the people in Washington state. For jobs. For the economy. For the environment. For everyone. Nikki's stomach roiled. Something stunk to the very gates of heaven. She was sure of it, and in a flash of memory she recalled that she had planned an exposé of Crowley, there was something…some scandal he had covered up. What was it? She worried her lip between her teeth and tried to concentrate, but other than her image of the cold man with the cane in the photography shop in Salvaje, she remembered nothing. Trent had said something about bribery. *Think, Nikki, think!*

Nothing came. Not one measly thought.

"Terrific," she growled in disgust and let out a perturbed sigh. Disgusted with her lack of memory, she rifled through the new stories she'd been given: an update on new bike paths near Lake Washington, an in-depth article on the new director of the symphony, a story on the import/export business in Seattle, with a note that she could use her own father as one of her sources as he owned one of the largest import/export houses on the Sound.

Nothing of any substance. No investigative journalism. No dirt. Not one thing that really mattered.

No wonder she'd been after Crowley. Tapping her pencil on her desk, she squinted at her computer monitor. But what was Trent's connection to the senator? He'd been in Salvaje, dogging Diamond Jim, just as she had. He'd been worried enough to pretend to be married to her. But worried about her safety? Or worried about what she might print about the senator? What was his ax to grind? She didn't know, she thought, leaning back in her chair and frowning at the screen, but she damned well planned to find out!

"Not really married!" Connie's jaw nearly dropped into her spinach salad. "But—you called. Said so." Her face crumpled into a mask of confusion and a wounded shadow crossed her eyes as she stared at Nikki.

"Look, I'm sorry. I didn't know myself." While picking at her crab Louie, Nikki confided in Connie, leaving out nothing save the very painful fact that she was falling in love with the very man who had started this phony charade in the first place. She even told her friend about her amnesia and the fact that she could remember little.

"You're kidding!" Connie whispered in the crowded restaurant. She glanced over her shoulder as if she expected to find, in the company of reporters, stockbrokers, secretaries and junior executives, a gun-toting mob hit man sitting in a caned-back chair, huddled over a plate of fettuccine, his gun and silencer visible when his jacket slid open as he reached for the garlic bread.

"Look, it's not that bad."

"Not that bad, are you out of your ever lovin' mind?" Connie hissed.

Nikki pronged a slice of egg with her fork.

"You fall or are shoved off a cliff, barely escape with your life, can't remember a damned thing, and your rescuer, nearly a total stranger who just happens to be on an island few people have ever heard of, claims you're married to him. Later, after you tell your family and friends that you're married, he admits it was all a lie. And why? To keep you safe? I think I'd take my chances with a barracuda."

"But you know him," Nikki said, feeling the unlikely urge to defend Trent. Rolling an olive over a bed of lettuce, she tried to explain. "Look, I know it sounds bad—"

"Bad isn't strong enough. Fantastic is more like it. Unbelievable is damned close, or downright deceitful is even better yet. God, the nerve of the guy. And, for the record, I don't know him. Yes, I met him when I had that auto claim. Someone stole my BMW, remember? The one my folks gave me when I graduated from college." She munched on some lettuce. "Did I tell you it was stolen by a guy who was involved with a ring of car thieves? Trent, working for my insurance company, exposed the entire operation."

"So he's not all bad."

"Few people are. And he's definitely not hard on the eyes. But I don't trust a liar, Nikki, and neither should you. This guy lied to you. In a major way. If you ask me he should be strung up by his...well, his hamstrings or worse!" She tore off a piece of bread and leaned across the table. "So tell me, when you thought you were married to him—"

Here it comes! Nikki picked up her water glass and swallowed against a dry throat.

"What did you do... Well, you were supposed to be on your honeymoon. How'd you handle all that?"

Nikki nearly choked, but this time the lie—the half truth, really—rolled easily off her tongue. "I was hurt. My face, my ankle, my whole body. Trent acted as if my injuries were reason enough not to get too involved. Besides, you should have seen me. I wish I had pictures. My face was so ugly, no man would be interested."

Connie lifted a skeptical brow, but didn't argue, and Nikki felt like a heel. Why couldn't she explain everything? Because the truth of the matter was she'd fallen for the louse.

"That's why I can't accept the wedding gift," she added as she pushed her half-eaten salad aside. "It's beautiful, but I'm not married."

Connie managed a smile. "Keep it," she said. "It was worth hearing all about this."

"I can't."

"Consider it an early birthday present."

"My birthday's in May."

"A late one, then."

They argued, and finally Nikki gave in, agreeing to buy lunch in partial trade, just to keep Connie happy.

"Now, about that missing memory of yours. Maybe I can fill in a few blanks," Connie said. "You were really unhappy before you left and you were on this... vendetta, I guess you'd call it, against Senator Crowley.

You wanted to do an exposé on the man, and Frank refused to let you. Even when Peggy went to bat for you, he insisted that Max or John be given the story, and we all know that Max thinks Diamond Jim can walk on water. When Peggy insisted that you be given a fair chance, Frank put his foot down. The quote went something like, 'Men just have a clearer insight into matters political.' You know, something pompous and asinine and way off base. It goes without saying that it caused your blood to boil." Connie cast Nikki a sly smile. "I think you were working on the story, anyway. You must've been if you found Crowley in Salvaje. What the devil was he doing down there?"

"I wish I knew," Nikki said as the waiter slipped their bill onto the table. She picked up the receipt, determined to find out everything she could about Senator James Crowley, as well as Trent McKenzie.

By late afternoon, the drizzle had disappeared. Sun began to dry the wet pavement, leaving puddles only in the deepest cracks and holes of the sidewalks and streets.

Nikki walked through the revolving door and took in great lungfuls of fresh air from the bay. The sky was still overcast, but a few rays of sunshine pierced through the clouds to sparkle on the concrete.

Tucking her umbrella under her arm, Nikki spied Trent, hips resting on the fender of his Jeep, arms folded over his chest. He was double-parked in an alley, but didn't seem the least concerned about a ticket. He lifted a hand when he saw her and she couldn't help the stupid little skip of her heartbeat at the sight of him. As if they truly were newlyweds. What a joke! When was this hoax going to end? Wrapping her arms close around her, as if she could guard her wayward heart, she sidestepped the deepest puddles.

He grinned at the sight of her, that sexy slash of white she found so unnerving. "Found your car."

"You did? At the airport?"

"Right where you left it."

She climbed into his rig, as if she truly belonged there, and the scents of leather and oil seemed suddenly familiar. This was getting dangerous. Though she was always a little unsettled by him, there was something intimate and secure in being with him.

He adjusted the seat, started the engine, flipped on his blinker and merged with southbound traffic, skirting the Sound.

True to his word, he drove her directly to one of the parking lots near the airport where her little Dodge ragtop was wedged between a Toyota wagon and a Cadillac.

"How'd you find this?" she asked.

He grinned. "Professional secret."

"Give me a break." She opened the passenger door of the Jeep but before she could step out, his hand surrounded her wrist. "I'll meet you at your apartment later," he said, and she felt her pulse jump a bit.

"I don't think that would be such a good idea."

"Got to keep up appearances, don't we?"

"For whom?" A part of her was anxious to be alone with him, to continue their little lie—make that *big* lie—to be with him in the apartment, to sit in front of the fire with a glass of wine, to kiss and hold him and touch every inch of him, and yet she knew that the longer she put off the inevitable, the more time she wasted pretending they were in love, the harder their eventual breakup would be. She needed to protect her heart.

He rounded the Jeep's hood and stood next to her as she forced her key into the compact's lock.

"Don't," she warned before he laid one finger on her.

"Nikki—" He tried to touch her, but she drew away.

"I really can't go on living this lie," she said, her voice hitching a little. Oh, Lord, she wasn't going to break down now, was she? She jammed the key harder into the lock and twisted.

"You have to."

She stiffened.

"For your safety."

That was too much. Whirling to face him, she left her keys dangling from the lock. "Oh, for crying out loud! Let's not get into this again. You know where I live, where I work, all about my parents, family, even my ex-boyfriend, for God's sake. And what do I know about you? Nothing! Not one blessed thing. But I'm supposed to feel 'safe' with you. Give it up, McKenzie."

"You can't get rid of me."

"Sure I can. As of now, we're divorced."

He barked out a laugh that bordered on cruel, then grabbed her quickly and swung her against him. She gasped as his mouth descended on hers, kissing her so hard she couldn't breathe. Her knees buckled and her head was spinning. *Don't let him do this to you!* a part of her brain screamed, but another part sighed in contentment.

Propped against the still-wet side of her car, the door handle and her keys digging into her buttocks, she tried to call up every reason in the world to push him away, attempted to recover her hard-nosed stance and insist that they had to end their affair, but her heart was pumping wildly, her body ached for the touch of him, and her determination seemed to slip away, inch by inch, just as the sun slid slowly beneath the horizon.

Her senses swam, and it seemed natural to wind her arms around his neck and tilt her head eagerly to feel his mouth against hers. His tongue parted her lips and she shivered with anticipation of that glorious invasion as it touched and danced with hers.

When he lifted his head, his breath came out in a rush and she swallowed with difficulty. This felt so right and she knew it was so wrong. Loving him would only cause more heartache, more pain.

Touching his forehead to hers, he held her close. "Let's not argue about this, okay. I'll meet you at home."

"*My* home," she clarified.

"Yes, Nikki, *your* home."

He didn't move as she slipped into the driver's seat of her convertible. The upholstery molded to her contours; the seat was the right distance from the throttle for the length of her legs. Shoving the gearshift into Reverse, she backed the car out of its tight slot, slammed into Drive and, with a squeal of tires, threaded her way through the parking lot.

Trent watched her go and wondered how in the hell he was ever going to ease back into his old routine. Once this Crowley mess was settled, there would be no reason to see her, no reason to find excuses to be with her, no reason to scheme ways to get her into his bed.

Angry at himself, the world in general, and most pointedly at Diamond Jim, he kicked at the tire of his Jeep, felt a jarring pain all the way from his foot to his hip and swore under his breath. From the first time he'd seen Nikki Carrothers he'd felt his heartbeat catch, suspected that she was a woman like no other he'd ever seen. When he'd found out that she was working on a story about Crowley, he'd learned everything he could about her. The more he knew, the more fascinated he'd become until, like Crowley, she had become his obsession. One good. One evil. A balance.

But Trent hadn't expected to become more entranced with her as the days had passed. His intuition had been right, he thought grimly as he stepped into the Jeep. She was different. Stubborn, determined, relentless—not exactly female qualities that he'd hoped to find in his wife.

His hands poised in midair over the steering wheel. Wife? What was he thinking? He didn't want a wife, never had and especially would never want a bullheaded, prideful, arrogant woman like Nikki. No, he'd always gone for the softly feminine type, curvy, flirtatious, not too many brains. Those kind of relationships were easy to end.

There had been a few intelligent women in his life, women who were attractive to him on a level he didn't trust, women who had a chance of toying with his heart and his mind, and he'd avoided them like the proverbial plague. But with Nikki, things were different.

He jammed his key into the ignition, punched the throttle and roared after her. A cynical smile curved his lips. At first he'd played the role of her protector for the singular reason of keeping her safe, but as the marriage charade had worked and he'd been forced into close contact with her, he'd found his attraction to her impossible to fight. She'd been vulnerable and alone in the hospital, frightened, but as the days had passed and she'd healed, Trent had caught a glimpse of the woman within, the woman who seemed to have wrapped her long fingers around his heart and given a hard tug.

Hell, what a mess! And now, here he was, chasing her. Fitting, he thought with more than a trace of irony curving his lips. He couldn't help wondering if he'd be chasing her for the rest of his life.

Nikki felt a new power as she drove. Following a nonending stream of glowing red taillights, working her way from freeway to exit, turning on the radio to stations that were as familiar as a favorite old robe, she realized she was beginning to understand herself. Memory flashes were coming as rapidly as the street signs, milestones of her past flashing through her brain.

She remembered a little black dog named Succotash, her favorite doll, her mother lighting a cigarette and warning her never to pick up the habit herself, the fights that seemed to wave from her parents' bedroom every night when she was in junior high school, her mother's increasing fascination with wine, the splitting of her family, painful and hard. She'd felt as if the underpinnings of her entire world had been ripped away, all the security she'd known had been stripped from her. That bleak period in her life was the only time she could remember seeing her father cry. Her chin wobbled a bit before her thoughts centered on happier moments, her senior prom and the sparkly white chiffon dress she'd worn only to spill orange punch on the skirt.

Tears studded her eyes as her life began to make sense and the holes and gaps in the jigsaw puzzle of her existence became smaller. She had a life—a life she could recall.

She remembered dating Dave Neumann. Dave. He was her first truly serious relationship, the first man she'd ever considered marrying. He was handsome and witty and they'd spent hours together, planning a future that somehow hadn't quite jelled. He'd wanted a condo in the city and she'd wanted a house in the suburbs. He'd wanted to wait at least ten years for children and wasn't sure that babies and diapers and midnight feedings would ever fit into his well-ordered life. He'd planned vacations around his work schedule and insisted that he go where he could "write off" the trip for business purposes rather than choosing a spot for fun or adventure.

No wonder the relationship had died a slow and painful death.

As she wheeled her little Dodge off the freeway, she considered herself lucky. They'd broken up "temporarily" to "test their relationship" to "find out for sure that they weren't making a big mistake." It had been Dave's idea and had all sounded so rational. So clinical. So lacking passion. Well, to hell with that. If Trent had taught her anything, it was that she was a passionate person. Sexually, intellectually and morally. For that, she supposed, she should be thankful.

Trent. Oh, God, what was she going to do with him? It had been easier to deal with him when she'd believed they were married, but now, knowing that there were decisions looming ahead—hard, painful, future-determining decisions—she was frightened. After the breakup with Dave, she'd told herself that she would never, *never* get involved with a man who tried to run her life. Well, Trent certainly had bulldozed his way past any barriers she'd put up and lied, *lied* to get what he wanted.

Her teeth gritted. She was still galled at the deception.

Then there was the matter of trust. For years she'd trusted and depended upon her father, never questioning his opinions, though recently, before the trip, they had argued, and it hadn't been the first time. She remembered Ted Carrothers's anger, not a red-hot fury, but a quiet seething that she'd suddenly become a woman with a mind of her own, as if he couldn't quite accept that his baby had developed into a free-thinking, high-spirited female.

"Leave Jim alone," he'd warned her just before she'd left for Salvaje.

Now, while driving into the parking lot, Nikki shook herself out of her reverie and stood on the brakes to avoid hitting the side of the apartment house. Her throat turned to dust as she thought about the argument. They'd been seated in the shade of a striped umbrella in a restaurant on the waterfront. The scent of brine had drifted upward through the plank decking and the wind had been brisk, ruffling her father's short hair. She and Ted Carrothers had been the only souls on the deck, all the other diners having been sane enough to seat themselves on the other side of thick glass windows.

"Jim's a friend of mine," her father had said as he'd motioned the waiter for another glass of gin and tonic.

"But he's involved in a lot of shady deals, Dad," she'd replied, tilting her chin up with determination, the wind whipping a long strand of hair over her eyes.

"He's a politician. It goes with the job."

"No way. I don't believe that. Just because someone's an elected official doesn't mean that he has to turn into a crook."

"The temptations—"

"Everyone has them, Dad. You do in business. I do in my job, in my life. It takes moral fiber to walk away from them."

Her father had shaken his head, then slipped into silence while the slim waiter, clad in a green polo shirt, white jacket and black slacks, had slid another drink in front of him. Ted had taken a long swallow, compressed his lips, then stared past her to the Sound, where noisy sea gulls floated on invisible air currents high above the water and ferries churned across the dark surface, leaving thick, foamy wakes. Pleasure craft and freighters had vied for space in the choppy waters and her father had smiled sadly as he viewed a sailboat skimming along the water. He glanced down at his drink. "I felt the same way you do thirty years ago, Nicole, but as you get older, have children, face the fact that the world isn't perfect, you accept the way things are."

Nikki hadn't conceded. She'd never thought of her father as weak, not once considered the fact that he might be getting old and world-weary. "I'll never believe that all men in power are corrupt."

"Not corrupt, Nicole. Just human. Take my advice. Leave Jim alone."

Now her stomach twisted into a painful knot as she locked her car and headed up the stairs to her apartment. She felt cold to the bone, as if a northern wind had howled through her soul, and for a second she had the same unsettling feeling, the same uncanny awareness, that she was being watched. Perhaps even followed. "That's paranoia, Carrothers," she told herself, but her skin crawled and she glanced over her shoulder, hoping to hear the roar of a Jeep's engine, or catch the wash of headlights splash over the shrubbery of the parking lot. She saw no eyes hidden in the thick rhododendrons and vine maples, no evidence that anyone was watching her. Still she shivered, but Trent didn't appear like some mystical medieval knight to save her.

Lord, she'd be grateful for him now and her heart nearly stopped beating at the thought. She stopped dead in her tracks, midway up the stairs.

She depended on him? Oh, no! Giving herself a swift mental shake she climbed the remaining stairs, unlocked the door, flipped on the lights and tossed her coat over the back of the couch. Opening the door of the refrigerator, she cringed, then yanked out a quart of milk gone sour and bread that had started to mold. So much for dinner.

She snapped on the disposal and poured globs of sour milk and slices of fuzzy white bread down the drain. Kitchen duty accomplished, she checked her messages and listened while her sister, Jan, started asking a dozen questions on the tiny tape. *"I thought you were going to call me. Come on, Nikki, I'm dying to know what's going on."*

Her mother, too, had called, expressing concern about Nikki's injuries and hasty marriage. *"I just hope you know what you're doing, and if your father decides to put on some kind of reception, you know that Fred and I will want to help. You're my daughter, too, you know."*

Funny how that sounded from a mother who had left three half-grown children to find herself and a new family in L.A.

The last message was from Dave. *"I don't know why I'm calling. Just a glutton for punishment, I guess. But I need to see you and know that you're happy."* Oh, sure.

The truth of the matter was, Nikki suspected, that Dave was suddenly interested in her because she was no longer available. Now that someone else wanted her, he did, too. She laughed a little. She wasn't married. Her relationship with Trent was doomed, but there wasn't a snowball's chance in hell that she'd ever try to patch things up with Dave again. If Trent had taught her anything, it was about her need for independence and the sorry fact that she needed a stronger man than Dave Neumann for a lifelong partner.

She didn't want to return any of the calls, but decided there was no time like the present. Besides, she'd rather speak without being overheard by Trent.

She dialed from memory and smiled to think that something so simple was such a relief. Jan was out, her mother was worried, and she had just left a simple message on Dave's recorder when there was a quick rap on the door, a click of the lock, and Trent, balancing two sacks of groceries, appeared on the other side of the threshold.

Startled, Nikki asked, "How'd you do that?" but, with a sinking sensation, she guessed the answer before he even replied.

"I have a key."

"You *what?*"

"When we were on Salvaje. I had one made."

She opened and closed her fists in frustration. Certain there was no male more maddening on the face of the earth, she narrowed her eyes on his arrogant expression. *As if he belonged here!* "You don't live here."

He didn't bother to answer, just set the bags on the table and began placing groceries in the refrigerator and cupboards. "I figured you were out of just about everything."

"Did you hear me?"

He sent her a sizzling glance over one leather-clad shoulder. "Loud and clear, lady."

"You can't just waltz in here like you own the place, like we're *married,* for the love of Mike. No way."

"Until this all dies down."

"What? Until what dies down?" she said, closing the distance between them in long, furious strides. "Crowley."

"Right."

"What the hell have you got to do with it?"

"Crowley's dangerous. You've figured that much out, I assume." His gaze skated down the side of her face that had been so bruised and battered.

Her shoulders stiffened involuntarily.

"I know you think you've got to do some damned exposé on him, but I think you'd better leave Crowley to me."

"What will you do with him?" she asked, shoving a sack of groceries out of the way, grabbing Trent's arm and forcing him to face her. A head of lettuce rolled off the counter and onto the floor, but she didn't care, didn't give a damn about the food.

Trent's face hardened. "I'll handle him."

"Will you?" she tossed back at him. Her piece on Crowley came back to her, a series of articles about bribery and special interests. If her sources were correct, the senator not only took care of the few and the wealthy, he also accepted large gifts from corporations in the state of Washington and all along the Pacific Rim.

She was still holding on to Trent's arm. "Look,

Nikki, you can believe what you want about me, I don't really care, but I don't want you getting hurt." His words were soothing, and she stepped away from him, away from the magic of his voice, the seduction in his eyes.

"Don't start this again, okay?"

"It's true, damn it!" Muttering under his breath, he dragged her into his arms and she froze. How easy it would be to let her knees and heart give way; to fall against him and rely upon him, to let him make decisions for her, to depend upon his judgment. She wanted to tell him to leave her alone, take his hands off her, take a long walk off a short pier...

But she couldn't. Bracing herself against the refrigerator door, she turned her head and her curtain of hair fell over one shoulder. He pressed his advantage, his lips brushing the back of her neck. Tingles of anticipation raced along her nerves and his arms wound around her waist, pulling her close, her buttocks wedging against the hardness forming in his jeans. She wanted to melt against him. Her bones were turning liquid as his mouth moved along the bend of her neck and his hands splayed over her abdomen, thumbs brushing the underside of her breasts.

"Don't," she whispered raggedly.

He didn't stop.

Swallowing against the urge to fall down on the floor and wrap her arms around him, she pulled his hands away. "Don't," she said more firmly, and he reluctantly stepped away.

Turning, she pressed her back against the refrigerator. "Don't use sex as a weapon."

"Is that what I was doing?"

She narrowed her eyes at him. "You know damn well

what you were doing. And I can't go along with you on this Crowley thing," she said, picking up the head of lettuce and tossing it into the sink. "It's too important."

"He's just one crooked senator."

A hard smile curved her lips. "But one I can take care of." She tossed her hair over her shoulder. "I must be doing something right, or he wouldn't have tried to do me in on Salvaje."

"He's dangerous, Nikki, and apparently desperate. You can't take any chances."

Waving away the argument she saw in his expression, she strode to her computer and snapped on the power switch. "There's got to be something," she said, drumming her fingers impatiently as the machine warmed up. "Something in here. If only I can find it."

Trent gave up arguing, and as she pulled up her chair, he propped his jean-clad hips along the side of the desk, bracing himself with his hands, crossing his ankles and watching her. She felt a rush of adrenaline as she settled her fingers over the keys and started entering commands. She'd been working on the Crowley piece for a couple of weeks behind her editor's back. Dissatisfied with the turn of her career, she'd decided to take matters into her own hands when she'd been denied, yet again, a chance to write something more interesting than a story about the winners of a local bake fair.

She intended to prove to God himself, Frank Pianzani, that she could work with the big boys. She'd been trained as an investigative journalist and never been able to prove what she could do. Well, this time, people at the *Observer* were going to sit up and take notice.

Unless she got herself killed first, she thought with a shiver.

She scanned her work files, but nothing showed up. She flipped through the disks near her desk, shoving each one into the computer and viewing the documents on each one. Still a big zero. "Where is it? Where? Where? Where?" she mumbled, biting off the urge to scream in frustration. Impatience surged through her. The story and her notes had to be here. Somewhere.

Unless everything had been conveniently erased. Trent had a key and access to her apartment when she was gone. There were times when she left him alone in this room. When she'd taken a shower, when she'd been at work... She ground her teeth together in frustration. He was a proven liar of the worst order and he would do anything to stop her, for whatever reasons, noble or otherwise.

Her fingers didn't move as her thoughts clicked steadily through her brain.

"Problems?" he asked, and when she looked up at him she expected to see mockery in his blue eyes, but he seemed genuinely concerned.

"I can't seem to locate my file."

Rubbing the stubble on his chin, he said, "Mind if I look?"

"Be my guest." Warily she rolled her chair away from the desk, stood and stretched her back as he slid in front of the machine. Fascinated, she watched as his long fingers moved quickly over the keys. He was as familiar with her machine as she was, or so it seemed.

"You must have it under some kind of code," he said, and she left him there, trusting him just a little. While he kept searching, she played the part of a domestic wife, washing the damned lettuce and using the groceries he'd picked up as the start of dinner. Her stomach rumbled in anticipation, but her mind was on the computer screen and her missing files.

She boiled linguine and cooked a shrimp, garlic and cream sauce while her thoughts swirled around Crowley. If he were behind her attack on the island, then good old Diamond Jim, her father's *friend,* had tried to kill her. So he knew she was onto him. How?

She glanced at Trent and her throat grew tight. He wouldn't! She licked the wooden spoon as she thought. What had Trent said—about a leak at the *Observer.* Connie? No! Frank? Max? "I can't remember any code," she said loud enough for Trent to hear. "It's one of the last foggy details, I guess." It was frustrating. Damned frustrating. Most of her memory had returned and yet this one important piece of information kept slipping her mind. "Come on, give it a rest. I'll feed you."

"Domestic? You?" He cracked his knuckles and stretched out, looking way too huge for her small desk chair.

"I figured I owed you, since you went to the trouble of restocking the larder." She motioned him into a chair at the small table, where she'd set out place mats and lit candles. "Don't get used to it," she teased, but her laughter died in her throat when she remembered that their relationship was only temporary. Surprisingly her heart felt a little prick of pain at that particular thought and she disguised her sudden rush of emotion by pasting a smile onto her face and setting a wooden bowl of salad next to the pasta and sauce.

It was silly really. She slid into her chair and waited as he poured them each a glass of wine. The clear chardonnay reflected the candlelight as it splashed into the bottom of her glass.

Oh, Lord, she would miss him, she realized with a sinking feeling that swept into the farthest reaches of her heart. She'd gotten used to him, looked forward to his laughter and his lovemaking.

He touched the rim of his wineglass to hers. "To marriage," he said, and her heart felt as if it had been smashed into a thousand painful shards. He was kidding, of course.

She painted on another false smile and said, "And to divorce."

"Can't wait to get rid of me, eh?" he asked, and she thought she saw a shadow of pain cross his eyes.

"As soon as possible." Tossing back the cool wine, she imagined the small circle of gold around her ring finger, and her throat grew so thick she could barely swallow. A new, fresh pain cut through her at the thought that no matter what, soon Trent would be just another murky memory in her mind.

They finished dinner in silence, each wrapped in private thoughts. As she put the dishes in the dishwasher, he started a fire, and they finished the bottle of wine with their backs propped against the couch and the flames crackling against dried moss.

When he turned to her, it was as natural as the wind shifting over the sea. His lips settled over hers and she fought a tide of tears that stung her lashes. His arms were strong and comforting, his hands possessive.

He slipped the buttons of her blouse from their bindings and she gave herself to him, body and soul, knowing deep in her heart that she'd never love another man with the same blind passion that now ruled her spirit as well as her life.

She was his wife. If only for a few more days. If only

because of the lie that bound them together and would, as surely as the moon tugged at the currents in the sea, pull them apart.

Nikki woke up with a start. Sweat streamed down her back, and her heart was pounding a thousand beats a minute. The nightmare had stolen into her sleep, burning through her conscious and terrifying her. Even now, snuggled against Trent, one of his arms flung around her, she shivered. Would the fear never go away?

She glanced at the clock and groaned. Four-thirty. The bed, tucked in the corner under the eaves, was warm, rumpled, smelling of sex and Trent, and through the window she saw stars, clear and bright, glittering above the city.

Letting out a long breath, she cuddled against Trent, when suddenly the memory slammed into her like a freight train running out of control. She remembered what she'd done with the Crowley file. The last wisps of her fear disappeared like night melting into the dawn. She slid from the bed. Trent growled and rolled over, his breathing never disturbed. Tossing on her robe, she walked to her computer, not bothering with lights. A few glowing embers smoldered in the fireplace, casting red shadows on candles that had burned down to pools of blue wax, their flames long ago extinguished, the wine bottle left empty on the coffee table, the wrinkled afghan where they'd made love left carelessly on the floor.

Her heart caught for a second before she told herself to quit being a romantic fool. She had work to do. On the day before she'd left for Salvaje, the very day she'd argued violently with her father, she'd decided to

hide her information on Crowley, just in case someone
from the *Observer,* or someone in Crowley's employ,
wanted to know what she was up to. She'd carefully
hidden all her notes and the computer disk in a box of
Christmas ornaments on the floor of one of the closets
tucked under the eaves.

Quietly, she opened the closet door and yanked on
the hanging chain dangling from the exposed rafters.
With a bare bulb for illumination, she worked around
the mousetraps and pulled out a heavy box with the
stand for the tree, then dug through another crate filled
with ornaments and lights.

On the very bottom, tucked in a cardboard envelope,
was the disk. In a manila folder were her notes. "Son of
a gun," she whispered, pleased that her memory had finally come through. Leaving the closet door open, she
carried her prize to the desk and snapped on the green-
shaded banker's light.

Trent snored softly and rolled over again.

Almost afraid of what she might find, she clicked
on the computer, and as it hummed to life, she rifled
through old newspaper articles, magazine clippings and
her own notes. "Great stuff," she congratulated herself.
She felt a sudden sense of pride in her job and in her
life, and she wanted to share it all with Trent.

She glanced over to the bed. He'd blinked his eyes
open and was watching her, his black hair mussed, his
beard dark, his naked torso bronze in the reflection of
the dying embers. Stretching, he glanced at the clock
and groaned. "You're out of your mind, Carrothers,"
he said, patting the warm spot on the bed that she'd recently vacated.

"I know, but I remembered!"

"Hallelujah!" he growled sarcastically as he rubbed the sleep from his eyes. "Couldn't it wait?"

"No way." She held up the old articles and pictures. "Evidence, McKenzie. That's what this is."

He levered up on one elbow and his brows drew over his eyes. "You're sure?"

"I think so. My guess is that good ol' Diamond Jim owes favors to some of the most influential businessmen in Tokyo, Seoul and Hong Kong." She couldn't restrain a smile of pride as she flipped through the articles taken from newspapers around the world.

"You've got old news," he said. "People have been trying to tie Crowley to a bribery scandal for years. Nothing ever sticks."

"This will," she said, as she skimmed her notes. "What ties it all together is a tip I received from someone who used to work for him. He claims that the senator did all his dirty deals, taking the cash and laundering it into a Swiss bank account, through a small island in the Caribbean."

"Let me guess," Trent said, his eyes no longer slumberous, every sinewy muscle of his shoulders and chest tense. "Salvaje."

"Bingo," she whispered. "That's why I was down there." She glanced through the window to the lights of the city winking through the trees. "That's why he tried to have me killed."

"Nothing you can prove."

"Yet," she said, determined to get the fat-cat senator. She dropped the clippings onto the desk beneath the lamp, and one yellowed article slid away from the rest. Along with the report was a picture of Senator Crowley with the head of an automobile company headquartered in Japan.

She reached for the article, but her fingers stopped in midair. Another man was in the grainy photograph, a man standing just behind the shorter industrialist, a man she recognized. Her world stopped and tilted as her future and past collided. She swallowed against the bitter taste of deception as she stared down at the unmistakable, rough-hewn features of Trent McKenzie.

Chapter 11

Nikki stared at the picture in disbelief. Anger surged through her bloodstream. He'd lied to her again! God, why had she trusted him, believed in him?

"What is it?" Trent asked, his voice rumbling and deep with recent sleep.

"I, um, found something interesting." A cold settled in the pit of her stomach. Her first impulse was to shove the damning piece of evidence under his nose, demand answers, rant and rave about truth and justice and the pain in her heart. Instead, she told herself to be calm, and with trembling fingers, she forced herself to tuck the picture deep into the notes.

"What?"

"More evidence. I have to talk to one of the aides who used to work for him. Barry Blackstone," she said, remembering a name she'd seen mentioned several times. "He quit working for Crowley a few months back and I've written a note to myself that indicates he can give me inside information."

"Blackstone?"

She stood and walked on wooden legs to the edge of the bed where she dropped onto the quilt near the lying son of a bitch...the man she loved. "What can you tell me about him?"

Trent's jaw tightened and his skin drew flat over his features. He tried to reach for her, but she pushed his hands firmly away.

"Not now," she said, disguising the fact that her heart was breaking, that she'd never let him hold her again, that they would never again make love. Here, with the scent of sex still clinging to the sheets, she vowed never to fall into his tempting trap again. To shove temptation from her grasp, she moved to the couch and leaned against its lumpy back. A world without Trent. It seemed so bleak. Suddenly world-weary, she crossed her arms over her chest. "You've heard of him, I assume."

"I've met Blackstone," Trent said, regarding her warily, as if he sensed the silent accusations charging the air. He slid into his faded Levi's. Threadbare at the knees and butt, the pants threatened to split as he strode barefoot to the fireplace, crouched down to lay a piece of dusty oak onto the grate and blew into the coals. Sparks glowed bright, catching on the moss and dry bark. "I used to work for our friend, the senator," Trent finally admitted, stirring the warm ashes with a poker.

Nikki couldn't believe his admission. Had he read her mind—known that she'd caught him in yet another evasion? Her heart began to pound and she didn't know if she wanted to hear the rest of his story. Would it be the truth or a lie? Would he admit that he was in league with the man who had tried to have her killed? "You never said anything."

"Never seemed like the right time." Red embers pulsed against the charred pieces of firewood. "A few years back, I was one of Crowley's bodyguards for a few weeks."

Too convenient. He must suspect that you saw a photo of him or read his name in one of the articles. Still, she played along, wondering whether if she kept giving him more rope, he would hang himself. "But you're off the payroll now?" Nikki asked. Betrayal, like a serpent, coiled around her insides and squeezed.

"Yep." He shoved another hunk of wood onto the crackling, hungry flames. "I quit four years ago."

"Why?"

He hazarded a glance over his shoulder. His mouth was drawn into a hard, cynical line. "I didn't like the working conditions."

"Meaning?" She knew she was pressing him, but she couldn't stop herself. After this one last time, she promised herself, she'd never again listen to his half truths and lies.

Standing, he dusted his hands on his rear, then slapped his palms together. "Meaning I was beginning to suspect that Jimbo wasn't on the up-and-up. A few things had happened that I didn't like. I suspected he was on the take, from international lobbyists as well as from corporations here in the States. I confronted him." A nostalgic, satisfied grin curved his lips. "He told me to take a hike."

"You were fired?"

"*Terminated* is the word he used, I think," Trent replied. "Nice, huh?"

Nikki shivered and rubbed her arms. *Don't believe him. Not a solitary word he says.*

"But it was too late, anyway. I'd already turned in my resignation." Shoving his hands into the front pockets of his jeans, he sauntered toward her, the firelight playing in red-and-gold shades upon the smooth skin and sleek muscles of his torso. She tried not to notice the webbing of black hair that swirled across his chest and narrowed to a thin line that dipped seductively past the straining waistband of his jeans. She avoided staring at the sinewy ridges in his shoulder muscles or the way his eyes, deep-set and so blue, stared at her.

Her heart did a stupid flip, but she didn't even smile. "You lied to me." The whisper echoed to the rafters and swirled around them like a cold whirlpool.

"We've established that already."

"No, I mean you lied to me again. You didn't want me to know that you were connected with Crowley. Why?" She angled her head up defiantly as he stopped just short of her, his bare toes nearly touching hers, his gaze delving deep into hers.

"I didn't want to talk about it."

"What about me? Didn't you think I might want to know?" she demanded, anger burning through her blood and controlling her tongue. The nerve of the man!

"What good would it have done?"

"This isn't about good and bad, Trent! This is about the truth and lies, about trust. You expect me to pretend you're my husband, let you live in my house, allow you to have a key to my door, for crying out loud, and you can't even show me the consideration of telling me how you're connected with Crowley!"

"You didn't ask."

"I did," she corrected, her lips curling. "You said it was personal."

"It was."

Throwing her hands up and grabbing the air in frustration, she shook her head. "How could I have been such a fool—such a damned fool?"

"You're not." His fingers folded over her arm. "I should have leveled with you, but it didn't seem important."

"Not important?" She yanked her arm away and strode to the fireplace, feeling a tide of misery swell in her heart. She loved him and he'd used her. Again. That was the sole basis of their relationship. It could never be anything more. "We're talking about my life here. Because of what I'm doing I was nearly killed, and you don't think it's important!"

A shadow crossed his eyes. "I'm trying to protect you."

"Then just stop. Okay? Get the hell out of my house and the hell out of my life! Leave me alone, Trent." *For God's sake, leave me alone to lick my wounds and start over.*

But he didn't. Cursing under his breath, he walked straight to her, and his expression was a mixture of anger, disgust and fear. "I can't, Nikki."

"Oh, spare me the protector routine. It's wearing a little thin."

"I love you."

The words echoed through her apartment and reverberated through her soul.

"I always have."

He reached for her, and she slapped him with a smack. "Don't say it, Trent. No more lies!" she cried as the red welt appeared on his cheek. Horrified that she'd struck him, she took a step backward but not before he caught her wrist and yanked her hard against him. His eyes slitted and she remembered once thinking that he was cruel.

"I've lied about a lot of things, Nikki, and I'm not proud of the fact, and I'm not going to tell you that all my reasons were noble, because they weren't. I slept with you, made love to you because I couldn't stop myself, damn it. I even rationalized that it was necessary, but I didn't count on falling in love with you." His fingers dug deep into her flesh. "If there was any way I could have prevented falling for you, you'd better believe I would have."

Her throat worked painfully. "I don't believe you," she choked out. How could she trust a man who had lied to cover lies? The words were music to her ears, but like a false melody they would fade quickly, disappear when the time was convenient, never to be recalled again.

"I love you, Nikki."

Again, those horrible, wonderful words. Her heart wanted to explode and tears filled the back of her eyes.

"I think I fell in love with you from the first time I saw you." He sighed loudly, playing out his role. "Don't get me wrong. I'm not a sentimental sap. This isn't like me, but I fell in love with you, and I swear, as long as I live, I'll never love another woman."

Oh, God! She wanted to believe him. With all of her heart, she wanted to trust and love this man, but she couldn't. As tears slid in tiny streams from her eyes, she tossed off his arm and shook her head. "And I swear to you, as long as I live, Trent McKenzie, I'll never trust you." Feeling as if she were shattering into a thousand pieces inside, she stepped away from him and brushed the tears from her eyes. "It's too late."

"Nikki—" He reached for her but she stood on wooden legs, refusing to go to him.

"Even if there was a chance for us once upon a time, it's over. Leave, Trent," she insisted, fighting the urge to run to him.

"But—"

"Just drop the key on the counter and walk out that damned door!"

He studied her long and hard, looking for cracks in her composure, then, grimacing, he turned on his heel, grabbed his jacket and walked out of her life. The door slammed with a thud, shaking the room.

Her knees started to give way. She grabbed the corner of a table and, afraid she might fall into a puddle and cry for him to come back to her, she ran to the bathroom, locked the door, turned on the shower and stripped off her robe. Steam billowed, filling the room and her lungs as she stepped under the warm spray and prayed that the hot needles of water would wash away the pain in her heart. She loved Trent, was destined and doomed to love him all of her life, but she wouldn't let him know how she felt. She had already experienced too much pain at his hands—she'd never be fool enough to give him the chance to hurt her again.

She cried in the shower, quietly sobbing and letting her tears mix with the water. These, she swore, were her last tears for a man who could lie and say he loved a woman without batting an eye.

When she finally turned off the spigots and shoved the wet hair from her face, she felt stronger. She would survive. Somehow she'd live each day without him and the pain would lessen, not quickly, but she would live with it and go on with her life. She'd learned long ago, during the pain of her parents' divorce, that she was a survivor and that she could accomplish just about anything she wanted to. Right now, she wanted Trent out of her life.

Cinching the belt of her robe around her waist, she clamped her teeth together and unlocked the bathroom door. She paused, took in a long, bracing breath and, in a cloud of steam, walked through the door.

Trent was gone. She knew it before she even glanced through the shadowy apartment. From the atmosphere in the room, the lack of life in the air, she knew that he'd left. And she realized that she'd been wrong. Just when she'd been foolish enough to think that she was fresh out of tears for Trent McKenzie, she found a few thousand more.

"I just don't see why I can't meet that husband of yours." Ted Carrothers touched the crook of his daughter's arm and propelled her across the street. He'd called while Nikki was at work and they'd agreed to have dinner together.

"He's busy," Nikki hedged as they threaded through the crowd of pedestrians hurrying along the sidewalks. Umbrellas, boots, newspapers and purses tucked beneath arms, raincoats billowing, everyone walked briskly, as if each person was in his own personal race with the world.

Unlike Salvaje, where the pace was slow, the weather warm and lazy, Seattle's gait was brisk, in tempo with the winds that blew chill off the Pacific. Fog was rolling through the streets and a slight drizzle threatened. Ted shoved open the door of his favorite Irish pub, and the sounds of hearty laughter, clink of glasses, and noise from a television where a boxing match was being shown, greeted Nikki. Smoke hovered over the bar and the smell of beer was heavy in the air.

"In the back. Rosie has a table for us," her father said as they moved past the long mahogany bar that had been a part of Rosie's Irish Pub since the great fire. "Here we go." Ted weaved through the tightly packed tables and, true to his word, found a booth in a corner near the back wall.

Nikki slid onto the wooden seat while Rosie, without asking, brought two frosty mugs of ale. Not believing that she could trust anyone to manage the place, Rosie worked day and night as a waitress and hostess. "Bless ya, Rose," Ted said with a wink.

"Come here often, do you?" Nikki teased, scanning her menu.

"As often as possible. And don't bother ordering. It's already done."

"Don't you think I might like a say in what I'm eating?"

His blue eyes twinkled. "Not when I'm paying the tab."

"This is the nineties, Dad."

"But I like the old ways better."

She wasn't in the mood for another fight. "Fair enough," she said, watching the small flame of a glass-encased candle flicker as they talked.

"Now, about Trent. Who the devil is he?"

Good question. "I met him through a friend." Not really a lie, just stretching the truth a bit. She took a long swallow of the dark ale. "You remember Connie Benson? I work with her, and she had her car stolen earlier in the year…" She perpetuated the lie and didn't have the heart to tell her father that her marriage was over. Or even that it had never existed. Over bowls of thick clam chowder and crusty bread, she rationalized that her love life wasn't any of her father's business and she would have to deal with Trent on her own. Rosie cleared the empty bottles and bowls and arrived with a platter of grilled salmon and planked potatoes. The conversation drifted back and forth, and each time Trent's name was mentioned, Nikki hid the quick stab of pain in her heart.

By the time she'd eaten half her salmon, Nikki thought she might burst.

"So where is Trent tonight?" her father asked as he pronged a potato and studied it. "Why couldn't he join us?"

"He's working late. Lots to catch up on."

"A private investigator…. Ah, well, I thought you'd marry someone…" He searched for the right word, and Nikki felt her temper start to simmer.

"Someone more conventional?" she asked. "Someone like Dave Neumann."

Her father lifted a big shoulder. "He's not a bad guy, but, hey, since you're married, let's leave him out of the conversation."

"Good idea." Nikki picked at the pieces of pink salmon flesh, but her appetite had disappeared. She felt like a fool and a fraud, defending a man who had not one ounce of compunction about lying to her.

Her father asked about her amnesia, tested her and, satisfied that her memory was intact, nodded to himself. "Glad you're feeling better. I was worried about you, Nicole."

"I know. But I'm okay. Really." They smiled at each other and some of the old feelings of love between them resurfaced. She remembered trusting him implicitly, never questioning his ultimate wisdom.

Finally, her father shoved his plate aside. Rosie, as if she'd been hovering nearby waiting, swooped down and swept up the dirty dishes. She asked about another round of drinks, but neither Nikki or her father was interested. When she finally left, Ted set his elbows on the table and tented his hands. "Aside from the honeymoon and the accident, how was your trip?"

"Salvaje's an interesting place. Semitropical. Warm. I'd like to go back someday."

Her father's lower lip protruded. "What about Jim Crowley?" Nikki's insides jelled and she looked up sharply, but her father just seemed to be making conversation as he swirled the remainder of his ale in his mug. "I know he was down there at the same time as you. I thought you might be dogging him."

"I was on my honeymoon, Dad," she said. "I didn't even talk to him." Nikki's tongue felt thick and twisted as she tried to evade the issue without lying to her father.

"He's…well, he's not really a friend of mine, but I know him. I've done business with his law firm for years. I deal with his son, James, Jr. Hell of an attorney. Smart as a whip."

"What you're saying, Dad, is that because Jim's son is a great attorney, I should back off on any story dealing with the senator. Especially if it shows our favorite son in a bad light?"

"Just don't hound the man, Nikki." Ted tossed back the remaining drops of his dark beer. "You people with the press, always digging, always looking for dirt."

"He's a politician, Dad."

"So he asked for it?"

"So he's got to keep his constituents' best interests at heart. He can't be playing to special interest groups and he's got to keep his nose clean. It comes with the territory."

"I think he's a good man, Nikki. I wouldn't want his reputation destroyed on some drummed-up charge. It wouldn't be fair and I wouldn't want my daughter a part of it."

"I'm a reporter, Dad." Her chin inched upward a notch in pride. "I try my level best to write the truth without being biased or opinionated. Now, that's tough given my gene pool, but the best I can promise you is that if Crowley's nose is clean, I won't harass him."

Her father sighed. "I guess that's the best I can expect."

"Damn straight."

Her father paid the bill and walked Nikki to her car. She gave him a quick peck on the cheek and wondered how they, who had been so close, had drifted so far apart politically. Age, probably. Disillusionment.

She drove to her apartment and had the uncanny feeling that she was being followed. Again. Lord, she was getting paranoid. If she didn't watch out she'd end up on some shrink's couch, paying big bucks to find out that she was insecure because her parents had split up when she was young.

And because a man deceived you into believing that you were married to him.

Oh, Lord. She tapped her fingers on the steering wheel and told herself that she should never see Trent again. Let the memories fade on their own. Let sleeping dogs lie.

As far back as she could remember, she'd never let one sleeping dog slumber in peace. Her curiosity, her sense of justice, her desire to set wrong to right, overcame her good judgment. She'd never been one to take the easy way out, or pussyfoot around an issue, and she wasn't going to start now. If she planned on being the best damned reporter that the *Seattle Observer* or, for that matter, the *New York Times* had ever seen, then she'd better quit thinking like a coward.

Sliding her jaw to the side in determination, she threw her convertible into Reverse, turned around and, tires screaming in protest, headed for Lake Washington. She was going to have it out with Trent McKenzie, right or wrong.

She drove with her foot heavy on the throttle, moving quickly in and out of traffic, suddenly anxious to see him. For weeks she'd been shackled by her injuries, by her amnesia, by Trent's lies and by the love that she'd begun to feel for him, but now she was in control, her life in her own hands again, though those very hands shook a little as she clutched the wheel.

A part of her still loved him. That stupid, female, trusting section of her brain still conjured up his face and thrilled at the memory of his touch. "Idiot," she growled, honking impatiently as a huge van pulled into the lane in front of her.

What would she say to Trent when she confronted him? She didn't know. Scowling, she caught her reflection in the rearview mirror and decided, when she caught the worry in her eyes, that she'd have to wing it. She'd done it before.

She ran a yellow light and turned off the main street. Pushing the speed limit, she drove onto the curvy road that wandered over the cliffs surrounding the lake. Steeling herself for another painful session, she wheeled her sporty car into the drive of his house.

The sun, already hidden by high clouds and clumps of thin fog, was beginning to set and the tall fir trees surrounding the rambling old house seemed gloomy and still. She slid to a stop near the garage and bit her lip. Trent's Jeep wasn't parked where he'd left it the previous night.

"Wonderful," she muttered, then walked to the front door and rapped loudly. No answer. She pushed hard on the doorbell, hearing the chimes ring. Still no footsteps or shouts from within.

She rubbed her arms and felt an overwhelming sense of disappointment. "Stop it," she chided herself. He wasn't going to weasel out of this showdown, not after she'd worked up her courage to face him. She walked to the back of the house and found a note on the back door, which she read out loud. "'Wait for me.'"

Her throat squeezed. He'd expected her. Or someone. The hairs on the back of her neck raised as she opened the door and stepped into the kitchen. Snapping on a few lights, she felt better, but the sight of the bedroom made her stomach wrench. The huge bed was made, the fire long-dead, the curtains drawn, but in her mind's eye she saw the room as it had been. A warm fire threw red and gold shadows across the bed that was mussed and warm. Trent's body, so hard and taut, was stretched over hers, his lips grazing her breast, his eyes gazing deeply into hers.

Love or lust?

She bit her lip in confusion. What she'd felt had been love. She'd welcomed his kisses, embraced his love-making, given her heart to him, and she'd do it time and time over, if she ever got the chance again. Sick at the thought, she realized she'd become one of those women who are inexplicably drawn to the wrong men, men who will only hurt and use them, men who are careless with their love, men who can never truly let a woman touch their souls.

Welcome to the real world.

The sound of a car in the drive brought her out of her reverie. Trent! Annoyed at the quick spark of anticipation in her pulse, she strode to the front door, intent on greeting him in person and giving him a healthy piece of her mind.

"Where the devil have you been?" she demanded, jerking the door open.

Standing on the front porch, his eyes a brittle blue, his expression a mirror of her own surprise, was Senator James Thaddeus Crowley.

Her insides shredded. "Oh," she whispered.

Crowley leaned heavily on his cane and his face was lined and weathered. A man stood next to him, one step back, and as Nikki's gaze moved to his face, her stomach clenched. She faced her own death. This tall man with the short-clipped black hair, feral eyes and long nose was the man who had been chasing her, the man whose swift steps had followed her through the steamy undergrowth of the jungle on Salvaje. In a blast of memory, she recognized him as the man who had placed his meaty hand on her shoulder and given her a shove. Oh, God!

"Miss Carrothers," the senator said smoothly, recovering as she began to sweat. "Well, well, what do you know? First on the island and now back here."

"What do you want?" Danger sizzled in the air around them and she looked for a chance of escape, but the two men blocked her way to her convertible and the senator's silver Mercedes was parked nearly on her car's bumper. No way out.

"I'm looking for McKenzie." Crowley's frigid eyes narrowed a fraction. "Your husband? Or is that just an ugly rumor?"

"He's not here right now," she said, trying vainly to calm the racing beat of her heart. Her fingers were slick with sweat where she still touched the edge of the door.

"No?" Crowley slid a grin of pure evil to his compatriot and said something in Spanish that caused Nikki's skin to crawl. She didn't understand the language, but the meaning was clear and deadly. She slammed the door shut, threw the deadbolt and tried to remember where all the doors in the house were. Oh, God, she couldn't. She didn't know how many entrances there were, how many ways a murderer could get into the house.

Trapped. Fear brought a metal taste to the back of her throat. Barely able to breathe, she ran to the bedroom, found the phone and dialed. "Please help me," she whispered as the dispatcher answered. "My life's in danger and—" She saw the face of Crowley's goon in the window and dropped the phone, running to the far end of the house. She heard a door creak open and her heart plummeted. She hadn't locked the kitchen door behind her.

It was only a matter of time until he tracked her down.

Fear, like ice, seemed to clog her blood and keep her feet from moving, but she forced herself to run. She found the door to the basement, left it open and quietly ran up the stairs to the second floor. On the landing she waited, her heart thudding loudly, her blood thundering in her ears. Holding her breath, waiting for her doom, she heard him. Inside. Walking like a predatory cat.

Trent, where are you?

She heard the steps creak and the door to the basement bang open farther.

She moved quickly, silently, diving into the first room she found. A bedroom with twin bunks and a window. Without thinking, she threw open the sash and stepped onto a shingled roof that was pitched gently. On her rump, she slid down the shakes, catching herself on the gutter. She had no choice but to jump. Wrapping her fingers on the sharp metal near a downspout, she lowered her body, heard the gutter groan in protest and dropped, landing in a crouch. She had no plan of escape, only hoped that she could run to a neighbor's house. But the neighbors on this stretch of the lake were few and far between, separated by dense forest or a long stretch of water.

Sprinting across the backyard, she raced into the thick shrubbery that rimmed the lake. In the distance she heard a car's engine roar to life and she thought that the senator had only been bluffing, that he was leaving. Through the leaves she saw the flash of silver. His Mercedes. Thank God. But her relief was short-lived.

In the upstairs window of the house, the very window she'd opened, she spied the henchman, his face set in an ugly anger, his eyes searching the grounds.

"God help me," she whispered silently, realizing that Diamond Jim had left this cruel man to do his work. He'd make tracks, be far from the scene when her next accident occured. Heart in her throat, she concentrated. *Think, Nikki, think! Use that damned brain of yours!*

She couldn't risk running to the front of the house. From his eagle's-nest view, the would-be assassin could see her. Her only chance was the forest. Surely she could make her way through the thicket to the next house.

Running quickly, shoving aside branches and berry vines, she plowed through the undergrowth. Dry leaves and cobwebs clung to her face, vines and sticks tripped her.

She heard a shout in Spanish and her heart turned to mush. He'd seen her! *Run, Nikki, run for your life!*

A limb behind her snapped. Oh, God. He was closing the distance. Her heart was beating like machine-gun fire. *Run! Run! Run!* Her legs couldn't move fast enough.

Déjà vu! This is how she'd felt in Salvaje and in her nightmares. Running, running, being chased by the evil. Footsteps pounded behind her. Closer. Closer. "Please, God, help me!" Her lungs felt ready to explode.

A gunshot cracked and she stumbled, scraping her knees and scrambling back to her feet.

She broke through the thicket and found herself on the edge of the cliff, looking down at the lake, far, far below. "No!" she cried as the footsteps plowed closer.

In terror, she looked over her shoulder and saw her

attacker, large and looming, his face, cut by twigs and thorns, twisted into a hideous snarl.

"Now you will not escape," he said, smiling and breathing hard.

Nikki stepped backward, felt her feet teeter and shifted her weight.

He lunged and she stepped to the side. "You bastard," she cried, kicking at him as she began to fall.

"Nikki!"

Another blast from a gun, the charge roaring in her ears as her attacker fell. Screaming, she felt strong arms surround her, saving her from sliding down the cliff. Trent dragged her back to safety. "You're all right," he whispered, his gun outstretched in one hand, his other arm a steel band around her middle.

"Oh, God, Trent!" She clung to him, sobbing, holding him as a spreading stain of dark red seeped from beneath Crowley's man. He groaned in pain and writhed.

"Don't move!" Trent warned him, and Nikki, collapsing, buried her face in his shoulder. He smelled of leather and sweat and gunpowder and he was shaking as violently as she. "Hang on, Nikki, I'm here," he whispered across her crown. "And I always will be."

She couldn't let go. Trembling, she clung to him as if to life itself. Time stretched endlessly, the minutes ticking by, her heartbeat slowing, the man on the ground moaning pitifully.

She listened to Trent's uneven breathing as, in the distance, sirens screamed loudly, people shouted and eventually the police and neighbors arrived. The events played out in slow motion in Nikki's mind. She remembered Trent talking to one of the officers, taking a drag from a cigarette and pointing toward the house.

A female officer took her statement, and Nikki was surprisingly calm as she gave it, though her mind seemed disjointed and she kept watching Trent. She was aware of the helicopter and the paramedics who life-flighted the attacker away, over the serene waters of the lake, to be deposited in a nearby hospital, but the events seemed surreal and confused and she was grateful when Trent helped her into his Jeep and they drove to the police station.

Under the harsh lights, answering harsher questions, Nikki drank several cups of bitter coffee, explaining over and over what had happened. There was talk between the officers, as if they found her story preposterous then finally believable. The man in the hospital had been willing to spill his guts, it seemed. He was going to survive, and his story corroborated Nikki's and Trent's.

According to the would-be assassin, Crowley had known that Nikki had followed him to Salvaje with the express purpose of gathering information to expose him. Crowley had ordered the "accident" to end her life even though he knew her father. Nikki was too determined, too dogged and Crowley recognized her for the enemy she was. The senator had learned of her obsession to expose him from a friend of his…good ol' Max who worked at the *Observer* and was jealous of Nikki's ambition and hard work.

Eventually, hours later, she and Trent were allowed to go home.

"You all right?" he asked as he tossed his jacket over her shoulders.

Bone weary, she offered him the shadow of a smile. "I think so."

He helped her into the passenger side of the Jeep,

then slid behind the wheel, but he paused before jamming the key into the ignition. Closing his eyes for a second, he turned to her, and when his blue gaze caressed hers, he sighed. "I'm sorry," he said, touching her cheek.

"For?"

"Everything. I shouldn't have left you alone."

"You didn't have a choice. I had to go to work. I have a life. You couldn't have followed me minute by minute."

"I should have." Guilt slid stealthily over his features. "I'd hoped you'd come back, but I wasn't sure, so I left the door open and went to your apartment. When you didn't show up there, I got worried, returned home and saw Crowley hightailing it out of there. Your car was in the drive and I thought..." his jaw clenched convulsively "... I thought I might be too late. Nikki, if anything would have happened to you..." He leaned heavily back against the seat. "That bastard will pay. He's come up with an alibi, you know. Good old slippery Diamond Jim." Trent's lips curled into a line of satisfaction. "However, his alibi isn't that airtight. I know the guy who claims to be having drinks with him, and he can be persuaded to tell the truth."

"How?" Nikki asked.

"The man has a gambling problem. Connected to the wrong circles, owes a lot of money. I know, because I used to deal with him those few weeks when I worked for Crowley. Jimbo's slipping. He could've bought himself a better story, but he didn't have a lot of time. He didn't know you'd be at the house or that you'd recognize Rodriguez as the man who'd tossed you over the cliff on Salvaje.

"Besides, Jim thought you wouldn't escape this time. He wanted it to look like an accident, just like before." Turning, he gazed deep into her eyes. "We'll nail them, Nikki. Together. You've got yourself the story of a life-time."

The story of a lifetime. Proof that she could be "one of the boys" at the *Observer*. Why did it seem so little? "And you. What did you get?"

"I've got a monkey off my back. At first when I worked for Crowley, I thought he was honest and up-right and the best man to represent the people of this state. But I found out he was dirty and crooked and I've spent the last few years determined to bring him down."

"So now your life's quest is over," she said, attempt-ing to sound lighthearted when her insides felt weighted with stones.

"Yep. Suppose so." He stepped on the throttle and twisted the ignition. The Jeep's engine caught, and within a few minutes they had merged into the slow stream of traffic heading away from the center of the city.

Through the night, Trent drove to her apartment. He parked, and without asking, helped her up the stairs and inside. "Why did you come back to see me?" he asked as she slid out of her jacket.

"I thought we needed to have it out."

"It?"

"Everything." She snapped on the lights, trying to break the intimacy, the spell of being with him. She looked into his eyes and wished that things were dif-ferent between them. "You lied to me."

"And you'll never forgive me."

Her teeth sunk into her lower lip. "I don't think I can."

He looked about to say something, changed his mind and turned toward the door. "I wasn't lying when I told you I loved you, Nikki. And I've never been so damned scared in my life. When I saw you on the cliff..." He leaned back against the door and his face turned the color of chalk.

Her heart turned over. *Love him! Trust him! Forgive him! He did it for you!*

"When I figured out that you were on Salvaje digging up dirt on Crowley I thought I should try to protect you. I didn't lie when I said that I took one look at you in Seattle and lost all perspective. Seeing you on the island only reinforced my feelings. That's why I came up with the cock-and-bull story about being married. I just wanted to get you safe and hustle you off the island as quickly as I could. I thought that if we traveled together, posed as husband and wife, Crowley and his men wouldn't be so suspicious. It might have worked, too, if it hadn't been for the storm." His mouth twisted into a sad smile.

"What if I hadn't lost my memory?"

A muscle twitched in his jaw. "I don't know. I would have come up with something else."

"You took one helluva chance."

He stared at her. And the words, *I did it for you* didn't come to his lips. Instead, he read the censure in her eyes, slid one final look down her body and said, "You know how I feel and you know where I live. Oh, by the way, it's not really my house."

Another lie.

"I rent it from a friend."

Well, not so bad.

He opened the door. "Goodbye, Nikki." With a quick glance over his shoulder, he was gone, the door shut behind him, and giving into the exhaustion that overcame her, she slid to the floor, dropped her head in her hands and cried.

Nikki sipped a cup of coffee and stared at the small television on Frank Pianzani's desk. It had been nearly a week since her story broke, and in that time she'd become Frank's new star reporter. Max, having been exposed for tipping off the senator, had been fired.

Frank was pleased with himself. Thanks to Nikki, the *Observer* had scooped all the competition, and now the outcome of her incredible work was on the evening news.

Nikki stared at the screen and watched as Senator Crowley's face, showing signs of strain, appeared. His voice, however, still rang like an orator's. "I categorically deny the charges. They are absolutely false and all the constituents of the state of Washington who have voted for me over the years know that I've never accepted a bribe, nor have I accepted gifts from special interest groups."

"What about the man in the hospital? Felipe Rodriguez?"

"I don't know much about him. He's only been on my payroll a month or two. But the man is obviously suffering from delusions. His story is too bizarre to be believed. Why, just look at my record—"

"Rodriguez claims that you met on Salvaje, that you were recently there and that you paid him to kill an

American citizen, Nicole Carrothers, a reporter for the *Observer*."

"As I said—delusions. His story is preposterous. Now, if you'll excuse me, I have no further comment."

Frank snapped off the set. "Looks like old Diamond Jim isn't going to seek reelection."

"Good."

"And the senate ethics committee will look into your allegations."

"More good news."

"It just keeps coming and coming," Frank said, standing and stretching. His white shirt was wrinkled, and he snapped his suspenders happily. "You know, I don't think I ever gave you enough credit around here."

"You didn't," Nikki said.

Frank rubbed the back of his neck. "Well, I'll make it up to you."

"Too late."

"What?"

Nikki offered him her most ingratiating smile. "I quit."

Frank looked as if she'd beaned him with a bowling ball. "Quit? You can't quit!"

Reaching into her purse, she pulled out a long, white envelope. "Just watch me."

"This has something to do with that husband of yours, doesn't it? Just because things aren't working out between you two…" Realizing he'd overstepped his bounds, Frank grabbed his reading glasses off his desk and shoved them onto his nose. "Don't tell me, the *Times* offered you more money."

She grinned, but the deep-seated satisfaction she hoped to feel didn't surface. How could she explain that she'd proved her point, made her statement, and now had to move on? Her life had been turned upside down and inside out in the last week and never once had she seen Trent.

Everyone else, but not Trent. Her father, mother and sisters had rallied around her in her time of need. Calling and visiting, sick at the thought that she'd nearly lost her life. There had been many questions about her husband, and Nikki had ducked them all, saying only that the marriage wasn't yet on stable ground and after the events of the past few weeks, they'd both decided they needed some space.

Her family had thought the reaction odd, but she'd muddled through, dealing with the police, other reporters, interviews and her job. Through it all, she'd felt lonely and empty inside.

Well, today her life was going to change. One way or the other. Grabbing her coat, she took the elevator to the parking garage and climbed into her little convertible. The back seat was filled with the clutter that had been her desk: notes, pens, paper, recorder, Rolodex file, books and general paraphernalia that she'd accumulated in her years with the *Observer*.

It was time to move on. Crossing her fingers, she put her car into gear and hoped that she would be moving in the direction she hoped to.

You know where I live.

Nerves strung tight, she eased her way through traffic, flipped on the radio and hummed along to an old Bruce Springsteen hit. But her thoughts weren't on the lyrics or even the melody; her thoughts were with Trent and what she had to say to him.

She turned into the drive of the house on Lake

Washington and her heart sank. His Jeep was missing and the house looked empty and cold, as if no one lived there. The police tape, denoting a crime scene, had been stripped away, but there was no sign of Trent.

She knocked loudly on the front door and waited.

Nothing. Not one sign of life. A few dry leaves rattled in the old oak trees before floating downward and being caught in a tiny gust to dance for a few seconds before landing on the ground. *Just like us,* Nikki thought, watching with sadness. She and Trent had danced for a few weeks and drifted apart.

Wrong. You pushed him away. She walked around the house and an uneasy feeling wrapped around her, a feeling that she was stepping on her own grave. Rubbing her arms, she followed the path she'd taken on the day she'd been attacked, saw the broken branches in the forest, noticed the footprints, observed the dark stain on the grass and dry leaves where the blood of her attacker had pooled.

Trent had risked his life to save her.

Shivering, she told herself she was lucky and she stared across the lake, past the steel-colored water to the opposite shore where houses were tucked in the evergreen forest.

"Nikki?" Trent's voice whispered on the wind. She turned and found him approaching, his hair ruffling in the breeze, his familiar leather jacket open at the throat. "What're you doing here? I saw your car and…" His voice drifted away as his gaze caught and held in hers.

"I thought we had some unfinished business," she said, feeling the ridiculous urge to break down and cry. Lord, she seemed to fall to pieces whenever she was around him. Blinking against that sudden rush of tears, she walked to him and linked her arm through his. "Come on, let's not stay here."

They followed the path to a point that had been unspoiled by the evil and malevolence that had trailed them from Salvaje to Seattle. "I, um, I've been thinking," she said, still holding his arm as she turned to face him. The wind caught her hair, blowing it over her face, brushing it against her cheeks.

"When have you had time?"

So he'd seen her on the news. Kept track of her busy life. "Things have been hectic," she admitted, "but I've had a lot of hours to do some heavy soul-searching."

"Have you?" He wasn't buying her story, obviously. "I heard you got a commendation and a promotion."

She shrugged. "I quit."

He didn't say a word, just stood there woodenly, not taking her into his arms, even when she was silently begging him to.

"It was time to change."

"Got another job?"

She shook her head. "Not yet."

"Seems to me you could have your pick."

"Doesn't matter." She felt his hand stiffen and held his fingers more tightly in her own. "I don't want a new job, Trent. I just want you." When he didn't respond, she took his face between her palms and forced him to stare into her eyes. "Those hours I spent soul-searching I was alone. In my bed, crying my eyes out. I decided if I wasn't going to wallow in my own misery any longer, I had to face the truth and that is—" she took in a shuddering breath, ready to bare her soul "—I love you, Trent McKenzie, and I want to marry you." His jaw clenched tight. "If you'll have me."

Swallowing the lump of pride that filled her throat, she reached into her purse and withdrew a packet. "Tickets to Salvaje," she said. "For you and me."

His lips cracked into a small, skeptical smile. "You want to go back there?"

"Mmm-hmm."

"When?"

"Right after we stop down at the courthouse and tie the knot."

His smile kicked up a little higher. "What if I don't want to get married?"

Pain sliced through her heart, but she tilted her chin upward defiantly. "Then come with me as my lover."

He barked out a short laugh and stepped away from her. "You're too much," he said, resting his hands on his hips and shaking his head.

Disappointment curdled her insides.

"I thought you never wanted to see me again."

"I had a change of heart." When he didn't respond, she tossed her hair out of her face. "Damn it, Trent, this wasn't easy for me, you know. I've swallowed my pride, told you that I love you, nearly begged you to marry me and you don't have a thing to say?"

"Oh, sure I do."

Here it comes. "And what's that?" she demanded, feeling fire leap in her eyes.

He slid a finger into the pocket of his jeans and withdrew the slim gold band, the very band that had been her wedding ring on Salvaje. "I just wondered what took you so long."

She let out a long, agonized breath. "You've been waiting for me to come back here. You knew I would, didn't you?"

"Thought you might."

"You arrogant, self-important—"

He cut off her insults with a kiss that caused her blood to turn to liquid fire. "Will you shut up a minute?" he asked as he slipped the ring that he'd sized to fit perfectly onto her finger. "I need to get this right this time." He looked down into her eyes and cradled her face in his hands. "Marry me, Nikki," he whispered, feeling the tremor of her body as it molded to his.

Wrapping his arms around her, he pressed anxious lips to hers and knew that now and forever Nikki would be his special woman.

* * * * *

B.J. Daniels is a *New York Times* and *USA TODAY* bestselling author. She wrote her first book after a career as an award-winning newspaper journalist and author of thirty-seven published short stories. She lives in Montana with her husband, Parker, and three springer spaniels. When not writing, she quilts, boats and plays tennis. Contact her at bjdaniels.com, on Facebook or on Twitter, @bjdanielsauthor.

Books by B.J. Daniels

Harlequin Intrigue

Whitehorse, Montana: The Clementine Sisters

Hard Rustler
Rogue Gunslinger
Rugged Defender

The Montana Cahills

Cowboy's Redemption

Whitehorse, Montana: The McGraw Kidnapping

Dark Horse
Dead Ringer
Rough Rider

HQN Books

The Montana Cahills

Renegade's Pride
Outlaw's Honor
Hero's Return
Rancher's Dream

Visit the Author Profile page at Harlequin.com.

UNDENIABLE PROOF

B.J. Daniels

This book is for Tim and Elise,
who told us about these waters and gave us
our first chart of the islands. Thank you for
many hours boating through a blur of
mangrove-green islands on endless water.
There is no neater place to be lost.

Chapter 1

He'd waited too long. They knew. The realization turned his blood to ice water. If they knew that he had the disk, then they also knew what he planned to do with it.

He felt the full weight of the disk in his breast pocket. In the right hands, the disk was gold. In the wrong hands, it was a death warrant.

Simon didn't look back but he knew they were behind him, following him. Two of them. He could hear them. Feel them working their way along the dark street.

All he could guess is that they weren't sure where he was headed. They would want to know who he'd planned to give the disk to. He had a pretty good idea that they knew exactly who he worked for—but just wanted proof.

He'd changed course the moment he'd heard them

behind and now found himself headed for the beach. Ahead was the artsy part of St. Pete Beach, the small southern Florida town at the edge of the Gulf of Mexico. Art galleries, studios, little shops. All closed this time of the night.

No place to hide.

He had to ditch the disk. It was his only chance. He was probably a dead man either way, but he might be able to talk his way out of this if the disk wasn't found on him.

Ahead Simon spotted a light burning in one of the art studios. Was it possible it was still open? Could he be that lucky?

He could hear the quickening of the men's steps behind him as he neared the shop entrance. Inside, the light silhouetted a figure at the back of the shop apparently working late. His good luck. That person's bad fortune.

It took everything in him not to run. But that would make him look guilty. That would get him killed before he could hide the disk.

Simon reached the front door of the shop and grasped the knob. He could see a woman working in the studio at the back. The men behind him were so close he thought he could feel their collective breaths on his neck. As he tried the door, he expected to feel a hand drop to his shoulder and a cold steel barrel press against his backbone.

Locked! He couldn't catch his breath. He jiggled the doorknob. His heart pounded so hard, all he could hear was the blood buzzing in his ears.

The woman who'd been working at the back looked up. Obviously she hadn't been expecting anyone.

Simon waved and called to her in a voice he didn't recognize as his own, "Sorry I'm late."

Surprise registered in her eyes, but she stopped what she was doing and walked toward the door.

He thought he heard the two men slide back into the darker shadows as the woman opened the door.

"I'm sorry I'm so late," he said, stepping in, forcing her to step aside as he pushed past and into the shop. "I was afraid you'd already gone home. I called about one of your—" he glanced to see what kind of work the woman did "—paintings," he said, and stuffed his hands into his pockets so she didn't see how badly they were shaking as he turned to look at her.

He'd thought her twenty-something but she could have been younger. It was hard to tell her age with such pale skin sprinkled with golden freckles and blond hair that she had pulled back in a single long braid that trailed down her back. She wore a sleeveless T-shirt, peach-colored, and a pair of denim cropped pants. He caught the scent of vanilla.

"I'm sorry," she said, looking confused. "Are you sure you have the right gallery?" Simon could see that she was scared. If she only knew. But she closed the door behind her, failing, he noted, to lock it, though. Would the two men come in here after him? He couldn't be sure.

But if they did, the woman was as good as dead.

"Yes, this is the shop," he said, improvising as he moved to look at one of the Florida landscapes done in pastels. "My wife said she was told someone would be here late." A man with a wife would make her feel safer, he hoped, as he saw that she hadn't moved. In fact, she seemed to hover by the phone on the desk by the door.

He thought of the real wife he'd had. She'd left him because she couldn't take the line of work he was in. Low pay, ridiculous hours and always the chance that tonight might be the night he didn't come home. Tonight might be the night she got the phone call. Or worse, opened the door in the wee hours of the morning to see one of his buddies at the door bearing the bad news.

He studied one of the signed paintings, trying to focus. Thinking about Evie right now was a really bad idea. Next to it was a poster announcing an art show at a gallery down the street tomorrow night. "Are you W. St. Clair?"

"Yes." She sounded shy, maybe a little embarrassed. Or maybe it was just nerves with him in her studio this late at night. He could see where she'd been framing some paintings at a workbench in the back.

"You say someone told your wife I would be here late?" she asked. He could hear her trying to come up with an explanation. "I can't imagine who would have told her that."

He shrugged and moved through the paintings, trying not to look out the front windows. Just act normal. The thought almost made him laugh. A normal man would be smart enough not to have gotten caught. And he was caught. Even if he ditched the disk, he wasn't sure he could save himself. Those men wouldn't be after him unless they knew he'd double-crossed them.

"I had to work late myself tonight," Simon said, making it up as he went. Nothing new there. "I was afraid I wouldn't get here in time. You see it's our anniversary. Ten years. My wife told me about a painting she saw here and I thought it would make a great anniversary present for her."

Evie had bailed after six years. Hadn't even waited for the seven-year itch.

"Your anniversary?" The artist smiled. She wanted to believe him. Simon knew he was laying it on a little thick but he needed her to feel safe. To act as if she'd known he was coming. Act as if nothing was wrong for the men who he knew were outside watching him. Watching them both.

The ploy seemed to be working. He saw her relax a little, her movements not as tense as she stepped away from the front windows.

"Do you mind if I just look around for a few minutes?" he asked. "I know I'll recognize the painting she fell in love with from the way she described it."

"If you tell me—"

"You do beautiful work. I can understand why she was so taken with your paintings," he said, cutting her off.

"Thank you," she said, sounding less suspicious although clearly still cautious. "I have a show coming up tomorrow night so I was working late framing. I'm afraid some of the paintings aren't for sale—at least until the show tomorrow night. I hope your wife didn't choose one that's tagged for the show."

"Well, if she did, I'm sure I'll find something that she'll love." Simon heard her go back to the bench. All she had to do was look up and see him from where she worked. He continued to move through the paintings, pretending to admire each as if in no hurry to find the one his wife wanted.

There was only one spot in the small shop where she wouldn't be able to see him. Nor would anyone outside have a clear view because of several large paintings that hung from a makeshift wall.

He found a painting that was marked For Show, Not For Sale and slipped the knife from his pocket. He quickly cut a small slot along the edge of the paper backing the framed painting—one of a colorful sailboat keeling over in the wind—and slid the disk inside between the paper and the artwork.

The disk fit snug enough that it made no sound when Simon picked up the painting as if inspecting it more closely. No one should notice the careful cut he'd made. Not that anyone would get the chance. He'd be back tonight for the painting just as soon as he got rid of the two men after him.

He breathed a sigh of relief as he picked up another small painting of a Florida street market, colorful and quaint and the painting was not tagged for the show.

"This is the one. What does the W. stand for?" he asked as he took it over to her.

"Willa." She smiled as she saw which painting he had selected. "An excellent choice."

Simon paid in cash and watched her carefully wrap it, priding himself on the fact that he hadn't once glanced toward the front windows. Anyone watching him from outside would think this had been his destination all along. At least he hoped so. Everything was riding on this.

"You really saved my life," he said, smiling at the young woman. "I can't tell you how relieved I was to see that you were still around tonight."

She handed him the package and smiled back. "Happy anniversary. I hope your wife enjoys the painting."

"Oh, she will." Evie would have had a fit if he'd brought home a painting by an unknown. Evie liked nice things. And Simon had failed to give her what she needed.

Swallowing down the bitterness, he idly picked up one of the flyers by the cash register announcing Willa St. Clair's gallery showing the next evening and pretended to study it before he folded the flyer and put it into the breast pocket of his jacket.

She followed him to the door.

"Good luck with your show tomorrow night," he said as she started to close the door. "Maybe my wife and I will stop by."

"It's just down the street, at the Seaside Seascapes Gallery."

Simon nodded as she closed and locked it behind him, then he turned and started back the way he'd come, taking his time, the small painting tucked under his arm.

He waited for the two men to accost him as he walked down the street. Two blocks from Willa St. Clair's art studio, and he hadn't seen anyone who wanted to kill him. Maybe he'd been wrong. Maybe he'd hidden the disk and blown off his delivery meeting for nothing.

He should have been relieved. But instead, it made him angry. He'd panicked for nothing. Now he would have to go back and get the damned disk after the studio was closed. Worse, he would have to set up another delivery meeting. Any change of plans always increased the danger.

At his car, he beeped open the doors, the lights flashed and he reached for the door handle.

They came at him from out of the darkness, surprising him. Simon reached for his weapon, but he wasn't fast enough. The small painting he'd bought fell to the ground with a thud as the larger of the two grabbed him, the smaller one taking his gun and searching him.

"What the hell do *you* want?" he bluffed, recognizing them both. "You scared the hell out of me. You're damned lucky I didn't shoot you both."

The smaller of the two men scooped up the painting from the sidewalk and tore the canvas from its frame, tossing it aside when he didn't find what he was looking for.

Simon considered whether he could take them both and decided he'd be dead before he even had one of them down. No, he thought, he had a much better chance if he could get them to take him to their boss. He'd managed to bluff his way this far. He had to believe he could get himself out of this, as well.

"Where is it?" the small one demanded as he jammed a gun into Simon's kidneys.

He groaned. "Where's what?" The big one hit him before Simon even saw him move. The punch dropped him to his knees.

"Not here," the smaller one snapped and Simon heard the sound of a car engine.

A moment later he was shoved onto the floorboard of the back seat, something heavy pressed on top of him.

He tried to breathe, to remain calm. The disk was hidden. If he played his cards right, he could get it back and still make delivery. Too much was at stake to give up now.

If there was one thing Simon Renton was good at it,

it was talking his way out of trouble. Didn't everyone say he was like a cat with nine lives?

He just hoped he hadn't run out of lives.

Chapter 2

Simon was dead.

Landry Jones stood in the large office of the Tampa warehouse fighting the urge to put a bullet hole into the brains of the two men who'd killed Simon. Stupid fools.

But then he'd have to take out their boss, Freddy D., and that wasn't part of the plan. At least not yet.

"We almost got him to tell us who he was working with," said the larger of the two thugs, who went by TNT or T for short, no doubt because of the man's short fuse.

The other man, known as Worm, was smaller, cagier and meaner if that were possible. "I told T to back off a little but Simon was giving him a lot of grief."

Knowing Simon, he would have purposely got T going, so the fool killed him before he gave up the names of the other undercover cops who'd infiltrated the organization.

Landry swore under his breath. "That's why I wanted to handle this. I would have gotten the names out of him."

Freddy D. studied him from beneath hooded gray eyes. "Maybe. Maybe not."

Landry shook his head angrily. "So where's the disk Simon supposedly made?" he asked the two thugs. "Or did you kill him before he told you that, as well?"

"Easy," Freddy D. said, but turned his big bald head to take in T and Worm. "Tell me you got the disk." The tone of his voice made it pretty clear that T and Worm might not be around long if they didn't.

Landry held his breath. T squirmed but Worm looked almost cocky. "He told us where to find it," Worm said.

Landry let out the breath he'd been holding. "Great. You don't have the disk, you don't even know if it exists or if Simon *was* a cop or not." He felt the corpse-gray eyes of Freddy D. shift to him again.

"My source said he *was* a cop and that there were two others working with him in my organization," Freddy D. said.

"Yeah? And what if your source just wanted Simon dead and you running scared of your own men?" Landry asked, knowing he was stepping over the line. "Simon was smart. He was good for business. Now he's dead and there might not even be a damned disk."

"Cool down…" Zeke said from where he lounged against the wall. Zeke Hartung, known affectionately as Zeke the Freak, was tall and slim with rebel good looks. Landry had never asked how he got the nickname. He didn't want to know.

"We all liked Simon," Zeke continued. "If he was a cop, then I'm a cop and I'm taking you all in."

The men in the room laughed nervously. Landry met Zeke's gaze. Zeke smiled. The bastard loved to bluff.

"If your source says there's a disk, Freddy D., then there's a disk," Zeke continued. "So let's find it. Find out what's on it. Find out where Simon got his information— or if these two morons killed the wrong man."

"Who you calling a moron?" T demanded, going for Zeke.

Freddy D. stopped it with a wave of his hand. "Zeke's right. Once we have the disk, then we'll know who we can trust. So where is this disk and why don't I have it yet?" Freddy D. asked, a knife edge to his voice.

Even Worm looked a little less sure of himself. "Simon said he hid it in a painting in one of those art studios down by the beach."

"You think he's a cop, you think he has information on a disk that will bring down the entire organization or make it possible for some other organization to move in on us, and you trusted him to tell you the truth about where he hid it?" Landry demanded incredulously.

Freddy D. shot Landry a look that dropped his blood temperature to just above freezing before turning that cold stare on T and Worm. "So why didn't you just get the painting and bring it to me?"

Worm swallowed, his Adam's apple bobbing up and down. "It's in this art studio. The thing is the shops are all open now. We can't just waltz in and take the painting in broad daylight."

Freddy D. sat up, his weight making the chair groan. "Don't *take* it, you fool. *Buy* it. How much money do you need?"

T and Worm exchanged a look. "It's not for sale."

Freddy D. sat back as if Worm had slapped him. "You aren't serious."

"The painting is part of an art show tonight at some gallery called Seaside Seascapes," Worm said. "I just thought I'd go to the show tonight and buy the painting."

Freddy D. groaned. "You? At an art show?"

"Better than sending T," Landry said.

Freddy D. swiveled around in his chair to pin Landry with that corpse-gray gaze again. "You go, Jones. T and Worm will be waiting for you in the alley to make sure there are no problems. You buy the painting, make sure you get it tonight, you hand it over. They'll be watching you the whole time. Have a problem with that?"

"That's assuming T and Worm aren't undercover cops," Landry said sarcastically.

Even Freddy D. laughed at that.

"I don't know. They're dumb enough to be cops," Zeke said.

Both men looked like they could kill Zeke, but were smart enough not to try. At least not right now in front of the boss.

"I don't want those two in the alley," Landry said. He knew the best thing he could do right now was to go along with Freddy D.'s plan. But it was too late in Landry's life to do the best thing. Far from it.

"Think about it, these two hanging out in the alley behind a fancy art gallery?" Landry said. "First off, anyone who sees them is going to call the cops, thinking they're staking out the place. Secondly, if your source is right and Simon was a cop working with the feds and had made a disk he planned to hand over, then the feds are looking for this disk, too."

Freddy D. narrowed his eyes at him, and for a moment Landry thought he might tell T and Worm to kill him. "While not eloquent or wise, you do make a good point. You're saying that Simon might have gotten the feds word where he hid the disk."

Landry doubted it. Otherwise the feds would be busting down the doors right now, guns blazing. "I think it would be a mistake to underestimate Simon. I know if I was him and I spotted these two behind me, guilty or not, I'd do whatever I could to cover my ass."

"I'll cover the alley," Zeke said. "Or better yet, I'll go to the art show and let Landry wait in the sidelines."

"Like you know squat about art," Landry said, then pretended not to care. "Whatever."

Freddy D. raised a hand. "Landry goes in. Zeke, you take the alley. T and Worm won't be far away just in case."

Just in case any of them thought about double-crossing him. "I want that disk," the boss said.

"If it exists," Landry added, and Freddy D. gave him a warning look before turning again to T and Worm. "What do we know about this artist where Simon said he hid the disk?"

The thugs exchanged confused looks.

"The painting he had on him was signed W. St. Clair," Worm said. "Simon said her name was Willow."

"Or something like that," T said. "He wasn't talking too clearly."

Freddy D. groaned. "What about the artist? Is it possible she's his contact?"

"You hear sirens?" Zeke asked sarcastically. "If the feds had the disk we'd all be facedown and handcuffed."

"Zeke's right," Landry said. "So what does this painting look like? You did get that, right?"

Worm looked like he was itching to punch Landry's ticket. "It's a painting of a sailboat. It had a red and white sail and the boat was blue. The boat is at full sail and there is a blond woman at the wheel. Her hair's blowing back and she's kind of hanging off to the side like she's having a great time."

Landry stared at Worm, amazed they'd gotten that much information out of Simon about the painting but weren't sure about the artist's name. He wanted to believe that Simon had made up every word of it. But Landry had seen T in action and knew that few men could withstand that form of torture. Even Simon.

"I'll find the painting," Landry said.

"I also think it would be wise to find out what the woman knows about Simon," Freddy D. said. "Either way, she's a loose end." Freddy D. was looking straight at him. "You have a way with the ladies, Landry. Take care of her."

Willa St. Clair glanced around the gallery at all her paintings hanging on the walls and could no longer suppress her excitement. She still couldn't believe it. All the hard work, the long hours painting then framing, had finally paid off.

Just when she thought that her life couldn't get any better than this, she saw the handsome dark-haired man standing by the door.

He'd caught her eye several times earlier, lifting his wineglass and giving her a nod. She'd felt herself warm, complimented by his attention.

Now he smiled and she saw that the crowd had

thinned. Clearly he was waiting for her. Her heart beat a little faster.

Several of the stragglers came over to congratulate her. Like her first two openings, this one had been an incredible success. She still couldn't believe it. Almost all of the paintings had small red dots on them, indicating they were sold.

Her dream had come true. She tried to calm her runaway heart, took a deep breath and turned to look toward the door.

He was gone.

Her disappointment pierced the helium high she'd been riding on just moments before. She'd taken too long. He'd gotten tired of waiting.

She couldn't help feeling regret. He'd made a point of getting her attention during the show. But each time she hadn't been able to get away to talk to him. She'd hoped he would find a way to talk to her before the evening was over.

"Great show, sweetie," the gallery owner, Evan Charles, said, coming over to give her an air kiss beside each cheek. "Everyone was just raving about your use of color. You're a hit."

She thanked Evan and promised to let him know when she had enough paintings ready for another show. Taking her wrap from the closet by the door, she stepped out into the Florida night air, closed her eyes and breathed it all in as he locked up behind her.

You're not in South Dakota anymore.

She smiled to herself. She would never tire of breathing sea air. She could hear the cry of the gulls and the lull of the surf not a block away. She loved Florida. And Florida, it seemed, loved her.

"Beautiful night," said a male voice as warm and silky as the night air. "Beautiful woman."

She opened her eyes and turned already smiling, knowing it was him. He *had* waited for her.

"Congratulations," he said. "I was hoping all evening to get a chance to meet you. You were much too popular. And I was much too shy." He grinned and extended his hand. "Landry Jones."

He was anything but shy, she thought as her hand disappeared into his large one. His touch was gentle but there was raw power behind it. She shivered as she looked into his dark eyes, and he grinned as if he knew exactly what she was thinking.

Amazingly, he was even more striking up close. Not classically handsome. Too rough around the edges for that. He wore khaki chinos and a palm-tree-print short-sleeved shirt and deck shoes. He was tanned and the fingers on his left hand were scraped as if he'd been in a fistfight. He looked like a man who could hold his own in a fight, she thought, as a niggling worry wormed its way into her perfect night.

Landry Jones wasn't the type of man a woman met at an art showing. Especially not hers.

"So, you're interested in Florida landscapes?" she asked, cocking her head to one side. "You don't seem the type."

He feigned hurt, laughed and gave her a sheepish grin. "Actually I'm more interested in the artist, although I find both intriguing."

She felt her cheeks heat under his compliment as well as his dark piercing gaze. If he was trying to charm her, he was doing a darned good job. "Thank you." She wanted to pinch herself. This night was just too good to be true.

"Any chance I could buy you a cup of coffee?" he asked. "Now that we've officially met? There's a coffee shop I know that's still open not far from here. Or if you'd like something stronger…"

If only this night never had to end. And Landry Jones was like the topping on the cake. And maybe the ice cream, as well.

So what if he wasn't the type to frequent art shows? For tonight he could be her type, she thought with a thrill.

"Coffee would be great." She couldn't trust herself with anything stronger, not while feeling as exhilarated as she was already.

"Coffee it is then," he said, his smile mesmerizing. "This night calls for a celebration. If you're feeling adventurous, we could even have a piece of key lime pie."

She was feeling adventurous, all right.

"My car is just over here." He pointed down the dark street and suddenly she wasn't so sure.

She knew she was being silly. But suddenly the reality of the situation hit her. This wasn't South Dakota and she didn't know this man from Adam.

The idea of getting into a car with a complete stranger was totally alien to her—and suddenly seemed more than a little dangerous.

Odd as it might seem, she knew everyone back in her small hometown in South Dakota and never dated anyone she didn't. Now she was about to get into a car with a stranger she'd met just moments before.

While she could hear traffic a few streets over, there

was no longer anyone around, all the shops and galleries were now closed and she was feeling a little vulnerable.

She turned, hoping Evan was still inside closing up. Even the gallery lights were out. She hadn't seen Evan leave, but then all her attention had been on Landry Jones, hadn't it?

Landry must have seen her indecision and the way her feet were rooted to the sidewalk. "Wait here. I'll get the car." He flashed a reassuring smile, then turned and keyed his remote. A set of headlights flashed down the street. She watched him walk toward a newer-model blue BMW, telling herself she was being very foolish.

Yes, she was taking a chance, but hadn't she had to take a chance when she'd left South Dakota to come to Florida? And look how that had worked out. Sometimes you had to take a chance.

Especially with a handsome man on one of the most exciting nights of her life.

She groaned as she took a few steps down the street away from the gallery—and Landry Jones. With her luck, the man would turn out to be a serial killer ax murderer. Otherwise, it was almost as if he was too perfect.

At the car, Landry climbed in and pulled out his cell. He punched speed dial as he watched Willa St. Clair.

"The painting wasn't in the show," he said the moment the line was answered. He could see Willa St. Clair waiting for him. "But don't worry. I'll find it. I have the artist in my crosshairs right now, so to speak. Tell Zeke I won't be needing him. I'll call when I have the disk." He snapped his cell shut before Freddy D. could argue.

With a start, he saw that Willa St. Clair was walking down the block toward the alley behind the gallery.

He swore as he noticed the change in her. She'd looked a little leery earlier when he'd asked her out. But now she appeared scared and, unless he missed his guess, about to change her mind.

She hadn't been what he'd expected. One look at her and he'd known he'd have to handle her with kid gloves. At least until he got her in the car.

Now he had to move fast. Once he had her under his control, he told himself, it would be smooth sailing. He grimaced at his own inside joke.

Where the hell was this sailboat painting that Simon had told T and Worm he'd hid the disk in? Landry had come to believe it existed. Simon was smart enough to know that by telling T and Worm, he would also be telling the rest of them. That could explain the intricate description Simon had given the two goons.

But as Landry's luck would have it, the painting T and Worm described wasn't in the gallery show.

So where was it?

T. and Worm had said that some blond woman had been working at the back of the art studio last night when Simon had gone in. Their description of her matched the artist's—Willa St. Clair.

She was the key to finding the painting—and ultimately the disk. And Willa St. Clair was going to tell him. One way or another, Landry would have that disk before the night was over.

As he reached to start the car engine and go after her, he heard a soft tap on his side window. He turned and glanced up, only half surprised to see Zeke standing next to his car.

"What the hell do you want?" he asked as he powered down his side window. "Didn't Freddy D. tell you to call it a night?"

Zeke smiled. "Change of plans, old buddy."

Willa knew she would hate herself in the morning if she didn't go out with Landry Jones. For the rest of her life, she would think of him, actually building him up in her memory—if that were possible—and always wonder what might have been.

She stopped walking up the block and turned, blinking as she looked back. The BMW hadn't moved but she could hear the purr of the engine. As her eyes adjusted to the darkness she saw that a man was standing beside the driver's side talking to Landry.

Now was her chance to just disappear. Take the coward's way out. Run!

Funny, but that's exactly what her instincts told her to do.

Pop! Pop! The sound took her by surprise. She stared, unable to move even when she saw the glint of a gun through the windshield, saw the flash as Landry Jones fired two more shots.

The man next to the car staggered back, slammed into the wall and slid slowly down, his head dropping to his chest.

Poleaxed, she stared at the dead man—her first dead man—her mind screaming: Landry shot him! He *shot* him!

She felt Landry shift his gaze to her and suddenly she was moving, kicking off her high heels and running for her life. She could hear the roar of the BMW engine as he came after her, the headlights washing over her.

A main street was only two blocks away. She could see the lights of the traffic. There would be people around. She could get away, get help. But she knew she would never reach it. The BMW was bearing down on her.

She glanced back and blinded by the headlights didn't see the man with two dogs on leashes appear out of the darkness off to her right.

The man avoided crashing into her, but she got caught up in the dogs' leashes and went down hard.

"Are you all right? I'm sorry I didn't see you," the man said, sounding distraught as he knelt beside her.

"Help me," she cried, not yet feeling the pain. "He's going to kill me."

"Who?" the man asked, glancing around.

She managed to sit up, vaguely aware that her hands and knees were scraped raw from hitting the sidewalk. The street was dark. No BMW. No Landry Jones.

Three sets of eyes stared at her at ground level, only one set human. The dogs were big and wonderfully muttlike. The man knelt next to her, looking scared and upset.

Willa began to cry. "That car that was chasing me...."

"It went on past," the man said.

Her hands and knees began to ache and she saw that her dress that she'd bought especially for the showing was ruined. Her new shoes were back down the street where she'd kicked them off.

"Are you sure the car was chasing you?"

One of the dogs licked her in the face. She put her

arm around its neck, hugging it tightly for a moment before she dug her cell phone out of her purse and punched in 911.

Chapter 3

Landry couldn't believe how badly things had gone. What a nightmare. Simon was dead. So was Zeke. Zeke.

He put his head in his hands. What the hell had happened?

Unfortunately, he knew the answer to that, he thought as he gingerly touched his side. He'd been lucky. Although the wound had bled like hell, it hadn't been life threatening. Still, he'd had a hell of a time finding a doctor to stitch him up and make sure it didn't get infected. It wasn't like he could just walk into an emergency room. By law, doctors were required to report gunshot wounds.

He'd had to find a doctor he could trust not to turn him in. He couldn't chance using Freddy D.'s or any of the ones the cops knew about.

The wound, though, had turned out to be the least of his problems. Since that night, he'd been a hunted man. Willa St. Clair's eyewitness testimony that he'd shot Zeke Hartung down in cold blood had every cop on the force and the feds after him—not to mention Freddy D. and his boys.

For days Landry had been on the run, keeping his head down, but he'd known from the get-go that he couldn't keep this up. He had to find that damned disk. The proof he needed was on it. Without the disk, he was a dead man.

He'd come close to getting the girl—and in the long run, the disk. He still had a few friends on the force he could trust, ones that wouldn't believe he was a dirty cop, even if he was, and one of them had given him the safe house location where Willa St. Clair was being held.

Unfortunately, Freddy D.'s men must have had an inside source as well because they hit the house before Landry could.

He'd almost had Willa St. Clair, though. He'd been so damned close he'd smelled the citrus scent of her shampoo in her long blond hair. But she'd managed to get away from not only him, but also Freddy D.'s men. The woman had either known about the hit on the safe house or she was damned lucky.

Like the night of her art show. If that fool with the two dogs hadn't come out of nowhere, Landry would have caught up to her, got her into the car and he'd have the disk by now and be calling the shots instead of running for his life.

But she'd seen him kill Zeke and he had known getting her into the car that night would have been near impossible if she'd been alone. Landry was good but he couldn't have taken on the guy with the two big dogs, too. And Freddy D. had said T and Worm would be nearby. If they'd seen him kill Zeke, then he couldn't be sure what those two fools would do.

He would be sitting behind bars right now or dead if he hadn't gotten the hell out of there.

So he'd disappeared into one of the small old-fashioned motels along the beach, blending in as best he could with the tourists, waiting for his cell phone to ring with news.

Since the safe house hit, he'd been hot on the trail of Willa St. Clair. His one fear was that someone would get to her before he did. There was no way she would last long out there on her own. That's why he had to get to her first. It was now a matter of life and death. His.

His cell rang. He took a breath, hoping that one of his cop friends he could trust had come through for him. But Zeke had friends too, friends who were taking his death personally and would shoot first and ask questions later if they found Landry.

"Hey," he said into the phone.

"This may be nothing…but I ran her cell phone. Willa St. Clair made a couple of calls. You want the numbers?"

Landry closed his eyes and let out the breath he'd been holding. "Oh, yeah. I owe you big-time."

"Yeah, you do." His friend read off the numbers. One in Naples. The other in South Dakota.

He hung up and tried the Naples one first. An answering machine picked up. She'd called a law firm? He almost hung up but heard something in the recording that caught his attention.

"…if you've called about the apartments on Cape Diablo island…"

Cape Diablo? Where the hell was that?

Five minutes later, a Florida map spread across the table in his motel, Landry Jones found Cape Diablo in an area known as Ten Thousand Islands at the end of the road on the Gulf Coast side almost to the tip of Florida.

The only other call Willa St. Clair made had been to South Dakota to probably friends or parents. So he was betting she'd rented one of the apartments on Cape Diablo.

Landry couldn't believe his luck. The woman was a novice at this. Plus she had no idea about the type of people after her. Or the resources they had at their disposal. She thought she'd found herself the perfect place to hide, did she? Instead, she'd just boxed herself in with no way out.

Willa pulled the baseball cap down on her now short curly auburn hair and squinted out across the rough water. The wind blew the tops off the waves in a spray of white mist. Past the bay she could see nothing but a line of green along the horizon.

She glanced at the small fishing boat and the man waiting for her to step in. He called himself Gator, wore flip-flops, colorful Bermuda shorts and a well-worn blue short-sleeved vented fishing shirt. His skin was dark from what he professed had been most of his fifty-some years in the south Florida sun.

"You want to go to the island or not?" he asked, seeming amused by her uncertainty.

"Maybe we should wait until it's not so rough out there," she suggested.

He laughed and shook his head. "We wait, the tide will go out and there is no going anywhere until she comes back in. You want to wait until the middle of the night?"

She didn't, and this time when he held out his hand she passed him the two suitcases and large cardboard box, containing what was most precious to her.

He set everything in the bottom of the boat and reached for her hand. She gave it to him and stepped in. The boat rocked wildly, forcing her to sit down hard on the wooden seat at the front of the boat. "I haven't been in a lot of boats."

"No kiddin'," he said, and started the outboard, flipping it around so the boat nosed backward into the waves.

She grabbed the metal sides and hung on.

"Might want to put on that jacket," he said as he tucked a tarp around her large cardboard box. "It could get a little wet."

A slight understatement. A wave slammed over the bow half drowning her in cold spray. She heard a chuckle behind her as she let go to hurriedly pull on the crumpled rain jacket he'd indicated, then drew a life preserver on over that. Both smelled of dead fish, and not for the first time, she wondered if this wasn't a mistake.

The boat swung around and cut bow first through the waves. Gator gave the motor more power. She gripped the seat under her as the boat rose and fell, jarring her each time it came down. She was glad she hadn't taken Gator's advice and eaten something first.

As they started across the bay, she turned to glance back at Chokoloskee, afraid she hadn't been as careful as she should have.

The wind snapped a flag hanging from the mast of

a small sailboat back at the dock. The half-dozen stone crab fishermen she'd seen mending a large net on the dirt near one of the fish shacks were still hard at work. Several of the men had been curious when she'd walked down the dock to talk to Gator, but soon lost interest.

There was no one else on the docks. No new cars parked along the street where she'd hired Gator to take her out to the island. She tried to assure herself that there was no way she'd been followed. But it was hard, given what had happened while she'd been in protective custody.

Landry had found her in what was supposed to be a safe house with two armed policemen guarding her. She'd been lucky to get out alive. From the shots she'd heard behind her, the two men guarding her hadn't been as lucky. She didn't kid herself. Landry was after her.

Especially now that she was on her own, unarmed and running for her life. Nor did she doubt that the next time he found her, he'd try to finish what he'd started back at the safe house.

That's why she couldn't let him find her. Even if it meant doing something that she now considered just as dangerous.

The green on the horizon grew closer and she saw that it wasn't one large island but dozens of small ones, all covered in mangrove forests.

Gator steered the boat into what looked more like a narrow ditch, just wide enough for the small fishing boat. As he winded his way through one waterway after another past one island after another, she tried to memorize the route in case she needed to ever take a boat and get to the mainland on her own.

It was impossible. When she looked back, the islands

melded together into nothing but what appeared to be an unbroken line of green. She couldn't even see where the water cut between the islands anymore.

Tamping down her growing panic that she'd jumped from the frying pan into the fire, she told herself she'd picked this island because it was hard to find. She'd wanted remote, and what was more remote than an island in the area known as Ten Thousand Islands along the Gulf side of the southern tip of Florida?

She'd heard about Cape Diablo through another artist she'd met. The woman, a graphic designer named Carrie Bishop, had rented an apartment in an old Spanish villa on the remote island. That's the last she saw of the artist but she remembered the woman telling her that the area had always been a haven for smugglers, drug runners and anyone who wanted to disappear and never be found.

That would be Willa St. Clair she thought, as watched the horizon, anxious to see what she'd gotten herself into. The rent had been supercheap. The apartment was described as furnished but basic. Not that beggars could be choosers. She was desperate, and that had meant taking desperate measures.

The sun dipped into the Gulf, turning the water's surface gold and silhouetting the islands ahead and behind her. Willa wondered how much farther it was to Cape Diablo and was about to ask when she felt the boat slow.

She looked up and caught a glimpse of red tile roof. A moment later the house came into view. Instantly she wanted to paint it. A haunting Spanish villa set among the palms.

With relief she saw a pier and beyond it an old two-story boathouse, thankful she would soon be off the rough water and on solid ground again.

Gator eased the boat, stepping out to tie off before he offered her a hand.

The boat wobbled wildly as she climbed out on the pier, making Gator chuckle again. She shot him a warning look, then turned her gaze to the villa.

It was truly breathtaking. Or at least it had been before it had fallen into disrepair. The Spanish-style structure now seemed to be battling back the vegetation growing up around it. Vines grew out of cracks or holes in the walls. Others climbed up the sides, hiding entire sections of the structure.

Palm trees swayed in the breeze and through an archway she could see what appeared to be a courtyard and possibly a swimming pool.

This had been the right decision, she thought, staring at the villa. It gave her the strangest feeling. Almost as if she was supposed to have come here. As if she had been born to paint it. Silly, but she felt as if the house had a story it needed told. That there was much more here than just crumbling walls.

Movement caught her eye. She looked upward and glimpsed someone watching her from a third-floor window.

"You change your mind?" Gator asked from behind her.

She turned to see that he'd put her suitcases on the dock and was sitting in his boat, obviously anxious to leave. Apparently this was as far as he went with her suitcases and box. So much for chivalry.

She turned to look at the villa again. "It's incredible, isn't it?"

He grunted.

She'd rented the apartment sight unseen through a phone number she'd called. Her rent had been paid via mail. So she wasn't surprised there was no one to meet her. She'd been told that the caretaker lived in the boathouse near the pier but that he might not be around. If there was an emergency or any problems, he was the man to see. Her rent money would be picked up each month when a supply boat came. She was told to talk to a man named Bull to order what she needed since there was no phone on the island. No electricity other than a generator. And cell phones didn't work from the island.

She'd wanted to disappear to someplace isolated— well, she had.

"Last chance," Gator said.

She shook her head.

He shrugged and glanced toward the Gulf of Mexico where the sun had sunk into the sea. "Then I'll shove off." He looked past her toward the house and seemed hesitant to leave her here—just as he'd been to bring her to the island in the first place. He'd tried to talk her out of it, asking if she knew anything about Cape Diablo.

"Why would you want to go out there?" he'd asked, pinning her with narrowed brown eyes. "Only people who are running from something or searching for it go out there. Few find what they're looking for. Usually just the opposite. Most wish they hadn't looked. Why do you think it is called Cape Diablo?"

"What are you telling me? That the island is haunted?" Her graphic artist friend had told her the island had an interesting history but hadn't elaborated.

"More like cursed."

Willa had anxiously looked over her shoulder, half expecting to see Landry.

"Running from something, huh?"

"Not that it's any of your business, but I'm trying to get away from my ex-boyfriend, if you must know." She'd touched the bruise on her cheek that she'd gotten when the safe house the cops had put her in had been attacked.

Gator had given her a slow knowing nod, reached for the cash she'd offered him and hadn't tried to talk her out of it.

But clearly he hadn't wanted to bring her out here. Nor did he seem to want to leave her here. She thought about asking him why as he paused, then started the outboard.

"Send word by a fisherman or anyone heading to the mainland and I'll come get you," he said, his gaze softening. "Even if it's in the middle of the night."

Why would she want to leave in the middle of the night? His look said it wouldn't be long before she couldn't wait to get out off the island.

He touched the brim of his cap and turned the bow back the way they'd come. At least she thought it was the way they'd come.

She picked up the suitcases from the pier and started toward the villa, figuring she would come back for the box with her paints and art supplies. She couldn't help but wonder what Gator would have said if he knew the truth.

That she was the only witness to the cold-blooded murder of a police officer named Zeke Hartung.

Make that *missing* witness.

The story, complete with sensational headlines, had

been splashed across every South Florida paper followed quickly she didn't doubt by the attack at the safe house and the death of two more officers.

As she looked up at the villa, she wondered if there was any place safe enough or far away from civilization to elude Landry Jones. If it wasn't Cape Diablo, then no place existed.

The sound of the boat's motor died off into the distance. She looked back once but the boat had already disappeared from sight. All she could see were mangrove islands on one horizon and the endless Gulf of Mexico on the other.

She couldn't remember ever feeling so isolated, so alone—not even in the middle of South Dakota, miles from the nearest town. Surely all the people looking for her would have a hard time finding her. But she didn't delude herself. She wouldn't be safe until Landry Jones was behind bars.

Willa stopped in front of the villa. She could hear the waves lapping at the dock and the wind whispering in the palms, but also the faint sound of music.

She looked up again to see an elderly woman through the sheer curtains. The woman wore a white gown and appeared to be waltzing to the music with an invisible partner.

"Hello."

Willa jumped at the sound of the male voice next to her, making her drop one of the suitcases.

"Here let me take that." He stepped around her and picked up the suitcase and reached for the second one. "I thought I heard a boat."

She could only stare at him, her heart thundering in

her chest. She'd been told there were four apartments in the villa, all vacant when she'd inquired.

"Sorry. I didn't mean to scare you," the man said. He appeared to be in his early thirties, blond, blue-eyed and tan—her original idea of what Florida men should all look like. "What's your apartment number?"

"Three."

"Then you're right up there." He pointed through an arch. She could see a wrought iron railing, a blood-red riot of bougainvillea flowers climbing the wall behind it and a weathered door with a 3 painted crudely on it.

He took the other suitcase from her and carrying both, headed through the archway into a tiled courtyard. She started to turn back to retrieve the box with her painting supplies from the dock. "I'll get that for you," he said.

Still a little unsteady after the boat ride, she decided to let him and followed him through the archway, seeing that she was right—there was a pool. Unfortunately it was dark and murky, apparently abandoned years ago but never drained.

"I'm Odell Grady," he said over his shoulder. "That's my apartment over there." He motioned across the pool to what had once been the pool house, she guessed.

"How many tenants are there?"

"Just you and me right now. Unless you count the old gal up there." He motioned to a third-floor tower section of the villa where she'd seen the woman dancing. "She's grandfathered in, so to speak."

He stopped partway up the stairs and turned to look back at her. "You were warned about her, weren't you?"

She hadn't been warned about anything except the isolation and no one to meet her at the dock, but she wasn't worried about some elderly woman who waltzed with a phantom lover. Odell was another story altogether.

"If you like peace and quiet, you definitely came to the right place," he said as he scaled the stairs. "That's why I came here. How about you?" He'd reached the landing and stopped next to one of the doors to turn to look back at her.

"Peace and quiet," she agreed as she topped the stairs. She wondered if it would be possible to get either with Odell Grady around.

He nodded, openly studying her. He had put down the suitcases just outside the door and held out his hand.

It took her a moment to realize he was waiting for the key to open her door.

"Thank you. I can take it from here."

He seemed to hesitate, then looked embarrassed. "Sorry, didn't mean to come on so strong. This place gets to you after a while. I hadn't realized what it would be like, not talking to another human being."

"How long have you been here?"

"Too long obviously. I've been talking your ear off, sorry." He stepped back, giving her space. "I'll get your other package." He turned and trotted down the stairs.

She opened the apartment door but didn't enter, instead watching him, worrying.

Odell returned with the box. "It's pretty heavy. Want me to set it inside?"

"Thank you." She let him enter but stayed outside until he'd put the box down and came back out.

He must have seen how uncomfortable she was having him in her apartment. Actually being pretty much alone on the island with him—since she doubted the elderly woman upstairs would be much help if she needed it.

"So, welcome to Cape Diablo," Odell said, dusting off his hands on his shorts. He met her gaze. He didn't look dangerous, but then she'd thought the same thing of Landry Jones, hadn't she.

"If you need anything, I'll be right down there pounding on my manual typewriter. I'm a writer," he said walking backward a few steps. "Fiction."

She relaxed a little and felt guilty for the rude way she'd reacted to his kindness.

"How about you?"

"You mean what I do for a living?" she asked, giving herself time to come up with an answer. "I've been a waitress, a barmaid, a receptionist, a grocery clerk. Right now I'm just taking a break to figure out what I want to do."

"Been there," he said. "You're still young. You'll figure it out." He cocked his head at her. "You look like an...artist to me." He must have seen her shocked expression because he laughed. "No, I'm not psychic. The box lid came open and I saw all your art supplies."

The box had come open? Not with the amount of tape she'd used. "It's just a hobby."

"Yeah, that's how my writing is. I just hope to turn it into something more," he said, and looked toward the Gulf. "This would be a great place to paint." He turned back to her. "I'd love to see your work."

"I don't let anyone see it," she said too quickly. "It's just...embarrassing at this point."

He laughed. "Probably the same reason I don't let anyone read my work." Another song drifted on the breeze. He glanced toward the third floor where the elderly woman was dancing again. "If you weren't crazy when you came here, you will be."

"I'm sorry. How long did you say you've been here?"

"Just since this afternoon, but long enough to go stir-crazy, although not as crazy as some people." He made a face and cocked his head toward the tower, making a circle with his finger next to his temple.

Since this afternoon? So he'd arrived only a little earlier than she had. She felt a chill at the thought that someone had found out where she was going and Odell had been sent to wait for her.

"Thank you again for your help."

He smiled and nodded. "My pleasure."

Almost apologetically she turned away from him. She picked up her suitcases and stepped inside the apartment. As she started to close the door, he called from the stairs, "Hey, I never caught your name."

"Will—Willie." It was out before she could call it back. She was tired and just wanted to be left alone and she hadn't thought before she'd spoken or she would have given him the name she'd planned to use. Too late for that.

"Short for something?" he asked turning on the stairs.

She was forced back out on the balcony to keep from yelling her answer. "Actually, it's a nickname. My real name is Cara Wilson. My friends started calling me Willie and it stuck."

"Cara," he said. "That's a pretty name. But Willie suits you."

She smiled nervously and gave him a nod as she stepped back into her apartment and closed the door, leaning against it, feeling like a fool.

She concluded Odell was more lonely than anything else. *Nosy* and lonely. Unless she was wrong about him—the way she'd been wrong about Landry Jones. To think she had almost gotten in the car with Landry.

She shivered at the memory, her gaze skittering over the rooms where she'd be living until Landry was caught. The apartment wasn't bad. If you liked living in a monastery. The walls had once been painted white, the ceilings were cracked and ten feet high at least. The temperature was nice and cool, though, so that meant the walls were thick.

That was a plus and the place *was* furnished. Kinda.

Not that any of that mattered. She would be safe here. At least she prayed that was true.

Dragging her suitcases into the bedroom, she was excited to see the wonderful light coming in through the window. She felt a sense of relief. She would be able to paint in here. In fact, she couldn't wait to get started.

She dragged the box in. As she started to open it, she noticed that the tape was open on one corner and the flap turned back. She ran her finger along the edge of the tape. It had been cut.

Chapter 4

Willa's heart began to pound a little harder. Someone had cut the tape to look inside the box. Odell? Was it possible he had a knife in the pocket of his shorts? A lot of men in South Dakota carried pocket knives. But in Florida?

Or could it have been someone else? The box had been on the dock unattended for some time while Odell had brought her suitcases up to her room. But who else was there?

She glanced toward the third floor. The music had stopped again. She recalled it stopping before, a break between songs before she saw the elderly woman dancing once again. Was it possible the woman had gone down to the dock to look in Willa's belongings?

What harm could a curious old woman do anyway? Willa liked that theory better than thinking Odell had purposely cut the tape to see what was in the box. The man was nosy, but whoever had cut the box was looking for something. Looking for her?

But if whoever had looked in the box was here to kill her, then that person already knew she painted. And not even her changed appearance would fool him.

She tried to put the incident out of her mind as she unloaded her painting supplies and set up an easel by the window.

Painting relaxed her, let her escape for a while from the reality of her life, the reality that Landry Jones was still out there on the loose and she was the only witness to the murder.

Until the police captured him, she wasn't safe. Even when he was caught, she wasn't sure she would feel safe, possibly ever again.

She stacked up all of her art supplies on the top of the chest of drawers, hoping they would last until she got to leave here. Eventually she would run out of rent money and be forced to leave and get a job.

She moved to the window by the bed and peered out. Through the palms she could see the Gulf of Mexico. It looked endless. How odd not to be able to see land on the horizon. Just water as far as the eye could see. No wonder early man feared sailing to the edge and falling off.

Turning back to the room, she considered making the bed and taking a nap. She'd been running on fear for so long, she felt drained. She needed her life back. All she had to do, she told herself, was stay alive until Landry was caught.

She stared at the empty canvas on her easel. She had

to paint. It had been days since she'd gotten the opportunity. She itched to pick up a brush.

Painting had always been her survival. When her father was killed in a tractor accident. When her first love married someone else. When her mother remarried and sold the farm, hacking away the roots that had held Willa in South Dakota.

Willa hurried to catch the last of the day's light coming in through the palms. She never knew what she was going to paint until she had a brush in her hand and the white empty canvas in front of her.

To her, painting was exploration. A voyage to an unknown part of herself. Her work was a combination of what she saw and what she didn't. It was a feeling captured like a thought out of thin air.

She set up her paints and went to work, the evening light fading until she was forced to turn on a lamp. It wasn't until then that she really looked at what she'd been working on—and felt a start.

What had begun as an old building along a narrow street had turned into the street where she'd witnessed the murder. A thin slice of pale light at the back illuminated what could have been a bundle of old rags but what she knew was a body slumped against a stucco wall, the dark BMW sitting at the curb.

She stepped back from the canvas. She'd been so lost in the physical joy of painting, she hadn't even realized that she'd been reliving the murder.

From this distance, she saw the face behind the windshield of the BMW. It was subtle, almost ghostlike, but definitely a face. Landry Jones's face. The same one she'd drawn for the police. She remembered the investigators' strange reactions. When she'd asked if they knew who he was, the detective who'd been questioning her assured her they knew Landry Jones only too well.

Just her luck that a known criminal had taken an interest in her. She had wanted to ask what other crimes he'd committed but didn't want to know. Wasn't murdering a man in cold blood on a St. Pete Beach street enough?

In the painting, Landry was peering out of the darkness not at the body of the man he'd just killed—but at her. She could almost feel the heat of his dark eyes.

She stumbled back from the painting, bumping into the sagging double bed and sitting down on the bare mattress, suddenly exhausted and near tears.

Had she been foolish to think she would be safe anywhere—let alone on this island? She would always be haunted by what had happened that night, would always see Landry Jones's face, if not in her paintings then in her nightmares.

A tap at the door startled her. She didn't want to answer it but knew she couldn't pretend she'd gone out. Another tap.

"Cara? Willie?"

Odell. She groaned. Where had she come up with Cara? "Just a minute." She glanced around the room as if there might be something lying around that would give away her true identity, but didn't see anything. She couldn't help the feeling that she'd already made a mistake that was going to get her in trouble. She couldn't keep living like this.

She opened the door. "Odell," she said as if seeing him was a surprise.

"Hi. Sorry to bother you, but I noticed you didn't bring any food," he said, looking sheepish. He held out a sandwich wrapped in plastic. "If you don't want it now, you can eat it later. Turkey and cheese."

She took the sandwich. "Thank you. It looks…great." She actually smiled and he seemed to relax. A part of her felt bad about being so unfriendly. Back home in South Dakota her behavior would have been outright rude.

The whisper of fabric made them both turn. All Willa caught was a blur of white.

"She sneaks around here all the time like that, I guess," Odell said of the elderly woman who passed on the third-floor balcony overhead. "Her name's Alma Garcia. She was the nanny."

"The nanny?"

"You don't know the story of Cape Diablo?" he asked, sounding surprised. "The island is cursed. At least according to local legend. There have always been reports of strange happenings out here, including storms that wash up all kinds of interesting things. For decades it was home to pirates and treasure seekers who looted ships that sank or were sunk just off shore, smugglers and drug runners."

"Who built the villa?" she asked, unable not to. The place had drawn her from the first glimpse.

"Andres Santiago, a rather notorious pirate and smuggler, and this is where it gets interesting," Odell said, warming to his story. "Back in the late sixties, early seventies, Andres smuggled guns, drugs, anything profitable in from Central America. The Ten Thousand Islands have always been home to smugglers of all kinds because it is so remote and easy to get lost in."

She nodded remembering how quickly she'd become

lost among the mangrove islands on the way here. "You said he had a nanny?"

Odell nodded. "He lived here with his wife, Medina, and three small children from his first marriage. That wife died in childbirth. Medina was the daughter of a Central American dictator. During a revolt, her father was killed but Andres managed to rescue Medina and a devoted lieutenant named Carlos Lazarro. He brought them both to the island. Carlos still lives in that old boathouse by the pier." Odell paused. "Do you really want to hear this?"

He didn't give her time to answer. But she would have said yes even if he had.

"The woman up there, Alma Garcia? She was the nanny for Andres's children." He glanced toward the third floor. Only a faint light glowed overhead. "She went crazy after what happened."

Willa felt a chill. "What happened?"

"First, Andres's only son drowned in the pool. Then the whole family went missing. No one ever knew what happened to them. Alma and Carlos had been inland that night. When they came home some time after midnight, they discovered everyone gone. There was blood… The authorities suspected foul play, of course, but the case was never solved. That was thirty years ago."

"How awful."

"There are lots of theories. Some say Medina's father's enemies came and killed the whole family. Others say Andres made it look as if they'd all been killed so he could disappear with his family. In Andres's will he made provisions for both Alma and Carlos to live on the island for the rest of their lives. That's why the villa was divided into apartments since the money Andres left has long since run out. A lawyer friend of the family handles everything."

Willa saw the woman sneak back into her apartment. The front of her white gown was covered with what appeared to be dirt.

"When I got here, I saw her digging," Odell said. "Local legend has it that Andres Santiago hid a small fortune on this island."

She felt her eyes widen.

Odell laughed. "If it were true, fortune hunters would have found it over the last thirty years."

"I'm surprised Alma and Carlos would want to stay here after what happened," Willa said, seeing the villa so differently now.

"I guess they had nowhere else to go. Alma spends her days creeping around here like some kind of ghost. Carlos is the caretaker but most of the time from what I can tell, he's on the other side of the island in his boat fishing." He seemed to notice that she was still holding her sandwich. "You probably want to get that in the fridge and I've talked your ear off again. Sorry."

"No, I enjoyed hearing the story, and thank you for the sandwich."

He smiled. "Holler if you need anything. And don't worry about Alma and Carlos. They seem harmless enough."

"Thanks." Willa stepped back into her apartment and closed the door. She waited a few moments, until she heard Odell's footfalls retreat, before she locked the door.

After she put the sandwich in the fridge, she dragged her suitcase over to the marred old chest of drawers and unpacked. At the bottom of her suitcase, she found the sheets and towels she'd brought. She made the bed and hung up the towels in the bathroom, surprised to see there was a huge clawfoot tub.

Some of her fatigue evaporated at the thought of sinking neck-deep into a tub of hot water scented with her favorite bath soap. She popped in the plug and turned on the water. The old pipes groaned and complained but after a few moments, wonderfully warm water began to fill the tub.

Quickly she checked to make sure she'd locked the door before she went back to the bathroom and stripped off her clothing and stepped into the tub.

Everything was going to be all right, she told herself as she immersed herself in the warm water and began to soap her body in the rich lather. From somewhere she heard music again, the song older than the woman on the third floor. Past the music, she heard voices, though too faint to make out the words.

She couldn't help but think about the story Odell had told her. The history of Cape Diablo and the Santiago family fascinated her. She'd felt something when she'd stepped off the boat and looked up at the crumbling old villa. A sense of mystery. A story unfolding. Or had she sensed something else? The spirits of the lost souls? Or a sense of foreboding as if she'd been drawn to this island for another purpose?

She shivered, wondering again what could have happened to the family and even more intrigued by the woman who'd stayed on upstairs.

Odell certainly was knowledgeable about Cape Diablo. She felt foolish for suspecting him of having other motives for being on the island. And yet, anyone could learn the history of the place. And pretending to be a writer gave him the perfect cover.

She shook her head at the path her mind had taken. She hated that she was suspicious of everyone now.

Finishing her bath, she toweled dry and dressed in a sleeveless nightshirt. She felt better, calmer, back in control somewhat, she thought as she started to wipe the steam from the mirror and was momentarily startled by her own unfamiliar image in the glass.

Her hand went to her short curly auburn hair. It did make her eyes seem larger. Or that could have been the fear.

She picked up the glasses from where she'd left them on the sink. The lenses were clear, but the plastic frames distracted from her face enough to make her look entirely different from the woman she'd been just weeks before.

She touched her hair again, missing the feel of her long, naturally straight blond hair inherited from her Swedish ancestors.

But she would let her hair grow out again. After Landry was caught, after the trial—when it was safe to go back to her life, she told herself, trying hard to believe she could ever reclaim it.

Glancing around the apartment, she decided the first item of business would be to make this place more her own. What little furniture there was had been shoved against each wall.

She grabbed the end of the couch and pulled it away from the wall and saw at once why it had been pushed against the wall as it had been.

There was a sizable hole in the wall behind it.

On closer inspection, she saw that the hole—four

inches wide, a good foot high and seemingly endless
in depth—had been chipped into the adobe wall. She
couldn't tell how deep it ran. Not without a flashlight.

As she straightened she noticed a scrap of paper on
the floor near the hole. She picked it up and saw that it
was a piece of a torn photograph. The piece appeared to
be part of a face covered with something like a gauzy
veil or a film of some kind.

She peered into the hole and thought she saw another
piece of the torn photograph. How odd.

Vaulting over the couch she dug in her purse for the
penlight on her key ring. In the kitchen she found a butter knife and returned to behind the couch.

Shining the tiny light into the hole, she began to dig
out the pieces of the photo with the butter knife. She
still couldn't tell how deep the hole was—obviously too
deep for her dim light. But there were more pieces of
the photograph in there, as if they'd fallen down from
the floor above.

Diligently she worked the pieces out until she
couldn't reach any more.

Just as she was starting to collect the scraps, a sliver
of light sliced down through the top of the hole. Willa
angled her gaze upward into the opening and saw light
coming through what appeared to be a crack in floorboards upstairs.

She'd thought no one lived directly above her. She
heard the creak of footsteps on the floor overhead. The
light went out. She listened, but heard nothing more.

Taking the pieces of the photograph over to the small
kitchen table, she pulled up a chair and began to fit the
pieces together like a puzzle, curious after seeing the
veiled face in the first piece.

The graphic artist who'd mentioned Cape Diablo had also been an avid photographer. Was it possible this was one of her photos? Or maybe that she'd even stayed in this very room?

The photograph began to take shape. Several of the edge pieces were missing but she was starting to see an image. What was it she was looking at?

She laid down the last piece and felt a jolt. It was a photo of the pool in the courtyard, the water murky and dark.

Funny, but the face that had spurred her curiosity enough to put the photograph back together in the first place seemed to have disappeared.

That was strange.

Carefully she turned the pieces of the photograph a hundred and eighty degrees and gasped.

A boy of about four was lying on the bottom of the pool in the deep end, the dark water like a mask over his face. There was no doubt that the child was dead.

Chapter 5

Abruptly Willa shoved back her chair and stumbled to her feet. Odell had said Andres Santiago's only son had died here. Drowned in the pool? But that had been more than thirty years ago.

Her hands were shaking. How long had this photo been in the wall? If the shot had been taken by her friend, then it would have been just weeks ago.

Suddenly scared, Willa looked at the photograph again.

The body on the bottom of the pool was gone. So was the little boy's terrified face.

She stared down at the photograph. Had she just imagined seeing the little boy? Could it have been a trick of the light? Or just her imagination after the terrible story Odell had told her?

She glanced toward the hole in the wall. But if it had

just been a photograph of the murky pool, then why had someone torn the photograph into tiny pieces then hidden them in the wall?

Unable to suppress a shudder, Willa thought of the woman on the third floor and the light that had bled down from overhead as the woman moved around up there. Alma Garcia. She'd been the child's nanny, Willa thought as her stomach knotted. Had she been caring for the little boy the day he drowned?

Willa glanced again at the photo, telling herself it was just a photograph of the pool. Nothing more.

Shivering from a nonexistent cold breeze that seemed to have crept into the room, Willa scooped up the pieces of photograph and dumped them into the trash can. She couldn't keep seeing death everywhere she looked.

The curtains billowed in at the window, startling her. The tropical breeze was warm. The chill gone from the room again.

She stepped to the window, surprised how quickly it had gotten dark. Through the palms, she could see the lights of a boat far out on the dark horizon. Below her, shadows moved restlessly across the courtyard. She could smell salt in the air coming in from the Gulf, hear the breeze rustling the palm fronds.

The music had stopped. She realized the voices she'd heard were coming from the other side of the villa behind her. Moving to the back of her small apartment, she opened the window as quietly as possible.

Two people were talking beneath the window in a low murmur. She couldn't make out their words. As her eyes adjusted to the darkness she could however make out two figures in the shadow of the house.

As they moved, Willa saw that one was wearing an

old-fashioned white gown like she'd seen the nanny wearing earlier while dancing. The other figure was that of a man. He too was older, his voice sounding gravelly.

He appeared to be trying to persuade the woman to go with him somewhere. After a moment they parted, the woman slipping through an archway back into the villa. The elderly man faded into the darkness and vegetation of the island as if he'd never existed.

The man must have been Carlos Lazarro, she realized who, according to Odell, lived in the old boathouse.

Willa closed the window and started to close the blinds as well, when something caught her eye. Movement. The old man? Had he come back? She watched someone moving through the vegetation, but it was too dark to make out who it was. Not the old man. The person moved too easily. Almost catlike, making little sound, the movement fluid and hinting of power. Whoever it was headed for the back of the villa.

Landry Jones.

Willa shook off the thought. Landry couldn't have found her. It had to be Odell. She moved to the door, unlocked it and stepped out onto the long balcony over the courtyard. Below her, the pool was cloudy and bottomless. She stared down into it, seeing nothing and glad of it.

As she glanced across the courtyard toward Odell's apartment, she saw that a single light shone through the cracks between the blinds in what she assumed was his living room. The window was open. She listened for the clack of an old manual typewriter, but there was no sound coming from his apartment.

But behind the house she could hear the purr of a motor. The generator that supplied the electricity. They'd had a generator on the farm for when bad weather took out their power lines. She knew the sound well growing up on the South Dakota prairie.

She moved away from her open apartment door, sneaking as quietly as possible along the balcony to the back wall of the villa to gaze out through the thick foliage in the direction where she'd seen the person going. No one. Could it have been an animal? Whatever it had been it certainly moved like one.

Another rhythmic sound drew her attention. She moved along the back of the second-story walkway away from her apartment. Through the trees she spotted a figure bent over digging a hole in the ground. The sound of the steady scrape of a shovel blade through the soil drifted on the night breeze.

As the figure straightened, she saw that it was Odell. Of course that was who she'd seen from the window, she thought with a wave of relief. He turned up another shovelful of dirt, stopped and looked back toward the villa as if he'd heard something. Or sensed her watching him.

She melted back into the dark shadows along the wall, hoping he hadn't seen her spying on him. What could he be digging up? Or was he burying something?

He resumed his digging but she stayed hidden, afraid he would look over his shoulder again and see her. The shoveling stopped, then resumed again.

She took a peek. He seemed to be covering up the hole now. She watched as he patted down the disturbed ground then covered it with several palm fronds.

As he started toward the villa, she flattened herself against the wall, not daring to move. She feared he would see her even in the dark shadows because of the light-colored nightshirt she wore. But he didn't look up in her direction. He seemed intent on hurrying back to his apartment.

She watched him come through an archway almost hidden by vegetation and keep to the shadows, not making a sound as he entered his apartment. He no longer had the shovel. Nor was he carrying anything she could see.

Willa stood there until he'd closed his apartment door. Another light came on deeper in the apartment, then went out. What was all that about?

Did she even want to know? For just an instant, she thought about sneaking down there and finding out. Wouldn't she sleep better if she did?

Yeah, right.

She shivered as she made her way back to her open apartment door. Slipping inside, she locked the door behind her.

Whatever it was Odell had dug up or buried, it was none of her business. Though it was odd. And even a little chilling.

As she padded barefoot toward her bedroom she caught an unfamiliar scent in the air and slowed. Perfume? It smelled like…gardenias? Had someone been in her apartment? She'd foolishly left the door wide open and hadn't been paying any attention during the time she'd been watching Odell.

Deeper into the apartment, the scent grew stronger then faded all together as if she'd only imagined it. Like she'd imagined the little boy's face in the photo?

She stopped in the middle of her bedroom. Her pulse jumped, her heart leaping to her throat. Someone had been in her apartment. She hadn't imagined the scent of gardenias and what she saw—or in this case didn't see.

Her easel stood empty.

The painting she'd done of Landry Jones and the murder was gone.

Trembling, Willa removed the shade from the lamp on the table next to the bed and hefting the base, quickly searched the small apartment to make sure the thief wasn't still there.

The apartment was small with few places to hide. Once she'd checked the bathroom and the closet and under the bed, that didn't leave much of a hiding place.

But still she moved the couch out away from the wall to look behind it, feeling foolish. Why would someone be hiding in the apartment after taking the painting? But why would anyone come into her apartment and take an unfinished painting to begin with?

Once she was sure there was no one lurking in the apartment, she put the lamp back beside her bed, the shade on again and turned on all the lights.

Her stomach felt queasy and she remembered the sandwich Odell had given her. The supply boat wouldn't be coming until tomorrow morning with her groceries.

She had bought a box of granola bars before she'd met Gator at the dock and several bottles of water. She took the water from her large purse, opened one and put the other in the fridge. Too antsy to sit, she ate the sandwich and one of the bars standing up.

She felt a bit better but still nervous as she listened to the sounds of the night and the creaks and groans of the old villa and thought of the story about the Santiago family. Overhead, she heard footfalls on the floor as if someone was creeping around up there, then silence.

On impulse, she checked the hole behind the couch. No light shone from the floor above. She slid the couch back, double-checked the door to make sure it was locked, then made sure all the windows were closed and locked before hooking a chair under the doorknob as an extra precaution before going to bed.

As exhausted as she was, she thought sleep would elude her, especially given that someone had taken the disturbing painting she'd planned to paint over in the morning. Who? And why? Alma Garcia? The same person who'd cut the tape on the painting supply box while it was on the dock? Maybe the poor old soul had a problem with taking things. Willa would have to keep her door locked. And keep an eye on the old woman.

And Odell. What had he buried? Or dug up? She knew she would have to find out. She thought about going out there now but suddenly she couldn't keep her eyes open. Sleep dragged her down as if she'd been drugged.

She tried to fight it, suddenly afraid that Odell had put something in the sandwich. She felt as if she were underwater desperately trying to swim to the surface. She thought she heard a sound at her door then someone calling her name but then she went under and there was nothing but blackness.

In the dream the water was dark. She stood on the edge of the pool. There was something just below the surface. She could almost make out what it was. She leaned closer.

A face began to take shape. The face of a little boy like the one she'd seen in the photograph except the boy seemed to be fighting to save himself, as if he was being held under. There was terror in his eyes and he was gasping.

Suddenly the child's face floated to the surface. Not the face of a little boy but the bloated, distended face of a monster, the decomposed skin slipping off, the face literally dissolving before her eyes.

Willa screamed and lurched backward but the child's hand came out of the fetid water and grabbed her wrist, pulling her toward the pool as if to drag her to the bottom with him.

Frantically she fought to free herself but the grip on her wrist was like a steel band. She screamed again as she was dragged to the lip of the pool, what was left of the child's face grinning grotesquely up at her.

"Hey! It's me!"

Suddenly her eyes flew open and she fell backward. Odell grabbed her and pulled her back from the edge of the pool. She struck out at him, still deep in the nightmare.

"Hey, what's wrong with you?"

He held her at arm's length until her eyes focused on him, then he let go. She stumbled back from him, confused and shaking with terror.

"Are you all right?"

She blinked and looked around, memory of where she was slowly coming back to her. "How did I get down here?"

He shook his head. "Oh, man, were you sleepwalking?"

Her gaze flickered over the moonlit courtyard. Still in the grip of the dream, she stared at the dark water of the pool, until she finally pulled her gaze away and looked at Odell. He was wearing only pajama bottoms, his chest and feet bare, hair mussed as if he'd just woken up.

"I heard a scream and I came running out...." He was staring at her, looking almost as scared of her as she was of him. "That was really creepy. I've never seen anyone sleepwalking before. You were looking right at me and yet you didn't seem to be seeing me at all. If I hadn't grabbed you, you looked like you were going to fall into the deep end of the pool."

She tried to make sense of what he was saying. "It was only a dream?"

He chuckled, looking relieved that she was no longer freaking. "More like a nightmare from the way you were screaming."

It had been so *real*. She shot a glance toward the stagnant water of the pool again and shuddered, hugging her bare arms. She glanced down and saw that her feet were bare and realized she was wearing only her nightshirt. Although it covered her from her shoulders to her knees, she felt half-naked in the hot humid night air with this man.

She remembered the sandwich and the feeling that she'd been drugged. Was it possible he'd put something in the sandwich to make her hallucinate? But why would he do that? If he'd been sent here to kill her, why not just drown her in the pool, get it over with? Why save her?

"Are you sure you're all right?" Odell asked.

She nodded, realizing that the last time she'd gotten even a little close to a stranger had colored her thinking. She used to be so trusting. But Landry Jones had changed all that.

Thoughts of what could have happened if she'd gotten into the car with Landry that night skittered past.

Another shudder ran through her as she stepped farther away from Odell.

"If you're all right, I'm going back to bed," he said, seeing her move away from him. He seemed irritated. After all, according to him, he'd just saved her.

She nodded and stumbled backward to the stairs, groping with one hand behind her as if blind, even though an almost full moon and a canopy of stars now lit the courtyard.

Odell said nothing, just watched her until she disappeared up the steps and through the open door of her apartment. She closed the door, locked it and moved to the window to peer through the blinds down on the courtyard and the pool. Had it really only been a nightmare?

Odell was still standing by the pool looking up at her apartment.

She retreated from the window, letting the blind fall back into place. She couldn't quit shaking. She hadn't walked in her sleep since she was a child.

Shuddering again at the memory of the child's face in the water, she hurried to turn on a lamp, sending the darkness skittering back to the far corners of the apartment. But no light could take away the chill the nightmare had left behind. Or rid her of the feeling that it hadn't been a dream at all.

The hand coming out of the pool had been Andres Santiago's dead son grabbing her—

Almost as if still asleep, she slowly looked down at her left wrist, not realizing until that moment that she'd been rubbing it.

A stifled cry escaped her lips. The skin was chafed red where something—someone—had grabbed her wrist, the skin already starting to bruise.

Chapter 6

Willa woke to the sound of a boat motor. She bolted upright in bed, momentarily confused. All the lights were on in her apartment and she realized she'd left them on all night. She was on top of the covers where she must have lain once she'd returned to her apartment last night.

Her memory was fuzzy. Had she dreamt all of it, including waking up by the pool? She looked down at her wrist, shocked again to see distinct bruises in the shape of fingertips. And calluses on her palms from shoveling.

She groaned. Some of it had definitely been real.

Last night she knew she wouldn't be able to get back to sleep until she found out if Odell had buried something behind the villa.

She'd waited until his lights went out, and then giving another thirty minutes to make sure everything was quiet in the villa, she dressed and sneaked down.

As she passed the pool, she hadn't dared look into the water as if it might cast a spell on her. Or even worse, that she might see the little boy and he might reach for her again as he'd done in the nightmare.

Past the pool, she'd slipped through the arch, just as Odell had done earlier. The moon had sent silver shafts of light down through the palms and dense vegetation close to the villa. Just as she'd suspected, Odell had left the shovel just outside the courtyard leaning against the wall.

Silently she took it and gazed into the darkness under the trees for the spot where she'd seen him digging. It was harder to find from this angle. But she was good with directions. It went with being raised in South Dakota. A person could get lost on the prairie with no trees or even a knoll to use as a marker.

A few yards from the villa, the darkness settled over her like a shroud. She stumbled to the spot and turned to look back at the villa.

No lights shone. Moonlight played along the edge of the back wall. She saw no dark figure watching her, heard nothing as she turned back to the spot and removed the palm fronds Odell had used to cover it.

The earth had obviously been turned here. She was more than having second thoughts as she took the shovel in her hands and began to dig. While she'd brought the penlight, she didn't want to use it unless she absolutely had to, fearing that the light might be seen from the villa. The last thing she needed was an audience for what she suspected would be one of her more foolish acts.

She tried to imagine what her friends back in South Dakota would say if they could see her now. Worse, her mother. Better to think about that instead of what she might be digging up.

The blade struck something, making a ringing sound that seemed too loud. Everyone back at the villa had to have heard. Worse, she started to imagine all kinds of things buried down there. She shuddered and carefully turned over another shovelful then another.

Something glittered in the dim light. She put down the shovel and, taking a chance, turned on the penlight and shone it down into the hole, her nerves on end.

What the heck? She bent closer. It appeared to be a pint jar full of something. She cringed, not wanting to pick it up and yet how could she not? As if she could just cover it back up now...

Gingerly she bent down and cautiously picked up the jar wondering why Odell would have gone to the trouble to bury it. In the glow of the penlight, she could now see that it was a small mayonnaise jar and it was full of nails and tacks, all swimming in a yellowish liquid. Talk about odd.

She tilted the jar, the contents rattling softly. This made no sense. Putting down the penlight, she tried the lid. It unscrewed easily. Bracing herself, she took a whiff and recoiled at the smell. It couldn't be! But she knew it was. The color. The smell.

She quickly screwed the lid back on and returned the jar to the hole. It didn't take long to rebury it. She tamped down the earth and then covered the spot with the palm fronds. Carrying the shovel, she walked back to the villa, watching to make sure no one had seen her. She felt like a fool.

After leaning the shovel against the wall where she'd found it, she returned to her apartment, washed her hands and changed back into her nightgown.

It wasn't until she climbed back into bed that she let herself think about what she'd discovered. Odell had filled a jar with sharp objects and urinated on them, then sealed up the jar and buried it outside the villa.

It was a talisman. Willa knew because of an old woman who lived down the road from her family's former farm when she was a kid. The woman lived alone and some people said she was a witch. She was always brewing up herbs and poultices. The one time Willa had been in the woman's house she'd seen books about spells and hexes—and ways to protect yourself against evil. One required burying a jar filled with sharp objects and urine in the backyard to keep you safe from anything—or anyone who might want to hurt you.

What did Odell Grady need to protect himself against? The evil of the house? Or the evil he was about to do?

Willa's head ached. She couldn't be sure if it was from a fitful night of sleep or being drugged. She'd been a fool to eat the sandwich, knowing that Odell Grady might be a hired killer who'd been sent to make sure she never testified against Landry Jones.

But would Landry Jones send someone to kill her? Or would he come himself?

The thought sent a shudder through her as she quickly dressed to meet the supply boat, reminding herself that if Odell was a hired killer, he certainly hadn't acted like one last night.

He could have drowned her. Or poisoned her. He had done neither. In fact, if he was telling the truth, he'd saved her from the pool. Wasn't it possible that she really had been walking in her sleep, dreaming about that torn-up photograph, thinking she saw a body at the bottom of the pool?

But that didn't explain why he'd buried a talisman against evil behind the villa. Hadn't Gator said people came to Cape Diablo because they were running from something? Maybe someone was after Odell Grady.

The sound of the boat motor grew louder. Hurriedly she opened her door on the beautiful Florida sunny day and took a deep breath of the salty air. On impulse, she decided to get rid of the trash on her way. She didn't want that stupid photograph in her apartment. The last thing she needed was another nightmare like last night.

But as she picked up the small trash basket, she saw with a start that it was empty. Had she taken it out last night?

Not that she remembered.

She glanced toward her empty easel. Had the scraps of photograph gone the way of the missing painting?

The boat motor grew even louder. She put down the trash basket, not even wanting to contemplate why whoever had taken her painting would have also taken the scraps of a photo of nothing more than a murky pool.

As she rushed down to the dock, the supply boat came into view. She was half hoping it was Gator. But as the boat came closer, she saw that the driver was a stranger and he wasn't alone. There were two others in the boat with him, both women. Visitors? Or new tenants?

"Good morning." Odell came up behind her, keeping a little distance between them as if wary of her after last night.

"Mornin'," she said, embarrassed. If he was telling the truth, he'd saved her from possibly drowning in that gross pool last night and she hadn't even thanked him. In fact, she'd been rude to him. "About last night... thanks."

"No problem."

At the memory she looked down at her wrist and saw the bruises where fingers had pressed into her flesh.

"Oh no. I hurt you," Odell said, sounding horrified as he grabbed her hand and turned her hand palm up to look at the bruises on her wrist. He grimaced. "I'm sorry. You were just pulling so hard. I couldn't let go and let you fall into that pool. In the state you were in I was afraid you would have drowned or at least died of something after being in that putrid water."

She had to smile. "I appreciate you not letting that happen." But the suspicious part of her mind still wondered if he was telling the truth.

"I'm just glad you were there," she said, reverting to the manners she'd been taught. "Thank you. I was so upset last night. I'm sorry if I seemed ungrateful."

He smiled. "I'm glad I could be of help. It must have been some nightmare."

She nodded.

Odell looked past her, his expression brightening. "Wow."

Just then the supply boat banged into the dock. Odell righted her as the dock rocked, then grabbed the bow of the boat to steady it. "Good morning," he said with much more enthusiasm than he'd shown her.

The greeting, she saw wasn't for the supply boat driver, who must be Bull. He was a younger version of Gator, although just as weather-beaten and no more friendly.

No, what had brightened Odell was the tall red-headed woman in short shorts and an even snugger red halter top. Thirty-something, the redhead could have been a model. The other passenger in the boat was apparently a teenager. The girl had the sullen Goth look going: her eyes rimmed with black, her nose, eyebrow and lower lip pierced, along with her ears, and her dyed black hair stringy and in her eyes. She wore black jeans and a black crocheted top that revealed a lot of sunless white skin and a black bra.

Willa's first thought was that the girl must be roasting in this heat dressed like that. She had a bored, annoyed expression as she ignored Odell's offer of a hand out and agilely stepped to the dock.

"You have got to be kidding," the teenager said as she looked toward the villa with disdain.

Meanwhile, the redhead smiled up at Odell as she took his hand and awkwardly stepped from the boat. The redhead stumbled into Odell. He caught her, his arms coming around her waist to steady her.

Willa rolled her eyes. The woman couldn't have been more obvious if she tried. And Odell... What a chivalrous guy, Willa thought, watching the little scene. First he'd rescued Willa last night. Or so he'd said. And now he was playing knight in armor to what appeared to be their new neighbor, if the three matching red suitcases were any indication.

The breeze picked up a few notes from an old classic song and Willa turned to glance back at the deteriorated Spanish villa. On the third floor, the elderly woman of their items from the dock and leave. Willa waited as she saw Goth Girl coming back down. The girl looked surlier than before, if that was possible.

"Hi, I'm Willie," Willa said, catching herself before she blurted out her real name. She held out her hand.

The girl just stared at it, but mumbled the word "Blossom." Goth Girl had one of those young faces that made it hard to gauge her age. The eyes had an old look, as if the girl had seen way too much during her short lifetime, Willa thought. Willa's heart went out to her. She knew firsthand what it was like to age almost overnight after witnessing something horrendous.

"Blossom. That's a unique name," Willa said, trying to be friendly and at the same time wondering what the girl was doing here. Blossom obviously wasn't pleased to be here.

"Blossom is my stage name," she said with a roll of her eyes. "Don't tell me you've never heard of me."

Willa wouldn't dare. She understood stage names. Like Cara was hers.

"You've never heard of me," Blossom accused with obvious contempt. "I've only like done a ton of films, plays and commercials. Are you one of those freaks who doesn't watch TV?"

"I've been too busy to watch much TV," Willa said, deciding befriending this girl had been a mistake. "So what brings you to Cape Diablo?"

Blossom made a face. "My agent, the bitch. She thinks I need a break. She just can't stand the idea of me having any fun. I'm just supposed to make money for her and my parents. They're in on it, too, the para-s. They all think my friends are dragging me down."

girl looked even younger as tears welled in her

looked out, then the curtain fall back into place. Willa would bet the woman smelled of gardenias.

"Odell Grady," she heard Mr. Chivalrous say to the redhead. "Welcome to Cape Diablo."

The woman gave him a demure nod as she stepped out of his arms, but not far. "Henrietta LaFrance, but my friends all call me Henri." She favored Willa with a glance.

"This is Cara," Odell said. "Or do you prefer Willie?"

Henrietta cocked her head. "You look more like a Willie not a Cara."

So she'd heard. "Willie is fine." She knew she would never remember to answer to Cara anyway and now wished she hadn't mentioned the other name.

Odell hurried to tie up the boat and help unload all of the supplies, including the three large red suitcases and two large army-green duffel bags that apparently belonged to Goth Girl.

Mother and daughter? Henri didn't look like the mother type. Nor had Willa seen the two women ex-change even a look, let alone a word. So did this mean that they had come out to rent the remaining two apart-ments?

It seemed odd that when Willa had called, all the apartments had been vacant and now were rented. Maybe that was normal. Still, it made her a little anx-ious. At least the two new renters were women, though Willa couldn't imagine what had brought either of them to Cape Diablo. Henri looked like a woman who would have been happier at Club Med. And Goth Girl didn't look like she'd be happy anywhere.

"I'll get that," Odell said when Willa reached for the box of supplies with her apartment number on it.

"I've got it." She softened her words. "Thanks, but it's not heavy. Anyway, Henrietta needs your help more than I do."

"Henri," the redhead corrected. "Thanks," she said as Odell attempted to carry all three of her heavy suitcases. Henri took the smaller one from him and they started toward the villa.

Goth Girl made a face at their backs, slung a duffel bag strap over each shoulder and followed at a distance.

Bull was watching Henri walk away. He hadn't said a word but what he was thinking was all too evident in his expression, especially the slack jaw.

"Is this customary?" she asked him.

He looked up at her as if seeing her for the first time. "What?"

"This many tenants."

He frowned. "People come and go. Right now they're all coming. Don't understand the attraction, though," he said, glancing toward the old villa. "That one won't stay long," he said, no doubt meaning the redhead. "Few do. Nothing to do here even if the place wasn't cursed."

"Cursed?" she asked, curious if he would tell her something different from what Odell had.

He didn't bother to look at her. "You really don't know? Ask Odell. He's writing a book about the place."

She frowned. That might explain then why he knew so much about Cape Diablo and the Santiago family.

Willa forced Bull to redirect his attention for a few minutes as she paid for her supplies and placed her order for the next week.

"How was your first night on the island?" Bull asked, shading his eyes to study her.

"Fine," she said a little too quickly.

He chuckled and pocketed her money and ⟨⟩ for next week's supplies. "I guess those dark ⟨⟩ under your eyes could be from staying up all night, Odell." He chuckled at his own joke. "He doesn't s⟨⟩ your type, though."

What did that mean?

Odell and Henri were headed back to the dock f⟨⟩ the rest of the load.

"See you next week then." Bull seemed to hesitate. "I guess Gator told you that if anything happens that you decide you don't want to stay here, you can get Carlos, you know the old fisherman who lives in the boathouse, to take you to the mainland if you are in trouble. He's okay."

She wanted to ask him more, like what kind of "trouble" he might be referring to, and if Carlos was "okay," was Odell not? But Henri and Odell had returned to pick up the supply boxes. "Thanks" was all she said to Bull. At least there was a way off the island in a hurry if she needed it. And for some reason, both Bull and Gator seemed to think she might need it.

Feeling uneasy, she watched Bull take off in the b⟨⟩ Both men seemed worried about her—and neither ⟨⟩ knew just how much trouble she was in. Within se⟨⟩ the boat disappeared into the line of green mar⟨⟩ islands and was gone.

Henri and Odell came back down to the doc⟨⟩ with the rest of the supply boxes. Both were ta⟨⟩ they were old friends. Maybe they were, Wi⟨⟩ Maybe nothing was as it seemed. Was Od⟨⟩ book about Cape Diablo and what had ha⟨⟩ If so, why didn't he just say so? She wat⟨⟩ Odell, both lost in conversation, pick u⟨⟩

eyes. "A week. I have to spend a frigging week here. It's blackmail. I should have them arrested. I can't wait until I'm old enough to dump them all."

Still feeling the effects of the headache she'd awakened with, Willa couldn't think of a thing to say as the girl spun around, picked up her supply box and headed for the villa.

After a moment, Willa picked up her own supply box from the dock again and followed. Avoiding the sour girl wouldn't be difficult and now that Odell had Henri to talk to, Willa wouldn't have anyone to bother her. She hurried back to her apartment, anxious to have some breakfast and start painting.

As she climbed the stairs, she could hear Henri's and Odell's voices in the apartment below her but couldn't make out the words. Blossom disappeared into a small apartment at the end under Willa's bedroom. Willa realized there were two small studios under her larger apartment. She'd been lucky to get the rental, it appeared.

After unpacking her food supplies, she made herself breakfast and went right to work painting. It surprised her sometimes how the paintings came to her. She worked furiously, caught up in the process, hardly paying any attention to what began to appear on the canvas.

She wasn't sure how much time had passed when she heard voices in the courtyard. She stepped back from the easel to stare at what she'd painted. The villa, the walls cloaked in what appeared to be a bright red spray of bougainvillea. She stared at the painting, disturbed by the feeling it gave her.

Leaving the painting and the uneasy feeling it gave her, her thoughts returned to what Bull had said about

Cape Diablo being cursed—and Odell writing a book about it. Unconsciously she massaged the bruises on her wrist.

She could still hear Odell downstairs with Henri. Glancing out the window, she saw that he'd left his door open. She could see a small desk with a typewriter right by the door. This might be her only chance.

Shocked by what she was about to do, Willa slipped out of her apartment and sneaked down the stairs and across the courtyard. She didn't look into the depths of the pool as she passed it. Nor did she turn to glance back until she reached the pool house and Odell's apartment.

The blinds in Henri's apartment were drawn. Willa could hear Henri laughing, as if she found Odell highly amusing. Which made Willa suspicious. But then she was suspicious of everyone, wasn't she?

Taking another quick look back at Henri's apartment to make sure no one had come out or was watching through the blinds, Willa stepped through Odell's open doorway.

It took a moment for her eyes to adjust in the cool darkness inside the apartment. She moved to the desk. Next to the old-fashioned manual typewriter was a ream of white paper that had yet to be opened. On the other side was a stack of newspapers.

Her heart jumped as she saw the newspapers. Some were yellowed with age and felt brittle in her fingers. She read the headline on the top one. Entire Family Disappears From Cape Diablo.

So Bull had been right apparently.

As she set the newspaper gingerly back down, she saw a more recent headline on a paper below it.

All breath rushed from her. She lifted the older newspaper and pulled out the more recent one and gasped.

Next to the headline, Key Witness Missing In Murder Of Undercover Cop: Hunt On Following Safe House Attack, was her photo.

Chapter 7

Willa grabbed the edge of the desk, her knees going weak as she stared at the photograph of her escaping the safe house. How had anyone gotten this? But she knew. It had to have been taken from one of the media helicopters.

She remembered one of the officers guarding her had called for backup just a few seconds after the safe house was attacked. The media must have picked up the call on the scanner.

She stared at the photo, her heart sinking. Vaguely she recalled looking up and seeing a helicopter overhead as she was running away. She'd thought it was the police and had kept running, acutely aware that the police couldn't protect her from the likes of Landry Jones or the men he worked for.

The shot of her had been blown up, the picture grainy,

but even with her hair no longer long and straight and blond, she had no trouble recognizing herself.

Had Odell recognized her?

She tried not to panic. On impulse she took the section with her photo and the story about Zeke Hartung's murder, quickly folded it and stuffed it under the waistband of her shorts, covering it with her shirt.

The rest of the paper she would leave. She started to slide it back into the spot where she'd found it then noticed there was a laptop computer under his desk. Was the old manual typewriter just for show?

"You a news junkie, too?" Odell asked from his apartment doorway.

She jumped and spun around to face him, the newspaper still in her hands, her mind racing for an explanation for being in his apartment.

"The door was open," she managed to say. She'd left it open on purpose so she would hear him coming. But she'd been so upset and busy trying to get the newspaper back in the right place that she *hadn't* heard him. How long had he been standing there watching her? Had he seen her take the front page and hide it under her shirt?

"I can do without a lot but not the news," Odell said, leaning against the doorjamb watching her. "I have to know what's happening back on the mainland. You're welcome to read that paper if you'd like. I'm finished with it."

She looked down at the newspaper in her hand and said the first thing that came to mind. "I was just checking my horoscope."

He smiled. "You do that, too? It's silly but I can't help myself. When I spill salt, I have to toss some of it over my left shoulder." He smiled. "I even knock on wood. Silly, huh?"

"No. We all have our own superstitions," she said, remembering what he'd buried behind the villa. "If you don't mind, I will take the newspaper. Might as well read 'Dear Abby' while I'm at it."

He wasn't looking at her but at his typewriter now. She hadn't noticed that there was a sheet of white paper sticking out of it. When she'd seen the ream of unopened paper she'd assumed he hadn't been writing yet.

She could almost read what he'd typed—

He stepped to her, blocking her view of the typewriter. "I'm glad you were just after the newspaper and not trying to read what I'd written on my book." His smile didn't seem to reach his eyes now.

She smiled, hers even more strained. "Okay, you caught me. I was curious. Bull said you were writing a book on Cape Diablo."

Odell laughed. "I should have known he would blab. Okay, now you know. I'm fictionalizing it since no one knows what really happened, except maybe that old woman upstairs or her boyfriend, the Ancient Mariner, as I call him. But neither of them is talking. At least not to anyone but themselves," he added, and laughed at his own joke.

"I'm sure the book will be a bestseller."

"You think?" He seemed to relax a little.

She nodded, still smiling. She wanted to ask him what had him so scared that he was worried about evil curses. She wanted to go back to her apartment. She could feel the newspaper article under her shirt growing damp against her bare skin.

"Well, thanks for the newspaper," she said, holding

it against her chest. She started to step away and heard the crinkle of the newspaper article she'd hidden under her T-shirt.

"Hey," Odell said.

She froze.

"You'd better watch the sun as fair as your skin is," he said, eyeing her. "You look flushed and a little unsteady on your feet. The sun and heat on this island will do a fair-skinned girl like you right in."

Or something would, she thought.

"You're obviously not from Florida," he said. "Some place up north?"

She could feel him studying her. Had he seen the resemblance to the page one photo of her? She hadn't had time to read the story and see if it mentioned her name or that she was from South Dakota. No doubt the police had been forced to be forthcoming after two of their officers had been gunned down at the safe house and the media had photos.

"No, actually I was born and raised here," she lied. "I just avoid the sun."

"Probably a good idea," he agreed, sounding like he knew she was lying. "You must have gone to a good college. No Floridian accent like most of us. But some accent I haven't been able to place yet." He was no longer smiling.

"I think I'll lie down for a while." She started for the stairs, feeling his gaze drilling into her back as she hugged the newspaper to her stomach and practically ran to get away.

"If you're really interested in the book I'm working on, maybe we could get together and talk about the ghosts that haunt this island," he called after her.

"What ghosts?" Henri said, sticking her head out the open door of her apartment as Willa ran up the stairs.

"Cape Diablo ghosts," Odell said with a chuckle. "Has to be told over a good bottle of wine, though."

"I have the wine," Henri offered. "What do you say, Willie?"

Willa had reached her apartment, opened the door and was almost safely inside. Just not quick enough. She thought of several reasons to decline as she looked down and saw Odell watching her, waiting.

"That is unless Willie is too scared," he said, as if trying to make it sound as if he was joking. His gaze met hers.

"I'm not afraid of ghosts," she said, meeting his eyes.

Odell lifted a brow. "Great. Later I'll get the barbecue grill going. We'll make it a party."

"You got yourself a date," Henri said.

"Sounds great," Willa agreed, just to be agreeable. She would come up with an excuse later.

She closed her door, heard the music coming from the third floor again and shivered as she remembered her stolen artwork and the smell of gardenias. Odell might be right about one thing. The elderly woman living in the tower did appear to be in her own world. What had she done with the painting she'd taken? Probably put it up on a wall. At least no one would see it.

Pulling the newspaper from under her shirt, she dropped it and the rest of the paper on the table before glancing out the window. She caught a glimpse of Alma Garcia standing at her window overlooking the courtyard. Had she been listening to the conversation about ghosts? Apparently she had since she looked upset.

Willa followed the older woman's gaze. Alma seemed

to be glaring down not at Odell and Henri who were talking by the pool but at Blossom, who was partially hidden from view where she stood in the shade along the back wall of the villa.

The girl looked as if she was eavesdropping on Odell's and Henri's conversation. Blossom looked up. Her piercing gaze seemed to meet Willa's, almost daring her.

Willa dropped the blind back into place and picked up the newspaper article she'd taken from Odell's room and turned it over.

All the breath rushed out of her. Earlier she'd been so shocked to see her own photo in the paper that she hadn't even noticed a second story—and photograph.

This one was of a younger Landry Jones.

He was wearing a police uniform!

Dropping in a chair, her gaze flew to the headline. Undercover Officer Wanted For Murder Of Partner: Manhunt Continues For Killer Cop—And Only Witness.

Willa quickly read the newspaper articles. The story had been broken by the news media after discovering that the police were involved in an intense but secret manhunt for plainclothes detective Landry Jones of the St. Petersburg Police Department.

Jones was wanted for the murder of his partner, Zeke Hartung after an eyewitness saw Jones kill Hartung outside a St. Pete Beach art gallery.

The police commissioner refused to discuss rumors that the two had been working undercover at the time of the murder or had turned on each other after infiltrating a criminal organization.

An inside source not to be named by the paper said Landry Jones had been working for known crime boss

Freddy Delgado and had been hired for the contracted killings of Zeke Hartung and another undercover police officer, Simon Renton. Simon Renton's mutilated body had been found at a favorite organized-crime dumping site the day after Zeke Hartung's murder.

An inside news source said Renton's body had been identified by a tattoo on the torso because it had been impossible to get prints from the badly mutilated body.

Willa felt sick. No wonder the police had insisted on putting her in protective custody. Unfortunately they'd failed to tell her anything about Landry Jones. Or what he was involved in. Organized crime. Contract killings of two police officers.

She looked at Landry Jones's photo. The caption under it read Dirty Cop? Landry Jones Wanted For Questioning In The Brutal Murders Of Two Other Officers.

As she turned the page to finish the story, her gaze fell on a third photograph.

Willa gasped. It was the same man who'd come into her art studio the night before her gallery show.

The caption under the photograph read Undercover Cop Simon Renton Found Dead.

Willa was shaking so hard she had to put down the newspaper. Simon Renton was the man who had come into her studio the night she was finishing the last of the framing for her gallery show the next night. Now he was dead? Murdered? She shuddered. His body mutilated.

She dropped the newspaper. Simon and Landry were both cops, both working undercover on the same case. An icy chill wrapped around her neck. One man had come into her shop saying he needed a painting for his wife for their anniversary. The other had come to her gallery showing saying he was interested in the artist and her work.

Her pulse jumped. Both had lied. According to the story, Simon wasn't married. And a man like Landry wasn't interested in Willa's art—or her.

What had Simon Renton being doing in her shop that night? She shivered, remembering how he'd almost pushed his way in. He'd made her uncomfortable although she had the feeling he'd been trying to do just the opposite.

Something connected her with the two men. But she had no idea what. Both men had supposedly taken an interest in her artwork and now she was running for her life.

Not just from the police who were apparently doing their best to protect her, but from Landry Jones and organized criminals who it seemed might have a reason also to want her dead. It made no sense.

According to the paper, the safe house had been attacked by two known organized-crime hit men, the article said. Percy "TNT" Armando and Emilio "Worm" Racini. Both were being sought by the police after appearing on media cameras at the scene.

Was it possible that no one had seen Landry Jones but her? She'd just assumed he'd killed her two guards. If not, then what was he doing at the safe house?

Chasing her, she thought with a shudder. Making sure his buddies got the job done.

She had to get off the island. She didn't know where she'd go—just that she had to keep moving. She'd been a fool to think she could hide out—even here—for a few weeks until Landry was caught.

But she'd run out of highway. Out of luck, as well.

Landry could find her here. He was a cop, a renegade cop, but still he was trained for this. He had resources that ordinary people like herself didn't have. And he had organized crime behind him. She didn't stand a chance.

She wanted to curl up in a ball. Hastily she wiped at her tears. She didn't have the time to break down let alone feel sorry for herself. And giving up wasn't an option. She would go across the island to where Odell said the old man fished in his boat.

She'd ask him to take her back to the mainland. If he agreed, she'd come back and pack.

Now that her picture was in the paper, she wouldn't feel safe anywhere.

Just the thought of Landry Jones sent a chill through her. Look how close he'd come to getting to her at the safe house. She could still remember the murderous look in his eyes. She felt another wave of hopelessness. If she had any hope of surviving, she had to be strong. She'd stayed alive this long, hadn't she?

At the window, she peeked out. The courtyard was empty. Odell's door was closed. Willa let the blind fall back into place and opened her door, listening for a moment before she started down the stairs.

She heard music, this time coming from Blossom's apartment. Some awful loud band yelling obscenities over the scream of guitar strings.

Willa took the stairs, stopping partway to check to see if Henri's door was closed. It was.

Something told Willa that Henri wasn't in her apartment—not with that horrible music blasting into her south side wall.

As Willa hurried out of the courtyard through the back arch, she caught a glimpse of Henri and Odell walking down the beach. They had their heads together as if they'd known each other longer than less than an hour.

The conversation looked pretty serious for two strangers.

Willa put the two of them out of her mind. Soon they wouldn't be a concern. Soon, she would be off the island. She would go to Miami, maybe catch a boat to anywhere it was headed, anywhere far from here.

She found a narrow path through the thick vegetation, hoping this was the way that the elderly man had gone and that the path would lead her to the boathouse and Carlos Lazarro.

Not far into the dense undergrowth the air became thick and humid. Mosquitoes buzzed around her. She swatted at them and tried to keep moving, her bare limbs glistening with perspiration.

At a turn in the trail, she stopped to wipe the sweat from her eyes and thought she heard a sound behind her on the trail. Quickening her pace, she wound through the trees and brush, the island becoming denser. She felt turned around, no longer able to see the sun, and had no idea which way she was headed. For all she knew she could be going in a circle. The island wasn't large. She should have reached the other side by now.

Willa stopped to catch her breath. The trail forked ahead and she wasn't sure which way to go. This time there was no mistake about it. She heard the brush of fabric against a tree branch. Someone was following her.

Fear paralyzed her. She looked back but could see nothing through the underbrush. After reading the newspaper articles she now knew that it wasn't just the cops and Landry Jones after her—but possibly organized crime killers who didn't want her testifying.

She started down one path, afraid she was only getting farther and farther away from the villa—and more and more in danger. A twig cracked not far down the trail behind her.

A soft pop was instantly followed by leaves and bark flying up on a tree trunk next to her. Another soft pop, then a limb next to her exploded.

Someone was shooting at her!

Run!

She took off, running as fast and hard as she could, running blindly as the path twisted and turned. She could hear footfalls behind her, then another pop as a bullet buzzed past her ear and ripped through the leaves of a bush ahead of her.

She stumbled and just as she thought she might go down was grabbed from behind. An arm came around her, picking her up off her feet as a hand covered her mouth. She was jerked backward into the bushes and trees, her body slamming into the solid form of a man's chest as he tightened his grip.

"Don't make a sound or you're as good as dead." Her blood froze as she recognized the male voice that whispered at her ear as she was dragged backward into the darkness of the dense tropical forest.

Landry Jones.

Hadn't she known it was only a matter of time before he found her?

Chapter 8

Landry dragged a struggling Willa St. Clair deep into the trees. She tried to bite his hand, connected several good kicks to his shins and jabbed him in the ribs with her elbow. Pain rocketed through him as she hit too close to his bandaged gunshot wound.

Angrily he tightened his grip on her and pressed his lips close to her ear. "Do that again and I will kill you myself right here."

Keeping his hand firmly over her mouth, he dragged her a little deeper into the dense undergrowth and threw her down, pinning her to the ground as he sprawled on top of her and drew his gun with his free hand.

Her eyes blazed with anger and stark terror. Even against the odds and his threats, she still struggled to free herself. The woman was a scrapper. Under other circumstances he might have admired that.

He leaned close. "Quiet," he whispered, and pressed his body down over hers as he listened. He thought he heard someone moving along the path not far from them. He held his breath, knowing how vulnerable he was in this position. All he could hope was that whoever was on the path didn't spot them. He wasn't sure he could get in a shot before someone else did.

Minutes passed. Finally he heard footfalls retreat back down the path. He waited until he was sure the person was gone before he holstered his gun and pulled Willa St. Clair to her feet. Still keeping her mouth covered, he dragged her back through the trees.

On this side of the island, the surf from the Gulf broke over the rocky shoreline. It was loud enough, it would muffle any sounds that she made. He dragged her to a short stretch of sandy beach where he'd pulled up the borrowed boat he'd hidden in the brush.

Tossing his weapon onto the duffel bag lying in the bottom of his boat, he dragged her out into the water until they were waist-deep.

"Now listen to me," he said next to her ear. "I'm going to remove my hand from your mouth. You're going to be smart and not scream or fight me. And then we're going to talk. Got it?"

Her body was still rigid with stubborn determination. But she nodded and he removed his hand, knowing without a doubt what she would do.

She took a swing at him and opened her mouth to scream.

He ducked the swing, grabbed her and hurled her into the deeper water, forcing her head under before she could get out a sound. He held her there, his hand tangled in her short curly dark hair, until some of the fight went out of her, then he dragged her to the surface.

She came up spitting and sputtering, murder in her eyes.

"What part of that didn't you get?" he demanded as he dunked her under again.

She gulped for air as he brought her up choking on the saltwater, but at the same time glaring at him. He watched her eyes and saw what she planned to do before she tried to scratch his eyes out.

He shoved her head under water again, holding her down longer this time, half-afraid he'd drown her before she'd give up. He jerked her to the surface and felt some of the fight go out of her.

"Why don't you just kill me and get it over with," she cried, choking and coughing as she came up. "First you shoot at me, then try to drown me?"

He shook his head. "I hit what I shoot at. If I wanted you dead, you'd already be dead. I saved your puny butt back there on the trail."

She gave a chortle of disbelief.

"Look, sweetheart, I could have broken your neck back there off the trail," he said, getting angry. "Or I could drown you right now. I'm not trying to kill you. I'm just trying to get you to quit fighting me. The last thing I want is you dead."

Willa stared at him, hating him. He'd turned her life upside down. How had she ever thought he was hand-some? He was cruel and horrible. She glared at him, wanting to hit him but he held her at arm's length, his fingers tangled in her hair, and she knew if she tried, he would just dunk her again. Her eyes burned from the saltwater—and anger.

"If I let go of you, are you going to attack me again? Scream? Try to get away?"

She narrowed her eyes at him. "Would it do me any good?"

"None. All you'd accomplish is making sure whoever was shooting at you knows where we are and get us both killed."

He let go of her hair and stepped toward the beach, extending his hand as if to help her ashore.

She took a step back, the water up to her breasts now.

"Look, I'm not going to hurt you, okay?"

"Isn't that what all killers say? You probably told your partner that before you shot him."

A flicker of pain crossed Landry Jones's face and she thought for a moment he *would* drown her. He looked like he wanted to. Instead, he turned and waded through the water up to the beach. Stopping, he turned to look at her.

"See?" he said, holding out his hands. "And for the record, Zeke tried to kill *me*. It was self-defense."

She eyed him suspiciously. "If that were true, then why are the police looking for you?"

He sighed heavily. "It's my word against yours. All you saw was me shoot him. You obviously didn't see him try to kill me."

"Right. That's probably why the police didn't find a gun on him."

Landry made a low animal-like sound. "I saw you panic and take off. I came after you. Obviously someone took Zeke's gun to make me look guilty."

"Obviously."

He shook his head. "I don't care what you believe,

all right? Now come out of the water. I already told you I'm not going to hurt you."

A wave slapped her in the back, throwing her forward. She took a few steps toward him and stopped. He retreated even farther up the beach to give her space.

Don't trust this guy. Do not—repeat—trust this guy.

"You still think I was the one shooting at you back there?" He walked over to where he'd tossed his weapon before dragging her into the Gulf, picked it up and held the gun out for her to look at it. "You see a silencer on here?"

She stared at the revolver in his hand. No silencer. The person shooting at her on the path had a silencer on his gun. She felt her body go limp with the realization that more than one person on this island wanted her dead.

"You are smart enough to know the sound a gun makes without one, aren't you?" he asked sarcastically.

"How do I know you didn't take off the silencer before you grabbed me?"

He rolled his eyes. "Why would I do that?"

She didn't know. In fact, all she knew about this man was that she'd seen him shoot his partner, that apparently before that he'd been a police officer, and that he was now wanted by the law. The fact that she was the only witness to that shooting put her in a precarious position to say the least.

"I have no reason to trust anything you say."

He stared at her as if she'd just said something astounding, then he groaned, pulled off the cap he'd been wearing and raked a hand through his full head of dark hair. "What am I going to do with you?"

"I was wondering the same thing."

"Sweetheart, do you have any idea how many people want you dead? There are people waiting in *line* to kill you."

"Don't call me sweetheart," she snapped back.

"What I'm trying to tell you is that there is a massive manhunt going on for you right now."

She lifted a brow. "For you, as well, it seems."

He smiled. And for just an instant she forgot that she didn't find him handsome. "Point taken."

He reached into the shorts pocket, drew out a wet crumpled photograph and held it out. Reluctantly she stepped close and took it, recognizing the man in the picture at once.

"You remember him." It wasn't a question. He'd seen her reaction to Simon Renton's photograph. "He came into your art studio the night before your gallery showing. He left something there. I need it back."

So that was why she was still alive. He needed something from her. "And you think I have it?"

"I *know* you have it. Or at least can help me find it and end all of this."

And she had a pretty good idea just how it would end.

She glanced down the beach. The tide was coming in. The surf pounded at the rocks off to her left. To her right the short sandy beach ended in a throng of mangroves. Her only chance was getting past Landry and making a run for it back up the trail.

But even if she managed to get past him, she knew she wouldn't get far back in the brush and trees. And taking off swimming would be suicide even if he didn't come after her and drown her. Not to mention, the person who'd been shooting at her could be waiting in the trees.

"Look, I know what you're thinking," he said, his voice softening. "But you're out of places to run. There's already someone on the island taking potshots at you. It's just a matter of time before they kill you."

This, at least, sounded true. She said nothing, just looked at him, wondering what it was he thought she had and what possible chance she had of surviving this.

"You have a problem?" he asked.

She glared at him, realizing she was beyond caring right now if he shot her or drowned her or broke her neck. "Kind of the same one. I don't believe anything you tell me."

"You have quite the mouth on you, Ms. Willa St. Clair." He took a step toward her, backing her to the edge of the water, his gaze locked on her lips. "Quite a nice mouth, actually."

She felt herself squirm under the heat of those dark eyes. She was at his mercy, completely alone with a man she knew was a killer. But she also sensed that backing down would only make her more vulnerable—if that were possible. She stood her ground as he stepped so close that she could see tiny gold flecks in that dark gaze and feel heat radiating from his body.

"If you expect me to help you, then I suggest you stop threatening me," she said, surprised her voice could sound so calm with her pulse thundering in her ears. "All you're doing is convincing me you're exactly the man I think you are and certainly not one to be trusted."

His hand came up so quickly it took everything in her not to flinch. His fingertips were cool and rough as they trailed across her cheek to her lips. He dragged one finger over her lower lip, his gaze never leaving her eyes, then trailed it down her throat, stopping at her collarbone.

She held her breath and wondered just how far Landry Jones would go to get whatever it was he thought she had.

He drew back his fingertips and stepped away.

She let herself take a breath, her body trembling, suddenly more afraid than when he'd held her under water. There were worse things than death.

Landry was losing patience—with this woman—and with himself. He was used to getting what he wanted. Even Freddy D.'s men knew better than to push him too far.

For most of the past two years, he'd worked undercover, using intimidation like a weapon. Maybe he'd been undercover and around men like Freddy D. for too long.

But this woman was also exasperating as all hell. She was nothing like the mild-mannered Willa St. Clair he'd asked out for coffee the night of her art showing. Funny how just a few days could change a person. Or had all this steel been under all that sweet innocence?

Well, if she'd changed, he had only himself to blame for it. Seeing a man shot down in front of her had to have an effect. Especially on a woman like Willa St. Clair. He'd had a friend of his on the force do some checking on the artist. He suspected she was as squeaky-clean and green behind the ears as she seemed to be.

Or had been. Now she was on the run and desperate. He knew from experience that that alone could change a person.

He raked a hand through his hair and sighed. "Let

me lay it out for you. I infiltrated a crime organization operating out of southern Florida. After a while Zeke came in and then Simon." He looked past her to the gulf, his eyes dark. "We worked for a man named Freddy D."

"Freddy Delgado," she said.

He nodded, wondering if she knew more than he did at this point. Was it possible she'd already found the disk?

"We knew Freddy had a cop in his pocket," he continued, watching her face for any sign that she was way ahead of him. "My job was to find the dirty cop." He touched his tongue to his lower lip, eyes darkening. Her expression hadn't changed. "I had several leads on cops who Freddy was paying off to look the other way, but they were small potatoes. The guy I was looking for would have to be close to Freddy. Real close. As it turns out, real close to me, as well."

"You're telling me Zeke was the dirty cop." She didn't sound like she believed it for a minute. "But you said he came into the organization undercover *after* you."

He smiled. The woman was sharp. And she'd been paying attention. "Yeah, so now you understand why I was blindsided. I never suspected Zeke. Why would I?"

Her hair was wet. It curled around her lightly freckled face. Her eyes were wide and blue. She couldn't have looked more adorable—even with the straight blond hair she'd had the night he met her. It hit him that under other circumstances, he really would have asked her out that night after the art show. She had that much of an impact on him.

"Give me one good reason to believe anything you're

telling me is the truth," she said, those big blues narrowing.

He studied her for a moment, then lifted his shirt to show her the wound in his side. "When Zeke walked up to the car that night, I didn't see the gun in his hand until it was almost too late."

She flinched at the sight of his wound. "How do I know you didn't get shot when you attacked the safe house where the police were keeping me?"

He raised his hands slowly as if in surrender. "What is it going to take to get through to you? Isn't it possible I was trying to save you?"

Her gaze said, *Not a chance in hell.*

The gunshot wound had surprised her. She could see where he'd been shot. The area was red and angry, although clearly starting to heal. *Someone* had shot him. Was it possible Zeke's had been one of the shots she'd heard that night?

She thought of Simon Renton, remembering how he'd lied about wanting a painting for his anniversary, a painting his wife had picked out. She'd foolishly opened the door and let him in that night even though every instinct warned her not to.

"What did Simon leave in my studio?" she asked as she realized her only hope was to find out what was going on, what Landry Jones wanted from her.

He seemed to relax a little. "A disk. Simon put it between a painting and the backing." Landry's gaze softened. "You saved him and the disk that night."

"At what cost to my own life since he still died?" she said angrily. "And for what? Some stupid disk?" She shuddered. "Do you think it was worth it for him to be tortured to death? He still told them about the disk and the painting, didn't he?"

Landry looked away. "Simon knew what was at stake. We were all risking our lives to bring down an organization that steals, kills and pollutes all of our lives."

She said nothing, not sure what to believe. "What's on this disk?"

"If I told you that, I would have to kill you."

She looked at him, narrowing her eyes. "You think that's funny?"

"Actually, truthful. I'm serious, Willa. That's why I have to find that disk before Freddy D. and his men do."

It was the first time he'd called her Willa. She hated that he used her name in that soft tone of his and it had an effect on her.

"Aren't the police looking for it, too?" she asked, and saw the answer in his expression. "You want to find it before the police do, and you tell me you have nothing to hide?"

"It's complicated. The bottom line is that the disk is worth killing—or dying—for. You're going to help me find it. One way or the other."

"Back to threats? What will you do to me? Try to drown me again? Torture me? Beat me up?"

He groaned. "What do you want?"

"How about the truth? What's on the disk?"

"Important information about organized crime in southern Florida—names, numbers, enough to shut down these people."

She waited, staring at him.

He groaned again. "There's also proof on the disk that I didn't kill Zeke in cold blood. Proof that it was self-defense because the name of the dirty cop is on that disk. That disk will clear me."

"Or condemn you," she said.

He smiled and settled his gaze on her. "Either way, I need the disk. I'm asking you to trust me and help me find it."

Trust him? How could she, given what she knew? "How do I know that once you have the disk you won't kill me?" She couldn't suppress a grimace.

He raised a brow. "You don't. But without me, sweetheart, you're dead. Someone on this island obviously knows who you are and has been paid to come here and kill you." He smiled. "You left a trail anyone could follow. You think they're going to let you off this island alive without my help?"

He had a point. He'd found her and obviously someone else had. Unless, of course, he was the one who'd shot at her. But would he take such a chance when he needed her alive to help him find the disk?

The alternative was that he was right. Someone on the island wanted her dead. Other than Landry Jones.

"We need each other," he said.

"At least until you find the disk."

He shook his head in obvious frustration. "You want to get off this island alive? Help me and I'll help you. Maybe by the time we find the disk, you'll realize you can trust me."

Maybe. But she doubted it. Even if Landry Jones wasn't a murderer, he was dangerous. Especially to a small-town girl from South Dakota.

She looked toward the trail and again thought about trying to make a break for it. If she could reach Carlos, get him to take her to the mainland…

As she started past Landry, he grabbed her wrist so quickly she hadn't even seen the movement. His fingers clamped down. "Don't underestimate me, though. That would be a mistake."

She winced in pain and he loosened his grip, turning her hand over and opening his fingers. He frowned down at the bruises on her wrist.

"Who did this?" he asked, sounding angry.

This from a man who had just held her under the water. "I almost fell in the pool last night at the villa. One of the residents grabbed me." She rubbed at her wrist as she pulled it free.

"One of the residents?" he repeated. "You sure he was trying to save you?"

She wasn't sure of anything, and it must have showed. "How did you know it was a he?"

Landry only smiled. "I think you'd better tell me about the other people on the island before we go back."

"We're going back to the villa?" she asked in surprise. She'd figured they would be going back to the mainland. And she would get away from him.

"Don't you think it would be wise to find out who on this island might have reason to want you dead?" he asked.

"You mean other than you." Her sarcasm wasn't wasted on him.

"I'm amazed you've stayed alive this long," he said, stepping past her to pick up his backpack.

Now that she knew what was at stake, Willa was surprised herself. But as she looked into Landry's handsome face she was reminded again that there were worse things than death. Taking him back to the villa with her could be one of them.

"And how exactly do you intend to explain your appearance on the island?" she asked. "All the apartments are full."

"You let me worry about that," he said. "Tell me about everyone on the island."

Willa told him about Odell, Henri and Blossom. Landry listened, and when she finished she had the strangest feeling that he'd already known all of it.

She recalled the animal-like movement she'd seen from the balcony last night. It hadn't been Odell. It had been Landry. She was sure of it. "How long have you been on the island?" she demanded.

Landry grinned. "Long enough to know what you sleep in."

She felt her face heat as she remembered her little foray behind the villa with the shovel. "You were spying on me last night?"

"Look, the tide is coming in. We're losing our beach. Pretty soon we'll be arguing about this underwater." He turned his back on her and started through the trees.

She didn't move even when she felt a wave wash around her ankles.

He disappeared into the trees and she was considering taking the boat and making a run for it, when he returned looking irritable at best.

"What?" he asked, hands on his hips.

"Did you see what happened by the pool last night?" she asked.

He shook his head. "I came running when I heard you scream but by then your friend Odell had already saved you."

"He isn't my friend," she snapped. She was angry at Landry for spying on her. But even more angry that he hadn't seen what had happened before Odell showed up at the pool. "So are you going to tell me which painting Simon hid the disk in?"

"No." He started to turn toward the trees again but must have seen that she wasn't moving an inch until he told her. "It's a painting of a sailboat. That's all you need to know right now."

A painting of sailboat? She had done dozens of those.

"You're just going to have to trust me."

She stared at him. Trust him? He had to be kidding. Did she even believe him? She believed he was after something. Possibly *that* was the only reason she was still alive. What she feared was that there was something on the disk that Landry Jones needed to save himself, all right. He needed the disk so he could destroy it for his boss Freddy D.—and save the truth from coming out about him. And once she was dead there wouldn't be anyone to testify against him. It would be his word against a dead man's.

He smiled. "Calculating the odds?" His question took her by surprise.

"What odds?"

"Whether I'm lying to you or not."

He'd hit too close to home and she knew it must have shown in her expression. "Just my luck that Simon picked *your* art studio."

"My thoughts exactly."

He shook his head and settled his gaze on her. "Look, if all I wanted was the disk, wouldn't I just kill you and go through your stuff? Apparently that's what the person who was shooting at you had planned." He raised a brow in question.

"And they would have been very disappointed," she said. "I don't have any of my paintings with me."

That got his attention. "Where are they?"

She just looked at him and said nothing.

His jaw muscle jumped, his eyes darkened.

Clearly they had reached a stalemate. It was her turn to smile. "Who doesn't trust whom?"

"You're starting to burn," he said, and cocked his head toward the sun beating down on them. "We need to get you back to the villa." But he didn't move. "Don't you want to hear my plan?"

From his pleased expression? No. "What?" Her voice cracked. She had a bad feeling she knew exactly what he was about to suggest.

"The way I see it, someone on this island knows who you are. They could be searching your apartment right now. Or maybe planning to wait until tonight to break in, kill you and search it."

"That's crazy," she said, but rubbed her wrist, remembering last night by the pool and the gunshots only minutes before.

"Is it crazy? If those bullets would have found their mark earlier, you'd be shark bait." He must have seen her surprise. "You think your body would ever be found?" He chuckled. "As far as everyone is concerned, you've disappeared. So the simplest thing is for your body to end up as fish food. No one would ever have to know what happened to you." He sounded as if he'd given this some thought. "You're in over your head, sweetheart. You've got one chance and that's me." He grinned wickedly at her.

She didn't like his smugness. Nor was she sure Landry Jones's help was what she needed at all. She dug her heels in, even though the water was now washing around her thighs. "It sounds to me like you need *mine* since I'm the only one who knows where the painting is."

"So we work together."

There was no doubt in her mind that once he had the disk he would be long gone. "What's in it for me?" she asked.

He blinked in surprise. "Excuse me? When I have the disk, I clear my name and put some major scumbags in prison. You, sweetheart, get to keep breathing."

"I told you not to call me sweetheart." She felt his gaze go to the front of her wet T-shirt. More specifically to her breasts poking against the thin fabric of her bra and the wet fabric.

She crossed her arms over her chest and he had the good grace to look sheepish as he raised his eyes to her face again.

"I'm sorry. What did you say?" he asked, eyes hooded.

She glared at him, knowing darn well he'd heard her.

"So where are your paintings?" he asked.

She gave him a like-I'm-just-going-to-tell-you look.

"Fine. Want to take your chances without me, sweetheart? Up to you. I'll track down your paintings without you since I'm betting you'll be swimming with the sharks by midnight."

"Stop calling me sweetheart and I'll consider your offer."

He raised a brow. "My offer?"

It was simple enough. Even if he was lying, he would keep her alive until they found the disk. If he was telling the truth, once she knew which painting Simon Renton had hid the disk in all she had to do was find it first and get it to the police....

His gaze lazily caressed her face, a grin tugging at his lips. He had a pretty great mouth on him, too, she noticed. "First, let's discuss my cover. I'm your boyfriend."

"No way."

He didn't seem to hear her. "I got a ride out to the island to meet you here." He reached into the boat and brought out a duffel bag reminding her of Blossom's duffel. "We're lovers just having a nice vacation."

His grin made her stomach flip-flop. "I told you the painting isn't on the island."

"I'd like to make sure myself. I'm from Missouri, you know, the Show Me State?"

So that's why they were going back to the villa. "Whatever. Don't believe me. What about the person who wants me dead?"

"I'll take care of that, as well."

She eyed him. "Like you did Zeke?" She saw at once that she'd hit a sore spot.

"Zeke was my friend. I don't know what the hell happened, what made him do what he did." Landry's eyes darkened. "But do me a favor, don't bring him up unless you want to make me mad, okay, sweet—" He caught himself. "Okay?"

She nodded.

They stood glaring at each other for a long moment, the water rising around them. Then he said, "Can we go meet your island mates now, darlin'?" Before she could protest, he added, "I can't call you Willa. I have to call you something and we *are* lovers." That wicked grin again.

She wanted to wipe it off his face. But instead, she stalked past him. He grabbed her arm and spun her around to face him.

"You should let me go first. Just in case we run into one of your neighbors, the one with the gun," he said with a lift of his brow. "If that's all right with you, darlin'."

Chapter 9

Willa groaned as she stared at his arrogant backside. She was sure she heard him chuckle and hated him all the more as she followed him through the trees and underbrush.

It was cool in the trees. She felt flushed. From the sun. From being around this impossible man. But if this stupid disk would get her life back, she would find it. What choice did she have but let Landry Jones accompany her? He knew which painting the disk was hidden in. She didn't. At least not yet.

The quiet in the trees unnerved her. Was the person who'd shot at her waiting nearby, planning to finish the job this time? More to the point, would Landry Jones save her again?

"Are you really?" she asked as she quickened her step so she was right behind his broad back.

"Am I really what?"

"From Missouri?"

He glanced over his shoulder at her. "Yeah." A bird squawked off to their right, making them both jump. "Gotta ask you, why'd you pick this island of all the damned islands? Ten Thousand Islands and you pick this one."

"What's wrong with it?"

"Are you serious? Can't you feel it? The place gives me the creeps. What horrible thing *hasn't* happened here? Only you would pick a haunted damned island to hide out on."

"You don't really believe the island is haunted," she said, scoffing at such foolishness.

He glanced around uneasily. "Bad things have happened here, darlin'. Maybe you can't sense it, but I can. And you know what they say about places like this…."

"No," she said, telling herself he was just trying to scare her. "What do they say?"

"Bad things will happen again. Evil attracts evil. It's a known fact."

He wasn't serious. The next thing she knew he'd be out burying a jar behind the villa. "You're a strange guy, Landry."

He turned to look at her and grinned. "You don't know the half of it."

And that's what worried her.

Landry slowed as they reached the rear of the villa. He could hear voices and music playing. His stomach growled as he caught the scent of barbecue.

"Looks like we made it back just in time," he said over his shoulder.

Odell looked up in surprise as Landry came through the archway into the courtyard. Odell and Henri were sitting together in a pair of old metal lawn chairs outside his apartment. There was a bottle of wine on a small table between them, two mismatched plastic glasses and a deck of cards.

"Nice pool," Landry whispered to Willa.

Her gaze went to the dark water, then Odell. He had turned and was watching them with interest. Too much interest.

Clearly the two of them had interrupted something because Henri looked surprised to see them and maybe a little suspicious. Landry had seen the redhead and the devil child arrive this morning by boat. Thanks to Willa, he now had their names. If only he could have easily found out what they were doing on the island.

But he was more interested in Odell. Everything about the man worried him. Especially Odell's obvious interest in Willa.

"I made it," Landry said cheerfully, and put his arm around Willa, pulling her close. She nudged him.

"Look who surprised me," she said, as if trying to match his cheerfulness. She looked scared and wary, as well, of her villa mates.

"You go swimming?" Odell asked, lifting a brow as he took in their wet clothing.

Landry grinned and pulled Willa closer. "I was so glad to see her I didn't even give her a chance to take off her clothes." He chuckled and let his gaze move appreciatively over her. That at least he didn't have to pretend. She had a great body and wet clothing left nothing to the imagination. "We really should get out of these clothes, darlin'."

Henri laughed. "My kind of man."

Odell turned his attention back to the redhead.

As Landry led Willa past the two, he saw that they had been playing poker. Strip poker from the little they were both wearing—and the pile of clothing beside the table.

Odell was down to his shorts. Henri was wearing a string bikini.

As Willa and Landry passed them, Landry took a good look at the full swell of Henri's breasts in the tiny bikini top.

Willa elbowed him even harder this time and smiled as he rewarded her with a satisfyingly painful grunt. She slipped out from under his arm and ran up the stairs ahead of him. At the top, she turned to look back and caught him admiring her butt. She glared at him.

He shook his head and laughed as he charged up the stairs and pinned her against the wall, leaning down to kiss her neck and whisper, "You can't have it both ways, darlin'."

"Well, we know what those two are going to be doing the rest of the day," Henri said, loud enough for them to hear.

"You should change and join us," Odell said. "Don't worry, I have enough steaks for everyone."

Landry didn't like what he heard in the man's invitation. Odell sounded upset. Because he was jealous? Or because the last thing Odell wanted was anyone in Willa's room tonight?

Willa was trying desperately to ignore Landry. It was more than difficult given that he was nibbling on her neck and sending tingles through her body. She tried to shove him away, but he was much stronger and he seemed to be enjoying what he was doing. Unfortunately her body was reacting. She felt her nipples harden.

Landry pulled back to look down at her chest then grinned as he met her eyes. "Glad to see you're getting into your role."

She would have hit him if he hadn't had her pinned against the wall with his body. "You really are despicable," she hissed so only he could hear.

His grin broadened. He bent again to tease her throat with kisses and suddenly froze. She turned her head in the direction he was looking and saw Alma Garcia. The woman stood as if poleaxed, staring in horror at Landry just feet from them.

She said something in Spanish, then quickly crossed herself.

Willa gripped Landry's arm, frightened by the crazed look in the older woman's eyes. Willa could feel Odell and Henri watching the scene from below, as if spellbound.

Landry said something to Alma also in Spanish. The woman drew back, her hand going to her throat, tears welling in her eyes and spilling down her cheeks. Then she turned and practically ran, her antique gown rustling as she disappeared through the arch at the end of the walk.

"What was *that* about?" Willa whispered on an expelled breath.

"Welcome to the looney bin," Odell called up.

"Wow, that was scary," Henri said. "What did she say to you?"

"Mistaken identity," Landry said with a laugh and

drew Willa down the walkway to the door of the apartment, keeping his hand firmly on her arm.

She fumbled out the key and the moment the door opened, Landry pushed her inside and closed the door after them.

"What the hell was that?" he whispered, even though no one could hear them.

"You tell *me*."

He looked pale and she felt a tremor go through him as he held on to her arm.

"She called me her amour, her love, then asked me what I was doing back here. Did you see the look in her eyes?"

Willa nodded. "Don't ever do that again."

He stared at her. "What?"

"That," she snapped, pointing back toward the balcony.

His eyes narrowed. "I thought I made it clear. Whoever is trying to kill you needs to believe we're lovers."

"Bull. Wouldn't it be more effective to tell them you're my brother the cop? Or even better, the FBI?"

He smiled. "We should have thought of that before we told them we were lovers."

She daggered a look at him, wondering if she could hate him any more.

"That old woman—she lives here?" he asked, obviously more shaken by that than any look Willa could fire at him.

"Her name is Alma Garcia. She used to be the nanny here." Willa shivered from her wet clothing. She sighed and told him a shortened version of the story that Odell had told her. "I think Odell is writing a book about the disappearance of the family. But I also found a recent newspaper about…us. Complete with photos." She went to the table and picked up the newspaper and handed it to him, watching him as he stared at his photograph.

"How'd you get this?"

She squirmed a little. "I took it from Odell's room."

Landry looked up at her. "He's going to realize it's missing."

She shook her head. "He offered me the rest of the newspaper. So I took it. I'm just afraid he recognized me."

"Neither of us looks like this now," he said.

Landry was right. With his hair much longer and the designer stubble that was starting to be a close-cropped beard, he looked nothing like the clean-cut, clean-shaven cop in the photo. Now he looked more like a beach bum.

Or a pirate.

Is that why Alma thought she knew him? Hadn't Odell said that Alma's boss, Andres Santiago, was a modern-day pirate? Then others like him would have visited the island and apparently Alma had fallen for one of them. Fallen hard, given the way she'd looked at Landry with both love—and fear.

But why fear? Did she think that her pirate had caused the deaths of Andres and Medina and their children? Did she live in fear that the killer would come back for her, as well?

Or had Alma been afraid because as delusional as she might be, she'd seen a killer when she looked at Landry?

Willa felt a chill as she met his eyes.

"You should get a shower and change."

She shook her head and crossed her arms over her

chest again. "You're going to tell me what painting we're looking for first."

Landry studied her, wondering what went on in that head of hers, suspecting he knew. "It's a blue sailboat bent in the wind with a red and white sail, small." He held his hands about eight inches apart, all the time watching her face. "It was marked for the art show but it wasn't there."

Her smile could have cut glass. "That's why you came to my show. You were only after the painting. Until you couldn't find it. Then you were after me." She looked like she might want to scratch his eyes out. "Just tell me this. What would have happened if Zeke hadn't come along when he did? If I would have gotten into your car with you?"

He didn't answer her. Instead, he glanced toward the bedroom. He could see her bed, a double all made up with pretty floral yellow-and-white sheets and a brightly colored spread of primary colors. It looked more than a little inviting since he hadn't had but a few fitful hours of sleep for the past seventy-two hours.

But unfortunately sleep was the last thing he thought of when he looked at Willa St. Clair's bed—and that made that bed damned dangerous.

Dragging his gaze away, he saw her easel, a painting on it. He stepped into the second room, glanced into the bathroom, then studied her artwork.

The painting was of the villa but there was something about it that made his stomach knot. One wall was blood-red. At first he thought it was bougainvillea, but on closer inspection it appeared to be splattered with blood as if a massacre had happened here.

He heard her step into the room, could feel her

watching him. The painting was haunting. He pulled his gaze away to look at her, surprised by the effect of her painting on him, but maybe even more surprised by her talent and the effect *she had* on him.

"Well?"

He frowned, having forgotten the question.

"What did you plan to do to me the night of the art show?" she demanded, meeting his hooded gaze with a furious one of her own.

"You know the answer," he said, waving it off. "I needed the disk." He hated the hurt he saw in her expression. "Darlin', I'm a cop. I was doing my job, just like I'm doing right now, whether you believe me or not."

He looked at the painting again. It was like looking at a car wreck. You didn't want to look but you couldn't help yourself. "What the hell is this?" he asked, pointing at the red splatters on the wall.

She seemed to pull her gaze away from him, focusing slowly on the painting. "I don't know. It's just what I see. I paint what I see in my...mind."

He swore softly. "All your other stuff was nice sailboats, sunny days, warm turquoise water."

"That was before I witnessed a murder."

He sobered, softening as he looked at her. "I'm sorry you had to see that. Believe me it's given me a few nightmares, as well."

A silence fell between them. Willa felt herself softening toward Landry and mentally slapped herself.

"I know which painting you're talking about," she said after a moment. "But I don't know what happened to it."

"What?"

"I remember the painting. It was supposed to be in the show but I don't remember seeing it after the paintings went to the gallery."

He swore again. "Was it possible Simon hid the painting somewhere in your studio? The police searched the place, right?"

She nodded.

"Freddy D.'s not in jail so he knows the disk hasn't turned up. So where the hell was it?" She could hear his frustration and his fear. "Did anyone else have access to your shop?"

She shook her head. "Another artist who worked next door would sometimes watch the shop if I had to leave for a few minutes.... But she wasn't in the shop between when Simon Renton came in and I packed the items for the show."

"Okay, let's walk through what happened after Simon left your shop, okay?"

She explained how she had finished the last of the framing. "I was too excited to sleep so I packed up the art for the show, then I went to bed."

"And you're sure that painting was one of them you packed?"

She nodded.

"You say you went to bed?"

"My apartment was just upstairs."

"You think you would have heard if anyone had come in during the night?"

"Of course. Anyway, the paintings were packed. It would have been impossible for someone to sneak in, find that particular painting and take it without me hearing them."

He groaned and raked a hand through his hair. "Okay, the painting was packed, then what?"

"The next morning, Evan came over and helped me load the paintings into a van and take them to the gallery. Evan is the gallery owner. I helped him put the boxes in the back of the shop. Then I left and he set up the show after the gallery closed that afternoon."

"He does everything himself?"

"It's a small gallery."

"What did you do?"

"I went back to my studio and worked. I like to paint when I'm anxious. It calms me. Later, I went over to the gallery to make sure Evan had everything he needed."

"But you don't remember seeing the sailboat painting."

"No, but then I can't be sure it wasn't there and disappeared later. Evan might remember."

Yes, Landry would have to talk to Evan. "Did all the paintings sell?"

"Almost all of them. Evan packed up the rest."

Landry felt his heart quicken. If the small painting had accidentally been overlooked in a box at the back of the gallery, Evan would have just packed the unsold ones with it. "What happened to those paintings, the unsold ones?"

She frowned. "I asked him to put them away for me until I came for them."

The painting had to be one of two places if it hadn't been found yet, which he was counting on. Either it had been misplaced at the gallery. Or Simon had hid it in the studio.

"Okay," he said, feeling better. "What happened to everything in your studio?"

"The police took me back there and I packed up everything."

"Did any of the officers help?" he asked.

"Two." She seemed to see where he was headed with this. "Yes, but no one walked away with a painting or a disk. They just made sure you didn't try to kill me while I told them what needed to be packed, and they did it. I watched the entire process."

He ignored the part about him killing her. As far as he knew, the police didn't know that Simon had hid the disk in a painting. Simon was dead so he couldn't have told them and Zeke wasn't about to tell them since he'd changed sides no doubt long before all of this had happened. So the police wouldn't be looking for the painting. That meant either of them could have unknowingly packed the painting with the disk, never suspecting what they had in their hands.

"Is it possible you missed the painting—it was small, so maybe you overlooked it and left it behind?" Especially if Simon had hidden it.

She shook her head. "I gave up the studio so everything was packed and cleaned out. There really wasn't anyplace to hide anything."

He nodded. "So where is everything you boxed up?"

"In storage."

He rolled his eyes. "I gathered that. Okay, darlin'," he said, his gaze locking with hers as he stepped toward her. "What do I have to do to get you to trust me?" he asked, his voice soft as he cupped her cheek.

She tried to step away from him, but he pressed her to the wall with his body. She smelled clean and a little citrusy. He sniffed her hair, breathing her in.

Her big blue eyes were on him. He removed her

glasses and tossed them aside; her eyes widened. He could feel her breath quicken. Her heart was a hammer in her chest. She really was something.

As he bent to kiss her, she tried to turn her head away but he was still cupping her cheek, still pinning her to the wall.

She glared at him as he lowered his mouth until his lips were only a hairbreadth above hers. He felt her breath catch as he lowered his mouth to hers.

He kissed her gently, slowly, carefully. At first it was to show her how things were going to be but somewhere along the way he felt things change. Not so much in her as in himself.

Her mouth was paradise. There was a shyness to her, an innocence he'd seen the first time he'd laid eyes on her and yet hadn't believed. It was still there though beneath the bravado. And he was surprisingly touched by it.

He drew back to look into her big blue eyes. She looked like a deer caught in headlights. Her tongue darted out to touch her lower lip. She looked scared and excited all at the same time. He could feel her heart pounding beneath his. Something had changed between them and he already regretted it.

Sometimes he hated his job, hated that he had to use people, to gain their trust, to hurt them.

He especially hated that in the end he would hurt Willa St. Clair.

Willa looked past him, her eyes growing wider. He swung around, going for his weapon, expecting to see someone behind them.

The room was empty. He blinked as he swung back around with the gun in his hand and faced her.

Willa stood smiling smugly. "I think we need to establish some ground rules," she said calmly, although he could see she was anything but.

"That was just a *ruse?*"

She cocked her head at him, still smiling. "Just like that kiss of yours was to make me think I could trust you."

He holstered his weapon, eyeing her warily. He understood now how she had managed to survive this long. And maybe the kiss had started out that way, but it had changed. He thought about calling her on it. She'd felt something. He knew because he'd felt it, too. But she was right about them needing some ground rules.

"Have you heard the story about the little boy who cried wolf?" he asked as he stepped closer.

"I like the one about the wolf in sheep's clothing better," she said, and held up her hand. "That's close enough. Rule number one: Keep your hands off me."

He grinned. "That won't be easy given that your neighbors think we're lovers and up here right now going at it on your bed."

She flushed and he had a flash of the two of them on the bed doing just that. He took a step back as he felt himself grow hard at the thought.

"What?" she asked, frowning.

He looked at her. Was she serious? "How many men have you been with?"

"What?"

He let out an oath and took another step back. "Don't tell me you're a virgin."

Landry looked horrified and Willa wanted to defend

virgins all over the world. Instead, she kept her mouth shut, her face flushing and giving her away.

He let out another curse. "How old are you anyway?"

"Twenty-five, and you're wrong. I've been with plenty of men." She groaned inwardly. Why had she said that?

He started to laugh, shaking his head as he stared at her. "Twenty-five? Aren't there any able-bodied men in South Dakota?"

"No, there's only sheep," she snapped. "Of course there are men, and I told you, I've been with my share." Her chin went up.

"Then all the men are with the sheep," he said with a laugh.

"That isn't funny." Her voice broke.

He stopped laughing. "Sorry."

"Could we just concentrate on finding the painting and you stop ruining my life?"

He nodded solemnly. "I haven't ruined your life. At least I hope not." He took another step back.

"Would you stop treating me like I have some communicable disease?"

"Sorry. It's just that you're an attractive woman and I don't want to be the one who deflowers you."

She groaned. Deflower? Could she be any more mortified? "Don't worry about it. It's not like I would want you anyway."

"You're right. The first time should be with someone you love. Someone who respects you and wants your first time to be something wonderful."

"Could you please *stop?*" His words were getting to her. How could he sound so sensitive when she knew he was just the opposite? And he was still looking at her as if she was a freak of nature.

Was it possible that she could hate Landry Jones any more? Obviously it was. She glared at him, wanting to convince him he was wrong about her, but at the same time knowing she would be wasting her breath.

"The storage unit is in Everglades City," she burst out.

He blinked at her.

"Let's go," she said, and started for the door.

"Hold on," he said, grabbing her arm and then quickly letting go of it. "Sorry, forgot the ground rules," he said, acting as if she'd burned him.

She narrowed her gaze at him. It wasn't the ground rules that had made him behave the way he had. Men like Landry Jones didn't obey rules. The man was probably a killer, a dirty cop; he certainly was no gentleman. So why was he acting as if she had the plague because he thought she was a virgin? She'd bet he'd taken his share of virgins. So why draw the line with her? She felt insulted.

"We have to wait until everyone goes to bed around here," he said. "We can't just take off. Not unless we want to be followed by whoever tried to kill you earlier."

She hadn't thought of that. She'd been too angry with Landry. "Fine."

"In the meantime I think we should take Odell up on his offer of a steak."

"You have to be kidding." Having dinner with someone who wanted to kill her was the last thing on her mind.

"I would think a woman from South Dakota would eat beef."

She glared at him, still too angry with him to be civil. "Lamb and mutton, remember, all those sheep."

He laughed and glanced in her fridge. "Cottage cheese and fruit or yogurt." He closed the door. "Definitely think we should go to the barbecue."

"Fine." She didn't give him a chance to say anything as she stalked into the bedroom and started to close the door.

"No!" she cried. The next thing she knew Landry was at her side, his weapon in hand.

"Wait." Landry reached for her but she dodged his outstretched hand and rushed to her box of supplies.

"Oh, no," she said again as she dropped to her knees and began going through the box of supplies.

"What is it?" Landry asked after he quickly searched the bedroom and bathroom.

"Someone's gone through my things, only this time at least they didn't take my painting."

"Someone took a painting?" He sounded panicked.

From the floor, she looked up at him and mugged a face. "Not the painting you're interested in. This was one I did yesterday." Her eyes narrowed. "Did you take it?"

"No, why would I?" He looked insulted.

"Maybe it was Alma then. I smelled gardenias."

"Gardenias," he repeated, looking lost.

Nothing appeared to be missing this time, but someone had definitely gone through her stuff and she had to wonder who else had a key to her apartment. She felt violated, which seemed crazy since she was already running for her life and now living with a possible killer. What could be worse than that? Having someone paw through her private things.

"What was the painting?" Landry asked, hunching down on the floor next to her. He seemed concerned by how upset she was. Or maybe he was just worried that the same thief had his painting.

"It was—" she hesitated, remembering the painting "—of the murder in front of the gallery."

He winced. "Of me?"

She nodded, and he swore softly.

"Great," he said.

She glanced toward the painting on the easel, wondering why whoever had taken the other painting hadn't taken this one.

He shoved to his feet with a sigh. "Show me all of the paintings you have."

She looked up at him. "I told you the one you want isn't here."

"Or I can look myself," he said, his jaw muscle tightening.

She stood, copying his sigh. She crossed her arms. Her clothing had finally dried out some but she still felt half-naked around him. She couldn't help but think of the kiss, of what it felt like being in his arms, or the look on his face when she'd rushed from those arms and fooled him, she thought with a smile.

"What?"

She shook her head. "Go ahead. I know you aren't going to be happy until you've convinced yourself the painting you're looking for isn't here, so do it. Why don't you start with the bathroom? Then I'd like to bathe and change into some other clothes."

"I don't see anything wrong with what you have on." His gaze swept over her.

She looked down, not surprised to see that her

nipples were hard in response to his look and now pressed against the thin material of her bra and shirt. She cursed her body for betraying her around him.

"I think I can dispense with searching the bathroom for a painting," he said, smiling smugly at her. He probably thought she enjoyed the kiss. Well, he was wrong. She was just playing along, letting him think he had her under his spell. No matter what her body thought, she was too smart to fall for anything Landry Jones was offering. But it did still annoy her the way he'd reacted when he thought she was a virgin.

She took some clothing from the chest of drawers—a pair of cropped pants, a shirt and some of the undergarments her mother had purchased for her back in South Dakota. She didn't feel safe in the skimpy underthings she'd bought since being in Florida.

As she shot a glance at Landry, she wasn't surprised to find he'd been watching her. He was looking smug, as if he knew why she'd chosen clothing that covered more of her body. What arrogance.

She groaned and stalked into the bathroom, closing the door and locking it. She could hear him searching the apartment and closed her eyes for a moment, imagining him going through the chest of drawers and her thong underwear.

Reminding herself that Landry in her underwear drawer was the least of her worries, she opened her eyes and reached in to turn on the shower—and screamed.

Chapter 10

Landry practically flew into the bathroom, throwing open the door and almost knocking Willa down as he burst in, weapon drawn.

The bathroom was small and it only took him an instant to see that none of Freddy D.'s men were hiding in it. He heard a soft rustle and looked toward the bathtub.

The shower curtain was partially drawn back—just enough that he couldn't miss what was lying in the tub.

He flinched at the sight of the huge snake coiled in the bottom of the bathtub. He gently stepped back, putting Willa behind him as he did so. The snake was watching him through narrow slits, its tongue flicking from its wide flat head.

He'd seen his share of rattlesnakes, but this one had to be over six feet long—and appeared ready to strike.

In one quick movement, he was through the bathroom door and had the door between he and Willa and the snake. He breathed a sigh of relief and turned to look at her.

Her face was stark white, her eyes wide and scared, her hands trembling.

"What was *that?*" she whispered.

He grinned. "Don't they have rattlesnakes in South Dakota?"

"Not that big."

He chuckled and looked around for something to get the snake out of her tub.

"How did it get in there?"

"It came up through the pipes." He turned to look at her. She didn't really believe that, did she?

She'd sat down on the end of the bed but instead of looking scared, she looked angry. "It's whoever shot at me in the trees."

He didn't correct her as he opened the broom closet in the kitchen and pulled out a mop with a strip of sponge held in by eight inches of metal.

"What are you going to do?" she asked, sounding scared again as he passed her.

"I'm going to get the snake out of the tub, unless you want to shower with it." He opened the bathroom door quietly and slipped into the bathroom, moving behind the shower curtain. He could hear the snake trying to get out of the high old-fashioned tub. He took a breath and drew back the shower curtain with one hand, the mop handle in the other.

The snake turned at the sound, but Landry was faster. He slammed down the base of the mop, pinning the snake's head to the bottom of the tub, then gingerly he reached in and grabbed the snake behind the head and picked it up.

It twisted in his grasp. It was one heavy snake. As he stepped out of the bathroom, Willa let out a startled cry.

"Is it dead?"

"Not hardly." He moved to the back window near the couch, opened the window and pushed out the screen. Standing on the couch, he raised the snake and slid it through the open window, grabbing its tail to slow its fall as the snake disappeared.

"You let it go?" She sounded horrified.

"It was just a snake," he said, stepping down off the couch. "No reason to kill it."

Willa stared at him as if she'd never seen Landry Jones before. What kind of man couldn't kill a rattlesnake?

"You can take your bath now," he said.

She stared at him a moment longer then turned toward the bathroom, a little leery of what else she might find in there. "Are you sure—"

"Would kind of be overkill to have anything else in there, don't you think?"

Still she looked around before she turned on the faucet. It was probably one of the faster showers she'd ever taken, quickly washing off the sand and salt, shampooing her short hair and rinsing off.

She dried herself and dressed, feeling better as if wearing armor in the old-lady bra and panties that came up to her waist could protect her from her emotions. She couldn't help but think about Landry Jones. Just about the time she thought she had him figured out, he surprised her.

She gazed at her image in the mirror, dressed in the

capris and tea-length sleeved blouse. She looked like the virgin she was, she thought with a self-deprecating smile.

As she stepped out of the bathroom, she found Landry standing by her bed holding a framed photograph. "These your parents?"

It was all she could do not to stomp over to him and snatch it from him. He already knew too much about her. "Yes."

"You grew up on a farm?" He seemed interested. Then she remembered that he was probably just wondering if she'd shipped some of her paintings home.

She walked over and took the photograph from him, unable to resist tracing her fingers over her father's face before setting it back down, then changing her mind and sticking it faceup in the top drawer.

"The paintings aren't in South Dakota," she snapped, angry with him for even pretending to care about her or her family.

"I wasn't—" He shook his head. "Never mind." He glanced around the apartment. "The painting isn't here."

She gave him a duh look. "I believe I already told you that."

He nodded. "Missouri, remember?"

She remembered.

"I grew up on a farm, too. Dirt-poor."

She felt her expression soften. "Me, too."

He nodded and chewed at his cheek. "It was tough. I never wanted to be rich but I knew I had to do better than that."

"I know what you mean."

"You're making it as an artist. That's really something," he said with what almost sounded like admiration in his voice.

"Well, I was *starting* to."

He winced. "Sorry, but once this is over, you can get another studio, have a bunch more shows. It will be great." He actually sounded like he believed that.

"Thanks. What about you?"

Landry sighed. "I really don't know. I can't see myself going back to it. Undercover work. I guess I didn't realize how much I was starting to really fit into the role of bad guy. Maybe that's what happened to Zeke. He got so used to playing the part, it became who he was." Landry shrugged. "What happened with him changed things for me."

She could see that. She just wasn't sure in what way. They both started at the knock on the apartment door, then Odell's voice. "Willie?"

"Willie?" Landry whispered.

"Willie?" Odell called again.

"Go ahead, answer him," Landry whispered.

"Just a minute," she called.

Landry smiled. "He's going to think we're in bed."

She felt her face heat as she pushed past him and went to the door. She'd rather take her chances with Odell than Landry anyday, she told herself.

"Hey," she said, smiling as she opened the door.

Odell seemed surprised by the greeting. True, she hadn't been even a little friendly before this. His gaze took her in. "You look…great."

Did she? She glanced toward the large stained mirror on the wall, surprised to see that her cheeks were flushed, her eyes bright. Past her reflection, she saw Landry's. He was watching her closely, grinning as if he knew exactly what had put the color in her cheeks, the gleam in her eyes.

She turned back to Odell and waited for him to remember what he was doing here.

"You're still up for a barbecue, right?" Odell hesitated and Willa felt Landry come up behind her. "I was about to put the steaks on."

"Steaks." Landry sounded so hopeful.

"I have them marinating."

"He's marinating the steaks," Landry said to her. Odell didn't notice but Willa could hear the sarcasm in Landry's voice.

"We'd love to join you," she said, knowing there was no graceful way out of this. Her other option was to spend the rest of the evening in this tiny apartment with Landry. Just the two of them.

"Great." Odell seemed surprised but happy they would be joining him.

"What can I bring?" Willa asked, then remembered how little food she had in the fridge. It had been just a reflex from South Dakota. "I have the makings for s'mores."

"Oh, girl, you'll kill me," Henri called up. "S'mores? I'm going to think I died and went to heaven. Can you believe I forgot chocolate? One of the basic food groups right up there with wine."

It sounded as if Henri had already been hitting the wine pretty hard.

"See you soon then," Odell said, glancing into the apartment. Actually glancing toward the bedroom.

Past Landry she saw that the covers were on the floor, the sheets rumpled. She stared back at the bed in shock.

Landry stepped in front of both hers and Odell's views, blocking the bed.

"Great," Odell repeated, sounding less enthusiastic as he turned to walk away. He spun back around almost at once though. "I'm sorry. I never caught your name," he said to Landry.

"Tim. Tim Patterson," Landry said without even blinking at the lie, and she was reminded that lying was second nature for him as an undercover cop. He held out his hand to Odell.

"Tim." Odell shook his hand then nodded to Willa. He looked suspicious. But then she thought everyone did.

She closed the door and leaned against it as she looked at Landry. "You did that to my bed?"

He grinned. "People believe what they see. You're safer if they think I'm your lover and I'm only interested in ravishing your body."

She hoped he didn't see her shiver at the thought.

"At least he has steak," Landry said. "So where is your other island mate? Blossom?"

"She's a teenage film and TV star," Willa said.

"Really?" He sounded interested. "I hope she's coming to the barbecue."

"I'm sure you do."

He shook his head. "I only have eyes for you, darlin'. Anyway, I'm more interested in who was shooting at you earlier than I am in a movie star."

Right.

She went into the tiny kitchen and got everything she needed for the s'mores. She could hear Landry in the tub. She tried not to imagine him naked.

When she had everything together, she heard the

water shut off. A few moments later he came out wearing nothing but a towel wrapped around his waist. She looked away. Just not quick enough. Something burned in his gaze. Desire?

She felt her cheeks flush at the heat of his gaze and turned away for fear he might see the same in her eyes. She caught her reflection again in the antique mirror hanging on the living room wall and saw that she looked…happy. Or at least excited. Both were dangerous.

Suddenly Landry appeared in the mirror as he stepped up behind her. He slipped his arm around her neck from behind. She froze. His hand hovered for a moment then touched the collar of her shirt as he moved closer until his body was warm against hers. She felt his breath on her neck, the soft touch of his lips making the tiny hairs lift and her skin ripple with gooseflesh.

She held her breath as he straightened her collar, his fingers brushing over the skin below her collarbone.

"There," he said meeting her gaze in the mirror. "That looks better."

He held her gaze for a moment longer then returned to the bedroom and without closing the door, dressed in shorts and a T-shirt and his deck shoes. "Ready?"

She felt bereft at the loss of his touch. She dropped her gaze, not wanting him to see what he was doing to her but afraid he knew only too well. Why hadn't she fessed up to her lack of sexual experience? It was certainly nothing to be ashamed of. Was she afraid he would take advantage of it? Or because from the way he'd acted she feared he wouldn't?

"So you're Blossom," Landry said a few minutes later when they joined the other residents down by the pool where Odell had pulled up several tables and some chairs and had a grill going. Loud obnoxious music blared from Blossom's room across the pool.

Blossom gave Landry a bored look from eyes rimmed in charcoal. She appeared drugged as she slouched in one of the lawn chairs and pouted behind a wall of kinky dyed-black hair. She wore the same black outfit she had on earlier. Willa wondered if everything the girl owned was black.

"Her agent forced her to come here for some down-time," Henri said, and chuckled as she lifted her glass of wine in a toast. "There are worse places to be. I've just never found them." She laughed and downed her wine.

Odell reached for the wine bottle and quickly re-filled her glass, then turned to offer some to Willa and Landry.

"You wouldn't have a beer, would you?" Landry asked.

"In the cooler," Henri said. "I always like to be pre-pared. Bloody Marys in the morning."

Landry popped the top on a beer and offered it to Willa. She shook her head and held up her drink of pref-erence. "I brought bottled water, thanks."

"Bottled water," Landry said. "That's my girl."

She ignored him and took a sip of her water to cool herself down. What was Landry up to? She was hav-ing trouble believing this was about finding whoever had shot at her earlier today. She suspected there was a whole lot more to it.

"This is really nice of you," Landry said as Odell cooked the steaks. "We hate to eat all your food."

"I have the supply boat coming back tomorrow. This

island might be isolated, but there isn't any reason not to be civilized," he said, and looked over at Willa.

Henri finished off the wine and went to get another bottle, weaving as she walked back to her apartment. Blossom continued to sulk in her lawn chair.

Willa tried to imagine which of the three could shoot at her, let alone put a huge rattlesnake in her bathtub.

"She's getting over a broken heart," Odell said, watching Henri stumble into her apartment.

"Willie tells me you're writing a book," Landry said, sipping at his beer and watching Odell cook the steaks.

"Did she?" Odell looked over at her. "I'm still at that stage where I'm not completely sure what I want to write about."

"I thought you were doing it on this place," Landry said. "Cape Diablo and the Villa Santiago. It's definitely creepy enough. So what is your theory?"

"My theory?" Odell asked.

"On what happened to Andres and…" Landry looked to Willa.

"Medina," she provided.

"Medina and the other two kids?"

Odell looked uncomfortable as he glanced at Willa. "I think they were murdered here, their bodies disposed of on the property."

Willa shivered, remembering the night before when Odell had buried something on the property.

"Could this place be any creepier?" Henri asked, returning with another bottle of wine. She handed it to Landry, smiling suggestively as she said, "Be a love and open that for me, will ya?"

Landry returned Henri's smile and took the cork-screw from her and slowly opened the bottle while

Henri watched, as if in fascination. Willa found herself watching, as well. His movements were skilled, his hands large and nicely shaped, the backs tanned from the sun, his fingers working the cork slowly, gently, patiently from the bottle.

He would be that kind of lover, Willa thought, then looked away, shocked by the very idea.

"Odell tells us you're here because of a broken heart?" Landry said to the redhead.

Henri nodded. "He turned out to be a real bastard."

"All men are bastards," Landry said. "It's only the degree of bastard that separates us." He shot a look at Willa. "Isn't that right, darlin'?"

"Absolutely," she said. "And if anyone knows, it's you, *sweet*heart."

He grinned meeting her gaze. "You can see why I love her."

Henri laughed and took the glass of wine Landry gave her before stumbling into her lawn chair again. Blossom hadn't moved but she did seem to be watching everything. Just as Willa had seen her apparently listening to everything the evening before.

The steaks ready, Odell handed everyone a plate. "It's not fancy," he said when he gave Willa hers. "Steak and salad. That's as fancy as we get out here in the middle of nowhere. Kind of like out West. Montana, Wyoming, the Dakotas. Not that I've ever been there." He smiled at her.

She took the plate, her fingers trembling. She hadn't told him she was from South Dakota, had she? Or was he just making small talk?

She glanced at Landry.

If he'd heard, he gave no indication. He was busy

cutting his steak. He took a bite. "Great steaks, Odell. You'll have to give me your marinade recipe."

Odell smiled and said, "Thanks," but Willa could see that he didn't like Landry. Not that she could blame him.

Henri didn't eat much of her dinner but was all over the s'mores. She was letting Landry make her another one when Odell touched Willa's shoulder and motioned her toward the open door of his apartment.

"Would you mind helping me a minute?" he asked quietly.

Landry and Henri didn't seem to notice. Blossom was watching them with apparent disinterest.

"Sure," Willa said, and stepped into his apartment.

He moved to the back where there was a small kitchenette. The moment she joined him, he turned to face her. "How long have you known him?"

Willa blinked, not sure at first who he was talking about.

"Tim," Odell said. "How long have you known him?"

"Not that long," she admitted. "Why?"

"I just have a bad feeling about him," Odell said. "I know it sounds silly. But he feels…dangerous."

She couldn't have agreed more. "Dangerous?" she repeated, just for something to say.

Odell grasped her forearm. "Don't trust him. I'm serious. I don't think he's right for you." He took his hand back quickly as if he realized he was overstepping his bounds. "I'm sorry. It isn't any of my business. You're obviously attracted to him. Maybe I'm all wrong about him."

"No," she said, and quickly added, "I appreciate your concern. I'll be careful."

"You just don't seem like the type of woman who

would go for that kind of man. You know, the crude, aggressive type." Was that how Odell saw Landry? "He isn't the one who hurt you, is he?"

Had she told Odell the same story she'd told Gator? Or had Odell gotten his information from Gator? She really had to try to remember who she was telling what to. Keeping track of her lies was exhausting.

"No, Tim's not the one who was abusive to me," she said.

Odell nodded, but he didn't look like he believed it.

Henri called that they'd better get back out to the fire or all of the s'mores would be gone. She sounded drunk.

Without another word Odell returned to poolside. Willa glanced around his kitchen, peeked into the bedroom, then wandered back out. Was Odell really who he said he was and was his concern real? Or was there a gun with a silencer hidden somewhere in his apartment, a gunny sack that once held a poisonous snake? She couldn't help but wonder if what Odell really wanted was Landry out of her life. But why?

Back outside, Willa found herself watching Landry. It wasn't until she saw him talking to Blossom that she realized what he was up to.

He'd said they had to find out who was trying to kill her. She just assumed he meant to stop them. But now she realized that if one of these people was willing to kill her before they got the disk then Landry was thinking they already had the painting and the disk and they were just tying up loose ends.

"You all right, darlin'?" Landry asked.

She swore some times it felt as if he could read her mind. He kissed her neck and whispered, "You aren't jealous, are you? I saw the way you were looking at me. If looks could kill."

She groaned. She hated being so transparent.

He chuckled. "Let's go somewhere private," he said just loud enough for everyone to hear.

Willa felt her face flame as he pulled her to her feet.

"Thanks for dinner," Landry said with a grin. "I know you'll understand if Willie and I call it a night."

Henri raised her wineglass in a silent salute.

Odell said nothing, his gaze on Willa. He'd been watching her all evening. And she would wager he knew she was from South Dakota. She shivered as she climbed the stairs ahead of Landry and wasn't even surprised when he cupped her buttock on the way up and swept her into his arms as they both stumbled into her apartment.

It was what he said once they were inside that surprised her.

Chapter 11

"Henri is as sober as I am," Landry said as he locked the door behind them. "And if she's getting over a heartbreak I'll eat your underwear."

Willa ignored that. "You think Henri is the one who shot at me, the one who put the snake in my bathtub?" she asked incredulously.

Landry was checking the apartment. For killers? Or snakes? "She could be just setting up Odell," he said as he checked the bathroom. "You know, pretending she's really drunk so he'll make his move." Landry shrugged. "She's wasting her time, though. Odell's not interested in her." His gaze settled on Willa's face. "He wants you."

"Not in the way you think," she said. "He let it slip tonight that he knows I'm from South Dakota. I never told him that. He must have gotten it from the newspaper articles, which means he knows who I am."

"That doesn't make him the shooter," Landry said. "Come on. You saw what he buried behind the villa. The guy's afraid of his shadow. He is no snake handler. No, trust me, the guy's got the hots for you."

"Do you always have to be so crude?"

He smiled as if he thought it was part of his charm. "Now, Blossom is something else. She looks like she could wrestle a snake. You ever see her in anything on TV or the big screen?"

Willa shook her head. "She acts like she's bored but I saw her watching everyone."

Landry nodded, eyeing her with what could have been respect. "So you *were* paying attention." He glanced at his watch. "We should try to get some sleep."

She glanced toward the bed.

"I'll take the couch," he said, as if reading her mind again.

"Fine," she said, heading for the bedroom.

"Leave the door open," he ordered.

She turned to look at him.

"In case someone tries to get you in the middle of the night," he said, and grinned. "I'll wake you when it's time to go."

Like she could sleep knowing he was in the next room, she thought after brushing her teeth, washing her face and applying a light night cream—her usual routine which she was determined to keep no matter how many killers were after her.

She had thought about changing into her longest nightshirt in the bathroom but since she and Landry would be leaving sometime in the middle of the night, she dressed in her darkest-colored jeans and shirt to be ready. Safer that way for everyone.

The living room light was out when she came from the bathroom. She couldn't see Landry on the couch but she knew he was there. Just as she knew his eyes were on her.

She slipped between the covers and turned out the light, pitching the apartment into darkness. He'd indicated that he didn't make love to virgins, and he was convinced she was one. She should have felt safe. But she feared it wasn't Landry Jones's willpower she had to worry about.

When she closed her eyes, she saw him grinning down at her as his lips moved closer and closer until he was kissing her again.

Landry heard her moan in her sleep and tiptoed to the bedroom door. A shaft of moonlight cut through a crack in the curtains and fell over the rounded curves beneath the thin sheet.

Watching her sleep, he had a hard time getting enough breath. The woman had no idea just how irresistible she was. Or how much danger she was in. She was determined that she could take care of herself. He shook his head at that foolish notion.

So far he hadn't seen T or Worm. He figured they could be underground until all this blew over since both had been made when they'd killed the two police officers at the safe house and let Willa St. Clair get away.

Suddenly he felt as if someone had knocked the air out of him. He stumbled from her bedroom doorway, the words echoing in his head.

Let her get away.

He swore. Of course that's what Freddy D. had ordered T and Worm to do. Let her get away so she could lead them to the disk. Freddy D. was too smart to use muscle like T and Worm to go after Willa St. Clair. He'd put someone with more finesse on her if he really wanted to catch her.

Someone like Landry himself.

He stepped to the window. Odell's light was on in his apartment. The poolside area where they'd had the barbecue was empty, bottles and glasses still on the tables, but no sign of Henri. Or Blossom.

Was it possible he was being played? His heart beat a little faster. Was it the only reason he was still alive? Still free?

He felt like a puppet. Someone was pulling his strings. He thought about Zeke trying to kill him at the gallery. It hadn't made any sense. It still didn't. Unless he and Zeke had both been set up that night. If Zeke thought Landry was the dirty cop, thought he was lying about having the painting and the disk, thought maybe he'd turned and was either taking the disk to Freddy D. or selling it to Freddy D.'s enemies.

Closing the blind, Landry went back to the couch, his mind whirling. The disk would be worth a small fortune if sold to the right people. If Zeke thought that Landry really had turned....

Landry knew he'd rather believe that than believe his friend had been the dirty cop.

The front door and the windows were all locked. He was a light sleeper. He'd hear anyone who tried to enter the apartment. He told himself that Willa was safe.

Lying down on the couch, he closed his eyes, trying to slow down his thoughts. Simon had gotten the disk from a reliable source. It would have valuable information about Freddy D.'s organization. But it would also have a list of who worked for him—including any cops.

Landry had to find that disk. Not just to prove his own innocence but to prove Zeke's. Zeke and Simon couldn't have died for nothing. If there was a dirty cop in Freddy D.'s organization, it couldn't have been Zeke.

Music started to play overhead. He could hear the soft scuff of feet. Someone was dancing. The old woman. Alma Garcia. She'd said something else that Landry hadn't told Willa, something that had shaken him.

She'd asked him if he'd come back to kill her.

He must have slept some. The music was no longer playing. Nor could he hear anyone dancing. Getting up, he checked outside. It was still dark, the moon high.

No lights shone in Odell's apartment. Opening the door, Landry glanced below the balcony. Nor were any lights burning in Henri's or Blossom's apartments.

Not that one or all of them might not be wide-awake. Would Freddy D. trust just one person with going after Willa and the disk? Even if that one person was Landry Jones? Landry didn't think so. If he were Freddy D., he would have sent a backup.

He stepped back into the apartment, quietly closing the door, and tiptoed into Willa's room, aware that Henri's and Blossom's smaller apartments were just below and the floor creaked.

"Ready?" he whispered next to Willa's ear. She smelled heavenly. His lips brushed her skin. Soft.

She came awake in an instant, looked scared, then annoyed to see him. Nothing new there.

She nodded, threw back the sheet and swung her legs over the side. It took a few moments to put on her tennis shoes. He was glad to see that she'd chosen dark jeans and a long-sleeved dark-colored shirt. She snugged a navy baseball cap down over her head and stood.

"The keys to the storage unit?" he whispered.

She held them up, along with a small penlight. She had to be kidding.

He handed her a real flashlight from his backpack and took the extra one for himself.

She pocketed her penlight and gave him a look that said she didn't like him much.

Better that way, he thought as he motioned for her to be as quiet as possible. She followed behind him, barely making a sound. At the door, he opened it and peered out again.

No sign of anyone. He led the way down the stairs and through the archway. Once past the house and under the canopy of the trees there was no light from the moon. He stopped to listen to make sure they hadn't been followed. He could hear Willa's soft breaths. He reached for her hand; it felt cool to his touch.

Willa felt his fingers search out her hand. She tried not to flinch at his unexpected touch. Or shiver at the tingle of that same touch as his fingers tightened around hers.

She could feel the dampness, hear the breeze moving through the trees high above them, and smell the Gulf.

Landry stopped, pulled her close and for one crazy moment, she thought he was going to kiss her. Instead, he appeared to be listening, as if he feared they'd been followed. All she could hear was the sound of her own pulse pounding in her ears.

After a moment, he drew her deeper into the trees. She could hear the surf ahead. The trees opened. Moonlight spilled over the water. Waves curled white and broke on the beach. The tide was out again.

Landry moved quickly to the brush. She heard the scrape of metal over the sound of the surf breaking on the rocks behind her farther up the beach.

He pulled a small boat from the bushes and motioned for her to get in.

She hesitated but only for a moment, then stepped into the boat. Landry pushed it out and hopped in. A wave crashed over the front of the bow sending up cold spray.

She shivered as Landry paddled away from the island before starting the motor. The boat purred through the moonlight. She watched Landry as he worked his way past mangrove island after mangrove island, surprised how at home he looked on the water. She wouldn't have been surprised if Landry was at home in almost any situation.

When she glanced back toward the island, she saw a figure at the edge of the trees.

"Landry," she said over the putt of the outboard. She motioned back toward the shore.

He turned, eyes narrowing as the figure melted back into the vegetation. "Did you see who it was?" he asked after they'd rounded one of the other islands.

She shook her head, hugging herself. Someone had followed them. Someone knew they'd left the island.

For a long while, she watched behind them, expecting to see another boat on the moon-slick surface or hear another motor. But there was nothing but islands and the gentle rock of the boat to the steady throb of the motor to lull her.

She must have closed her eyes, lying back in the boat,

looking up at the moon riding high in the sky. As she drifted off, she tried not to think about what would happen once Landry had the painting and the disk.

Her eyes opened as she became aware that the boat had slowed. Landry brought the bow up to the dock. She grabbed hold of the ladder and held on as Landry hopped out and tied up the boat before reaching for her hand.

They walked through Everglades City, the town deserted at this hour of the night. Willa felt as if they might be the only two people still alive anywhere. It was a strange feeling, this closeness to Landry, this feeling that they were in this together.

She knew it wouldn't last but for tonight she breathed in the exotic scents, Landry Jones's among them, and didn't think about tomorrow. Or even the rest of tonight.

As they walked, she noticed Landry turning to look over his shoulder just as she had been doing for days. But she saw no one. She heard no other boat or even a car. It was off-season and most of the houses along the water were boarded-up and empty.

When they reached the storage facility, she took the keys from her pocket. The units were one long row of metal compartments behind a chain-link fence. She went to the gate and used a key to get them inside, locking it behind them.

Several large outdoor lights shone at each end of the property. Only moonlight lit the middle section and only on the east side. It was pitch-black on the west side where her unit was located. They stayed to the shadows, Landry watching behind them as she moved along the shell lane. She started at the sound of a dog barking in the distance.

She used another key to open the padlock on the door to her storage unit. It made a soft click. She froze, listened, then stepped aside as Landry rolled the door upward, the sound loud as a gunshot.

They quickly stepped in, closed the door and turned on the flashlights Landry had supplied.

The storage unit was nearly empty. Only a half-dozen boxes sat in one corner. Willa quickly moved to them not sure what they would find since all of the boxes had been packed by the police.

Landry pulled a knife and cut the tape on each box. She stared at the knife, remembering her cut art supply box, then shaking off her suspicion, began to go through the contents quickly, hoping she would find the painting or a disk—and yet afraid what would happen once she did.

It didn't take long to go through the six boxes that she'd left here only days before. The painting wasn't there.

She closed the last box and turned to look at Landry. He'd been going through the boxes after her. He swore as he looked through the last one, then he glanced up at her, a look of both disappointment and fear on his face.

"It's not here," she said because someone needed to say it.

He nodded. "You packed it for the show. The gallery owner must still have it."

From his tone she knew going anywhere near St. Pete Beach would be dangerous. And not just for her. Landry was more well-known there than she was. He would be at an even greater risk.

"I can go try to find it," she said, realizing that on

some level she believed his story about Zeke's death. Otherwise why risk her life to save his?

He smiled and turned off his flashlight. Hers was pointed at the concrete floor, leaving his handsome face in shadow, his eyes looking even darker than usual.

"There is no way I'd let you go alone," he said.

"If you're worried about me not coming back with the painting—"

"It's not that. It's too dangerous for you to go at all, let alone by yourself."

She felt a prickling of suspicion. "You want to go alone?"

"You can call Evan, tell him to cooperate with me," Landry said.

She stared at him, hating that he could so quickly make her feel uncertain of him.

"Isn't it possible that I want to protect you?" He was staring at her as if it made a difference what she thought.

Don't do this, Willa. Don't trust him. You know he'll only end up hurting you.

She couldn't look into his face. She turned off her flashlight, pitching the inside of the storage unit into blackness. She could hear him breathing, knew he was close, closer than he'd been just moments before. She swallowed, her nerves raw with just the thought of him, her body alive with the thought of his touch.

"We should get back to the island," she said, her voice barely a whisper.

"Not yet." His voice was rough with emotion and so close, she felt his breath warm her cheek.

She jumped at the brush of fingertips along her arm, then his arm was around her waist, dragging her to him as his mouth dropped unerringly to hers.

He groaned as if kissing her had been the least of his plans. She could barely breathe, the way he held her so tightly against him, her breasts crushed to his chest. He parted her lips with his tongue, and she opened to him.

Her heart was pounding so hard, she knew he had to feel it in his chest. Her body melted against his, her arms going around his neck as the kiss deepened and her pulse made a buzzing sound in her ears.

He shifted his body, his hand slipping between them to cup her breast. Heat shot through her, her breast aching, her nipples hard as pebbles, sending a fire shooting through her veins straight to her center.

She moaned against his mouth as he thumbed the hard peak of her nipple, the pleasure almost unbearable. "Landry," she breathed against the hot pressure of his mouth.

Lifting her, he pressed her against the Sheetrock wall and shoved her shirt up to get to the old-lady bra she'd put on earlier. He jerked it up and freed her breasts in one swift motion. She leaned her head back, arching her body against him as the night air blew across her bare breasts, dimpling her flesh an instant before she felt the hot wet suction of his mouth on her nipple.

She gasped, the intensity of the sensation making her dizzy. She could feel his fingers working at the zipper on her black jeans, feel his hardness through his own jeans against her bare belly.

Without warning, he stopped, cursed and drew back, his hands on her hips the only thing holding her up since her legs had gone to rubber.

She let out a small cry of frustration and fear that he wouldn't continue. She couldn't see his face—just hear him breathing hard. She wanted him like she'd never wanted anything in her life.

"Tell me about all the men you've had," he whispered.

She began to cry, great big tears silently rolling down her cheeks.

He leaned into her again, his lips brushing across hers, but she knew whatever had possessed him moments ago had passed. He'd changed his mind. She wanted to beat his chest with her fists. She wanted to beg him to take her.

He gently kissed her lips, then her tears. "Not here. Not like this. Not your first time."

She started to protest but he covered her lips with his in a silencing kiss, then pulled back as if he heard something. He turned on the flashlight, pointing it at their feet, but his gaze was on her face.

"Someday you'll thank me," he said as he laid down the flashlight, the beam shooting across the floor to the back of the shedlike room.

He reached to button her jeans but she pushed his hand away as she pulled her bra down over her breasts, covering herself, fingers trembling as she fought to get her balance and jeans buttoned. She'd never slept with a man because she'd never wanted one badly enough. Until now.

The faint clink of metal on metal made them both freeze. Landry quickly motioned to her to be quiet as he reached down and shut off his flashlight. A clank of metal on metal. Someone had just come in through the gate to the storage units.

Landry moved quickly to the large door and lifted it a few feet off the ground. Moonlight bled into the opening. He checked outside, then motioned for her to slip through and followed her. She heard him quietly close and snap the padlock into place, then move along the shadowed side toward the front of the property, motioning for her to wait.

He returned a few moments later. "It's an armed security guard," he whispered, and motioned for her to follow him toward the back of the property.

Her heart lodged in her throat. If they were caught, Landry would go to jail. She would go to another safe house. Neither of them would be safe. In fact, she suspected they wouldn't last long, given the powerful people after them.

A breeze stirred the palms that lined the back of the chain-link fence. She could hear mosquitoes buzzing next to her ear and smell the swampy stew that bordered the property. In the moonlight, she caught a glimpse of one alligator, then another. The tourist wild-animal park she'd seen was right next door.

Back here the fence surrounding the storage units was ten feet high but there was no razor wire along the top. There were just alligators lounging in the swamp on the other side of the fence.

Willa saw at once what Landry had planned and balked at even the idea. "Alligators," she whispered, just in case he hadn't noticed.

He knelt down, his fingers weaved together as he motioned for her to put her foot in for a boost up the fence. "Trust me," he whispered.

Right. She heard the sound of footfalls coming along the edge of the storage units and quickly weighed her options before putting her foot into his hands. He boosted her up. She grabbed hold of the fence and climbed to the top, swung a leg over and teetered there for a moment before gingerly working her way down the other side, all the while keeping an eye on the alligators.

Landry bounded up the fence, over the top and down the other side. He caught her as she dropped to the ground. She heard the scurry of the alligators nearest the fence and for a moment she thought they were scurrying after her instead of away.

"Come on." Landry took her hand, dragging her through the swamp toward the small shack that acted as a ticket booth for the wildlife exhibit. At one point, he stopped and pulled her down next to a large fake rock. She held her breath, listening not just for the security guard but for any alligators sneaking up on them. Off to her left, she saw a huge gator yawn, his massive jaws opening and finally closing again.

They slipped under the gate by the ticket booth and ran across the street, losing themselves in the shadows of the buildings as they wove through the small residential area.

"Neither of us can go to St. Pete Beach," he said when they finally quit running. He'd stopped by a fishing shack near the canal. The area was a web of canals. The night was deathly quiet. No lights or vehicles anywhere. "They'll be waiting for us." His gaze met hers in the darkness, his dark eyes shining. "We have to try to get the paintings sent to us."

She hated the thought of involving Evan Charles in all this. Keeping her voice down, she asked, "Are you sure the police or Freddy D. don't already have the disk?"

"If the police did, then Freddy and his crew would

be behind bars. No one would want us dead. Just the opposite."

"And if Freddy has it?"

He shook his head. "If he did then he wouldn't have any reason to want you dead. If anything, he'd want to keep you alive so you could testify against me."

He touched her cheek, his hand cool, his touch making her shiver but not from the cold. "Trust me. The disk hasn't been found. That's why you and I are still alive. That's why we have to contact the gallery owner—and not go there. Come on." He took her hand. "I saw a pay phone back by that closed motel."

Pop. Wood splintered on the shack wall beside her. Landry knocked her to the ground, landing hard on top of her and rolled them both down the slope toward the water. *Pop. Pop.*

The last thing she heard was Landry whisper next to her ear, "Hold your breath."

Chapter 12

They hit the water.

Landry pulled her under, dragging her deeper and deeper, forcing her to swim after him, the water growing colder and colder as they dove down toward the bottom.

Her head buzzed. She needed desperately to take a breath but he had a death grip on her wrist. Even if she thought about going to the surface and taking her chances against the would-be killer with the gun, Landry wasn't letting her go.

Suddenly he stopped swimming and pulled her upward. Her eyes were open but all she could see was blackness as her head broke the surface. She gasped for breath, her lungs burning. Her free hand struck something hard.

"Quiet," Landry whispered and she realized they'd come up under one of the docks along the canal.

She sucked in air, her body trembling from fear and lack of oxygen, as she treaded water, unable to touch bottom. The water was cold and she kept going under.

Landry pulled her to him, holding her up so her head was above water. His body felt warm and strong. She let him take her weight and fought the need to cry. She'd gone twenty-five years without anyone trying to kill her and now every time she turned around someone was shooting at her or putting snakes in her bathtub. She wasn't sure how much more of this she could take.

As if Landry sensed her despair, he pulled her closer, pressing his cheek to hers, holding her gently. She wrapped her arms around him and closed her eyes.

Overhead someone stepped onto the dock. It rocked, making the water under the dock splash. Landry pulled her out deeper into the water until they were almost to the end of the dock, never letting go of her.

The footsteps were slow, purposeful. Did the killer know they were under the dock? Had he seen them? The dock pushed down as the would-be killer walked to the end, leaving little space above their heads for air. But in Landry's arms, Willa felt safe. The irony of it wasn't lost on her.

She leaned back, trying not to panic. Landry was still holding her, his touch calming. She thanked God she wasn't alone or she knew she would have been dead. He'd saved her again. Her heart swelled, tears burning her eyes.

The dock buoyed upward as the footsteps retreated back down the dock.

They waited, listening. Water lapped softly at the

sides of the dock. A dog barked in the distance. Finally there was the sound of a car engine, the crunch of gravel beneath the tires and then the growl of the car's motor dying away in the distance.

"Wait here for just a second," Landry whispered and disappeared below the water.

He was gone for more than a second. She was getting ready to panic when he reappeared.

"Looks clear. Take my hand."

She did as he told her, swimming down before heading again to the surface. They came up on the lee side of the dock out of the moonlight. Quietly they swam to shore.

She was shaking hard now, the cold, the fear, all her adrenaline long gone. He helped her up onto the shore. Her legs trembled. She stumbled and would have gladly sat down for a while but he dragged her up along the side of the fish shack, then across the street, moving fast.

It would be light soon, surprising her how much time had gone by since they'd left the island.

The phone booth was an old-fashioned one, the kind that were hard to find, thanks to cell phones and vandalism. Landry dug out a handful of coins and dropped them on the metal tray.

Keeping the door open so the overhead light didn't come on, she dialed Information, waited and then asked for Evan Charles's number. She repeated it out loud to Landry, then still shaking, dialed Evan's number, using the coins Landry supplied as he stood guard. The answering machine picked up after the fifth ring.

"Evan. It's Willa St. Clair. I need to talk to you. If you're there, could you—"

"Willa?" Evan sounded groggy.

"I'm sorry to call you at this hour but I need your help."

"Oh, girl, I heard what happened. It's in the all papers. You must be scared to death, sweetie. Was it just awful?"

She had to smile, imagining him sitting up in bed now, eating up the drama. "Evan, what did you do with my paintings that didn't sell?"

"You need money. Of course you do. I told you I could sell them if you let me keep them in the shop."

Her heart fell. "Is that what you did?"

"Of course not. You told me you wanted to wait until you could have another show and we agreed that would give you the most play."

She breathed a sigh of relief. "How many are left?"

"Not even half a dozen."

Landry was motioning to her. "Evan, was there one painting that didn't get hung at the show?"

"Oh, sweetie, I just feel awful about that. I found it later when I went to pack up the others. Do you hate me?"

"Of course not." She nodded to Landry. Relief washed over him, softening the hard lines of his face. He couldn't have been more handsome.

"Can you just describe the painting for me?" she asked, and listened while he confirmed that it was the one they had all been looking for.

"It had a tear in the backing, I guess that's why my assistant didn't put it up," Evan said. "I am just sick about it. I'm positive it would have sold, sweetie."

"It's not a problem, really. I have a terribly big favor to ask of you. Would it be possible for you to send me the paintings without anyone knowing? I could give you an address."

"Not on his home line, in case it's tapped," Landry whispered.

"Could I call you back on your cell and tell you where to send them?" she asked.

"Oh, such intrigue. I'm just shivering all over," he cried. He rattled off his cell number, Willa repeating it.

"I'll call you right back."

"I'll get a pen and paper. Don't worry, sweetie, I'll destroy the evidence. I'll shred it. Or burn it. If you want, I'll shred it and eat it with a nice marinara sauce."

She hung up, half shaking her head. Evan was such a trip. She adored him. She just prayed that she wasn't endangering him.

"Wait," Landry said as she started to dial Evan's cell. "The safest way to do this is have Evan send the box by special courier to the marina so Bull can bring it out tomorrow when he brings the rest of the supplies. If he does it tonight, it will get here in time."

She nodded and called Evan's cell, gave him the address for Bull. "Address the box to Cara Wilson. That's the name I'm using."

"I'll do it right now. Not to worry. You really must let me know how this all turns out. I'll just be on pins and needles until I hear."

She promised, hung up and looked at Landry. This was almost over but she knew her life would never be the same.

There was one regret she was determined she wouldn't have when it was all over, she told herself as she leaned into Landry and kissed him.

"You all right?" Landry asked, seeming surprised.

She just looked at him. Was she all right? He had to be kidding. She was soaked to the skin, half-drowned, some kind of seaweed stuff in her hair and at least one person was trying to kill her—more than likely more.

He smiled and picked something green from her hair. "Think you can make it back to the boat?"

Like she had a choice. She nodded. The sky behind them paled as they reached the boat. She'd half expected someone to be waiting for them in ambush but apparently no one knew what Landry's boat looked like, and there were dozens of boats tied up along the canal.

She climbed in, surprised that she was starting to get her sea legs. He untied the boat and stepped in after her, quickly starting the motor and turning the bow out toward the watery horizon.

He tossed her an old towel from the bottom of the boat. It smelled of gas and oil. She didn't even care. She wrapped it around her and slid down in the boat. Sleep took her at once, dragging her down into a dreamless cold darkness.

She woke with a start, blinded by the light and jarred awake as the boat hit the sand. Struggling to sit up, she looked around. They were back on the island. She was awed and surprised that Landry had managed to get them back here alive. Daylight broke over the tops of the mangrove islands to the east. She felt as if she'd been dragged through the mud, like an alley cat sneaking home after a rough night on the streets.

As she turned to look at Landry, she saw the blood. "My God, you're shot!"

Landry smiled at the concern in her voice. "It's all right," he said as he stepped out into the water and pulled the boat partway up on shore. "It's just a flesh wound."

She climbed out, looking unsteady and a little green around the gills. "Why didn't you tell me you were shot?" She sounded angry now.

"It's no big deal. Anyway, what would you have done? You aren't one of those women who faint at the sight of blood, are you?" He reached for her as she seemed to wobble. "Oh, hell," he said as she sank to the sand.

He dropped beside her and forced her head between her knees. "Take deep breaths."

She was crying softly, gasping for breath. "My mother wanted me to be a nurse."

He laughed, and rubbed the back of her neck with his palm. "Yeah, you would have made a great nurse." When she was breathing normally, he hid the boat in the bushes again and then helped her up. "Can you walk?"

She looked offended. "Of course I can walk." She glanced at his upper arm, the shirtsleeve soaked with blood, and started to go faint on him again.

"Come on," he said, leading her through the brush, using his uninjured arm to guide her. They had to bushwhack for a ways through the brush before they hit the trail, skirting around the swamp and unstable ground.

"Watch out. There are parts of this island that are like quicksand," he told her. "You wander in there and you're never coming out again."

He was glad to see that the tide was coming in, the waves washing away any sign of their footprints in the sand. Soon the small beach would be covered in water.

He'd had time to think about the attack at Everglades City. Whoever had seen them leave the island had to have contacted someone onshore. First the security guard at the storage facility. Then the shooter.

What bothered him was that the two incidents didn't seem connected. The guard hadn't seemed alarmed. He might have just been checking things after being called about a possible break-in.

The shooter was a whole other story. He'd tried to kill them both. One of Zeke's friends from the force? Definitely someone who didn't give a damn about the disk—and just wanted Landry dead.

Landry was sure he'd been the target. Willa's mistake was being with him. And here he'd thought he could protect her. The way things were going, he would get her killed.

But the painting was on its way. All they had to do was wait for Bull to bring it to them then get off this island. He thought about the person he and Willa had seen watching them leave the island. Was it possible they'd been followed?

He hadn't heard another boat but no reason to take a chance. On the way back to the villa, he took a detour. "Stay here," he whispered, and sneaked down to the old fisherman's dock and checked the boat motor. Ice-cold. The boat hadn't been out.

"What?" Willa said when he returned and they were headed for the villa again.

"Is there another boat on the island that you know of because that one hasn't been anywhere," he said.

She shook her head. "You think the person who saw us leave somehow contacted whoever was shooting at us? But there is no cell phone service out here."

He smiled. "Exactly. That's what makes me think there's a boat we don't know about."

The villa was silent as they slipped through the archway and made their way up to her apartment. Once inside, Landry locked the door.

Willa looked beat and worse there was something so endearing about her he just wanted to hold her and promise her that everything was going to be all right.

It was a promise he couldn't make though, and holding her right now when they were both feeling vulnerable was the last thing he should do.

He walked through the bedroom and turned on the water in the tub. She was still standing where he'd left her looking lost. He motioned her into the bathroom. "Strip down and get in there. You can get hypothermia even this far south, and right now you look like you might tip over at any moment." He stripped off his shirt.

Willa's eyes widened.

"Don't worry, I'm not getting in with you. I'm just going to clean up the wound and then go see if I can find another boat on the island. I'll lock the door as I leave. You get some rest. I'll be back before you know it."

She nodded and he turned his back to her. He cranked on some water in the sink and began to gingerly wash the flesh wound to his shoulder. This was the second bullet he'd taken in a matter of days. Not a good sign.

"There's a first-aid kit in the cabinet," she said behind him.

He opened the medicine cabinet over the sink and took out the box, amused to see what all was in it— including a note that read "Be careful. Love, Mom xoxox."

He smiled to himself as he took out the gauze and replaced the box, note and all.

Just before the mirror steamed completely over, he

saw Willa slip out of her shirt and bra. He looked away, but not before he'd seen the pale creamy flesh of her breasts and remembered the warm soft weight of her breast in his palm. Just the sight of her half-naked sent a stab of desire through him like a hot knife blade.

He ducked his head, waiting until he heard her step into the tub and close the curtain before he looked up again. Fighting the urge to join her in the tub no matter what he'd said, he quickly cleaned the wound. It hurt like hell but it was exactly what he needed to exorcise the memory of Willa half-naked and remind him what was at stake here. He had to keep his mind on finding the disk. The last thing he needed was to let Willa St. Clair, South Dakota virgin, distract him.

The thought made him laugh. She more than distracted him.

"What's so funny?" she asked from in the tub.

"You, darlin'," he said as he shut off the water in the sink and covered the wound to his arm with the bandage before pulling on a clean shirt.

"I was just thinking about you and all those men you've been with," he said, and stepped out of the bathroom as the shower curtain opened a crack and a bar of soap flew past his head. He closed the door just in time, smiling to himself as the soap smacked the bathroom door.

In his duffel bag he took out his second gun, the one *with* the silencer, feeling surprisingly guilty. He'd had to do what needed to be done and yet... He stuck the weapon in the waistband of his shorts, covering it with the tail of his shirt.

He heard Willa get out of the tub to retrieve the soap as he left, locking the door behind him. The villa was quiet, no one apparently up yet, as he left. The sun rose behind the palms to the east in a burst of hot orange.

As Landry walked, he mulled over the same thoughts that had been haunting him since they'd left Everglades City. What if he was wrong about being the target? But who would want Willa dead? It made no sense.

If his theory was right Freddy D. had made sure both he and Willa were free so they could find the disk for him. Even Zeke's buddies wouldn't kill Willa.

So who did that leave?

Someone who didn't want the disk to ever be found. Or for Landry or Willa to live long enough to talk.

Landry swore as he circled the island looking for a boat. Who the hell was after them?

Willa finished her bath although she was so exhausted that just drying off took all her effort. All the adrenaline rushes, being shot at, running for her life, being almost made love to—all of it was taking a toll on her body.

Her mind wouldn't shut down, though. Her thoughts circled around Landry refusing to rest. She'd been wrong about him. He'd saved her life twice now. How could she doubt him anymore?

She thought about Odell and what he'd said to her in his kitchen. He had been acting so strangely during the barbecue. Almost jealous. Maybe definitely jealous.

The truth was she had little to no experience with men. As much as she hated to admit it, Landry had been right about her. She'd dated some in high school, all neighboring ranch boys who attended the same church she did. A couple of them she would have let get to first base—if they had tried. They hadn't.

She'd heard a rumor her senior year that she was frigid. She hadn't really known what that meant since she felt anything but. The rumor had persisted, and by the time she went away to college, she'd started to believe it.

She seemed to intimidate men. At least some of them. Men like Odell, who seemed to put her on a pedestal and wanted to protect her. Not men like Landry Jones, she thought as she slipped on a cotton nightshirt and climbed between the covers.

Overhead she heard the creak of footsteps, but she didn't even give Cape Diablo's ghosts a second thought as sleep took her again, this time even more deeply than in the boat on the way back to the island.

Landry took the main path down to the pier, then circled the island counterclockwise. He waded around fallen trees, mangroves, swampy bogs of quicksand and mud and finally rocks, sometimes having to almost swim to keep going.

As he reached the end of the island near the deep water cover, he spotted an older man. Carlos.

That was all he could remember. Carlos, the faithful friend, who had been given the right to stay on the island until he died—just like the old lady who lived on the third floor, Alma Garcia.

Willa said she'd seen the two talking, seeming to be arguing as if the old man was trying to convince the woman of something.

Now Landry watched Carlos pull his small fishing boat up on the beach. The elderly man seemed lost in his own world, making Landry wonder if both of the elderly on the island weren't senile. Or was that just what they both wanted everyone to think?

Did Carlos know the true story of the disappearance of his best friend, wife and children? Supposedly he and Alma hadn't been on the island when it had happened. Maybe that was true. Maybe Carlos was as much in the dark as Landry was about the events that had happened around him.

Landry stepped back into the trees as he watched Carlos look around then head into the thick underbrush. Where was he going?

Carlos wasn't gone but a few minutes before he returned with a fishing pole. He put it in the boat, then pushed out and climbed in.

The boat motor purred to life. Carlos spun the motor to point the bow of the boat toward a far island. He gave it full throttle and sped off to disappear into the horizon.

Landry waited for a few minutes longer, then trailed along the edge of the cove to the spot where he'd seen Carlos disappear into the underbrush. There was only a faint path, not even noticeable if you hadn't seen someone just emerge from it.

Bending low to avoid limbs, he pushed back through the dense vegetation. At first he didn't see it. Probably because the old fishing shack was grown over, the island reclaiming it.

He recalled how secretive the old man had been and felt a shiver of dread work its way through him as he reached for the door.

Chapter 13

Landry found the latch on the old fishing shack and slowly opened the door.

The shack was small and dark inside. All he could see were old bait buckets, weather-ruined life preservers from another era, a few fishing poles and odds and ends.

He wasn't sure what he was looking for. Maybe an unfinished painting by W. St. Clair. One of him. Stolen from her room.

It was just large enough that he could step inside. He stood in the darkness, not sure what he was looking for, just that he didn't like this place any more than he did the villa.

The island gave him the creeps and he wasn't sure if it was the people on it—or the evil he felt that permeated the place. He hadn't been kidding when he told

Willa he could feel that something horrible had happened here.

He found the small wooden box under a shelf hidden behind the life preservers. The lock was rusty, the hinges creaking loudly as he lifted the lid.

Old letters. Envelopes yellowed with age. Gingerly he picked up one, lifted the flap and carefully pulled out the thin sheet of paper.

The letter was written in Spanish, but he could make out enough of it to see that it was a love letter addressed to "My Dear One" and signed "Your Faithful." The writing was neat but neither masculine or feminine, the paper plain.

He put it back in the envelope, noting that the letters had never been mailed. Had they been delivered?

Putting the letters back, he returned the box to its hiding place and checked to make sure no one was waiting for him outside. The island seemed too quiet, as if even the birds held their breath. It gave him a strange, anxious feeling, and suddenly he couldn't wait to get back to Willa.

Slipping out, he stole back out to the beach. No sign of Carlos.

After circling the entire island, he hadn't found any sign of another person on the island or a boat. Maybe there wasn't anyone on the island he had to fear. Not that he was taking any chances with the odd group living here.

For now they were safe here. Bull would be arriving soon with the package from the gallery owner. Once they had the painting it would just be a matter of getting the disk to the right people.

As he neared the villa, he felt the heat bearing down

on him. He needed a bath. The thought brought back an image of Willa in the tub. Not a good idea. A swim. That's what he needed. He would get Willa and go down to the sandy part of the beach. The tide was going out. It would be nice to swim and maybe lie in the shade for a while. Better than staying alone in that small apartment with her.

Henri's door was open, but there was no sign of her or of the others as Landry crossed the courtyard. Loud music throbbed from Blossom's apartment. There was no other sound as he climbed the stairs.

He tapped at the door, wondering if he would wake Willa. He'd been gone for quite a while. She should be awake by now. She'd been so obviously exhausted earlier he figured she'd gone right to bed.

"Yes?"

"It's me," he said quietly.

She opened the door, a paintbrush in her hand.

He stepped in, her look questioning. He shook his head. "You're working?" He glanced toward the bedroom and her easel, relieved to see a picturesque painting of the villa. No splashes of red. No hint of a bloodbath.

"Want to go for a swim?"

She cocked her head at him.

"We can talk on the beach." He made it sound as if he thought the apartment might be bugged. It might be, but that wasn't his reason for wanting out of here right now. Willa smelled and looked wonderful and the apartment was cool, the bed too inviting.

She studied him for a moment, then said, "I'll put on my suit."

When she came out of the bathroom, she was wearing

a two-piece—chaste compared to that string thing that Henri was wearing yesterday.

But Willa in her two-piece was so damned sexy he felt poleaxed standing there looking at her. How the hell was he going to keep his hands off her?

"What?" Willa asked.

He shook his head, afraid to trust his voice.

She picked up a beach cover from behind the door and pulled it around her, leaving nothing exposed but a lot of leg.

He turned away, let out a long breath and couldn't wait to hit the water. He just hoped it would be cold enough, he thought as he followed her down a short path to a secluded stretch of beach, the sun golden over the top of the palms.

Running past her, he dove into the surf. As hot as he was, it felt icy, but as he surfaced and looked back at Willa, he realized the dip had done little to cool his desire for her.

What was wrong with him? He'd gone all these years without needing anyone. Hell, he hadn't seen his family in months. Talk about a loner.

So now he was going to let some South Dakota farm girl twist him all up inside? A virgin farm girl, he thought with a grin as he waded toward her.

He plopped down on the beach and squinted out at the Gulf. Out of the corner of his eye, he watched her drop her beach cover and walk slowly into the surf. He closed his eyes and lay back in the sand, concentrating on each breath the way he did when he was shooting a sniper rifle.

Over the sound of the surf, the breeze in the palms overhead and the cry of seagulls on the rocks nearby, he heard her return from the water and lay down on the sand next to him.

The sun beat down on his bare chest, legs and arms. He tried to concentrate on the rise and fall of his chest as he breathed slowly, carefully, too aware of her next to him.

Whose stupid idea had this been? A secluded beach in paradise? What had he been thinking? At the time he'd thought anything was better than staying another minute in that small apartment with her.

He flinched as a cool damp fingertip touched his shoulder. Eyes still closed, he felt her shadow fall over him only an instant before her lips brushed his.

He opened his eyes and looked into a whole lot of blue. He'd been able to read her from the first time he'd seen her. She was incapable of hiding her feelings. Even her thoughts. Just as she wasn't hiding any now.

He groaned and cupped the back of her head as he brought her mouth down to his again.

She tasted salty, her palm cool as she rested it on his chest. He parted her lips with his tongue and drew her down on him, her cool body on his sun-hot one as he kissed her deeply, aroused by her lush body clad in the still-wet old-fashioned two-piece swimsuit.

As he freed her of the two-piece suit, he rolled over so he was on top. Tossed the suit aside—top and bottom. Her eyes widened a little as he pressed his chest to hers. She felt so good.

He'd promised himself he wouldn't do this. She must have seen his moment of hesitation.

"Are you sure about this, St. Clair?"

"I need a man who doesn't own any sheep," she said on a breath.

He grinned down at her. Damn, she was sexy as hell in that innocent, naive South Dakota way of hers. "What you need, darlin', is a man who can promise you tomorrow. I'm not that man."

"Don't go gallant on me now," she said, and grinned up at him. "I want you to be my first. Set the bar for those other poor fools."

He didn't want to even think about another man making love to this woman. He dropped his mouth to hers, stunned by the sensation of just kissing her, and all the while telling himself that this wouldn't change anything between them.

Willa had often dreamed of the first time a man would make love to her. Frustration and fear combined. But kissing Landry, she let herself enjoy the feel of him, the new sensations that sent shock waves through her body, tremors of exquisite pleasure. She'd challenged him and he'd taken it. No other man would ever be able to surpass this, she thought as he dropped his mouth to her breast and she felt his wonderfully talented tongue begin its journey over her body.

After that, she had no clear thoughts. He touched and licked and caressed and kissed, leaving trails of heat up and down her body. She gasped, sometimes out of shock at the places he went, the things he did, until she lost herself entirely in the building volcano he'd started inside her.

And just when she thought she couldn't take any more, he made her explode, showered every cell in her body with pleasure as she quaked in the aftermath.

Then he kissed her, held her and started all over again. This time as she clung to him, he entered her.

She felt a sharp jab of pain, then slowly he took her higher and higher until she could no longer hold back, the two of them, their bodies locked in ecstasy on her swimsuit cover, the warm sand beneath.

He rolled to the side, taking her with him, pressing her face into the sweaty warmth of his chest. She breathed him in so she never forgot his scent, the feel of him, the sound of his voice next to her ear. She never wanted to forget.

"Are you all right?" he asked.

"Hmm," she said. "I just feel sorry for those other men. That will be a hard act to follow." She giggled and tried to remember a time she felt this wonderful. "Not even Christmas in South Dakota could top this."

He chuckled, a deep throaty sound, and pulled her closer. She sensed a sadness in him. Did he feel guilty for taking her virginity? She smiled at the thought, grateful to him, not that she would ever tell him that. But it made her wonder if Landry Jones wasn't as tough as he let on. She let herself drift in a cloud of contentment, forgetting for a while that anyone wanted her dead.

He must have dozed off. Landry woke with a start as cold water dropped on his chest, on his face. He reached for the gun he'd wrapped up in his T-shirt as he squinted up at the dark silhouette standing over him.

His T-shirt was empty.

He came all the way up into a sitting position, eyes focusing as he raised one hand to block out the sun and saw Willa standing over him holding his gun. His gun with the *silencer* on it.

He swore and met her gaze.

"You," she gasped as if she couldn't catch her breath. She was soaking wet, obviously having gone swimming. He hadn't felt her leave his side and that, it turned out, was a huge mistake on his part. "You're the one who shot at me."

She pointed the gun at him, her finger on the trigger. "I wondered when you didn't seem overly concerned about a killer being on the island with us. It was because you're the one who took those shots at me!"

He groaned. "I did it because I needed to gain your trust quickly."

"My trust?" She spat the words at him. "You took shots at me to gain my trust? Did you make love to me for the same reason?"

"You know better than that."

"Do I?" Her hand holding the gun was trembling. "You could have killed me."

"I'm a better shot than that." He gave her a grin, hoping to lighten this moment.

Her eyes narrowed, the gun in her hand steadied as she pointed it at his heart.

He wiped the grin off his face. "Look, I'm sorry I lied to you. I didn't know you then." He lifted up, getting his feet under him and slowly rising. "I was desperate and you were just a means to an end. But somewhere along the way, that changed." He reached out to her, needing to get that gun away from her before she accidentally pulled the trigger. Or pulled it on purpose.

She stepped back, the gun still aimed at his heart.

In the distance, he heard the sound of a boat headed this way. Bull. He glanced toward the sun. It was high overhead, bathing the island with golden heat.

"That will be Bull with the paintings," he said.

She nodded, her eyes sparking with anger and pain. She handed him the gun, slapping it into his palm, her blue eyes cold and hard enough to chip ice. "Let's get this over with."

Finally something they could agree on. She didn't give him a chance to say anything else, which was good because there was nothing he *could* say. He was a bastard. He liked to believe that all men were on some level, but right now he had the feeling he was wrong about that, too.

He stuffed the gun into his shorts as he watched her walk away, mentally kicking himself. As she was swallowed up in the vegetation, he quickly picked up his T-shirt from the sand, shook it out and went after her as he pulled it on.

His skin felt raw with sensation, their lovemaking imprinted on his flesh—and embedded forever in his brain. Talk about raising the bar. He couldn't imagine being with another woman without thinking of Willa and this sunlit beach.

Willa heard him behind her but didn't turn. She had every right to be angry with him. It didn't matter that he'd done what he had for supposedly a higher purpose—getting the disk and taking down the bad guys. Or that he'd been shot defending himself and was now being wrongly accused. Or that there were still people out there who wanted him dead—and her, as well, and that he'd taken those shots at her to protect her. Or that he *had* protected her, even saved her life last night by the canal.

The bottom line was that he'd lied to her. He'd deceived her.

It wasn't him she was so angry with and she knew it. Nor was it the fact that she'd made love with him, wanted him to be the first man and wasn't sorry one iota for it.

No, what had her furious with herself was that she'd made Landry Jones into some kind of hero in her mind. She'd needed a hero and she'd let herself believe he was one.

And that hadn't even been her worst mistake.

No, her worst mistake was... She slowed, tears burning her eyes. She felt his hand on her shoulder and didn't even have the energy to shrug it off. He came around in front of her, his gaze going straight to her tears. He looked like his heart would break, as if he could read the truth in her eyes.

Her worst mistake was falling in love with him.

She jerked away from him and wiped angrily at the tears as she bit her lower lip and gave herself a good mental talking-to.

"You want me to pick up the supply box?" he asked behind her, sounding uncomfortable, as if half-afraid to touch her and even more confused as to what to say.

"You do that," she said, lifting her chin into the air and stalking toward the villa. She could feel his gaze burning into her backside. He'd looked scared back there, as if he couldn't bear what he'd done to her—but she would bet if she glanced back, he'd be looking at her butt. Landry, everything else aside, was all male.

She cursed his black heart silently as she passed through the archway and ran up the stairs. She heard Odell come out of his apartment to go down and get the supplies he'd ordered, but she hurriedly unlocked her door and rushed in before he could call to her.

She went straight to the tub and stood under the spray, washing away the sand and the scent of Landry Jones. If only it was that easy to wash away the feelings. They had come on her so quickly. But spending time with a man under a dock under these kind of circumstances put feelings on fast-forward. At least that was her excuse.

It didn't help that he was so darned handsome. Or often pretty witty. And that grin—

She shut off the water and heard the door to the apartment open. She'd left it unlocked so he could come in when he returned from the dock. The painting was in the box. Evan had said it was. So there was no more looking for the disk. Soon, no reason to be together.

She heard Landry cutting into the box and reached for a towel. Within moments, Landry would have what he wanted, and if she knew him the way she thought she did, he would be gone.

She leaned against the wall and waited for the sound of the front door closing. Maybe he'd already left and she just hadn't heard the door close. He could be halfway to his boat right now.

The bathroom door opened. Her heart did a little leap inside her chest. At least he had come to say goodbye.

He drew back the shower curtain, seeming a little surprised to see her standing in the tub holding a towel to her. She met his gaze and felt another start.

"The disk isn't in the painting."

"What?" She plowed past him out of the shower and into the living room, still holding the towel in front of her, indifferent to her otherwise nudity.

The box was open, a half-dozen of her paintings standing up along the front of the couch. The one painting, the one that Simon Renton had supposedly hid the disk behind, was on the floor, the back ripped, revealing the space under the paper. It was empty.

She bent down and picked up the painting, seeing at once where the paper backing had been slit. The disk *had* been inside it.

She turned to stare at Landry. He looked like he'd been kicked in the gut as he lowered himself into one of the chairs just feet from her.

"Where is the disk?" she said stupidly.

He shrugged. "Maybe it fell out. Maybe Simon lied. Who knows?"

She felt chilled suddenly. Putting down the painting, she went into the bedroom, closed the door and dressed. The ramifications were just starting to hit her. Without the disk, Landry could never clear himself. Both of their lives would remain in danger.

Unless someone already had the disk and that was why she and Landry were almost killed last night. They had become too much of a liability.

As she came out, she found Landry sitting in the chair, his head in his hands. She desperately wanted to ask him what he was thinking of doing now. But she was afraid to hear his answer.

"Okay," she said, unwilling to give up, needing something to do, to say. "What if the disk did fall out?"

He looked up at her as if she had to be kidding, even thinking there was somewhere to go from here.

"Seriously, what if it did?" She went over to the box and looked inside, although she was sure Landry had already done that. "Then it must have fallen out before it left my studio, so it would be…" She glanced toward the box the police had packed, knowing the disk wasn't in the bottom of it. Both she and Landry had gone through that box, as well.

A thought struck her. "Why didn't the police know about the disk?"

"What?"

"You said the police didn't know about the disk so they wouldn't have been looking for it," she pressed. "But if you and Simon were working undercover to get information out about organized crime—and who the dirty cop was—then why wouldn't the police be on the lookout for a disk?"

"Because the disk just kind of fell into our laps from one of Freddy D.'s disgruntled associates. The guy contacted me but Simon insisted he be the pick-up man because I was too visible in the organization. He hadn't been in long and was low on the totem pole."

"So neither you nor Simon had told your bosses that you had the disk?" she said.

He nodded. "We hadn't gotten a chance. Then after what went down… The cops had no way of knowing how you were really involved. They would just assume you were in the wrong place at the wrong time."

"So…" she said, glancing toward one of the boxes that the police had packed for her. "If one of them picked up the disk, they would just think it was mine. All this time, we've been looking for a painting. Not a disk."

Landry watched her with interest now.

She stepped over to her box of supplies and dug down to the box marked "Bookkeeping." She came back to the table and set it down, half-afraid to open it for fear she was only going to get both of their hopes up for nothing.

Slowly she lifted the lid. Under all the papers was a small disk box with the imprint of one of the more popular home business accounting systems. Inside were a half-dozen disks.

"You own a computer?" Landry asked.

"A laptop. I had it shipped back to South Dakota. My stepfather was going to do my taxes for me if this dragged out until April. But I forgot to send him the disks."

Landry watched her as she removed the disks from the box and sorted through them.

Her fingers froze. She swallowed around the lump in her throat. "This one isn't mine." She handed it to him as if it were made of glass.

He swore. "If we had a computer we could check to see if it is the right one."

"Odell has a laptop." She remembered seeing it under his desk and wondering at the time why he was doing the book on an old typewriter instead of the computer.

Landry looked from her to the disk and back again. "You think you could distract him long enough for me to make sure this is the disk?"

She went to the window and peered out. Odell had come back with the supplies he'd ordered. Through a crack in the blinds she could see him unloading some things.

"Go out now. I'll call him up to my apartment and try to give you as much time as possible," she said, meeting his gaze.

He eyed her. "You're not thinking of—"

"Of course not. I'll think of something."

He nodded, something passing between them that felt like trust. "I'll come up as soon as I know for sure."

She smiled. He seemed to think she would be needing his help to keep Odell off her. "Take this." She tossed him her camera. "It will give me an excuse for you being gone."

Landry caught the small digital camera and tucked it into his pocket, then reached into the duffel he had by the end of the couch. "Put this someplace where you can get to it if you need it."

"I'm touched by your concern," she said, actually meaning it as she took the gun he handed her.

He grinned. "I know I really know how to treat a girl." And he was out the door.

Willa put the gun in a drawer in the end table by the couch, then waited until Landry disappeared before she went down the stairs to Odell's apartment. The door was partially ajar. She could see him inside putting food in the fridge.

"We owe you steaks," she said from the doorway and then tapped on the door slightly. "Sorry to catch you in the middle of something." She couldn't help but glance toward the typewriter. There wasn't any paper in it. Out of the corner of her eye, she caught a glimpse of the laptop right where she'd seen it before.

"Come on in," Odell said, putting the rest of his food inside and closing the fridge door. "Can I offer you something to drink?"

"Thanks. Landry took off to try to photograph the sunset and…" She feared she was a horrible liar and Odell could see right through her.

"Do you need something?" he asked, coming right over to her.

"You're going to think I'm silly, but I started to re-arrange the furniture and I found a hole behind the couch," she said. At least that much was true. "I'm

afraid there might be something in it. Like rats. Or—"
she shuddered for real "—a snake?"

He smiled. "Do you have a good flashlight?"

She shook her head and he quickly went to his desk,
pulled out a drawer and took out a large flashlight.

"Let's go see what's in your wall," he said, sounding
excited—and not the least bit afraid of snakes.

"You're sure you don't mind?"

Odell laughed. "Not at all. I'm honored actually—"
he said as she led him across the courtyard and up the
stairs "—that you would ask me."

She felt guilty at once. He'd been nothing but nice to
her and now that she knew he hadn't taken potshots at
her, she felt even worse. But there was still that snake
someone had put in her tub… "You have been so nice to
me. I really appreciate it." She opened her door, let him
go in and entered behind him, leaving the door open.

He stopped in the middle of the room. "You've been
through a lot, it sounds like. I figured you might need
a friend."

She smiled at him. "I do."

Silence stretched between them as they just stood
looking at each other. For a moment Willa had the
strangest feeling that she might need the gun she'd hidden. She took a step toward it.

Odell seemed to come out of a daze. "The hole behind
your couch. Right." He turned and surveyed the couch.
"Looks even worse than mine."

All Willa could think about was Landry. Was he
in Odell's apartment? She'd noticed that Odell had
closed his door, but hadn't locked it—just as she knew
he wouldn't. Unless he was working, his door was usually open.

She helped Odell pull the couch away from the wall. While he went behind it to peer into the hole, she stayed on the other side near the end table and the gun.

Landry, she realized, hadn't even asked her if she could shoot a gun. She guessed he'd just assumed that since she was from South Dakota...

"This is quite the hole," Odell said. "Goes back in quite a ways. Don't see any indication there has been any kind of creature in here, though."

"What do you think made it?" she asked, getting on her knees on the cushions to peer over the back of the couch.

To her surprise she saw that Odell had a small pocket knife in his hand. She recalled the knife cut in the tape on her box of supplies from the dock. Odell. He'd opened the box. That's how he knew she was an artist. Was that also how he knew she was from South Dakota? Something in her supply box gave her away?

Or had Odell known long before then? Was she the real reason he'd come to Cape Diablo? And Landry thought Odell's interest in her was romantic. Willa suspected he couldn't be more wrong.

Odell sat down, his back against the wall as he looked at her. "I'd say a person made the hole in your wall."

"Why?" She tried to hide her surprise at seeing the pocket knife that Odell had folded and put into his pocket again.

"I don't know if you've noticed but the old gal upstairs doesn't just sneak around a lot at night," Odell said. "She's looking for something."

Willa thought about her missing painting. "Like what?"

"I saw her digging around the villa, poking in the

walls," he said. "It wouldn't be that unusual for a smuggler and pirate like Andres Santiago to have hidden all kinds of things in these walls—gold, coins, even jewels or I suppose currency."

Willa feigned interest. "Are we talking a lot of money?"

He laughed and leaned toward her conspiratorially. "There are those rumors that Andres hid a small fortune on this island before his disappearance. Seems he didn't trust banks. So it's not too surprising that there were also rumors after that about fortune hunters who came out to the island disappearing, as well."

"You don't think—?"

"That the old gal would kill to keep a treasure she felt was rightly hers? You better believe it. Not to mention the Ancient Mariner from the boathouse. I think he's in love with Alma. And we all know what a man will do to protect the woman he loves."

"That is very true," Landry said as he leaned over the couch to smile at Odell. "Honey, there is a man behind our couch. I hope you can explain this."

Willa hadn't heard Landry come in and obviously neither had Odell. Odell looked both startled and embarrassed, quickly getting to his feet and dusting himself off as he retrieved his flashlight.

"I found a hole behind the couch when I started rearranging the living room and I was worried there might be something in there," she quickly explained with a grimace. "Something icky."

Landry shook his head and grinned at Odell. "Just like a woman. What is it that makes them want to rearrange the furniture all the time?"

Odell shook his head. "Nothing in the hole to worry

about anyway," he said to Willa, and smiled. "Let me know if you need help again."

"I doubt that will be necessary," Landry said, his smile gone. He tossed Willa her camera. "Got that photo you wanted, darlin'."

Odell left, but not before stealing a glance at Willa.

"You made him think I was coming on to him," she whispered the minute the door was closed.

"If I hadn't acted jealous, he would have been suspicious and you have to admit, having him look into a hole behind the couch is suspect. Brilliant," Landry added quickly. "But later when he's over there by himself, he's going to wonder."

She stared at him, trying to gauge what he'd found out, pretty sure by his mood that she already knew. "Was it the disk?"

He nodded. "I didn't have time to read it—just confirm that it is the disk that got Simon killed. And Zeke."

She saw the pain in his eyes. "I'm sorry."

He shook his head. "Finally the truth will come out."

She let herself breathe a sigh of relief, then instantly felt a stab of acute disappointment. If he had been telling her the truth about the disk and it clearing him, then all of this would be behind them once he turned it over to the police. He could go back to his life. She could go back to hers. Isn't that what they both wanted?

She told him her theory about Odell.

Landry didn't seem that surprised. Or that worried.

"What happens now?" she asked.

He pulled the disk from his pocket and turned it slowly in his fingers. "We get off this island." He looked up at her, pocketed the disk and smiled. "I'll go get the boat. Pack what you have to take and I'll pick you up at the dock."

She nodded, feeling a wave of doubt. Landry was leaving with the disk. She had the strangest feeling that he wouldn't be back for her. That she wouldn't ever see him again.

"Hey," he said, lifting her chin with his finger. "You don't think I'll come back for you?"

Mind reader. She opened her mouth. Nothing came out.

Landry looked disappointed in her as he reached into his pocket and took out the disk. He opened the drawer where she'd put the gun and put the disk in the back, then held up his hands to show that he wasn't doing some disappearing act with it.

"Lock the door behind me. I'll be back for you," he said and taking the gun with the silencer on it left.

Chapter 14

The sun glided slowly across the sky toward the Gulf as Landry left. Wind moaned in the tops of the palms and the air seemed heavier, as if a storm was coming in. A big tropical one from the feel of it. He moved quickly, the growing storm making him all the more anxious to get off this island.

It was dark in the trees, the trail deep in shadow as Landry left through the archway, taking the path where he'd first found Willa.

So much had changed since then. *He* had changed. He couldn't believe she'd found the disk. Even if the painting would have made Willa's show, the disk wouldn't have been in it. Landry shook his head, imagining how that would have gone over if he'd purchased the painting and found no disk inside.

Now all he had to do was get the disk to the right

people. No small chore since someone knew where they were. Those shots at them in Everglades City had been to kill. They couldn't go back there.

As he reached the beach where he'd hidden the boat, he realized what had been nagging at him all day. Why hadn't the shooter followed them to the island to finish the job?

He froze as he looked into the bushes and saw that his boat was gone and knew why the shooter hadn't followed them to the island.

Because there was already someone planted on the island to make sure he never left here with the disk.

His mind racing, he ran toward the old fisherman's shack. As far as he knew Carlos's was the only other boat on the island. He had to get Willa and the disk off this island and fast and he hadn't heard Carlos return to the boathouse. Landry would check this side of the island before heading back. With luck he would find the old man and persuade him to either take them off the island—or lend them his boat.

Who was the killer on the island? Odell? The guy would be his first choice. Willa wouldn't let him back in the apartment again, would she? What about the women? Either of the women looked like they could bite a man's head off in a single bite.

As he reached the beach where he'd seen Carlos pull up his boat, Landry saw that it was empty. No boat. No Carlos.

He'd been so sure he would find the old man here, get the boat and get back to Willa. Once they were on the water, he planned to head up the coast. He'd rather take his chances out in the Gulf than go back to Everglades City.

But now he worried that there was no way off the island. No boat. No chance to get the disk into the right hands before it was too late.

Landry swore and started to turn back toward the trail and the villa when he saw something in the water. His pulse jumped as he stepped toward it. A piece of dark fabric washed in the waves. Kneeling down, he reached into the water and grabbed a piece of the fabric, half-afraid it would have a body attached to it.

He lifted out the black top Blossom had been wearing and looked toward the storm-blackened horizon for her body, his heart in his throat.

Dropping the top back into the water, he dove through the trees for the villa. He didn't know what the hell was going on but he had a bad feeling the killer on the island was about to make himself known.

Landry hadn't gone but a few feet when he heard a noise off to his right. He wasn't alone.

Hoping a moving target would be harder for whoever was out there to hit, he took off in a crouched run down the winding trail.

Willa couldn't sit still. All she wanted to do was get off the island with the disk. She could come back for anything she left behind.

She dressed for the boat ride, packed a few essentials, then waited for Landry, listening for the sound of a boat and growing more anxious every minute when she didn't hear one.

It was the quiet that eventually got to her. Blossom wasn't playing her music. In fact, Willa had seen neither Blossom nor Henri all day.

She peeked out through the blinds. A light was on

at Odell's apartment. She could see it through his partially opened doorway. But no sign of him, either. The villa was too quiet.

Her heart began to pound. Where was Henri? And Blossom? And why didn't Landry come back?

Her fear growing, she went to the end table and took out the gun he'd left with her. She checked to make sure it was loaded, thankful that Landry had been right. She did know how to use a gun.

Darkness settled over the villa. She realized there was someone else she hadn't seen—or heard all day. Alma Garcia. There was no light that she could see on the third floor. Where was everyone?

She glanced again at Odell's. No sign of life. He must have gone somewhere with Henri and Blossom, though she couldn't imagine a more unlikely trio. As she waited, she fought the need to find one of them just to reassure herself that everything was fine.

Wait until Landry comes back.

She went back to the couch and had just sat down when she heard the scream. Leaping up, she ran to the window and looked out. She could see Henri down by Odell's open doorway. Henri was walking backward, her hands over her mouth, a wounded animal sound coming out of her.

Grabbing the gun and keeping it by her side out of view, Willa opened the door and stepped out on the balcony.

"What is it?" she called down to Henri.

The redhead spun around, terror in her eyes. Her hands fell away from her mouth and she began to cry as she stumbled to the bottom of the stairs, sitting down on the bottom step. "It's Odell," she managed to say between sobs. "I think he's dead."

"Did you check for a pulse?" Willa called down.

Henri looked up at her, her face pale, her eyes red from crying and shook her head. "I couldn't. I faint at the sight of blood and there's blood all over." She started crying again.

"I thought you left. I haven't seen you all day," Willa said as she descended the stairs behind the other woman.

"I had a hangover," she said, sniffing and wiping her face on the sleeve of her robe. "I took a sleeping pill with some wine. It knocked me out."

"Have you seen Blossom?" Willa asked.

Henri noticed the gun and shook her head slowly. "She was with Bull earlier. But I thought Bull left alone."

"Okay," Willa said, and with the gun still at her side started across the courtyard toward Odell's open doorway. She listened for the sound of a boat, praying that Landry would return before she reached Odell's apartment.

She saw no one, heard no boat motor. And Landry should have been back by now.

Willa glanced back. Henri now stood in her apartment doorway looking scared.

"Stay there," Willa said unnecessarily to Henri as she neared Odell's open doorway. "Odell?" she called. "Odell?"

At the door she stopped, took a breath and let it out slowly, her fingers tightening on the grip of the gun. With her free hand, she pushed the door open with one finger. It swung in.

The smell of blood hit her first.

The second thing was Odell lying on the floor, his typewriter next to his head. Henri was right. There was blood everywhere.

Willa stepped in trying to ignore the blood as she hurried to check Odell's wrist for a pulse. She could see that the side of his head had been smashed in and there was blood on the typewriter and the sheet of paper was sticking out of it. Like Henri, she fainted at the sight of blood under normal circumstances.

She had just touched his wrist and found what she'd expected—no pulse—when the typed words came into focus. She drew her hand back as she read the byline: Odell Grady, *St. Petersburg Times* Investigative Reporter.

Below it was the beginning of a newspaper story about her and Landry. No wonder Odell Grady had to have a paper every day. A news junkie, huh?

A sound startled her. She couldn't tell where it had come from. But it had sounded like hurried movement. Her gaze flicked to the cool shadows at the back of the apartment. The killer wouldn't be foolish enough to hide in here. After Henri had found Odell and come for help, the killer would have had plenty of time to get out. Unless, of course, he was waiting for Willa.

She heard the sound again, so close it made the hair stand up on the back of her neck. She swung around as a hand dropped to her shoulder. She screamed, her hand tightening on the gun, her finger going to the trigger.

"Easy, darlin', it's me," Landry said as he caught the gun before she could turn and fire.

He looked past her to where Odell Grady was

sprawled on the floor, clearly dead. "Was it something he said?"

She buried her face in Landry's chest. He put his arms around her, holding her tight.

"I didn't hear the boat."

"My boat is gone and the old fisherman hasn't returned."

She drew back to stare in shock and fear at him.

"Not to worry. We're getting out of here," he said as he drew her out of Odell's apartment and into the courtyard. "Where are Henri and Blossom?"

"Henri's the one who found Odell. She's in her apartment. No one has seen Blossom since she was talking to Bull earlier." Willa seemed to choke on a sob. "Odell lied. He was a newspaper reporter. He was doing a story on us."

Landry heard the panic rising in her voice. "Okay," he said, sounding much calmer than he felt. "Let's go get Henri and see if we can find Blossom."

She nodded as he pocketed her gun and they started across the courtyard toward Henri's apartment.

"Her door's closed," Willa said, slowing. "When I left her it was open. She was standing in the doorway, waiting for me."

Landry felt his pulse jump.

"She said she fainted at the sight of blood."

He wondered why Willa hadn't. Because she could be strong when she had to be. He was counting on that.

There was no light coming from inside Henri's apartment and the storm had snuffed out the sun, filling the courtyard with a kind of ominous darkness.

Landry tapped at Henri's door, realizing he couldn't hear the power generator. The only light in any of the apartments was one on the third floor. An old oil lamp, he thought, watching the light flicker.

Someone had shut down the generator. Or forgot to refill it with gas. Either way, it didn't bode well, given that Odell Grady had been murdered and it appeared Henri was now missing. He didn't even want to think about what had happened to Blossom.

He tapped again. No answer.

"She wouldn't have left, Landry," Willa cried, grabbing his arm. "She was upset and scared and she said she would wait."

Right. Unless she killed Odell and Blossom.

He tried the knob. It was unlocked. Pushing open the door, he took the flashlight from his pocket and shone it into the room. "Henri?"

No answer but then he hadn't expected one.

The apartment was smaller than Willa's, the bathroom door standing open, the shower curtain pulled back exposing an empty shall. Henri was gone.

"Let's try Blossom's." He knew she wasn't going to answer the door but he could hope.

He knocked, then tried the knob. Also unlocked. He was starting to see a pattern here. He pushed open the door and shone the flashlight in. The light bobbed around the small apartment with the same results. Empty.

"Okay," he said seeing the fear in Willa's eyes. "Where is the disk?"

"In my pocket. I thought it would be safer on me."

He smiled down at her. "Good." As he glanced toward the third floor, he couldn't help but recall the noise he'd heard out in the woods. Someone had followed him back here.

Through the third-floor window he saw a shape cross in front of the lantern light. "I think we'd better pay a visit to the old gal upstairs," he said, and handed her back the gun he'd taken from her earlier. "Just in case."

Willa didn't like the stormy darkness that had settled over the villa. Or the fact that Landry had given her a weapon. She could see her own fears mirrored in his face as the wind whipped the tops of the palms in a low howl.

Landry thought Henri and Blossom were dead. She had seen it in his expression when he'd checked their apartments.

She glanced up the stairs. It was the last place she wanted to go. But she also knew that Landry wasn't about to leave her alone while he checked on the old woman. Look what had happened when she'd left Henri alone.

Willa had seen someone upstairs—just a dark shape silhouetted against the lantern light for an instant. The old woman? Was it possible Henri had gone up there? Maybe Blossom, too.

As she started up the stairs, Willa couldn't shake the feeling that going up there was a mistake. Someone could be waiting for them. What if it was the old woman? With all that digging for treasure, Alma could be stronger than any of them suspected. Strong enough to lift an ancient manual typewriter and kill Odell.

At Alma's door, Landry tapped softly. No answer. He tapped again. Willa thought she could hear music playing faintly inside the apartment.

Landry tried the knob. The door swung open and Willa was hit with an old musty smell. But what surprised her were the furnishings. It was as if time had stopped in this room thirty years ago.

"Alma?" Landry called. No answer. Willa felt her stomach clench as she and Landry moved through the living room deeper into the apartment toward the sound of the music. Alma must be in the area over Willa's apartment. She could see a closed door at the end of the room. The music seemed to be coming from behind there.

"Wait," Landry whispered.

She had reached for the knob on the closed door, but when she turned she saw that Landry had stopped in front of a painting on the wall.

Her *unfinished painting!* The one stolen from her apartment.

Landry was frowning at the painting, no doubt rocketed back to the night he killed his partner, Zeke Hartung.

Willa closed her hand over the knob to the closed door just before she heard the rustle of fabric off to her right and swung her head in the direction of the archway into the kitchen.

Alma Garcia came flying out of the kitchen, a butcher knife clutched in her fist, her eyes wide and wild.

Willa had just enough time to jump to the side as the woman rushed her. She caught a glimpse of Landry's surprise as the woman spun on her heel, more agile than Willa would have expected, given her apparent age.

Alma lunged for Willa again, but Willa managed to get one of the living room chairs between her and the knife-wielding woman. She could see that the older woman's hands were shaking, the knife blade flickering in the light from the oil lamp.

Landry grabbed Alma from behind. He said something to Alma in Spanish. The knife fell to the floor and he kicked it toward Willa who quickly picked it up, her heart in her throat.

The older woman's eyes filled with tears. She shook her head and answered him in English. "I will never leave you. Kill me so that my spirit might remain here always."

Landry spoke again in Spanish, cajoling. Alma began to cry. He let go of the older woman.

"Come on. We'll have to leave her," he said. "Henri and Blossom aren't here."

Willa moved to the door, keeping an eye on the woman and vice versa. She put the knife down as she went out the door, the scent of another time wafting out as Landry closed the door.

They went back down to Willa's apartment. Landry checked to make sure they were alone before he locked the door.

"You don't think Alma killed…"

He shook his head.

She saw something in his expression and felt her stomach lurch. "What aren't you telling me?"

"I found that crocheted black top of Blossom's floating in the water by the old fisherman's shack."

Willa covered her mouth with her hand. "Henri?"

"At this point, I'd say there's a good chance she's our killer."

Willa shivered. Outside her window, the wind howled, the palm trees slapping the side of the house, the air inside the apartment seeming too thick to breathe. They were on an island, trapped with a killer. "What do we do now?" she asked in a whisper.

He cocked his head and went to the window, opening it. The wind blew in, making the blinds flap. "That sounds like the old fisherman's boat motor."

"I don't hear anything," she said, trying to listen over the wind.

"Carlos didn't come in at the boathouse. The wind is carrying the sound from the cove. With the storm getting worse, he would be smart enough not to try to get back around the island by boat."

Fear jolted through her. "But that's exactly what you're planning to do. Let me go with you."

He shook his head, grinning. "Me and boats are like that," he said, crossing his fingers and holding them in front of her. "Not to worry, I'll be back before you know it."

She looked at Landry, suddenly even more afraid because she knew what he was thinking. "Henri will be waiting for us knowing we're trying to get off the island. That's why you won't let me go with you."

He brushed cool fingers over her cheek, his gaze locked with hers. "I want you to stay here. Lock the door. And if anyone, and I mean *anyone* tries to get in, shoot them." He released her hands to pick up the gun from where she'd set it down, and he pressed it into her palm.

"Landry—"

He cut her words off with a kiss. Pulling back he gave her a grin. "I'll be back. I can't bear the thought of all those other men competing with me if I don't."

She couldn't help but smile. She leaned into him, aching for him. Right now she just wanted him to hold her and never let her go but she was smart enough to know **their only chance was to get off the island. Everyone** was dead except a killer, a crazy old woman and a possibly equally demented old fisherman. Neither would be of any help.

She and Landry were on their own against— That was just it. They had no idea what they were up against.

Landry let go of her and moved to the door. He checked out the window first. The sky was dark with the storm. She could hear the roar of the Gulf as he opened the door. Past him, darkness pooled in the corners of the courtyard.

Henri could be out there anywhere.

Landry glanced back at her. What she saw in his eyes tore at her heart. But before she could say a word, he was out the door, locking it behind him.

She stood in the middle of the room feeling bereft, listening for…what? Gunfire? That pop she'd become so familiar with? A grunt? A cry?

She could hear nothing over the wind as it rattled the windows and rain began to pelt the glass. Overhead she heard the squeak of floorboards and froze.

Landry moved through the rain and stormy darkness, quiet as a cat. If he didn't make it back to the villa he feared Willa wouldn't stand a chance. Whoever had killed the others would wait her out. The supply boat wasn't scheduled to come back for days. There would be no one on the island who could help her because unless Landry missed his guess, the old fisherman and his boat would disappear, as well.

The wind groaned in the trees overhead, the canopy swaying above him. He could hear the rain hitting the leaves, but couldn't feel it except through the occasional hole in the canopy. It was dark under the storm and trees, the air thick and humid, buzzing with mosquitoes.

He tried to see ahead, to listen for the sound of a killer stalking him. He could hear nothing but the storm and see nothing in the darkness that lay ahead.

Moving swiftly, he ran along the trail, his gun drawn. He was surprised when he reached the cove and saw that the boat was pulled up on the beach. No sign of Carlos.

Landry made a run through the driving rain to the boat, he pushed it out, jumped in and started the motor.

Carlos appeared out of the dense vegetation. He seemed confused. He didn't go for a gun. Nor did any-one else appear. No bullets whizzed past as Landry turned the boat out into the huge waves that now swelled in the cove. It would be a rough trip around to the pier. An even rougher trip up the coast once he had Willa.

And the disk.

For a while, he'd almost forgotten about it.

Rain soaked him, the driving wind chilled him. He hit a large wave and spray cascaded over him, salty and cold. He rounded the end of the island and looked back.

He could see no one as he pointed the boat toward the first channel marker. Getting the boat had almost seemed too easy. So why hadn't Henri tried to stop him? His fear spiked at the obvious answer.

Because Henri had her sights set on someone else.

The person who had the disk. Willa.

Chapter 15

The floor overhead groaned. Willa could hear some-one moving around on the floor above her. She stared upward, her heart pounding.

Something was different. When Alma had been up there moving around, the floor hadn't groaned like this.

Willa stumbled over to the table where she'd put down the gun. She picked it up, holding it in front of her as she stared at the ceiling.

Someone was up there. Not the old woman. Some-one heavier. The floor groaned. She could hear the foot-falls reverse their path across the floor and then there was silence.

Willa jumped as something crashed into the door behind her. She heard a cry then the faint words, "Help me."

Her heart leapt to her throat as she moved to the door. "Who's there?"

"Help me."

She reached for the doorknob, remembering Landry's admonition not to open the door no matter what.

Hurrying to the window, she looked out. Blossom lay at her door. She was soaked to the skin, wearing nothing but a black bra and black jeans, barefoot, holding her hand to her side, bleeding. The gun bumped against the window.

Blossom looked up at her, pleading in her gaze as she mouthed, "Help me."

Willa looked past Blossom at the storm-whipped courtyard, the rain sheeting down, and made the only decision she could. She put down the gun and hurriedly opened the door.

Blossom hadn't moved, her eyes closed and for one horrible moment, Willa thought the girl was dead.

"Blossom!" She knelt at the girl's side, glancing at the balcony, afraid Henri would appear out of the rain.

Blossom's eyes fluttered. Willa grabbed Blossom by the feet and pulled her into the apartment, slamming the door and locking it behind them.

"Henri," Blossom said, her voice faint.

Willa knelt again beside the girl. "How badly are you hurt?"

"Stabbed," she whispered, and Willa saw that Blossom had both of her hands clutching her side.

"I'll get the first-aid kit." Willa ran into the bathroom and found the kit where Landry had used it. It was a small metal six-inch square can her mother had sent with her when she'd left home. Her mother had personally stocked it with items she feared her daughter might someday need.

As she turned, she heard a sound as if Blossom had bumped into the kitchen table. The table where Willa had left the gun.

On impulse, she slipped the disk from her pocket and hid it in the bathroom in a small hole behind the toilet.

Then she turned and stepped out of the bathroom, the first-aid kit in her hands.

Blossom stood at the table, the gun in her hands. A red stain ran down her bare skin where the stab wound should have been.

Willa looked from the woman's white unmarked skin to the gun pointing at her and finally met Blossom's gaze.

It was the first time she'd seen those eyes without the black coils of hair covering most of her face.

She was older than she had appeared before and the hand holding the gun was strong and sure.

"Where is Henri?" Willa asked, fear making her throat tight and dry. She was still holding the first-aid kit.

Blossom didn't seem to notice. Nor did she seem to hear Willa's question. She appeared to be listening, as if she heard—

Willa froze as she picked up the sound of a boat motor. Landry! He was headed for the dock.

"What do you want?"

Blossom focused on her and smiled. "Don't screw with me. I want the disk."

Willa looked down at the first-aid kit in her hands. She could hear the boat motor growing louder. She couldn't let Landry walk into a trap. Nor could she give up the disk.

"So all of that stuff about you being a star was just bunk?" she asked as she stepped a little closer to Blossom.

Goth Girl smiled. "Gotta admit I am one hell of an actress."

"You work for Freddy Delgado?"

Blossom laughed. "Yeah, right."

Willa was close enough that she could have gone for the gun. If she'd been crazy. "Well, you're not a cop."

"Not hardly. Come on, let's get this over with before your *boy*friend gets back," Blossom said, still pointing the gun at Willa's heart.

"I guess you won't be needing this," Willa said looking down at the metal first-aid kit in her hands. She'd popped the lid, remembering the small sharp metal objects her mother had put in the kit: scissors, clippers, tweezers, pins. Everything a South Dakota girl might need in the big city.

Blossom's gaze went to the first-aid kit just an instant before Willa flung it at her face. Willa had expected to hear the boom of the gun as she slammed into Blossom, driving her back. Taken by surprise, Blossom fell over the chair behind her and went down hard. The gun skittered across the floor and disappeared under the couch.

Willa launched herself at the door, grabbing the knob and jerking the door open. She caught only a glimpse of Blossom scrambling to her feet with a knife in her hand as the door slammed behind her.

Landry brought the boat into the dock, fighting the waves kicked up by the storm. The wind howled as rain lashed down. He could barely make out the villa through the driving rain as he hurriedly secured the boat to the lee side of the dock and ran up the beach.

His mind had been racing ever since he'd taken the boat and started back. So much about the missing disk and the people after it hadn't made any sense. But as he'd fought the storm waves, running the boat back as fast as he could without swamping it, he'd had time to think.

His thoughts had taken a turn that had curdled his stomach. He had to be wrong.

He heard a creaking sound off to his right and swung his weapon as he turned toward it, half expecting Henri to come at him out of the storm.

He couldn't make out what it was but he slowed, moving toward the sound. *Creak. Creak. Creak.*

And then he saw it.

His heart leapt to his throat and he let out a cry of alarm as the body swung into view. Henri. She hung by her neck from a rope tied to the ornate wrought iron along the front of the villa. Her body swung in the wind.

Henri was dead?

If Henri hadn't killed Odell and Blossom, then…

The steps were wet and slick. Willa fell, tumbling down the last few. She scraped her arm on the wrought-iron railing and cut her leg open. Her blood mixed with the rain as she struggled to get to her feet. Behind her, she heard her apartment door bang open. In a flash of lightning, she saw Blossom silhouetted against the storm. The light caught on the knife blade, glittering wickedly as Blossom descended the stairs at a run.

Willa was on her feet but Blossom leapt over the

stair railing, tackling her and taking them both to the tile next to the pool. Willa rolled Blossom over, both hands on Blossom's wrist holding the knife as she tried to wrestle it away from her.

But Blossom was strong and had obviously done this before. She bucked Willa off, throwing them both over the lip of the pool and into the putrid water.

Willa gasped as she hit the surface, dragged under by Blossom as they continued to fight for the knife. She opened her eyes but could see nothing in the darkness at the bottom of the pool as she and Blossom struggled.

Something brushed past her arm, wet and slimy. She choked, desperately needing air, but unable to let go of Blossom and the knife. She felt dizzy and could feel her grip weakening. And suddenly she saw something next to her in the water. The waterlogged face of the little boy from the photograph.

Landry sprinted through the arch into the villa, fear propelling him like a rocket into the courtyard.

Through the pouring rain, he glimpsed the two forms struggling by the pool, heard the splash as the two fell in.

Blossom and Willa.

He ran and dove headfirst into the rain-dimpled dark water. It was pitch-black beneath the surface. He swam blindly toward the spot where he'd seen the two go under, shoving away limbs and leaves that had decayed in the pool, feeling as if he was swimming through a decomposing soup.

His hand brushed against something that felt like hair and he brought himself up short as he felt pain slice across his arm.

Blossom had a knife and appeared to be frantically trying to swim to the surface, but something was holding her down. He didn't see Willa anywhere.

Hurriedly he swam around Blossom, staying out of reach of the knife she was swinging in a frenzied arch.

No Willa.

He could barely make out Blossom, who was fighting desperately to free herself from something he couldn't see. Needing air, he surfaced, and in a rush of relief, saw Willa hanging on the edge of the pool, choking and gasping, but alive.

He swam to her, pulled her into his arms. "Are you hurt?"

She shook her head, blinking through the driving rain at him as he let her go and pushing himself out of the water, pulled her out beside him.

He took one last look into the pool as he helped Willa up the stairs. The water had stilled except for the rain falling on it. Just below the surface he could see the dim gleam of silver from the knife still clutched in Blossom's hand and her hair floating around her pale face.

Landry turned away from the look of horror on her face and helped Willa into her apartment.

"You're bleeding again," she said, her voice sounding far away as she slumped into a chair.

"I'm fine." He locked the door and stooped to pick up the contents of the first-aid kit. His arm wasn't cut badly but he knew he had to get some disinfectant on it after being in that pool. "Come on."

He helped Willa to her feet and undressed her and himself on the way to the bathroom. Turning on the shower, he regulated the water then climbed in with her. They stood, holding each other as the water washed over them. Slowly he began to soap her wonderful body, desire washing away the horror of what he'd seen in the pool, the terror of what could have happened if Willa hadn't fought off Blossom and somehow escaped to the surface. How had she done that? he wondered.

Something in the pool had saved her.

He shook off the thought as she took the soap from him and began to lather it over him. He closed his eyes.

Later, lying in bed, warm and dry and sated, his arm bandaged, his heart beginning to slow, he looked over at Willa. Her blue eyes were filled with tears.

Alarmed, he sat up and stared down at her. "What is it? Did I hurt you?"

She shook her head, her lips turning up a little at the corners as she looked at him. "You could never hurt me."

He wasn't so sure about that.

"So much death," she whispered. "I have seen so much death."

He pulled her into his arms and held her tightly. "The storm is letting up. We have to leave here. The disk? I know you had it in your pocket. It wasn't there when I undressed you. It must be in the bottom of the pool, huh?"

"I hid it in the bathroom."

He let out a breath, not realizing how afraid he'd been that the disk had been lost, that all of this had been for nothing. "Then everything is going to be all right." He drew back to look at her. "We survived it, darlin'."

Willa looked into his dark eyes and cupped his cheek with her palm. Her heart felt as if it would break, she loved him so much. She'd been afraid in the pool. Not for her own life, but Landry's. Willa had known she couldn't fight Blossom off any longer in the pool. She was out of air, weak and losing hope.

"What is it?" Landry asked.

She wanted to tell him about what she'd seen in the pool. About what had happened when the boy had appeared. But she couldn't bring herself to say the words.

"Can we please get off this island?" she said instead.

He smiled and nodded. "The rain sounds like it is letting up. We should be able to see well enough to make it up the coast."

She started to pull away from him, but he drew her close again and kissed her.

"I'll get the disk," she said. Everything else could stay here. She could buy new art supplies. If she ever painted again.

The rain had stopped by the time they were dressed and ready to leave. Landry got the gun from under the couch, insisting she keep it on her. "Just in case."

She tried to tell him she wouldn't be able to pull the trigger even if she had to. Not today. But she'd taken the gun and stuffed it into the pocket of her jacket.

Landry led the way out of the apartment. Willa glanced down at the pool and quickly looked away. She felt a chill as she followed Landry down the stairs, and when she looked up she wasn't surprised to see the face at the window on the third floor.

Alma Garcia looked terrified, her eyes appearing even more crazed in the glow of the lamplight. She was staring at the pool as if hypnotized. Willa shuddered as she realized that the elderly woman had seen everything. Even the child in the water who had drowned thirty years ago?

Willa grabbed Landry's arm as they hurried from the courtyard. The boat was at the dock. She could see a strip of green in the distance as the other islands appeared from out of the storm.

"Don't get in yet," Landry said as he began to bail the water out of the boat.

She stood, afraid to turn around and look back at the villa for fear of what she might see. Landry was bent over, scooping rainwater from the bottom of the boat. She could tell by his movements that he wanted off this island as badly as she did.

The dock swayed. Willa froze as she realized that someone had just stepped onto it. No. She squeezed her eyes shut, shoving her hands deep into the pockets of her jacket. *No.* This was going to be over as soon as they reached the mainland. It *had* to be over. She felt powerless, too close to the edge. She couldn't take any more today.

She opened her eyes as the dock swayed again. Landry was still bent over, unaware they were no longer alone.

Slowly she turned and gasped as she recognized the ghost moving down the dock toward her. It was the man who'd come into her art studio that night before her gallery showing.

"Hello," Simon Renton said.

Landry swung around, his hand going for his gun.

"I wouldn't do that if I were you," Simon said.

Landry froze, his face a mask of shock and then slow realization. "No."

Simon laughed. "Sorry to disappoint you. I'll take that disk now."

"Why?" Landry asked on a breath, not moving to give him the disk.

"Isn't it obvious? I'm *dead* and that disk is worth a small fortune on the market."

"You'd sell it to Freddy D.'s competitors?"

"Or Freddy D. if he can come up with enough money."

Neither man seemed to have remembered Willa was even there. She could understand why. She felt small and insignificant, huddled in her jacket, standing on the end of the dock next to the boat watching the two as if all of this was nothing but a very bad nightmare. Any minute she would wake up and be in her art studio apartment upstairs planning her showing that coming night.

"You were the dirty cop," Landry said with a shake of his head. "Not Zeke. But why did he try to kill me?"

"Could have been because of the information I leaked to him about you. I told him not to trust you. That I'd heard you were shopping the disk and that if you got your hands on it…." Simon shrugged.

"Zeke tried to kill me."

Simon nodded. "I thought he just might. He hated dirty cops." He held out his hand. "I'll take the disk now."

"Without the disk, I will always be a hunted man," Landry said.

"But you'll be alive."

"Will I?" Landry said with a laugh. "You can't let me live. You know I'll go to the cops, the feds, I'll tell them about you faking your death. How did you do that anyway?"

"It's all about money. You pay the right guys the right amount and they will find a homeless guy your size, even get him a tattoo just like yours," Simon said with a grin as he lifted his shirt, exposing a dragon tattoo that curled around his side. "All you need is two not real bright goons to help you fake your death and tell their boss they killed you."

"T and Worm. So why didn't you go back and get the painting and the disk that night then?"

Simon sighed. "It took a while to convince them they would be better off playing on my team. By then it was morning and I needed to lay low. After all, I was dead. But I knew if I sent the info to Freddy D. he'd send you to get the disk. And if I could depend on anyone to get it, it would be you." He wiggled the fingers of his out-stretched hand. "Come on, Landry. The disk for your life and your girlfriend's here."

"You're the one who hired Blossom—or whatever her name was."

Simon smiled. "What happened to her anyway? I really thought I'd be hearing from her and not have to take things into my own hands, so to speak. Doesn't matter. You can give me the disk or I can take it off your body. Which is it going to be?"

The gunshot startled Willa, bringing her out of her lethargy as she saw the bullet punch the water's surface next to the boat.

"Landry!" she cried, afraid he'd been hit.

"It's okay, darlin'," he said, not looking at her. "You want the disk, Simon. Fine. But let her go. I'll start the boat. You let her get in and leave. Then I will give you the disk."

Simon smiled. "So it's like that, is it?"

Landry reached back and pulled the cord on the motor. The air filled with the throb of the engine. Holding up his hands, Landry stepped from the boat and reached for Willa's hand, his gaze meeting hers.

She saw the warning, felt it in his body as he drew her to him, wrapping his arms around her tightly for a moment before helping her into the boat. She stood in the boat, numb from the cold, the terror, the exhaustion.

"You can drive a boat, can't you? Keep land in sight until you reach a town," he said. "Keep going." He shoved the boat out.

She swayed and almost fell as the boat drifted slowly away from the dock. She steadied herself as she saw Landry reach in his pocket for the disk. *No.*

She reached into her pocket for the gun.

It was gone.

Landry. He'd taken it. He'd known she would try to kill Simon. And probably fail.

She was floating away, the motor on the boat idling. Did Landry really believe that Simon would let him go? Let her go, as well? Simon would come after her. She and Landry knew he was alive. He couldn't let either of them live.

Landry started to hand Simon the disk.

She grabbed the handle on the motor, spinning it around as she'd seen Gator do, and hit the throttle. The bow of the boat shot up. She couldn't see the pier but she heard a startled sound come from it as the boat roared toward the two men.

The bow hit the pier and sent a shockwave through

her as it glanced off throwing her to the side. As she fell she heard the pop of a gun going off. It was the last thing she remembered before waking up in Landry's arms.

Epilogue

Landry walked out of the police station, stopping on the steps to breathe in the warm Florida morning. He was free. Free of false charges. Free of being an undercover cop.

He wasn't sure how he felt yet. Everything that had happened had taken its toll on him. He wasn't sure he would ever get over Zeke's death. Or Simon's for that matter. Landry had ended up killing them both. They'd been his partners. He'd trusted them.

It had taken days to make his statement. Thank God for the disk that proved that Simon was the cop who'd gone bad—not Landry. Not Zeke. It was little consolation. A lot of people had died unnecessarily, Zeke among them.

The body of Blossom—real name Angela Warren—was brought up from the bottom of the pool on Cape

Diablo. The police found that part of the baggy black garb she'd been wearing as her Blossom disguise had gotten caught on a large limb that had fallen into the pool.

Landry remembered the look on Willa's face when she'd been told that. She didn't seem to believe it. He wasn't sure he did when he recalled how Blossom had been fighting to surface, striking out at water as if she thought someone was holding her down.

Blossom, that is Angela Warren, turned out to be a young prostitute whom Simon had once arrested. A hundred thousand dollars was found in her checking account supporting what Landry said about Simon hiring Angela to pose as Blossom at Cape Diablo to get the disk—and get rid of Willa and Landry.

Odell, it was assumed, had either run across Angela as an investigative reporter and recognized her when she came to the island or let it slip what he was working on and it had gotten him killed.

Henri had been exactly who she said she was. Nothing more than a guest on the island. While Landry had been suspicious when she'd pretended to be drunker than she was, he suspected she was just hoping Odell would take advantage.

Maybe she really had come to the island thinking she wanted solitude to get over her recent breakup. But once she'd met Odell she must have decided she wouldn't mind a little male comfort. Instead, she'd only met death.

Henri had definitely picked the wrong island for any kind of peace. Willa had made the same mistake. Only, he thanked God, with a different ending.

While Willa gave her statement and was released,

Landry had been held for more questioning. With the information on the disk, the police and feds were able to throw a wide net over organized crime in Florida, bringing down Freddy D. and his associates and underlings, except for T and Worm.

Their bodies were found in a dump, both shot, gangland-style, in the back of their heads. Freddy D. no doubt had heard about Simon Renton's "second" death on Cape Diablo and realized T and Worm had double-crossed him.

When the cops were finally satisfied with what was on the disk and Landry's and Willa's statement, the chief broke the story, dragged him in front of the blazing lights of the media and gave him a medal. The story made headlines across the state. He was a hero.

He hadn't wanted any of it.

But once labeled as a dirty cop, it took a hell of a lot of fanfare to clear his name and he wanted that more than anything. He *needed* that before he could go find Willa St. Clair.

He'd heard she'd gone back to South Dakota, some tiny town he couldn't even find on a map. He'd had to fly into the capital of Pierre at the center of the state and rent a car, driving north until he spotted a grain elevator with Alkali Butte printed on it.

After that, he'd only had to ask for directions, then taken a series of dirt roads until he spotted the white farmhouse on the horizon and slowed to pull into the drive.

Willa heard the vehicle pull into the farm yard and looked up from her painting to see the unfamiliar car stop in a cloud of dust.

She'd never thought she'd come back to South Dakota. But after everything that had happened, she realized a true home didn't have to be one you'd been raised in all your life. It was anywhere there were people who loved you.

Her mother and stepfather had been wonderful through all of this. She'd seen how much her stepfather loved her mother and it had made her realize she'd never given him a chance.

Being around family had helped her regain her strength if not heal her aching heart. But she was painting again and that she knew was a sign that she would be all right.

"Who's that?" her mother called from the kitchen. The house smelled of homemade bread and beef stew since it was almost suppertime.

"Someone lost," Willa called back as she put down her paintbrush. No other unfamiliar cars ended up in the yard otherwise. "I'll take care of it."

She left the small room off the living room where she'd set up her studio and walked to the door, pushing open the screen to squint out at the car, the sun glinting off the windshield.

The driver's door slowly opened.

She blinked, her heart soaring as Landry Jones climbed out. Over the weeks since she'd seen him she'd heard he'd cleared his name. But she'd never expected to see him again. Because she never planned to go back to Florida. And she'd never dreamed he'd come all the way to South Dakota.

"Hello, darlin'," he said, stopping on the bottom porch step. "You're a hard woman to find, Willa St. Clair."

She tried to swallow the lump in her throat as tears welled in her eyes. "Landry, what—" That's all she got out before he was up the steps and she was in his arms.

"I love you, Willa St. Clair," he said, and then he was kissing her.

Behind her she heard the screen door creak open. "This must be Landry Jones," she heard her mother say. "I'll set another plate." The screen door closed with another creak.

Landry pulled back from the kiss and grinned at her. "I already like your mother," he whispered. "But then I adore her daughter."

Her heart leaped.

Landry turned serious. "I quit my job. I've got some money saved, though. But at this moment, I have no plans for the future." He grinned again. "Except one."

Willa held her breath and thought about the painting on her easel inside the house. She hadn't painted since she left Cape Diablo. Until this morning.

On her easel now was a painting of a two-story white house, a tire swing in the big tree next to it, an assortment of toys scattered across the green lawn. There were red-and-white gingham curtains at the kitchen window and a man and woman sitting together on the front porch swing. They were faceless, the painting not yet finished.

"Willa," Landry said, and swallowed.

She'd never seen him nervous before.

"I know the timing is awful. Why would you want to marry a former undercover cop, let alone one who is jobless and isn't even sure what he's going to do now?"

"Landry," she said, smiling up into his wonderfully

handsome face. "Is there something you wanted to ask me?"

He laughed. "Oh, yeah, darlin'. Would you consider being my wife? I love you. I need you. I don't care what tomorrow brings as long as I'm with you." He dropped to one knee. "Marry me, Willa St. Clair."

She laughed as she cupped his face in her hands and leaned down to kiss that amazing mouth.

"Was that a yes?" he asked as she pulled back from the kiss.

"No," she said as she drew him to his feet, wrapped her arms around his neck and started to kiss him again. "*This,* my love, is a yes."

* * * * *

SPECIAL EXCERPT FROM

⊞ HARLEQUIN®

INTRIGUE

Jen Delaney and Ty Carson were once sweethearts, but that's in the past. When Ty starts receiving threatening letters that focus more and more on Jen, he'll do whatever it takes to keep her safe—even kidnap her.

Read on for a sneak preview of
Wyoming Cowboy Ranger *by Nicole Helm.*

Jen Delaney loved Bent, Wyoming, the town she'd been born in, grown up in. She was a respected member of the community, in part because she ran the only store that sold groceries and other essentials within a twenty-mile radius of town.

From her position crouched on the linoleum while she stocked shelves, she looked around the small store she'd taken over at the ripe age of eighteen. For the past ten years it had been her baby, with its narrow aisles and hodgepodge of necessities.

She'd always known she'd spend the entirety of her life happily ensconced in Bent and her store, no matter what happened around her.

The reappearance of Ty Carson didn't change that knowledge so much as make it...annoying. No, annoying would have been just his being in town again. The fact their families had somehow intermingled in the last year was...a catastrophe.

Her sister, Laurel, marrying Ty's cousin Grady had been a shock, very close to a betrayal, though it was hard to hold it against Laurel when Grady was so head over heels for her it was comical. They both glowed with love and happiness and impending parenthood.

Jen tried not to hate them for it.

She could forgive Cam, her eldest brother, for his serious relationship with Hilly. Hilly was biologically a Carson, but she'd only just found that out. Besides, Hilly wasn't like other Carsons. She was so sweet and earnest.

But Dylan and Vanessa… Her business-minded, sophisticated older brother *impregnating* and marrying snarky bad girl Vanessa Carson… *That* was a nightmare.

And none of it was fair. Jen was now, out of nowhere, surrounded by Carsons and Delaneys intermingling—which went against everything Bent had ever stood for. Carsons and Delaneys hated each other. They didn't fall in love and get married and have *babies*.

And still, she could have handled all that in a certain amount of stride if it weren't for *Ty* Carson. Everywhere she turned he seemed to be right there, his stoic gaze always locked on *her*, reminding her of a past she'd spent a lot of time trying to bury and forget.

When she'd been seventeen and the stupidest girl alive, she would have done anything for Ty Carson. Risked the Delaney-Carson curse that, even with all these Carson-Delaney marriages, Bent still had their heart set on. She would have risked her father's wrath over daring to connect herself with a *Carson*. She would have given up anything and everything for Ty.

Instead he'd made promises to love her forever, then disappeared to join the army—which she'd found out only a good month after the fact. He hadn't just broken her heart—he'd crushed it to bits.

But Ty was a blip of her past she'd been able to forget about, mostly, for the past ten years. She'd accepted his choices and moved on with her life. For a decade she had grown into the adult who didn't care at all about Ty Carson.

Then Ty had come home for good, and all she'd convinced herself of faded away.

She was half convinced he'd returned simply to make her miserable.

"You look angry. Must be thinking about me."

Don't miss
Wyoming Cowboy Ranger *by Nicole Helm,*
available June 2019 wherever
Harlequin® Intrigue books and ebooks are sold.

www.Harlequin.com

Eva Kendall slowed her pace as she approached the training facility where she worked training guide dogs.

Using her key, she entered the training center, thinking about the male chocolate Lab named Cocoa that she would work with this morning. Cocoa was a ten-week-old puppy born to Stella, a gift from the Czech Republic to the NYC K-9 Command Unit located in Queens. Most of Stella's pups were being trained as police dogs, but not Cocoa. In less than a month after basic puppy training, Cocoa would be able to go home with Eva to be fostered during his initial first-year training to become a full-fledged guide dog. Once that year passed, guide dogs like Cocoa would return to the center to train with their new owners.

A few steps into the building, Eva frowned at the loud thumps interspersed between a cacophony of barking. The raucous noise from the various canines contained a level of panic and fear rather than excitement.

Concerned, she moved quickly through the dimly lit training center to the back hallway, where the kennels were located. Normally she was the first one in every morning, but maybe one of the other trainers had gotten an early start.

Rounding the corner, she paused in the doorway when she saw a tall, heavyset stranger scooping Cocoa out of his kennel. Panic squeezed her chest. "Hey! What are you doing?"

The ferocious barking increased in volume, echoing off the walls and ceiling. The stranger must have heard her. He turned to look at her, then roughly tucked Cocoa under his arm like a football.

"No! Stop!" Panicked, Eva charged toward the man, desperately wishing she had a weapon of some sort.

"Get out of my way," he said in a guttural voice.

"No. Put that puppy down right now!" Eva stopped and stood her ground.

"Last chance," he taunted, coming closer.

Don't miss
Blind Trust *by Laura Scott,*
available June 2019 wherever
Love Inspired® *Suspense books and ebooks are sold.*

www.LoveInspired.com

LISEXP0519

Want to give in to temptation with
steamy tales of irresistible desire?

Check out **Harlequin® Presents®**,
Harlequin® Desire and
Harlequin® Kimani™ Romance books!

New books available every month!

CONNECT WITH US AT:

Facebook.com/groups/HarlequinConnection

 Facebook.com/HarlequinBooks

 Twitter.com/HarlequinBooks

 Instagram.com/HarlequinBooks

Pinterest.com/HarlequinBooks

ReaderService.com

**ROMANCE WHEN
YOU NEED IT**

PGENRE2018

Love Harlequin romance?

DISCOVER.

Be the first to find out about promotions, news and exclusive content!

Facebook.com/HarlequinBooks

Twitter.com/HarlequinBooks

Instagram.com/HarlequinBooks

Pinterest.com/HarlequinBooks

ReaderService.com

EXPLORE.

Sign up for the Harlequin e-newsletter and download a free book from any series at **TryHarlequin.com.**

CONNECT.

Join our Harlequin community to share your thoughts and connect with other romance readers! **Facebook.com/groups/HarlequinConnection**

HARLEQUIN®

ROMANCE WHEN YOU NEED IT

HSOCIAL2018

Earn points on your purchase of new Harlequin books from participating retailers.

Turn your points into **FREE BOOKS** of your choice!

Join for FREE today at
www.HarlequinMyRewards.com.

Harlequin My Rewards is a free program (no fees) without any commitments or obligations.

MYR18